# BRENDA NOVAK

## *The Heart of Christmas*

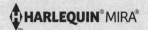

Recycling programs
for this product may
not exist in your area.

ISBN-13: 978-0-7783-1639-8

The Heart of Christmas

Copyright © 2014 by Brenda Novak, Inc.

Printed in U.S.A.

www.Harlequin.com

To Marilyn Burrows—for her love of reading
and her friendship with Ruth Carlson.

Dear Reader,

In one of my romantic suspense trilogies—*Inside, In Seconds* and *In Close*—I created a character named Rex McCready who was a good friend to Virgil Skinner (the lead character in *Inside*). Rex had a tragic past, one that led him into trouble early on. And sadly, it was the kind of trouble that doesn't disappear easily. That made him, at least on the surface, appear to be less than the kind of man most people would admire, but I always saw him as a diamond in the rough. I wanted him to have his own happily-ever-after, but I wasn't sure my readers would agree that he deserved it—until I started receiving so many letters and emails requesting his story. Ever since then, I've been looking for just the right home and situation for this particular character, the place where he can finally shed his old skin completely, be the man he was destined to be and find peace. I discovered that place in Whiskey Creek, so you'll get to meet him in this book (if you don't already know him from *Inside, In Seconds* and *In Close*).

Those of you who've been following the Whiskey Creek series will be happy to learn that this is also Eve's story. Not only does Eve find the right man for her in a very unlikely stranger, she also learns the answer to the 1870s mystery that has plagued her B & B since her parents bought it when she was a child.

I would like to extend a special thanks to my Aunt Channie for purchasing the chance to name a character in this book via my annual online auction for diabetes research. She chose the name of one of her best friends, Marilyn Burrows, whom you'll see in the story as Rex's assistant. Like every other person who's helped me raise money for this important cause, my Aunt Channie (Ruth Carlson) is a hero to me.

I love to hear from my readers. Please feel free to visit my website at www.brendanovak.com, where you can use the contact button, enter various monthly giveaways, learn more about this novel as well as all my others (I've now written fifty books!) or get involved in my online auctions for diabetes research. Thanks to everyone who has gotten involved so far, we've been able to raise $2.4 million. My youngest son has this disease, as well as 350 million people worldwide, so here's to finding a cure.

Happy reading!

Brenda Novak

# Whiskey Creek Cast of Characters

## Major Characters

**Aaron Amos:** Second-oldest Amos brother (one of the "Fearsome Five"); works with Dylan and brothers at their auto-body shop. Had a relationship with **Presley Christensen** some years earlier and is now engaged to her.

**Cheyenne Christensen (now Amos):** Helps Eve Harmon run Little Mary's B & B (formerly the Gold Nugget). Married to **Dylan Amos**, who owns Amos Auto Body.

**Sophia DeBussi:** Jilted **Ted Dixon** years ago to marry investment guru Skip DeBussi—later revealed as a fraud. Mother of **Alexa.** Reconnected with Ted and is now married to him.

**Gail DeMarco:** Owns a public relations firm in LA. Married to movie star **Simon O'Neal**.

**Ted Dixon:** Bestselling thriller writer.

**Eve Harmon:** Manages Little Mary's B & B, which is owned by her family.

**Kyle Houseman:** Owns a solar panel business. Formerly married to Noelle Arnold.

**Rex McCready (aka Brent Taylor):** New to town.

**Baxter North:** Stockbroker in San Francisco.

**Presley Christensen:** Former "bad girl" who left town and recently returned. Mother of **Wyatt.**

**Noah Rackham:** Professional cyclist. Owns Crank It Up bike shop. Married to **Adelaide Davies**, chef and manager of Just Like Mom's restaurant, owned by her grandmother.

**Riley Stinson:** Contractor.

**Callie Vanetta:** Photographer. Married to **Levi McCloud/Pendleton,** veteran of Afghanistan.

**Other Recurring Characters**

**The Amos Brothers: Dylan, Aaron, Rodney, Grady** and **Mack.**

**Olivia Arnold:** Kyle Houseman's true love but married to **Brandon Lucero,** Kyle's stepbrother.

**Joe DeMarco:** Gail DeMarco's older brother, owns the Whiskey Creek Gas-n-Go.

**Phoenix Fuller:** In prison. Mother of **Jacob Stinson,** being raised by his father, Riley.

# 1

There was a naked man in her bed.

Eve Harmon's stomach tensed, and her heart skipped a beat—but she was pretty sure she'd invited him. From the way their clothes were strewn carelessly around the room, it was obvious that, not long ago, she'd been happy to have him with her.

She nearly groaned as her eyes swept over him. What had she done? She didn't have a boyfriend and she never slept around. She hadn't been with anyone since Ted Dixon—an old friend who had briefly turned into more a year ago. And before him, it had been much longer. Most people, at least those younger than her parents, would consider her extended periods of celibacy rather pathetic for a woman her age. But she lived in a small town, cared about her reputation and had been holding out for the kind of love that came with a white picket fence.

She just hadn't found the right guy, and she was beginning to think maybe she never would. The odds weren't in her favor. Now that most of her friends were married, she didn't get out all that often.

But she had a lot to be grateful for in spite of her dismal love life, she quickly reminded herself. Although she'd never been the type who wanted work to become her sole focus in life, she liked her job. She ran Little Mary's, a B and B in a converted Victorian owned by her retired parents. They lived in the house a hundred yards in front of her own small bungalow—when they weren't traveling in their RV like they were at the moment. Thanks to them, and the quaint, bucolic area where she'd been raised, her life had always been pleasant and safe—and predictable. Absolutely predictable.

Until now.

God, she hadn't even slept with someone she knew. And since there were only about two thousand people in Whiskey Creek, it was hard to find someone she didn't.

Shifting carefully so she wouldn't wake the man lying next to her—she needed to regain her bearings before confronting him—she tried to get a look at his face, but a thunderous headache made it difficult to sit up. That headache also explained how she'd ended up in this predicament. Last night she'd made the mistake of going out to celebrate her thirty-fifth birthday even though her friends weren't available until tonight, and she'd drunk too much. She'd been determined to do something wild and fun and completely out of character before reaching such a significant age, the age at which some doctors advised against getting pregnant.

Now she was paying the price for her out-of-control evening.

Had they even used birth control?

Briefly squeezing her eyes shut, she sent up a silent prayer that she'd had the presence of mind for *that* at least. It would be entirely *too* ironic for someone like her—someone so cautious—to get pregnant because of a one-night stand.

*What have you done?* And what should she do now? Should she wake him? What would she say when he was looking back at her? She'd never been in this situation before. But she couldn't let him sleep much longer. She needed to get rid of him so she could shower for work.

Thank goodness her parents had had engine trouble and hadn't made it home from her brother's house yet. She'd lamented that yesterday, when she'd been bored and lonely while setting up her little Christmas tree. Today she was glad.

Moving slowly to compensate for her hangover, she managed to prop herself against the headboard and, once there, frowned at her bedmate.

Who the heck was he?

She had no idea, but she was relieved to see that he was no bum off the street. He wasn't even one of those "he looked a lot more attractive last night" kind of pick-ups everyone joked about. This guy was so far above average that she began to wonder why he wasn't already taken. Heaven forbid that was the case! She didn't see a ring on his left hand, which rested on the pillow above his head. But he had to have *some* story. If he looked *this* good sleep-tousled, she could only imagine what he'd be like once he had a chance to clean up.

It was his bone structure, she decided. Those pro-nounced cheekbones. The narrow bridge across his nicely shaped nose. The distinct ridge of his upper eye sockets. He also had a strong chin and a manly jaw, which cer-tainly didn't detract.

So maybe she couldn't point to just one or two fea-tures. With his long, sandy-colored hair spread across his pillow, he resembled a fallen angel—and his body further enhanced that image. Although bedding covered his lower half—thank goodness—she could see his torso. He was built like a greyhound or panther, lean and sin-ewy and ideally proportioned with very little body hair.

What body hair he did have was golden and downy, as appealing as his tanned skin.

He'd make a nice subject for a painter, she mused, someone looking for refined masculine beauty—a man who could even be called *elegant*.

But not *everything* about him was elegant. When she looked closer, she could see that he had some very unusual scars....

What types of injuries could've caused *those?* she wondered. It seemed to her that he'd been shot, and more than once. Several round, bullet-size marks dotted his chest. Then there was a long, jagged scar on his side that must've come from something else....

Out of nowhere—he didn't open his eyes first, so she had no warning—he grabbed her wrists in a crushing grip and slammed her onto her back.

Eve gasped as she stared up at him. Gone was the image of an angel, fallen or otherwise. Shocked at being so easily and unexpectedly overpowered, she couldn't even scream. His fierce expression, as if he was intent on causing her bodily harm, made it worse.

Had she brought home a homicidal maniac? Was he about to *kill* her?

The terror that surged up must've shown on her face because he suddenly came to his senses. He gave his head a shake. His expression cleared and, letting go, he eased off her and slid back onto his side of the bed.

"Sorry about that. I thought..." His words trailed off, and he covered his eyes with one arm as if he needed a moment to pull himself together.

Her heart was now pounding in unison with her head. But once she could speak somewhat normally, she prompted him to finish his sentence. "Thought *what?*"

His lips turned down. "Never mind. I was dreaming."

She pressed a hand to her chest as though she could slow her galloping pulse. "It couldn't have been a pleasant dream."

"They never are," he muttered.

He dropped his arm and looked over at her, and—intriguing as that statement was—she was too concerned about her nudity to pursue more of an explanation. She drew up the blankets, but he didn't seem interested in ogling her. His gaze circled the room, taking in the gauzy fabric that wound around the top of her canopy bed, the Christmas gifts she'd already wrapped and stacked in the corner, the many photographs of friends and family scattered across her dresser and the plantation shutters she'd recently had installed. He seemed to be taking stock of everything, weighing it, evaluating it—especially the closet and the door leading into the hall—as if he might encounter some threat.

"Where am I?" His voice, although more commanding than before, hadn't quite lost the rasp that came from having just awakened.

"Whiskey Creek."

He held three fingers to his forehead. She guessed he had a headache, too, although, suddenly, she could scarcely feel hers, thanks to that recent burst of adrenaline.

"I can remember the *town*," he said wryly. "It's not like I think I'm in China."

Fortunately, he sounded as normal as he looked. "Really? Whiskey Creek is where you're supposed to be? Because I've lived here my whole my life, and I don't ever remember seeing you."

"You say that like you know *everyone*."

"I do. Or just about."

As he proceeded to rub his face, she wished he'd cover

up. The bedding had fallen away when he rolled on top of her. She could see far more of him than she wanted to—at least now that she was sober. But he didn't seem to notice or care about his state of undress.

"I'm new here," he said.

"When did you move in?" she asked.

"I didn't. I should've said I'm visiting."

A lot of tourists came through. The quaint shops beyond the graveyard next door to her B and B catered to them, particularly in the summer. So an unfamiliar face in town, even in the first part of winter, wasn't remarkable enough for anyone to make a fuss.

"Where are you staying?"

He hesitated. "I don't remember the name of the place," he muttered. He had to be at her competitor's or one of the small inns or B and Bs out in the country. She hadn't seen him at her place. "How long will you be in town?"

"A short time."

His answers were clipped, terse and noticeably skimpy on the details. She might've asked what had brought him here. But he was being so evasive she didn't see the point. Was he putting her on notice not to expect any follow-up to their night together?

Eve told herself she didn't care that the first romantic encounter she'd had since her big mistake with Ted Dixon wasn't shaping up to be any more promising than the false starts she'd experienced before. She just wanted to make sure that her "no way am I going to stay home and watch TV on my birthday" mutiny hadn't left her with an STD. As soon as she felt reasonably assured that she hadn't ruined her life, they could part ways— and she'd try to forget that she'd felt desperate enough to sleep with a stranger.

"I don't see anything in here that belongs to a man," he said.

She gave him a curious look. "A man?"

"I'm safe to assume you're not married? You aren't wearing a ring, but not everyone does."

Particularly a woman hoping to pick up a guy in a bar. Now she understood. She'd been too busy berating herself to clue in, or his meaning would've been clear from the beginning. "Do you make a habit of sleeping with married women?"

"Not when I can think straight. But last night I wasn't using a great deal of discretion. I don't even remember how I got here." He lifted a hand. "Wait, yes, I do. There was some waitress from that hole-in-the-wall honky-tonk who—"

"Sexy Sadie's."

"What?"

When his eyes flicked to her, she noticed that they were a startling shade of green, far lighter than the more common hazel. His eyelashes and eyebrows matched the darker streaks in his hair.

"That's the name of the bar," she clarified.

He shrugged. Apparently he found that information irrelevant—as though a bar was a bar and he'd frequented many. "Anyway, I have this vision of some waitress driving us over here and dumping us on what appeared to be a very long driveway, and that's about it."

When Eve's mind conjured up the same memory, she barely managed to stifle a groan. "Noelle Arnold." That Noelle, of all people, would know what they'd done made it so much worse....

"You don't like her?"

Her tone had revealed more than she'd intended. "Not

a great deal. Not since she seduced her sister's boyfriend, then claimed she was pregnant so he'd marry her."

"Small towns…"

She didn't like the way he said that. It seemed to imply that they were too backward to behave with as much sophistication as city folk. "I happen to be close friends with Kyle, the man she duped. Of course I'd feel defensive."

"You can feel defensive all you want, but this Noelle person did us a favor. She could easily have left us to our own devices. *I* certainly deserved it. I haven't gotten that wasted in—" without bothering to ask, he rummaged on the nightstand and helped himself to one of her elastic ties so he could pull back his hair "—a couple of years."

She could've pointed out that if Noelle had *really* been looking out for her, she would've seen to it that she got home safe *and* alone. But then she remembered making out with this man in the backseat of Noelle's car. No wonder Noelle had dropped them off together. Now she was probably running around, telling everyone she could think of that Eve Harmon, of all people, had picked up a stranger and taken him home to bed.

His eyes narrowed. Something about her had caught his interest. "What's wrong?" he asked.

She combed her fingers through her hair in an attempt to untangle it. While she had far bigger concerns than her appearance, she couldn't entirely resist her female vanity. Because her hair was jet black and her eyes blue, people often told her that she reminded them of the Disney version of Snow White. Some red lipstick added to the effect; she'd often capitalized on that when she needed a costume.

But maybe he didn't find Snow White all that appealing. He didn't seem too impressed.

"Nothing. Why?"

"You're blushing."

"No, I'm not."

"You absolutely are," he said. "Did I say something to embarrass you?"

She stopped trying to act as if discovering him in her bed was no big deal. "This whole situation embarrasses me," she admitted. "I've never taken anyone home from a bar before and, unlike you, I won't be leaving this town any time soon. That means I'll have to face all the people who witnessed my licentious behavior."

He raised one eyebrow. *"Licentious?"*

"Promiscuous, debauched. Whatever you want to call it. Waking up with a total stranger isn't something that's normal for me."

He studied her, his gaze...thoughtful. "Last night you told me it was your birthday."

"And?"

"Quit being so hard on yourself. From what I could gather, it was a rough one. And with the holidays coming up, and knowing you're going to spend another year alone, you said it wasn't likely to get any easier."

Damn. She'd shared that? Hadn't she revealed enough when she took off her clothes? "My birthday was fine. Spending another Christmas as a single woman is fine. *Everything's* fine." How could she complain when she'd always had it so good?

She could hear the scrape of his beard growth as he ran a hand over his chin. "What's that saying about protesting too much?"

"I'm not protesting."

"If you say so."

Holding the sheet in place, she slid a few more inches away from him, but she couldn't go far. She was about to fall out of bed. He wasn't bulky, but he had wide shoulders and he didn't seem to be concerned about giving her space. "If you know it was my birthday, you remember more than getting dropped off here," she said.

"It's coming back to me."

Bits and pieces were coming back to her, too. How she'd noticed him watching her from where he sat alone at the bar. How she'd danced for him in such a seductive manner, reveling in the appreciation she kindled in his eyes. How he'd eventually gotten up and walked over to join her. How he'd danced with her, so cautiously and respectfully even though the sparks between them felt like they were about to burn the place down.

How she'd slipped through the crush of bodies on the dance floor to catch her breath outside and he'd followed....

There were still things she couldn't recall, however, and his name was one of them. Had he ever told her what it was?

"Who are you?" she asked.

Without even a stretch or a concluding peck on the cheek, he climbed out of bed and started to dress.

At least she wouldn't have to ask him to leave, she told herself. It looked as if he planned on walking into the sunset—or sunrise since it was early—as soon as possible. But this wasn't New York or Los Angeles. He couldn't just hail a taxi. She lived in the Sierra Nevada foothills of Northern California in one of the many mining towns along Highway 49 that had sprung up when gold was discovered a century and a half ago. It was a community that hadn't changed as much as one might expect in such a modern, technologically advanced world. And if the lack of urban conveniences *in* Whiskey Creek wasn't enough of an obstacle, she lived several miles *out-*

*side* town. There was very little traffic out here and no buses or other public transit.

He'd have a long hike if he intended to make his way back to Whiskey Creek without catching a ride from her.

Or maybe he planned to call someone. He had a cell phone and, for the most part, there was service.

"You won't answer?" she asked.

"What difference does my name make?" he finally responded.

That set off alarm bells, since one of the other things she couldn't recall was whether they'd used any birth control. He wasn't one of those weirdoes who went around purposely infecting people with HIV, was he?

"You don't want me to know who you are?"

Having donned his boxers, he jammed one leg and then the other into a pair of well-worn jeans. "I don't see any purpose in exchanging personal information."

So he'd already decided he wasn't going to see her again. She hadn't been entirely sure she wanted to see *him*. He hadn't been that friendly so far, but she felt a measure of disappointment all the same. She had enjoyed what she could remember of last night—and what she remembered more than anything else was the way he kissed. It was so good, so completely bone-melting, that she grew warm just thinking about it. A man who really knew how to kiss a woman seemed like a nice place to start a love affair.

"What if I need to reach you?" she asked. To tell him he'd given her herpes, for instance.

He lowered his voice. "I'm sorry, but last night…I shouldn't have let it go the way it did. I knew better and…I wasn't going to, but…God, you can *dance*."

"So you do have one nice thing to say.…"

"I told you not to take what we were doing seriously,

but…I'm sure that's all forgotten. So I'll say it again. I'm not interested in a relationship."

He couldn't even take her to dinner before calling it quits?

Obviously her luck with men wasn't improving—even when she opened herself up to a random encounter.

"Why?" she asked. "Are you married?" At this point, his rejection was so unequivocal she almost hoped he was. Then she wouldn't have to credit it to some failing on her part.

"No." He didn't even look over when he responded.

"You have a girlfriend, then?" Jared. She was almost certain he'd said his name was Jared….

"No. I might be a lot of things, but I've never been a cheater."

Great. She must've acted like a desperate idiot last night. Or maybe she wasn't nearly as good at kissing—or other activities—as she was at dancing.

"Was it something *I* did?" Normally, she wouldn't have asked. It was difficult to lower her pride. But if he was going to brush her off anyway, what could it hurt to learn the reason? Maybe that information would help her know why she couldn't seem to find Mr. Right.

"No."

That was it? That was all the feedback he was willing to give her? "You're far too generous. Thanks for the reassurance."

He glanced up at her sarcasm. "At least I meant what I said. It's not you. It has nothing to do with you."

But he still wasn't interested. *Why?* "Just tell me we used some protection, *Jared*," she said. "Then you can take off."

"Of course we used protection." He scowled, but she couldn't tell if that was in reaction to her remembering his name or the nature of her question. "I wouldn't leave either of us vulnerable to what could happen without it."

She clutched the sheet tighter. "How do I know you're telling the truth?"

"Condom wrapper's on the floor. I'll leave it for you to throw away, if that makes you feel any more secure. And just to reassure you, I'm clean."

Seeing the wrapper he'd mentioned peeking out from under her nightstand, she breathed a sigh of relief. "Not that you seem worried but...just in case, so am I."

"What?" He was searching for the rest of his clothes.

"Clean. Well, to be totally honest I've never been tested. I wouldn't even know where to go to get tested. But I've only been with three other guys, and one of them was clear back in high school, when we were both virgins."

He got down to peer under the bed and came up with a missing sock. "Going by what you told me last night, they were all from around here."

"What difference does that make?"

"This place doesn't strike me as a hotbed for venereal disease."

She watched as he sat down and pulled on his hiking-style boots. He stood without lacing them. "Don't tell me I gave you my whole sexual history," she said.

"Why? You don't have much of one. It didn't take long."

"Sounds as if I was a bit of a blabbermouth." That wasn't appealing. She probably wasn't experienced enough for him.

"You were trying to explain why you were so hungry for a man."

There was no judgment or accusation in his tone. It sounded as though he was merely trying to jog her memory. But she didn't want to be perceived as sexually aggressive. Most people didn't consider that a positive trait, especially when it was associated with a woman. "I'm sorry if I was too…uninhibited or—or overeager."

"You were honest about your needs, which is why I thought I could fulfill them. Our exchange was simple. Straightforward. Nothing wrong with that."

"I'm glad you're satisfied."

He reached for his shirt. "You're not?"

She knew he was referring to the many orgasms he'd given her and changed the subject. "Why are you here? In Whiskey Creek, I mean. What brought you to this area?"

"I wanted a change of pace. Heard it was pretty up this way."

"So it's not because of your job."

"I'm taking some time off."

She noticed another scar, this one on his back. "Were you in a car accident or something?"

He didn't seem surprised by the question. She could only assume he heard it every time he bared his upper body. "No."

"What happened?"

"Shark attack."

What she saw didn't look like a shark bite. It looked like he'd been cut by a knife, or maybe he'd been caught in barbed wire. "Really?"

"No."

For whatever reason, he didn't want her to know anything about him. "Are you like this with all women—or is it just me?"

He didn't answer. After shrugging into his shirt, he buttoned it and then paused at the foot of the bed. "Last night was—" he seemed to be putting some effort into choosing the right words "—a welcome diversion. Thank you."

"And thank *you* for making me feel like a worthless piece of trash you tossed aside." Those words rushed out of her mouth before she could stop them. She was offended that he wouldn't even tell her his name, that she'd had to remember it without any help from him, but she could only blame herself for this situation. She was the one who'd extended the invitation. Actually, she'd done more than that. She'd *enticed* him. She'd never acted so wanton in her life.

She thought he'd walk out on her. But he didn't. As he stood there, staring at her, a muscle moved in his cheek. "Do you ever have any thoughts that *don't* come out of your mouth?"

She raised her chin to let him know she didn't care if he approved of her or not. The fact that last night really hadn't meant anything to him, not even enough that he'd want to have a cup of coffee together, stung and she'd reacted. She wasn't going to beat herself up over it. "Not often. Why, does my frank approach wound your sensitive nature?"

"Some things are better left unsaid."

The disappointment and anger he inspired bubbled to the surface again. "If I was as good at feeling nothing as you seem to be, I wouldn't have any trouble divorcing my mouth from my heart. Maybe not caring is something you get better at with practice."

"This isn't my fault," he said. "You needed an escape last night as badly as I did."

"Says you."

As his gaze moved over her, she got the impression he was speculating on whether she needed another escape now. There was a flutter in her stomach, her breath caught in her throat and it seemed as though time stood still. As though…she wasn't sure what. She didn't like him, resented how he'd treated her this morning, and yet…the sizzling attraction that had brought them together in the first place hadn't disappeared. That was suddenly obvious.

The intensity on his face made her think he might return to the bed. But then he reined himself in, hard, and that hungry expression was hidden by a stoic mask. "Just because I don't say everything you want me to doesn't mean I feel nothing."

It took a moment for her to collect herself, but as he started down the hall, she called out, "It's a long walk to town. And it's December. Are you sure you don't want me to give you a ride?"

"No, I'll make my own way back," he replied.

# 2

That was a mistake. Rex McCready knew better than to let himself get involved with a woman like the one he'd just slept with. But last night he'd been craving more than a perfunctory encounter. He'd been hoping to assuage the aching loneliness that plagued him, to finally connect on an emotionally honest and intimate level.

It'd been so long since he'd felt close to anyone. To make matters worse, he'd been traveling from town to town for over a week, which meant he'd spent Thanksgiving in a hotel room, alone. The holidays were always rough, regardless of where he happened to be.

But if he wasn't careful, he'd drag another innocent party into the mess he'd created. And he couldn't do that. Four years ago, he'd almost lost the only woman he'd ever loved to the men who were looking for him. Allowing himself to care about someone else merely threw him back into the same situation, a situation that left him vulnerable—and made anyone he cared about vulnerable, too.

Last night he'd acted selfishly and he'd gotten drunk to give himself the excuse. But he had a sneaking suspicion that even without the whiskey, it would've been

impossible to resist the beautiful woman who'd singled
him out at the bar.

Eve. That was her name. He'd heard the waitress who
drove them back to her place call her that, and he'd found
it as ironic then as he did now. She'd tempted him and
he'd fallen, although she wasn't the kind of woman he
should be with. She was far too innocent, too trusting,
too conservative in her ideals. She hung on to the people
in her life; he could tell that from the little she'd told him.

He glanced back at her bungalow with a regret he
didn't want to feel. If he could've stayed a bit longer,
made love to her when they were both sober—that
would've done a lot more to fill the gaping hole inside
him. But he was only driving himself crazy by dwelling
on what he couldn't have. He didn't want to be responsible for bringing danger into anyone's life—and if he'd
learned anything since being released from prison, it was
that associating with him could be dangerous.

At least the hours they'd been together had given him
a much-needed escape, even if it was far too brief.

A truck came rumbling up from behind. He stuck out
his thumb, hoping to catch a ride, but the driver squinted
at him through the dirty windshield as if he couldn't
imagine any normal person hitchhiking these back roads
in the chilly dawn, and drove on.

So much for people in the country being more trusting
than those in the city, Rex thought. In his travels, he'd
discovered that it was often the opposite. But he wasn't
worried about having to make the long trek to town on
foot. He could travel five miles in an hour. According to
his smartphone, Whiskey Creek was 4.1 miles due north.
Besides, he enjoyed being in motion. There was a cathar-
tic quality about covering the ground with a quick, purposeful stride. It appeased the restless wanderer inside

him who never seemed to be content, never seemed to be comfortable coming to a complete stop. Even when he remained in one place, he found himself jiggling his knee to siphon off excess energy.

But if he didn't make good time, he'd leave his assistant hanging around the park where he was supposed to meet her, and he didn't want her to panic, thinking something had happened to him. He'd never had to go into hiding like this before, not since she'd come to work for him, so she was already a little freaked out.

He phoned her at home, hoping he could catch her before she left.

"Marilyn?"

"How's the prospecting?"

A lot of people came to this area to look for gold in the rivers and streams of the Sierra Nevada foothills. Some did quite well. Although that was ostensibly his reason for choosing this particular spot for his "vacation," it was too cold in December and he didn't really know what he was doing. "I tried it once." And nearly froze his nuts off. "Found nothing. About this morning—"

"I'm glad you called," she broke in. "I'm running late. My husband left the interior light on in my car, and it wouldn't start, even after a jump. He's putting in a new battery."

She sounded frustrated. She liked coming to work early so she could head home at three-thirty. But the fact that she was behind schedule suited him fine. "No worries, since I can't make our original meeting time, either."

"Why not? Is everything okay?"

She knew he wouldn't have stepped away from the helm of his company, especially in such a hurry, unless he had no choice. She just didn't know the nature of the threat he faced. Working in personal security for several years, he'd come up against some pretty bad dudes, any one of whom could want to even the score. Marilyn probably assumed he was dealing with a situation like that. But this particular problem was much bigger than anything he'd ever encountered with a client and it stemmed from before he'd started All About Security, Inc. This went all the way back to a time when he'd been a different sort of man.

"It's fine—for the moment." He grimaced at the ribbon of road winding through the hills in front of him and blew on his hands to warm them. There was no snow on the ground, but there was plenty of frost. "So when will you get here?"

"That'll depend on whether or not a new battery does the trick."

"Fine. Text me when you leave." Since she was coming from the Bay Area, where his office was located, he'd have two hours from that point.

"I will."

"Perfect."

"Are we still meeting in the little park you told me about?" she asked before he could end the call.

"Yes. Right next to the giant gold-panning statue." He preferred public places in case she'd been followed. That was for her safety *and* his; he didn't like the idea of someone kicking in the door to his room and shooting him before he could draw his own weapon. Although it wasn't legal for an ex-con to own a firearm in California, let alone carry concealed, he wasn't nearly as afraid of the cops as he was of the other side. He disregarded that no-firearms stipulation whenever he felt the situation warranted it. He'd been fighting to preserve his own life so long that he simply did what he had to do.

But, as vulnerable as it made him feel, he didn't have

his gun with him now. He'd certainly known not to take it into a bar. These days a lot of places screened patrons before letting them in and, last night, he'd needed a break badly enough to go unarmed.

"I'm sure I won't miss it," she said. "I'll see you soon."

He was just putting his phone away when he heard the approach of another vehicle. This one slowed before he could stick out his thumb, and the driver, an old man, leaned across the seat and lowered the window.

"Hey, you need a ride?"

"I do." Flashing the guy a grateful smile, Rex climbed in.

"Why didn't you come to coffee this morning?"

Eve turned to see Cheyenne, her very pregnant best friend, waddle into the small office at the back of the B and B and bend down to put her purse under the desk. Although Cheyenne had cut back on her hours, first when she got married and then when her sister returned to town so she could help out by babysitting her toddler nephew, she still came in four days a week. Her schedule would change again, however, once she had the baby. As much as Eve hated the thought, she would probably have to find a replacement, at least temporarily. She was already working all the hours she could to compensate.

"I woke up late." She feigned more interest than she really had in the bill-paying process she'd started as soon as she arrived. Ever since her competitor, A Room with a View, opened up down the street, it had been a struggle to remain solvent. But she'd fought long and hard and wasn't about to give up any time soon. Not only would this B and B one day be her inheritance, it felt like a member of the family. And since her siblings, two brothers, were nearly fifteen years older and had lived in Texas since they both joined the air force, she didn't feel she had any family members to spare.

"It wasn't the same without you," Cheyenne commented.

"Who came?"

"Dylan, of course."

Chey's husband had joined them ever since the two started dating.

"Then there were Ted and Sophia," Chey went on, glossing over those two names as she always did since Eve had dated Ted last Christmas. "Brandon and Olivia, Callie and Levi, Noah and Addy."

All couples. In the past few years, the dynamic of the whole group had changed.

"Oh, and Presley stopped by," Cheyenne added. "She was passing out invites to her wedding. I have yours in my purse."

Eve swiveled her chair around to accept it. *Another* wedding. Presley wasn't a member of their original clique. She was Cheyenne's older sister by two years. But that didn't matter. Eve felt she'd soon be the only single person in Whiskey Creek, other than their friends Kyle and Riley. Thank God neither of them had tied the knot. Actually, Kyle had been married briefly to Noelle, the waitress who'd given her and her mystery lover a ride home last night. And Riley had once been engaged.

Eve hadn't even gotten *that* close to the altar.

"Where were they?" she asked, setting Presley's wedding invitation aside. "They're almost as regular as I am."

"I don't know, but we thought it was strange that all three of you didn't show up."

All three of you *singles*. Crazy how quickly they'd become the minority....

"I don't miss often." Eve was one of the driving forces

behind their weekly coffee date. She looked forward to catching up with the people she'd hung out with since forever—although, more and more, visiting with them made her feel she was being left behind. These days, instead of who was seeing whom and what they had planned for next weekend, the conversation revolved around babies and purchasing houses and the ups and downs of marriage.

Eve had nothing to contribute to that.

Still, she would've attended but she could all too easily imagine everyone wishing her a happy birthday and asking what she did last night, and she didn't want to be reminded of it. This evening the whole gang was taking her to San Francisco for dinner, in a limo no less. She preferred to start the celebration fresh, as if she'd never gone to Sexy Sadie's.

"I'll see everyone later. I'm sorry I missed out, but…I was feeling pressure to get caught up around here."

Cheyenne frowned at her. "Is there a problem?"

Was she acting unusual? "No, just the day-to-day stuff," she said. "You know how tough it is to survive the off-season."

"But I thought you were feeling encouraged. We've been full almost every weekend, and we were full last night, on a Thursday. That's better than a year ago. Offering afternoon tea has definitely improved our occupancy rate."

The tea had been Eve's idea. Besides the boost it gave her business, she enjoyed going to secondhand shops looking for vintage items she could use in unexpected ways. Most recently she'd been collecting old plates and fastening them to various candleholders and other bases to make elegant stacking trays or elevated dishes.

"With luck, word will spread and our tea will really

bring in some business when spring hits," she said. As Cheyenne had mentioned, they'd already noticed a spike. "But we have to get by until then."

Fortunately, A Room with a View was no longer undercutting her prices. For months after it first opened, the owners—a European couple relatively new to the area—had tried to drive her out of business. They'd finally given up, but she wasn't under the illusion that they'd backed off out of kindness or compassion. They must not have had deep enough pockets to continue.

Thank God. She couldn't have hung on much longer. As it was, only the nineteenth-century mystery of Little Mary's murder, and the rumor that her ghost might be haunting the place, had saved the inn from foreclosure. *Unsolved Mysteries* had come out to film an episode, and the publicity from that had enabled Eve to continue to pay the mortgage.

"How's Deb getting on with breakfast?" Cheyenne asked.

Hungover and sleep-deprived, Eve hid a yawn. "She was doing okay when I checked on her a few minutes ago." Fortunately, their "new" cook had been with them for nearly six months, so she was well accustomed to the demands of the job.

Cheyenne's chair creaked as she settled in. "I can't remember—what's on the menu?" She sniffed. "Whatever it is smells great."

"Ricotta pancakes with lemon curd and fresh raspberries. A fruit and yogurt parfait with handmade granola. Two sausages and fresh-squeezed orange juice."

"Oh, right." Cheyenne gave an exasperated laugh at her forgetfulness. She was the one who'd planned this particular meal; she'd chosen the ricotta pancakes last week. "I take it the taste-test went well yesterday?"

"Those pancakes are delicious!"

"I can't wait to try them."

Eve glanced at her watch. "Most of our guests signed up for a nine-thirty breakfast. We should go to the kitchen in another twenty minutes or so to help Deb." They had only seven rooms, but with such a small staff—three of them to cook, handle the food and clean during the day and two people who traded off as night manager and covered for Eve when she was gone—it could be tricky to get everyone served at once.

"Are most of them eating in the dining room?" Chey asked.

"All but 1 and 5." Room 1 was the smallest. Located at the back of the inn, it overlooked the garden, arbor and hot tub. Room 5 was their wedding suite, or could be turned into one if they had a bride and groom.

"Maybe we should do a sign-up sheet with two slots for each half hour so that the most we'll ever serve at one time is—"

The buzz of Cheyenne's phone interrupted. When she looked down at it and fell silent, Eve twisted around to see why.

"What is it?" she asked.

"Kyle texted me."

"Where was he this morning?"

"He says he had to give Noelle her spousal maintenance."

Eve froze at the mention of Noelle. She didn't want Kyle coming into contact with his ex-wife. Not so soon after last night. She was hoping that, with the passage of time, Noelle might forget what she'd witnessed—or forget to say anything about it. "His spousal maintenance isn't due until the middle of the month. He's told us that more than once."

"She always tries to get it out of him early. That's why we know when it's due. We've heard him complain that he's supposed to have until the fifteenth. Anyway, this time she told him the utility company was going to shut off her electricity."

"He fell for that old trick?"

"Kyle's a big softie. And he still feels guilty for getting involved with her in the first place." She took a moment to text him back.

Hoping Cheyenne and Kyle's conversation would end there, Eve entered a few more checks in her electronic register, but heard Cheyenne say her name a few seconds later.

*"Eve?"*

She curved her fingernails into her palms. "Yes?"

"Noelle's been telling Kyle some crazy stuff."

A knot formed in Eve's stomach, but she had to answer. "Like what?"

Eve could hear the change in Cheyenne's voice, even though she wasn't facing in that direction. "You didn't go out last night, did you?"

"For a while," she hedged, and then did what she could to take control of the conversation. "But if Kyle wants to know what I did for my birthday, why isn't he texting *me?*"

"He says he tried and got no response. It has him worried."

After surveying her desk, she realized she must've left her phone in her car.

"He wanted to know if you were at coffee this morning. Wants to make sure you're okay."

"You can tell him I'm fine." And to butt out. But she knew that wasn't going to happen when Cheyenne gave a cry of surprise.

"Noelle is claiming you took some guy home from Sexy Sadie's!" With her extended abdomen, it was a struggle for Cheyenne to get to her feet. "Is that true?"

Damn Noelle! Eve had suspected she wouldn't keep her mouth shut, not while she was privy to such a delicious secret. And now that she'd blabbed, everyone in town would hear about Eve's mistake.

*"Is it?"* Cheyenne asked.

Letting her breath go in a sigh, Eve stopped pretending to work and turned. "I'm afraid I had a little too much to drink."

"Who were you with?"

"Jared Somebody."

*"Somebody?* You don't know his last name?"

"We didn't get that far," Eve said with a shrug. "It was just a…a quick encounter. He left almost right away."

"But not before…"

Eve was tempted to lie. But this was Chey. If she couldn't tell her best friend when she screwed up, who could she tell? "No."

"Wow, that's *so* unlike you." Eyes wide with shock, she sank back into her seat. "I don't think you've ever done anything like that in your life."

"I haven't."

"What made you do it last night?"

"That's hard to explain." She rubbed her temples.

"Give it a try."

"You know how I feel about turning thirty-five."

"I do. And I understand why. But lots of women are marrying later in life. And they're having children, too." She touched her belly. "Look at me."

True. However, Chey's situation was anything but typical. If not for the fact that Aaron, her brother-in-law, had donated sperm for an artificial insemination, which had

happened in secret, she would be childless. Her husband
didn't know he wasn't really the father. Eve wouldn't
know, either, if Cheyenne hadn't broken down and told
her during a brief scare when she began to spot at three
months and feared she was about to have a miscarriage.

"I was determined not to spend my birthday alone,
so—"

"I feel terrible," Cheyenne broke in. "I should've been
there for you."

"You couldn't. You have a husband and other responsibilities now." Not that it made the loss of her best friend's
time and attention any easier. Eve was more alone than
she'd ever been. With her parents traveling so much, and
her friends busy with their own lives, all she had to de-
vote herself to was the B and B. Since she'd dated Ted
last year, and he'd broken up with her for Sophia, she'd
been even lonelier.

"It wasn't Dylan who pulled me away," Cheyenne clarified. "His brothers were arguing with their father and
stepmother, and we were trying to act as intermediaries."

"Well, helping in that situation was more important
than hanging out with me last night," Eve said. "Trust
me, what I did wasn't your fault. It was mine. As I said,
I was drinking. And this guy was…"

Worry creased Cheyenne's forehead. "Pushy? He
didn't press you too hard or…or make you feel you had
no choice…."

"Not at all," she said. "The moment I noticed him, I
wanted him—more than I've ever wanted anyone else.
It had to be the booze. I'm not usually like that, not with
a stranger. But everything—my mood, the alcohol, the
fact that I was alone and the handsomest guy I'd ever
seen was sitting at the bar… It all sort of undermined
my good sense."

Cheyenne bit her lip. "So you invited him over?"

"More or less. We wound up together. Let's just say that."

"I'm happy you met someone you were attracted to. But taking a stranger home… That's so dangerous, Eve. He could've hurt you or…worse."

Eve had swallowed two ibuprofen tablets to help her recover from her hangover. She'd been feeling better since then, but the tension of having to confess to something she'd much rather forget was bringing back the pain. "He didn't do anything I didn't want him to, so there's nothing to worry about there. I made a mistake. It's that simple. I was stupid and foolhardy, but it's over now, and I can't take it back."

She returned to her computer, hoping the discussion was now at an end. But Cheyenne didn't go back to work.

"So you're okay?"

"As okay as I can be when I'm embarrassed and humiliated," Eve replied. "I'm hoping my parents won't hear about it once they're home. They'd be just as embarrassed. And disappointed. They don't need that at their age."

"Did they get the RV fixed?"

"Not yet. They had to order one of the parts."

"Lucky for you. Hopefully, this will blow over before they return."

"From your lips to God's ears."

Cheyenne groaned as she stretched. Then, obviously attempting to be nonchalant about it, she asked, "Do you think you'll be seeing this guy again?"

"No. He's only in town temporarily." She didn't want to add that he'd also made clear he wasn't interested, which was hitting her hard after Ted's defection. Until the past few years, she'd been the one to call the shots with the men she dated. But maybe she'd been too picky for too long and deserved the reversal. Maybe karma was coming back to bite her. It certainly seemed that way, because there'd been Joe DeMarco, who'd dated her just once—by his choice—and Ted, who'd done *more* than date her, only to break it off right when she'd decided she was finally falling in love.

Counting this guy, she was zero for three.

"What brought him here?"

Eve felt herself flush. "We didn't do much talking."

"Apparently not." Cheyenne seemed to be fighting a smile.

"Stop!" Eve scowled at her. "This isn't funny. Let's just…pretend it never happened."

"*We* can do that. And I'm confident we can convince Kyle to keep *his* mouth shut. He knows what it's like to make that kind of mistake. But Noelle? If you take someone home with you, don't ever do it in front of her."

Eve didn't volunteer that Noelle was the one who'd given them a ride. "If I'd had any brain cells that were still functioning, we wouldn't be having this conversation!"

Cheyenne came up behind her and began to massage her shoulders. "Everything will be okay. Try not to let it ruin your birthday."

Turning thirty-five had already done that. But she had more to worry about than the memory of a birthday gone sour. Even if she could forget what she'd done, she couldn't escape what had caused her to act that way in the first place. There was a void in her life and she was trying to fill it with something meaningful. Last night hadn't helped, however. If anything, it'd made things worse because it had highlighted, once again, the companionship she was missing, as if watching her friends move on with their lives wasn't difficult enough. "I never saw this coming."

"Neither did I," Cheyenne admitted. "But…maybe you needed to cut loose."

"Thanks for looking on the bright side." Eve took a moment to smile gratefully. Then she shoved last night into the back of her mind. They needed to get through the most challenging part of the day—and for any B and B that was pulling off a fabulous breakfast. "We'd better go help Deb."

Cheyenne gave her a final squeeze and they headed to the kitchen, where Eve insisted on being the one to deliver the meal trays to the guests who'd requested breakfast in their rooms. She didn't want Cheyenne climbing such a long flight of stairs if she didn't have to.

Trying not to obsess about who else Noelle might be telling about her faux pas of last night, Eve hurried to Room 1 with a single tray for a Brent Taylor. B and Bs primarily hosted couples, but that wasn't necessarily the case in Whiskey Creek. Because there were no regular motels, she rented to anyone who needed a room, and that sometimes included a husband or wife who'd been kicked out of the house or had stormed off for whatever reason, people who came to pan for gold, business travelers and others who were passing through for one reason or another.

With her mind on returning to the kitchen for the other two trays she had to deliver to the couple in Room 5, she donned a polite expression as soon as the door opened. But the words she was about to utter—"Good morning. I hope you enjoy your breakfast"—never passed her lips.

There, looking like he'd just stepped out of the shower, was the man who'd shared her bed last night.

# 3

"How'd you find me?"

When she heard the accusation in his voice, Eve realized her mouth was hanging open and closed it. She was so used to being associated with Little Mary's it took her aback that he thought *she* was the one out of place. *"What?"*

"I said, how did you find me? Did you *follow* me?"

Judging by the impatience on his face, he wasn't happy about that idea. Perhaps he'd connected with other women who hadn't understood the meaning of "I'm not interested."

"Of course not! I would never force my attentions on you or any man."

His gaze shifted to the tray she was carrying. "Then how come you're here, bringing me breakfast?"

"I own this place! I serve a lot of people breakfast," she said. "I had no idea you were one of my guests, *Mr. Taylor.* If you'll remember, you told me your name was Jared." She met most of the people who stayed at Little Mary's. She bumped into them as they wandered around the property, enjoying the garden, walking to or from the private hot tub, sitting in the alcoves where they could watch the sunset or having breakfast or tea in the dining room. But the only place she'd ever seen Mr. Taylor was at the bar once she'd left work. She'd assumed he was at A Room with a View if he was in town. "When did you check in?"

"Last night around seven."

That explained it. He'd come when Cecelia was on duty. "Meeting up again like this is…is merely an unfortunate coincidence," she said. "But there's a second B and B in Whiskey Creek, so you have another option. It's called A Room with a View and it's just down the street. You might want to move there." She handed him his tray. "Come downstairs when you're done and I'll get you checked out."

When his eyes widened, she could tell she'd managed to surprise him, but she didn't care. She meant what she'd said. She wanted him gone. Losing his business would cost her a few bucks, but at least she'd be able to avoid him.

"Wait, are you kicking me out?" he called after her.

She'd started for the stairs, but she turned and lowered her voice so their exchange wouldn't be heard by any guests who might be in nearby rooms. Staying at Little Mary's was all about peace and beauty and tranquility. For most people, anyway. The rumor that the place was haunted brought others. But she sold an experience, and she was determined to make that experience one her clientele could rely on.

"I wouldn't state it quite that strongly," she whispered, tossing a worried glance at the closest door. Hopefully, the couple staying in Room 3 was at breakfast. That was where they should be, since they'd signed up for the nine-thirty sitting. "I'm just suggesting you find other accommodations."

"Because…"

"I wouldn't want to ruin your stay by fawning over you the way you obviously assume I will." She manufactured an exaggerated wink. "This is your chance to escape another man-hungry woman."

He raised his eyebrows, but she didn't stick around to witness any more of his reaction. She wanted to get away as quickly as possible. She had things to do. And the faster he ate and packed, the faster she could put last night behind her and go on with life as usual. She didn't need a love interest. She'd find other worthwhile things to fill her life. Things like—

"Eve…"

He was standing at the top of the stairs when she turned back.

"I'll be waiting whenever you're ready," she responded. Then she was too far away for him to say more.

But when he appeared a half hour later, he wasn't carrying any luggage—not even a duffel bag. And he didn't approach her to check out. He cut through the dining room, nodding to Deb when she wished him a good morning and strode out the front door.

What the heck?

Eve started after him. She'd been serious when she suggested he go elsewhere. But he was walking so fast, she'd have to run to catch up with him—and she wasn't prepared to go that far. The last thing she wanted was to cause a scene.

Maybe he had plans. Maybe he'd move later.

Cheyenne came up beside her as she hesitated at the front desk, wondering whether he would or wouldn't check out—and what she could do to make her life feel more complete.

"I'm going to start cleaning the downstairs rooms," she said. "Deb's tackling the upstairs."

"Sounds good."

"Did you meet the people in Room 1? Do you think we'll be able to get in there soon to make the bed and straighten up?"

She could've explained to Cheyenne that the bed hadn't been slept in, that there was only one occupant and it was the stranger she'd taken home last night. But she didn't. Since she preferred to let it all fade away, she figured she might as well let that process begin now.

"Eve? Did you hear me?" Cheyenne asked.

She'd been too preoccupied to answer. "Room 1 is empty," she said.

"Okay. I'll have Deb do that room while she's up there."

"That'd be great," Eve mumbled. But then she called Cheyenne back. "Never mind. I'll do it myself."

"Are you sure?"

"Yeah, I've got it." If Mr. Taylor wasn't going to leave, as she'd requested, she'd start her new lease on life by satisfying what she could of her curiosity.


"You're going to go crazy here."

Rex looked up from the picnic table where he was signing the payroll checks for All About Security, Inc. "Why?"

His middle-aged assistant—a wife and mother of three who reminded him of Melissa McCarthy with her big red hair and the pound of hairspray that shellacked it—smirked as she gazed around. She'd worked for him since he first opened his doors three years ago and always took good care of him. But he'd never appreciated her more than he did now that he'd been flushed out of his comfort zone. Although she had an opinion about everything and generally felt free to voice it, she could also use discretion when necessary. "It's beautiful," she said. "So Christmassy, with all the lights on the old-fashioned shops and stuff. But you like the city, and you normally work 24/7. If this hiding-out thing goes on much longer, you won't know what to do with yourself."

He gave her a sardonic smile. "Hiding out? Come on. This is my dream vacation. Loads of people would love to get away and enjoy nature as they pan for gold."

"Dream vacation, my ass," she muttered.

Her choice of words shocked him a little when she swore, but he found her language kind of funny, too, coming from someone who looked like a 1950s house-wife with her floral button-up shirts and ankle pants.

"For you, this is hell," she added with even more con-viction. "You've been traveling from one town to the next for more than a week. And it's been too cold to do much outside."

"At least I'm still in one piece." So far, he'd whiled away the hours by working on his laptop. After posting a help-wanted ad on Craigslist, he'd been poring through résumés—pondering each one much longer than usual. He needed to fill the open slot Eric James left when he got stabbed in the shoulder and his wife insisted he find safer work. But it was difficult to do any meaningful evaluation when he couldn't meet the applicants face-to-face. He had to refer the candidates who had promise to Marilyn. She interviewed them, then called him to report.

He'd also been dealing with his accountant, at long last getting caught up on his books, something he rarely took the time to do when living his normal life. He pre-ferred to be on the phone or answering email queries, booking jobs for himself and the six bodyguards he em-ployed. Business had never been better, which was part of the reason he was dying to get back to it. There were times he felt so much like a regular person, like a regular *businessman,* he could almost forget the past.

Almost but not quite. There were some incidents he could never forget and people who wouldn't let him forget others.

"You could take up mountain biking," she suggested. "My two sons love it."

"That's outdoors, too."

"But you don't do it standing in a river. And if you ride hard enough, you stay warm. They bike year-round. We live in California, after all."

He moved the check he'd just signed to the bottom of the stack. "I won't be vacationing long enough to take up a new sport."

She looked across the park toward the maple and dogwood trees that lined one side. Those trees blocked the sight of the Victorian where he was staying, but Marilyn had no idea. He wasn't telling anyone where he slept at night—for their safety as well as his.

Not that he'd actually spent the night at Little Mary's... And he wouldn't. Eve had asked him to leave.

"How do you know?" Marilyn asked.

Finished with the payroll, he tapped the edges of the checks on the table to even the stack. "What do you mean?"

"How do you know how long you'll be here? You weren't planning to be gone in the first place, just up and left in the middle of the night. Yet we're both here in this park. *Something* must be wrong. Are you sure you'll be able to fix it?"

Maybe not. He'd been fighting the same battle for years; he'd thought things had finally settled down—until he heard otherwise from an old friend. In a different time, a different place, he would've closed down his business, sold his house and moved. Anything less was gambling with his life.

But he wasn't about to sacrifice everything he'd created now that he'd hit his stride. At thirty-six, he was getting too old to be constantly starting over. Not only that, but he was afraid of what another uprooting would do to him. Afraid he'd no longer have the determination or the energy to keep plowing forward.

No way could he allow the gang he'd joined in prison to cost him the ground he'd already gained. He just had to lie low for a while, make sure The Crew never found him. With luck, he'd stay one step ahead, and they'd never get the revenge they were after.

"I'm hoping for the best," he said.

She sent him a "give me a break" look, what he guessed her adult sons saw when they tried to put one over on her. "I wish that assured me," she said, but then concern pushed aside the skepticism. "I know you won't tell me what's going on, but I'm getting the impression you're really in a mess this time."

He'd been in a mess since long before he knew her. It'd started when he'd been a lost and confused teenager and then spiraled out of control. But the men who wanted him dead also had a business to run—several businesses. Prostitution. Gun and drug smuggling. Money laundering. Theft. Whatever would make them a buck. Although killing him would give the banger who did it ultimate bragging rights, chasing him around didn't net The Crew any money. If he continued to elude them, they'd eventually quit, wouldn't they?

It was possible. But the opposite was more likely. The longer he lived, the more of a legend he became, and that only increased their desire to put him in a body bag. As far as they were concerned, he and his best friend, Virgil Skinner, had done the unpardonable when they defected and then assisted the authorities—and that demanded retribution. The member who accomplished it would be a hero, at least in their small, sordid world.

"Depends," he said. "Has anyone come by the office, asking for me? Any strange calls?"

"There are always strange calls," she said. "You own a personal security firm. Some of our clients are delusional as well as paranoid."

"So nothing out of the ordinary."

She studied him for several seconds. "It would help if I understood what you were dealing with. Maybe then I could figure out what to look for."

"You know I can't tell you. Some people are after me. That's all."

"There've been no red flags on my end."

He took a deep breath, held it for a few seconds and let it go. He'd stay away from his usual haunts for another week, see if there was any sign of his former "brothers." If all remained quiet, he'd head home. Mona Livingston, the friend who'd warned him that several members of The Crew claimed to have new information on his whereabouts, was still using drugs, so he wasn't sure her information was all that reliable. She could've imagined what she'd heard. Or maybe it was nothing but a bunch of street soldiers trying to impress everyone else by vowing they were going to bring him down. There was always that chance, since putting a bullet in him or Virgil, who now lived on the east coast with his wife and kids, would make them the envy of all they admired.

"So how'd it go with Frick?" he asked.

"That's Jason, right? For the job? Physically, he's per-

48       *Brenda Novak*

fect. He's an absolute Goliath! But mentally?" She made a clicking sound with her tongue. "He seems a little trigger-happy to me. I'd worry about him shooting someone without a legitimate reason."

Rex had sensed that same reckless element when they'd chatted briefly on the phone, but he'd wanted to give the guy the benefit of the doubt. It wasn't easy to come by someone who was six-six and built like a Mack truck. "What about the others? Anyone else a good fit?"

"Peter Viselli seems like he has the right temperament."

He grimaced. "Peter's what…five-eleven?"

"Yes, but that's just a couple of inches shorter than you. You also weigh less than every other man in our company—and yet no one's better at security than you are."

Size wasn't a man's only weapon. Rex found speed, agility, experience and intelligence to be more important. But appearance counted, too. Size gave All About Security, Inc., the intimidation factor, and enough of an intimidation factor could head off problems before they started. Being surrounded by a couple of muscle-bound giants also helped foster client confidence.

Still…

"I don't want any loose cannons on my team." Besides the moral implications of having someone use a firearm without sufficient provocation, there were liability issues. Rex preferred to avoid both. "Set up a second interview with Peter for when I get back next week—say, Friday?"

"You think you might be back *that* soon?"

"Yes. I'll call you if anything changes."

Lips pursed, she slipped the checks he'd signed into a file and put them in her oversize bag. "We definitely need you. You're what makes us successful."

"I'll be back soon."

"The question is…will you be safe?"

He nodded to placate her, but he hadn't been safe in years.


Brent Taylor didn't have much luggage. A leather satchel lay open on the bed. From what Eve could tell without digging through it, he'd packed jeans, T-shirts and at least one sweatshirt.

The bed was made, as she'd known it would be. The shower was damp. She also found wet towels in the bathroom, where she could smell his deodorant and the shampoo she provided for her guests.

Now that she was here, she felt silly taking careful note of such mundane things—the same things she saw when she cleaned other clients' rooms. She wasn't sure what she'd expected to learn or why any of it would matter. If he hadn't been so secretive and standoffish, she probably wouldn't have bothered.

There was nothing that revealed a great deal about him, but a few clues gave her more information than she'd had. The type of pan used for prospecting sat on his nightstand. That told her what he was likely doing in Gold Country. On the small desk by the window overlooking the backyard was a laptop, and on the Little Mary's writing pad by the phone, he'd jotted down some names and numbers.

He wrote like a typical guy, she decided. He printed, but it wasn't particularly legible. The name Jason Frick topped the short list. His area code suggested he was from the Bay Area, which was just a couple of hours away. She recognized it because so many of her patrons came from there.

Was Frick a friend of Mr. Taylor's, or a business associate? The other names were male, too, also from the Bay Area. Peter Viselli and Dom Chandler—although Dom's name was crossed out.

Eve "accidentally" ran her finger over the mouse section of the laptop while dusting, hoping his screensaver would dissolve into whatever he'd been working on, but it didn't. The demand for a password popped up instead.

She didn't protect her own computers with a password, even the one she worked on here at the B and B. But there was hardly any crime in Whiskey Creek, and *she* had nothing to hide.

So who was this Mr. Taylor?

Obviously someone who lived in the city.

Knowing she didn't have long before Cheyenne or Deb came to find her—or Brent Taylor returned—she replaced his towels and minicontainers of soap, shampoo and conditioner and threw away the ones he'd used. Then she ran a vacuum over the carpet.

When she was finished, she could hear Deb speaking to some guests in the hall. The usual morning sounds made her feel a bit embarrassed for poking around Mr. Taylor's room. Had she crossed the line? Was she acting like a stalker?

She really needed to get a life, she told herself, and, for the first time ever, considered hiring someone to run the inn for a few months so she could try something else before settling down for good and letting her life harden like cement.

Maybe last night was a sign that she needed to broaden her horizons, embrace change, try new things.

Maybe if she didn't, she'd regret it later. Cheyenne would be having her baby soon. It wasn't as if they'd get to work together after that, anyway. Or at least not for a while—

"Hey."

Eve jumped and turned to see the very person she'd been thinking about standing at the door. "What are you doing up here?" she asked. "You're not supposed to be climbing the stairs."

"Who said? The exercise is good for me, as long as I don't fall."

"Falling's what I'm worried about." After trying for two years to get this baby, and resorting to what she'd resorted to, Cheyenne would be devastated if she lost it.

"I'm being careful. I just wanted to let you know…" She winced as if what she had to say wouldn't be welcome news.

"What?" Eve prompted.

"Your parents are back."

Eve's hand flew to her mouth and she spoke through her fingers. "No!"

"Yes. They're waiting downstairs in the small parlor. They feel terrible that they didn't make it in time for your birthday, so they had the part for the RV flown in, which cost them a lot more, and now they're anxious to give you their present."

Her parents were too good. They had to be the best, most supportive people in the world, which was partly why Eve felt so embarrassed about her recent behavior.

"You don't think they'll hear about last night…."

"No! Of course not! Who'd tell them?" Cheyenne plastered a reassuring smile on her face, but Eve could see right through it.

"You *do* think they'll hear."

She let her smile wilt. "I'm afraid they might. We *are* talking about Noelle. When Kyle dropped by to give her his spousal maintenance, she had that other waitress over—Casey? He said they were talking and laughing about…the situation."

Casey hadn't even been working on Thursday night.

Eve closed her eyes as she pinched the bridge of her nose. She had to get out of this town. She felt trapped, stifled. As much as she loved Little Mary's and Whiskey Creek and all the people she'd grown up with, she needed something new. But it seemed odd that this realization had burst upon her so suddenly. Did other people question where they were in life at only thirty-five? Was she having a midlife crisis before she ever hit midlife?

Maybe she should take whatever money she'd saved and travel across Europe….

"I'll finish up," Cheyenne said. "What's left?"

"Nothing." As Eve wound up the vacuum cord, she thought once more about telling Cheyenne that Brent Taylor was the man she'd slept with, but changed her mind. She didn't want Cheyenne to find out that he'd lied to her about his name. And even if he didn't check out today, he wouldn't be in Whiskey Creek for long.

"Want me to go down with you?" Cheyenne asked. "Would that help you face them?"

"No. I've got to put the vacuum away first—and I'm not going to let you carry it down those stairs so don't even offer. Just tell them I'm coming."

Cheyenne gave her a quick hug. "You're in your thirties. If they do hear about last night, they probably won't say anything."

Of course they wouldn't. They weren't intrusive. It was what they'd *think* that troubled Eve.

Again, she felt a desperate need for more space, a change of scenery, a chance to figure out if the person she'd become was the person she wanted to be. Maybe she'd been treading water, hoping for the kind of love some of her friends had found, but it didn't look as though that was going to happen for her. At least not here… Maybe it took her thirty-fifth birthday to make her realize she had to go in a different direction.

She listened to Cheyenne's footsteps recede. Then she lifted up the vacuum. But before she could collect her cleaning bucket, she noticed the luggage tag on Brent Taylor's suitcase and set the vacuum down.

*There* was his personal information. She should make a note of it in case there was some reason he didn't want to give it out. Say…if the FBI happened to be looking for him. If she was going to be stupid enough to sleep with a stranger, a possible fugitive from the law, she should do what she could to point the police in the right direction if they came knocking at her door.

But the tag didn't say the suitcase belonged to a Brent Taylor, or even a Jared. Taylor Jackson was written in the same handwriting as the names on the pad. There was no address. Just a number, which she keyed into the notes section of her phone.

Had he borrowed someone else's luggage?

It was possible. But the fact that he'd used two names already gave her the feeling it was more significant than that.

What was going on with this guy? Last night he'd been the perfect lover. Attentive and responsive. The more she remembered about being with him, the more convinced she became that he'd provided the best sex she'd ever had. He'd seemed to enjoy himself, too. Yet this morning, after everything they'd done, he would scarcely give her the time of day, had acted particularly odd when she asked for his full name and, even though he'd said he was Jared, he'd checked in as Brent Taylor and his bag indicated it belonged to a Taylor Jackson.

Knowing she had to go and greet her parents, she grabbed her cleaning stuff and hurried out, closing the door behind her. But as she descended the stairs, she figured she was probably lucky that Jared or Brent or Taylor—whoever he was—didn't want anything more to do with her.

# 4

"Honey, we're so sorry we missed your birthday. I can't believe we had engine trouble!" Eve's mother looked genuinely distraught as she pulled Eve in for a hug. "We got back as soon as we could."

"You shouldn't have gone to the extra expense of having that engine part flown in," Eve said. "I can't believe you did. I assumed we'd just celebrate whenever you could get back."

Her father embraced her as soon as her mother let go. "Your birthday's in December, so that means it can get swallowed up by the holidays. We try not to let that happen. You're too important to us."

She cringed as she thought of Noelle and the pleasure she was likely taking in ruining Eve's reputation. "Thanks, Dad."

He shoved his hands in his pockets and jingled his change. "The B and B looks great, by the way. You've done an outstanding job, created the very picture of a Victorian Christmas."

They'd been in Texas for three weeks, having Thanksgiving with her brothers, who now owned a bar together in Austin. "Better than usual?"

"I'd say so," he replied.

"It's the new icicle lights," she told him. "They're pretty hanging from such a steeply pitched roof." She'd hired a company to hang those lights, and all the others on the exterior. But she and Cheyenne had done everything else. The tree alone had taken one full day—the Sunday after Thanksgiving, when they traditionally made the switch from harvest decor to evergreen and holly. The day after that, she'd added wreaths with red ribbon at every window, garland above each door, on every mantel and around every banister and mistletoe hanging over the tables in the dining room. This was usually Eve's favorite time of year. The entire town waited to see what she'd do with the inn, and she took great pride in making it stand out like a beacon of hope for the weary traveler—or even just the weary of heart.

"It's everything," he said. "We drove past A Room with A View. It can't even compare."

Because the owners didn't understand how the beauty she created encouraged the whole town to stop and reflect. Her competitor gave the season a passing nod by putting up a bunch of plastic Santas and reindeer and hanging giant ornaments from the tree in the front yard, all of which looked tacky rather than elegant. But as Eve followed her father's eye to the candles she'd placed so they could be seen from the street, she didn't feel the wonder and magic she used to feel. She was afraid she might be going through the exact same motions for the rest of her life—only without Cheyenne, because she knew that Cheyenne wouldn't work at the inn forever.

"You told us you're planning to go to San Francisco with your friends tonight," her mother said, "so I was hoping we could have you over for dinner tomorrow after you get off work. I'll make your favorite cake, the carrot one, and get some ice cream."

"Of course," Eve said. "Thank you. That sounds delicious."

"And…" Her mother rummaged in her huge purse and finally pulled out a small, wrapped gift. "I'd like you to open your present right now, since you couldn't do it yesterday."

Guilt for behaving in a manner that would reflect poorly on her parents once again swept over Eve. What had she been thinking last night? She'd acted no better than Noelle.…

"Go ahead," her father urged as her mother handed her a small box.

Eve hoped it wasn't expensive. Her parents often tried to do too much. But as soon as she tore off the wrapping and opened the gift, she could see that it was pricy. A gold watch, with diamonds around the face. "Wow," she breathed.

"Do you like it?" The twinkle in her mother's eye showed how excited she was to give her daughter such a wonderful gift.

"I *love* it," Eve said, "but…it's too generous. You guys have to be careful now that you're retired, especially with what we've been through trying to save the inn. You don't have the savings you used to—"

"Don't worry about that," her father interrupted. "You deserve whatever we can give you. You've worked so hard, been the perfect daughter."

*Perfect.* That word pricked her conscience, and she went over and closed the door. "I really love the watch. It's beautiful."

Her mother and father exchanged a look. "But…"

They'd heard the resignation in her tone.

"I'm definitely not perfect. As a matter of fact, I've

done something I need to tell you about before you hear it from someone else."

She felt bad about the fear that entered their faces, and the way they sank slowly onto the sofa. "Good. I was going to suggest you sit down."

"Is it that bad?" her mother asked.

"It's nothing to be proud of."

Her father seemed baffled. "What could it be? We know you. We know who you are."

"You don't know this. I went out last night...by myself and...and got a little drunk."

They sat blinking at her, saying nothing. No doubt they could tell there was more coming.

"And I met someone," she continued. "A...a stranger. He was handsome and charming and he'd also had too much to drink."

"You've met someone?" her mother echoed.

The hope in that question didn't make this any easier. Her parents wanted her to marry and start a family almost as much as she wanted the same thing. Grandchildren had been mentioned on a number of occasions. Since her brothers were fifty and fifty-two, one an avowed bachelor and the other divorced without children, her parents probably wouldn't have any grandkids unless they came from her—although they viewed Cheyenne as a daughter and were excited to welcome her first child into the world.

"No. Not really," Eve said. "It's not what you might think."

"Then what is it?" her father asked.

Throwing back her shoulders, she blurted out the truth. "I took him home with me."

There was a moment of awkward silence. Then her father cleared his throat. "Eve, we've never gotten involved in your personal life. I mean, in *that* part of your personal life. This isn't something you have to report to us, especially at thirty-five. In fact, I'd prefer *not* to know, and I think I can speak for your mother on that, as well."

Eve couldn't help smiling at his response. "I wouldn't have said anything except…I'm afraid you'll hear it around town in the next few days, and I didn't want you to be blindsided. Or disappointed," she added, "but there's no way to avoid that now."

"I see," he said. "And why would someone tell *us?* Why is it any of their business?"

"It's not. But Noelle Arnold works at Sexy Sadie's and—"

"Ah, I see," her mother piped up. "Olivia's sister is spreading the news."

"Yes."

Her mother frowned. "I've never thought very highly of her."

That was a scathing rebuke, coming from her sweet mother. "You're in good company," Eve responded.

"So…that's it?" her father asked. "That's what has you so upset?" He studied her carefully. "It doesn't get any worse, does it?"

"Isn't that *enough?*" she said, surprised that they weren't more upset themselves.

"Honey, everybody makes a mistake now and then," he said. "It's not up to us to judge you or to…to tell you how to run your life. We had our chance to guide you when you were little, and we did our best. Now you're in charge, and while I can't say I'm happy about what you did last night, I can understand how it happened and why."

"It's not as if your father was a virgin when he met me," her mother said. "He slept with loads of women."

"Adele!" her father snapped, obviously appalled. Then

Eve had to laugh and, once she started, she couldn't seem to stop. She recognized how her parents felt about her confession, because she felt the same about what her mother had just revealed. She didn't want to view either one of them as sexual in any way, not even with each other.

"I'm sorry," she said as she wiped away the tears streaming down her face. "I don't mean to laugh, and I don't want you to think I'm not taking what I did seriously, but—"

Her mother got up to hug her again. "I'm *glad* you can laugh. Let it go, honey. We know it hasn't been easy watching all your friends get married. We were as disappointed as you were last year when things didn't work out between you and Ted. He's a good man. But there'll be someone else, someone very special."

She caught hold of her mother's arm before Adele could release her. "What do you think about me…going somewhere else and…trying something new?"

"You mean leave Whiskey Creek?" her dad asked.

"I love it here, but…I'm not sure it's the only life I want to know."

This seemed to sadden them more than the news of how she'd spent last night. Her brothers had gone to Texas A&M on football scholarships, then joined the air force and never returned to California. Her parents often lamented how little they saw of Darren and Dusty.

"We would certainly miss you," her father said. "But we don't want to hold you here if it's not where you want to be. We don't want Little Mary's to hold you here, either."

She glanced around. She loved the B and B almost as much as she loved them. But there had to be some way to vanquish the dissatisfaction that had crept into her life and seemed to be growing stronger by the day. She didn't want to wake up one morning when she was sixty-five and wonder why she'd never made a change.

"You're not saying... Should we put the inn on the market?" her mother asked.

"No, no. Nothing that drastic," she said. "I'm just thinking of hiring someone to run it for a year so I can try something else before I settle down, you know?"

Her parents wore somber expressions as they nodded. "We understand. And we want whatever will make you happy," her father said.

Eve couldn't imagine she'd be happy leaving Whiskey Creek. Besides her parents, she had so many good friends here—and she'd be the godmother to Chey's baby, which would bring a great deal of joy into her life. But would that be enough? Suddenly, it felt as if she was living off the crumbs of other people's lives and trying to tell herself that she would be content with that indefinitely. "We can talk more about it after the holidays."

Her mother managed a smile. "So there's no hurry?"

"None whatsoever." Eve held up the watch. "Thanks for this. I've never seen anything quite so lovely."

"You're ten times as lovely," her mother said.

She made a face. "Oh, yeah? Be prepared for the rumors that are swirling around town."

"No one can change our opinion of you," her father insisted.

Cheyenne walked into the parlor almost as soon as Eve's parents left. The Christmas music playing in the dining room grew louder when the door opened, causing Eve to look up. She was sitting on the antique Eastlake chair she'd purchased from an estate sale in Sacramento last year. She'd been gazing down at her new watch, thinking about how lucky she was to have such wonderful parents and wondering if she'd be doing the right thing by leaving them. She had a responsibility to herself but, since her brothers seemed to feel no obligation to their aging parents, she had to make sure they were happy and well cared for, too.

They had their RV, however. They could come and see her....

"How'd it go?" Cheyenne asked.

"I told them I slept with a stranger," Eve said.

Her friend stopped in her tracks. "Are you kidding?"

"No. I figured it would be better for them to hear it from me."

"But they might never have heard it at all!"

"I didn't want to take that chance."

"I see," Cheyenne said slowly. "That was probably wise. How did they take the news?"

"Much better than I expected. I guess I underestimated them."

"Or you set even higher standards for yourself than they do."

Cheyenne took the seat opposite her. "Is that your present?"

Eve handed over the watch so Chey could take a closer look. "Stunning, isn't it?"

"Gorgeous!"

"They're *such* great parents."

"You just made a mistake, Eve. We all know what you're really like," Cheyenne said, giving back the watch.

Eve smiled at the compliment. Her friends and family all thought they knew her, but she wasn't sure she knew herself anymore. Who was the woman who'd let go of all inhibition and thrown everything she had into making love with a complete stranger?

\* \* \*

Rex was in his room, packing up his stuff, when he received a call from Marilyn. He thought maybe he'd accidentally skipped a check he was supposed to sign, and hoped it wasn't because she'd run into trouble with her car. Her engine had started fine when she gave him a ride to Sexy Sadie's to pick up his Land Rover....

Pausing to sit on the edge of the bed, he hit the answer button. "'Lo?"

"You're never going to believe this," she said.

After what he'd been through in his life, he could believe just about anything. But he tensed, wondering if she'd run across proof that The Crew was indeed coming after him. "What is it?"

"I got a call from Scarlet Jones, the photographer from San Francisco."

He let his breath slowly seep out. "I provided security for her some time ago."

"You remember."

"Of course." After splitting off from Virgil back east, where they'd run the same kind of business, he'd hung out his own shingle here in the west and she'd been one of his first clients. "She was getting some strange mail, felt she was being followed. What's going on with her now?" He knew everything had been okay after his contract ended because he'd checked in with her periodically, although not in the past year.

"Apparently she's being harassed again. The first incident happened a few months ago, in September, when she received an email containing a picture of a man's penis."

"So this guy's another Anthony Weiner? That's not particularly creative."

"She forwarded it to me. What he sent wasn't particularly *impressive,* either."

Rex had to chuckle. "Sounds like he should have stolen more than Anthony's idea, maybe something from a porn site. But if this happened in September, why'd Scarlet wait so long to contact us?"

"The threats she got before never amounted to anything. She thought if she ignored it, this would go away, too."

"Let me guess—it hasn't."

"No. It's getting worse. But what I don't understand is why whoever it was stopped in the first place."

"Maybe the guy went to prison."

"That would explain it. Because he's taking up where he left off, except the letters she's receiving are even more personal," Marilyn said. "One mentioned a mole on her, um…"

"Breast? Ass? What? You're seldom at a loss for words."

"It's somewhere even more intimate."

"So whoever is doing this has been *quite* close to her." He raked his fingers through his hair. "Or talked to someone who has."

"That's just…creepy."

"At least it narrows the list of potentials. She still has no idea who it might be?"

"No. She says that none of her past lovers would do anything like this." She cleared her throat. "You, uh, weren't aware of the mole?"

"I don't get sexually involved with our clients. You know that."

"I do. But I thought this client might be an exception. She's extremely attractive. And she's not married."

He had a soft spot for Scarlet, but she was more like a younger sister to him. When he'd watched over her before, he'd still been in love with Laurel, Virgil's sister, but he wasn't remotely tempted to change his relationship with Scarlet, even now. "You said it was getting worse. What else has happened?"

"Yesterday someone broke into her house and urinated on her bed. That's why she finally called."

"Was anything taken?"

"Several pairs of underwear."

What he'd just learned made Rex itch to get back to work. It had always bothered him that the police hadn't been able to find the guy who'd tormented Scarlet. "What'd you tell her?"

"I said I'd be happy to arrange for a bodyguard until the police can find out who's behind it, but when she realized the bodyguard wouldn't be you, she started to cry."

This type of security was very up close and personal. He could see why she'd want somebody she already knew and trusted.

He wished he could help her, but he couldn't ask her to sit tight and wait until he felt safe to return to the Bay Area. He couldn't drag her around the Sierra Nevada foothills with him while he tried to keep a low profile, either. He was about to say he was sorry but there was nothing he could do when a flyer he'd found pinned to the public message board at the local coffee shop popped into his mind. It had advertised rooms for rent in a private residence....

Why not answer that ad? He could hunker down in this quaint town and have Scarlet join him. That would remove them both from their usual circles—take them out of the flow of motel life, too, which added a degree of security. He might not come up with such a perfect solution, at least not such a perfect and *immediate* solution, anywhere else, especially during the holidays.

"Text me her number. Given these latest problems, I'm guessing she's changed it since I spoke to her last."

"What are you going to do?" Marilyn asked, sounding surprised.

"I'm going to take the job."

*"How?"*

"By inviting her to come and spend some time with me here in Whiskey Creek."

"You think she'll do that?"

"If she's truly scared, I don't see that she has a better choice."

"But how can you ask her to leave her home with Christmas coming?"

"If the police do their job, she should be able to return by the big day."

She harrumphed. Then she said, "Whiskey Creek, huh?"

"Why not? Getting her away from her usual routine should give us an advantage. Maybe her stalker will get frustrated when he can't torment her and then he'll do something that'll give him away."

"But I thought you were moving on, that moving on is what keeps *you* safe."

He turned to frown at his packed bags. *This* latest move wasn't about that. This move was more about what he'd done last night. He didn't want to fall back into bed with Eve Whoever She Was—well, actually, he *did* want to fall back into bed with her. That was the problem. What he *didn't* want was to get her hopes up, make her think they might have a future together. Considering his limitations, he knew that wasn't fair.

But if he moved out of the B and B and into a house or some other situation with his client—a client he enjoyed as a friend—surely he'd be able to avoid Eve, maybe forget about her, too. His work had always been enough for him before.

# 5

Meeting with Ted was awkward. After their failed attempt at romance, Eve had grown accustomed to coping with the strain in their relationship when she saw him and the rest of their friends on Fridays at Black Gold Coffee. She just directed her comments to the group in general, when she could, and avoided sitting too close to him and Sophia. But there was no getting around a direct confrontation now. He'd asked if he could come over. He wanted to write a book about the mysterious murder of the child who had died in the basement in 1871.

But he was already a successful suspense writer. Eve couldn't understand why he didn't stick with fiction and leave her alone.

"I'm not sure a book about Mary will be worth your time," she said as she sat across from him in the parlor where she'd spoken to her parents earlier.

He'd been fiddling with his phone, trying to find the record app. "Why not?" he asked, glancing up. "I've been intrigued by it since I was a kid."

"Because you're doing so well with your fiction," she explained. "Wouldn't it make more sense to put out another serial-killer book or something in the time it would take you to write this?"

"I'm not doing it for pay. The proceeds will go to the historical society so they can preserve more buildings like this one."

He was donating the money?

Damn, she couldn't even feel justified in remaining mad at him. That was always the problem. He was too nice.

He gave her a look that told her he was suspicious of her resistance. "Don't tell me you're still holding a grudge."

"You say that as if I'd have no right to."

"You're not the kind of person who hangs on to resentment."

That was true. And he'd already apologized several times. He'd also tried very hard to maintain their friendship. But she couldn't help feeling like an old shoe that had been cast aside. Maybe if she'd been able to move on like he had, or if the guy she'd been with last night hadn't treated her the same way, it wouldn't be a problem.

"Of course. I'm happy for you and Sophia." Part of her really was. She'd known Ted since childhood. And she had to take partial responsibility for getting romantically involved with him. On some level, she'd realized he still had a thing for Sophia. She'd just chosen to ignore her instincts hoping that she would indeed find a good husband.

"When I walked in and hugged you, you were stiff as a board," he pointed out.

"So I'm having a bad day."

Some of the suspicion disappeared, replaced by concern. "Is there something serious going on?"

"Not really." She tried to wave his question away. "I'm always under a lot of pressure around the holidays."

"You *love* the holidays."

She said nothing. She wasn't enjoying them this year.

"Do you want me to come back in January?" he asked.

Why? Why not get this out of the way? He'd already explained that he'd turned in his latest book and didn't need to start the next one until January. It was the fact that he had time during the Christmas period that made him want to get moving with this—and it was all for charity. His gift to the town they both loved. "No. I'm sorry. I'll give you what you need."

"Suffer through it, huh?"

"I didn't mean it like that. It's just that even *Unsolved Mysteries,* and all the crime analysts they brought to town, couldn't figure out who murdered Little Mary, so I'm not sure what more you'll be able to do."

"This isn't so much about *solving* the crime as chronicling the mystery and suggesting possible scenarios." He tilted his head as he studied her. "It should be good publicity for the B and B," he said by way of enticement.

But he'd been talking about doing a book on Little Mary for several years. Did he really have to come and talk to her right *now?* The day after she'd slept with a total stranger? Make her worry that he might have heard the news? Make her wonder if he found what she'd done as pathetic as she did?

Mr. Taylor had returned earlier. Eve had watched him come in. But he didn't look at her or acknowledge her. He'd walked right past her and marched up the stairs. Then he'd gone out again shortly after—without his bags. Since checkout was at noon and it was after two, she could only assume that he planned on staying another night.

She wasn't quite sure how she felt about that, whether she should do anything to enforce her request that he leave or just pretend, like he seemed to be doing, that last night had never happened. Their encounter was probably so meaningless to him that he didn't care whether he ran into her every time he passed through the lobby.

"The B and B is doing better these days," she told Ted. "The tea I'm offering is generating some interest. We're getting groups of Red Hat Society ladies, and we've had an increase in couples ever since we started advertising in bridal magazines."

"I'm glad to hear it, but advertising is expensive, and this will be free. If this book takes off, you could get a steady stream of visitors, curious to see whether this place really is haunted. That's how it worked after *Unsolved Mysteries* aired, didn't it?"

"For a while." She supposed she should be grateful to him for taking an interest—on behalf of her and the town. She would have been if she didn't already have so much on her mind.

"So…shall we get started?" he asked.

She sat back. "Of course. Ask away."

"Why don't we go over the basics, just to make sure I've got them straight?"

"You should know the basics. The whole town does."

"I'm aware that Mary Hatfield was six when she was found strangled in the basement in December of 1871. Her birth and death are engraved on her headstone in the cemetery next door. But you lived here when you were little, too. I'm actually hoping you'll tell me what that was like."

"We were only here for a few years, until the first round of renovations were completed. Then my parents bought the property where we live today, and we moved out there."

"I remember when that happened. We were still in

grade school. But you didn't move because of Mary's ghost...."

"No, my parents wanted a regular family life, where they could be off work sometimes—and we could have some privacy as a family."

"Are you glad they did that?"

She nodded. "I am. I love this place, and I did even then. But...it would've been difficult facing guests constantly with no break. And making sure three little kids were behaving perfectly at all times was too tall an order for any mother."

"Can you tell me about some of your earliest memories of this place?"

"I remember the musty smell of it more than anything else. And I remember playing with the old stuff in the attic. Dressing up in the clothes I found in various trunks, taking my Barbie dolls up there, that sort of thing. Being in that space made me a bit uneasy, even back then, but it was the perfect size for a child and the only place I wouldn't be bothered by my brothers. I could play for hours."

"What about the basement?"

She shivered. "I never played here. But I remember my brothers locking me in once, just to frighten me."

"That was where Mary's body was found."

"Yes. So you can imagine how terrified I was. They called through the door, telling me that her ghost was going to get me, and I was absolutely convinced they were right."

"How'd you get out?"

"My mother heard me screaming and came to the rescue."

A faint smile curved his lips. "I bet she was angry."

"She was."

"What happened to your brothers?"

"They were put on restriction." She shook her head at the memory. They'd found her terror so funny.

Ted made a few quick notes. "Okay, so Mary's parents built this place—and it wasn't ever renovated until your parents took over. Is that correct?"

"It is."

"How old was Mary when John and Harriett moved in?"

"She wasn't born yet. But even after she was, she didn't have any older brothers to torment her. She was an only child."

"After her death, rumors circulated—and persisted—that her father might have killed her. Since he also discovered the body, and it was nearly Christmas, I always think of it as the nineteenth-century JonBenét Ramsey case."

"Was there any evidence to suggest he did the deed?"

"Not really. He was known to have a violent temper and knocked her mother around a bit. He also didn't seem to grieve much. But not all men show their pain."

She'd left the doors to the parlor open. She almost always did that, so her staff would feel free to approach her, if necessary. But today it meant that when Brent Taylor came through the front door, returning for the second time, she happened to see him. He saw her, too, and paused as if he had something to say, so she stood up and hurried over.

"You're late for checkout, but I can take care of that now, if you're ready."

His gaze shifted to Ted before coming back to her. "Would you mind if I stayed one more night?"

Couldn't *anything* go her way? "A Room with a View has no openings?"

He frowned as if recognizing the disappointment in her voice. "I was just over there. They're booked."

Of course they would be—despite their cheesy decorations. Full occupancy seemed to come so easy for them. But they also spent a great deal more on advertising. They always *had* more to spend.

She wanted to refuse but Ted was looking on, and she knew she wouldn't be able to come up with a good excuse for turning away business. Ted and the rest of her friends had been privy to her financial difficulties in the past few years. "That's fine, I guess."

"Thanks. Do you know a good place for dinner?"

"Just Like Mom's has delicious home-style food, if you like that sort of thing. It's down the street."

He hesitated briefly. Then he took her elbow and pulled her close so he could whisper in her ear. "I could've handled this morning at your place a lot better. I'm sorry," he said, then headed up the stairs to his room.

"What was that all about?" Ted asked.

Eve shut the doors in spite of her usual policy and resumed her seat. "Nothing. He's just a…a patron."

"Do all patrons whisper in your ear like that? It looked sort of intimate."

"It wasn't." She considered admitting what she'd done, as she had with her parents, but couldn't bring herself to do it. These days, Ted was happily married and the proud stepfather of a beautiful teenage girl. She didn't want to be perceived as still struggling. Of course, he'd likely hear the rumor, so there was probably no way to prevent him from finding out. But she'd deal with that if and when it happened. She just hoped no one would bring it up or tease her tonight at her party or at their weekly coffee date. Her friends were wonderful, but they'd been so close for so long that nothing was off-limits.

"I only have a few more minutes," she told him, "so we should get on with this."

They talked about what *Unsolved Mysteries* had discovered when they came to town, which was virtually nothing as far as forensic evidence was concerned. Then they discussed the bits and pieces of information that had been recorded in the journals of various people who'd known the Hatfields at the time. These mostly contained venomous recriminations against John Hatfield, who was wealthy and austere and not particularly well liked. Although Eve couldn't say there were any solid leads in those journals, she'd kept copies of everything she'd come across relating to the history of the B and B. She even had a laminated photocopy of a newspaper from the late 1800s that regurgitated the story, and a box of research material *Unsolved Mysteries* had given her when they were done with the shoot.

She went to her office to get the box but she couldn't find it. So she'd brought back only the things she'd collected over the years.

"I can't imagine where I put the stuff *Unsolved Mysteries* left," she told Ted.

"But you'll find it for me?"

"I will. I'll check the attic when I have a minute."

He accepted what she did have. "You seem to go back and forth on this, but, for the record, do you think the inn is haunted?" This had always been a difficult question for Eve. She didn't want to commit herself because, crazy though it sounded, sometimes it *did* seem as if Mary's spirit lingered. She told him about the drapes moving without being touched, about various doors closing and other noises she'd heard when there shouldn't be anyone else about. One time, she was positive she'd heard someone moaning in the basement. That had been chilling.

Unless there was something she absolutely *had* to get, she never went down there alone.

"I honestly don't know. But I feel angry with whoever killed Mary and I hope justice will, somehow, some way, prevail, even at this late date," she told him.

"Do you think the father did it?"

"I think Mary's mother believed he did."

His eyebrows shot up. "What makes you say that?"

"She wouldn't speak a word after Mary's death."

Ted leaned forward. "I've never heard you or anyone else say that before."

"I just found out about it. It was in an email I received a few days ago from a couple who come here every summer—a historian and his wife who once had family living in the area. He stumbled across a letter from his great-great-grandmother dated several years after Mary's death. It refers to Harriett Hatfield and her enduring silence, and he thought I might be interested. According to this letter, Harriett became a hermit and would scarcely go out after that, which is probably why more people didn't mention it. They didn't really have any contact with her."

"Her silence and withdrawal could be a reaction to her grief," Ted suggested.

"True, but she could also have been an abused wife, rebelling in the only way she could without risking her own life."

"It's something to consider." He stood and slipped his phone in his pocket. "That's it for today. I'll call if I need anything else."

She gave him a weak smile. "You know where to find me."

"Are you looking forward to going out for your birthday tonight?" he asked, changing the subject.

A trip to San Francisco didn't sound as enjoyable as it had before last night. Although she'd get to see Baxter, who used to be part of their group but moved to the city two years ago, she'd had about as much of turning thirty-five as she could take. Still, she lied to protect his feelings. There was nothing to be gained from making her friends feel sorry for her. "I am."

"You don't sound too enthusiastic." He stopped her as she opened the parlor doors. "Are you planning to tell me what's going on?"

He knew her even better than the rest of their friends did, since they'd once been lovers. But that was exactly the reason she no longer felt comfortable confiding in him. "No. Thanks, anyway."

"Regardless of what you might be feeling right now, Sophia and I care about you," he said. "We all care about you."

He was referring to their entire circle. "I appreciate you saying so."

"Hmm…a polite dodge." He retained his hold on her arm. "You're really not going to tell me?"

"No. But answer me this. If you were going to leave Whiskey Creek, where would you go?"

He dropped his hand. "You're thinking of moving away?"

"Probably not forever."

"*Probably?* God, Eve, I hope this has nothing to do with me. I thought we'd gotten past last year, but…you seem angry again."

She wasn't angry so much as frustrated with her loneliness. And the Christmas season only made it worse. "This isn't about you. It's just time I figured out what to do with the rest of my life."

"Has that been in question? I always thought you'd

spend it here, with us." He gestured at the B and B. "I can't imagine anyone else running this place. You do such a good job."

Cheyenne approached before Eve could respond, a look of wonder on her face. "The baby's really active!" she said, and pressed their hands up against her belly.

Eve could feel the child's foot. Or maybe that was an elbow jutting out. "Oh, wow," she breathed. "That's exciting, isn't it?"

"I can't wait to…" Ted's words drifted off as she glanced up at him, but that sudden catch told her what he'd been about to say. He couldn't wait to have a child with Sophia.

"This kid is strong." Cheyenne filled the awkward silence. "Just like his daddy."

She meant his daddy's *brother,* who was also her sister's fiancé, but she would *never* admit how she'd gotten pregnant. She didn't want Dylan to face the fact that he couldn't give her a child, which was why she'd performed the artificial insemination without his knowledge. Other than Eve, only Presley and Aaron knew how she'd gotten pregnant, because they'd helped facilitate it.

"You've been talking like it's a boy the whole pregnancy," Ted said, "but Dylan wants a girl. Do you know something you haven't shared with us?"

"No," Cheyenne said. "It's just easier to refer to him as one or the other, and flip-flopping feels weird."

Eve could have stood there indefinitely, marveling at the baby's movements. Creating life was such a miracle, a miracle she longed to experience herself.

She wanted a baby—but she didn't want to have one on her own. Suddenly she sucked in her breath.

"What is it?" Cheyenne asked.

Eve pulled her hand away, but she couldn't answer

immediately. Something was going through her mind, something that hadn't struck her before and filled her with concern.

"Eve?" Ted said.

"I'm fine," she mumbled, but she wasn't so sure. This morning Brent Taylor had pointed out the condom wrapper on the floor when he told her they'd used protection. But there'd only been one, and she was positive they'd made love more than once. She definitely remembered that much. And yet…when she'd thrown away that wrapper, she hadn't noticed any others.

# 6

Eve's heart was pounding in her throat when she knocked, rather timidly, at Brent Taylor's door. She didn't want to bother him again. He'd apologized for his rudeness this morning, and she preferred to leave it at that.

But if there was a possibility that she might be pregnant, she needed some way to notify him.

She was actually hoping he could tell her there'd been other condoms he'd somehow disposed of himself, by flushing them down the toilet or whatever. But that didn't seem very likely. How many men carried more than one or two condoms in their wallets?

The door cracked open, and he peered out at her.

"It's me." Bracing herself for whatever reaction she was going to get, she drew a deep breath. "I need to speak with you for a minute."

He said nothing, just swung the door wide enough to let her in, and stepped back.

She walked in and closed it behind her. Lord knew she didn't want anyone else overhearing what she planned to discuss.

"What is it?" he asked, immediately defensive. "I can't stay tonight? You want me to move out right now? What?"

"No." She tucked her hair behind her ears. "You're fine here until…tomorrow. Or…whenever."

His face cleared as he sat on the bed. "You seem nervous."

"I am, a little," she admitted.

He studied her closely. "If you're here because… because you want more of what we shared last night, you don't have to be nervous. The answer's yes—as long as there are no strings attached. I have certain…limitations."

Was he *serious?* From what Eve could tell, he was. But how could he believe she might come back for more after the way he'd tried to distance himself? And what made him think she'd settle for an offer like *that?*

The shock must've shown on her face, because a smile slanted his lips. "I guess your expression answers that question."

"I'm not…coming on to you," she explained. "I'm not a 'no strings attached' kind of girl."

"You're here for some reason."

"Yes." She wandered over to the window so she could break eye contact with him. "I'm here because…because I was wondering…"

The bed creaked as he got up. "About…"

She made herself turn to face him. "You know that condom wrapper?"

"We're back to that?"

"Do you carry quite a few of those?"

"I can always get more," he said, eyebrows raised.

She rubbed her hands on her thighs. "I'm wondering how many you had to begin with?"

It wasn't difficult to discern the exact moment he clued in to what she was trying to establish. A distinct wariness entered his eyes. *"Why?"*

"Why do you think?" she asked. "I don't know what

you remember about last night, but I remember making love three different times."

"You're sure?"

"Yes! Did you have that many condoms?"

When he didn't respond, she added, "And if you did, did we use them? I mean…maybe you sleep around enough that you carry a whole box. But it wasn't as if you had your vehicle, so…that means you had only what you were carrying on your person."

He bowed his head as he leaned against the wall. "Shit."

She winced. "That's a *no,* right?"

"I had just the one. And it was pretty old. But are you certain—"

"I'm positive. There was—" she lowered her voice "—the first time when we didn't quite make it to the bedroom, remember? And then the second time, we did find the bed. After that, I'm pretty sure there was one more, when we woke up a couple of hours later."

"That was when I had to move you down so you didn't hit the headboard."

She felt her face flush. "Yeah. So at least three."

He nodded solemnly. "That's when I used the condom."

Her stomach knotted. "But you didn't use anything before?"

"I couldn't have."

"And you didn't know that?"

He threw up a hand. "Maybe I was mentally avoiding the possibility of…consequences by assuming they were all one time."

She bit her lip. "Oh, boy."

"So I take it you're not on birth control or anything—" He cut himself off. "Never mind. I don't even have to ask.

If you haven't been sleeping with anyone, you wouldn't need to."

He rubbed his forehead. "So where are you at with your…you know…your cycle? Is there any chance you might have been fertile?"

She'd already counted the days. She'd wanted to be prepared before she spoke with him. "I'm afraid we couldn't have planned it any better if we'd been *trying* to conceive."

At that, he went pale. "I see."

"That doesn't mean I *am* pregnant," she said. "Chances are just as good that I'm not. We'll hope for the best. But if I am…I won't have an abortion or put the baby up for adoption."

"Okay," he said, as if that news was as unwelcome as the possibility of a pregnancy.

"I'm sorry that disappoints you."

"I'm not sure it does. I just…I don't know what to say to all this."

"You don't have to say anything until we find out. If I'm pregnant, I'll have and raise the baby alone. But… since you're in a situation where you'll be leaving soon, I'd like to know exactly who I'm dealing with."

He began to pace, head down. "I showed my ID when I checked in," he muttered, but that was hardly convincing.

"So you're Brent Taylor? Or are you Taylor Jackson?"

He stopped to look at her, his jaw hard. "You've been snooping through my things?"

"Not like you think. But someone had to clean your room, and I noticed the luggage tag."

"I borrowed a suitcase from a friend."

"Brent Taylor is your real name, then."

*"Yes."*

"Okay. Can I get some contact information, too? Just in case."

He rubbed his forehead again, as if he needed a moment to regroup, or didn't like the thought of giving her what she'd asked. That was more than slightly off-putting.

"I promise I won't contact you unless absolutely necessary," she added, her voice showing her irritation.

"You don't understand," he started, but then he stopped. "Never mind. I don't have any good contact information right now. I'm in a…transitional period. I'll have to check back with you. But I'll do my part. Don't worry about that."

Did he expect her to rely on his integrity when she didn't even know if he had any? She opened her mouth to tell him that was asking a bit much, but he didn't let her get that far.

"I realize that requires a great deal of trust," he said. "But I'm hoping you can manage it if…if I'm also trusting you."

Feeling a chill, although it wasn't that cold in the room, she rubbed her arms. "In what way?"

He seemed to be thinking fast, trying to come up with an arrangement that would be fair. "Do you have medical insurance?"

"I do. I provide it for all my employees, too," she said. That was partly what made it so difficult to stay afloat.

"The birth would be covered, then?"

"Yes."

"There's that, at least. But still…there'll be plenty of other expenses. What if I leave you with some money? If you're pregnant, you can keep it for the baby. And I'll send more, of course. Like I said, I'm not trying to dodge my responsibilities."

Eve hated that she'd screwed up so badly that her life,

in a matter of twenty-four hours, had been reduced to this kind of negotiation. "Does that mean you wouldn't want contact with the...um, child?"

He closed his eyes. "I can't even think about, I mean that right now—what *I* want. I just need to take care of what you want. We'll worry about the rest later, if there is a baby."

"Then how much are you planning to leave?"

"Enough that you'll feel confident, or optimistic if not quite confident, that I'll follow up. You name the amount."

She had no idea how much to request, but there was something very odd going on with Brent Taylor. This proved it, and made her raise the figure that came into her head by several grand. "Five thousand?"

To her surprise, he didn't argue. He just got the money—stacks of hundred-dollar bills separated by paper clips—out of his duffel bag. After handing her two of those piles, he counted out the final thousand. "Here you go."

"I can't believe you happened to have this on hand!" She couldn't begin to guess how he was going to explain that, but she stopped him before he could even try. "Never mind. I don't want you to lie to me." He had to be a drug dealer or something, not exactly the type of person she'd want as the father of her baby, so maybe it was a good thing he'd be leaving. She could only hope he *wouldn't* want contact.

After she slipped out of his room, she hid the money under her waistband so no one would see it and hauled in a deep breath. She might be looking at an entirely different future than the one she'd been contemplating when she was thinking about traipsing off to Europe. But worrying about what might or might not be wasn't going to change anything. She might as well go by the bank and deposit what he'd given her for safekeeping, then get ready for the trip to San Francisco. Because of her birthday celebration, she had the night manager coming in early. Once the evening got under way, maybe she'd be able to enjoy dinner and dancing and, at least for a few hours, forget Brent Taylor and the changes that might be taking place inside her own body.

If she was pregnant, she'd deal with it. She could be a single mother. She'd longed to move on to the next stage of life for some time now; she'd just never dreamed she might do it without a husband.

That night Rex was more restless than usual. He attempted to do some work on his computer. He'd made all the arrangements for Scarlet to join him tomorrow— rented them each a room at that house he'd seen advertised at Black Gold Coffee. Their new landlady, an elderly widow, was willing to let them move in right away. But, as the minutes ticked slowly by, tomorrow and his impending move across town seemed like a long way off. His mind kept straying back to Eve.

Could she be pregnant with his child? And what would he do if she was?

He'd send money, of course. Like he'd promised. But he couldn't imagine having a son or daughter, especially when he wouldn't be able to know that child—not without putting him or her in jeopardy.

Thirty minutes before Just Like Mom's closed, he went over to grab a bite to eat. The gal who served him had a nametag on her shirt that read Tilly. She blushed every time he looked at her, but she was young. Too young for him. He guessed she was about...twenty-one.

"Where are you staying?" she asked, showing him her dimples when she brought his check.

"Little Mary's."

"Oh, Eve's place. That's a great B and B."

He toyed with the salt and pepper shakers as he asked, "How well do you know Eve?"

"I didn't go to school with her or anything. She's ten years older than I am, but I often see her around town. She's a supernice person."

"Is she?"

"Definitely! I don't know anyone who doesn't like her. Have you met her?"

"I have." He suddenly realized that Eve reminded him of Laurel, even though their coloring was opposite. And God knew how much he'd loved Virgil's sister. That had to be the reason he'd been so attracted to Eve last night. "She seems like a good person."

"She is."

"Why do you think she hasn't married?"

She twisted her mouth as she searched for an answer. Most people would consider this an odd question—too intrusive coming from a stranger—but she was trying too hard to be helpful to consider it critically. "I'm not sure. *I* think she's the prettiest in that group."

*"Group?"*

"She's part of a tight-knit bunch of friends who grew up here. Most of them are married now so…I have no idea why she hasn't found someone."

"She could be difficult to get along with," he suggested, just to see what kind of response he'd get.

Tilly shook her head firmly. "No way. If anything, I'm guessing it's because she's still stuck on Ted."

"Ted's an old boyfriend?"

"They dated last year, briefly. But he wasn't over Sophia, a girlfriend he had years before. So after Eve got Sophia a job working for Ted—she was just trying to help—Ted decided he wanted Sophia instead."

Rex had never met Sophia or Ted, but he couldn't imagine anyone passing over Eve. He took a long drink of his Coke so his next question would seem as casual as he wanted it to. "Was she torn up about it?"

"She pretended she wasn't, but everyone pretty much understood that he'd broken her heart."

"That's too bad."

"Ted would've been quite a catch," she said. "He's a famous suspense writer, you know."

"He is?"

"Has ten books out. Or maybe more. I'm losing track." She noticed that he'd finished his Coke and picked up the glass. "Can I get you a refill?"

"No, thanks. I'm ready to go."

She hesitated, shifted on her feet, then cleared her throat. "You new in town?"

"Just passing through."

"I see. Well, if you're looking for something to do tonight, I'm partying at the local bar with some girlfriends after I get off. You should join us."

He wished she appealed to him half as much as Eve, but she didn't. He had enough problems, anyway.

Smiling with a hint of regret so he could let her down easy, he said, "That sounds like fun, but I'm afraid I have to be up early."

"Okay. No problem. If you change your mind, anyone can tell you how to get to Sexy Sadie's. And if I don't see you, I hope you enjoy your stay in Whiskey Creek. Come back soon."

"Thanks." He tossed a twenty on the table to cover his meal and her tip and walked out.

When he climbed into his Land Rover, Rex intended to head back to the B and B and get some sleep. But that wasn't what he did. He drove past the turnoff and kept on driving, out into the country where he'd been that morning.

# 7

Since Eve lived the farthest from town, the limo dropped her friends off first. It was raining by the time they pulled into her drive, but at midnight it was early yet, considering how late they used to stay out for special events.

A night on the town with the gang wasn't what it used to be. Now that Cheyenne was pregnant and couldn't stand for very long, Addy had a newborn she didn't like to leave for more than a couple of hours and Ted and Sophia had a fifteen-year-old who was home alone, the fun ended a lot sooner than it would have a couple of years ago. Much to Baxter's consternation, they'd left San Francisco before all the good parties had even started.

But Eve couldn't blame her friends. If she were in their shoes, she'd want to get back, too. She just didn't have anything to rush home for—unless she wanted to continue worrying about last night. And she really didn't. She'd told herself she wouldn't even think about it until she knew whether or not she was pregnant. But she'd thought of little else all evening.

Her phone pinged, signaling an incoming text message.

So much for your big birthday bash.

It was from Baxter. She'd texted him to thank him for the earrings he'd given her.

It's fine, she wrote. We're all getting older. Our lives are changing.

Screw that! The others can get old without us, he responded. Come stay with me next weekend. I'll show you a good time.

He said that as if his life hadn't changed, too, but he had a partner these days, and Eve got the impression that Scott wasn't particularly interested in Baxter's "old" friends. Bax had built a separate life in the city. But as sad as Eve was to lose so much of his time and focus, she was happy for him. He'd struggled to get over Noah, who didn't have the slightest gay tendency and was now married to Addy. Eve hoped that with Scott, Baxter had found someone who could return his interest on *all* levels.

Weekends are hard during the holidays, she wrote. The B and B gets busy. But I'll see you when you're home for Christmas. I like Scott, by the way. You did well.

Scott likes you, too.

"Sure he does," she grumbled. He'd barely acknowledged any of them....

A second text came immediately, and it sounded as if Bax was signing off, so she didn't text him back. Happy birthday! it read. And call me if you need anything, even if it's just to bitch about life.

She smiled at her phone. He'd clued in to how she was feeling, but she was pretty sure she'd fooled everyone else.

The limo driver put the transmission in Park and came around to open her door.

Her friends had tipped him when they got out—they

said they didn't want her paying for anything—so she merely thanked him and sighed as she watched him pull away. She was about to remove her high heels so she wouldn't twist an ankle on the gravel drive when she noticed a Land Rover parked beside her parents' RV.

"Whose is *that?*" No one she knew owned a Land Rover.

She'd worn only a light sweater to the Bay Area because it looked better with her dress than her big wool coat. She regretted that decision now that it was wet and cold, but she was too curious to let the weather drive her inside quite so soon. This Land Rover didn't belong at her house....

She was making her way over when the driver's-side door opened. Brent Taylor got out, but he didn't come toward her. He didn't even step away from the vehicle so he could close the door. He simply stood there, waiting to see if he'd be welcomed.

"What...what are you doing here?" she asked in surprise.

"I wish I knew exactly," he replied.

"You must have some idea."

He didn't respond; he just gave her a look that said it should be obvious.

"You're back for more...."

"Why not? We both enjoyed last night."

"You were drunk. We both were. And I thought you didn't want to see me again, that you wanted what happened between us to be over. You grabbed your clothes and ran out of my house this morning as if I might try to tie you to the bed."

"I know. I *did* want it to be over."

She thought he should be a little more contrite and embarrassed after making it so clear that he didn't want her contacting him. This guy didn't do contrite or embarrassed, though. He was far too bold for that. "But…" she prompted.

He rested one arm on the door and the other on the top of his vehicle. "I can't quit thinking about you."

She took off her shoes. The rocks cut into the bottoms of her feet, but at least she wouldn't trip and fall. "We're already worried about a possible pregnancy."

"I'm prepared this time."

"So…you want to be with me. You just don't want it to mean anything."

He glanced away and rubbed his forehead. "I won't be around for long."

*No strings attached.* He'd said that earlier. Would she *never* meet a man who was willing to fall in love?

The same old disappointment welled up, making her want to tell him what she thought of the meaningless encounters he seemed to prefer. But she didn't have any right to judge him. She was the one who'd started this by bringing him home last night. They were different people who wanted different things. In any event, she was determined to continue to be polite. "Thanks for going to the trouble of coming all the way out here. I can see why you would. I probably sounded like a desperate fool last night when I was telling you about my birthday and… all of that. But there are other women who can give you what you're looking for, and I think you'll have a much better time."

He straightened. "You're saying I should seek out someone else?"

"I am. I can even help you find someone, if you want. Noelle, the waitress from Sexy Sadie's who brought us home last night, would be a good bet. It's common knowledge that she sleeps around. And in case you didn't notice, she has these *huge* implants."

"That should be exciting for a guy as shallow as me, huh?"

"For a guy who's just looking for a good time," she clarified. "And if she's not working tonight, I'm sure if you hang out at the bar long enough, you won't go home alone."

When he didn't say anything, she drew a deep breath. "I'll tell you how to get there from here."

He swore and hung his head. Then he met her eyes again. "I'm not interested in Noelle or her implants—or anyone else at Sexy Sadie's, Eve. I know what I want, and I want you."

He seemed taken aback when she laughed outright and shook her head. "No, you don't. The way I behaved last night might seem to contradict this, but I'm actually very old-fashioned. For me, making love is still about getting close to someone, being vulnerable, sharing concerns and fears and lives, making a commitment. You *definitely* don't want to be with me."

No response.

"Noelle would be better suited to what you're looking for," she said since she couldn't tell whether she'd convinced him. "I can call over there to see if she's working. She'll think she's died and gone to heaven if you walked in and asked to take her home. Especially if she felt she was stealing something from me."

"I may not be able to give you a future, but that doesn't mean I don't want meaningful contact, just like you do. Let me hold you tonight. Please," he added softly.

They were both getting wet. Eve wrapped her thin sweater tightly around her as she blinked against the rain. "But this is crazy. I may already be pregnant...."

"I told you, I have birth control. So being together now won't make that situation any worse."

"Still—"

"Do you *want* to be with me?" he asked. "Be honest."

She was reluctant to say yes, although that was the truth, so she said nothing. But he understood what her silence meant.

"Then don't send me away. And stop talking about women like Noelle. My life feels empty enough already."

Rex held his breath, hoping he'd managed to persuade her. He needed something to fight the sense that he was constantly drifting. Eve could offer him a respite. He knew that. He felt a connection with her similar to the one he'd felt with Laurel. But Virgil's sister had come into his life too soon, when it was still a mess, when *he* was a mess and couldn't seem to vanquish his demons.

"Well?" he asked.

She was still standing there in the rain, gaping at him.

"I don't know what to say. Except for last night, I've never…engaged in a temporary arrangement like this. I'm not even sure I can…meet your expectations."

"What expectations? It's not as if you suddenly have to perform like a porn star. I want one honest engagement. That's it. Then, tomorrow, I'll do what's best for both of us and leave you alone."

She rubbed her arms, trying to ward off the cold. "Why is that best?"

"I have certain…practical concerns, reasons I need to keep moving."

"Are you wanted by the police?"

"No. I can promise you I'm not a criminal." He'd been in WitSec at one time, but he'd left when they couldn't provide the protection he needed. He found he was better off living by his wits. No one was more motivated to save his own skin than he was.

"Then what?" she asked.

"Call it wanderlust." He had to tell her *something* she'd believe, or she'd keep questioning him, or wondering silently. "Anyway, I'll never be the kind of man you need."

She'd agree if she knew his background. He struggled every day to overcome everything he'd done and been. That didn't make him a good romantic candidate for anyone, especially such a nice girl. She deserved someone as uncomplicated and innocent as she was, not a man with the baggage he carried. Not someone who hadn't spoken to his family in years. Not an ex-con, ex–gang member, ex–OxyContin addict. He doubted she'd even let him in the house if he told her. He didn't look like a man who'd have those kinds of skeletons in his closet, which was lucky for him. He probably wouldn't have been able to start his bodyguard business and be so successful at it otherwise.

"So what do you say?" he asked.

When she nodded, he released his breath. *I have one night,* he told himself. One night to pretend he was as normal as anyone else.

She was really going to do this.

Eve's heart threatened to pound right out of her chest as Brent Taylor swung her into his arms to save her feet from the sharp rocks and carried her across the yard. This had to be the craziest, riskiest thing she'd ever done—particularly with her parents at home and asleep in their house just a hundred yards away. But it was also exciting. The smell of Brent's skin, that hint of aftershave or deodorant or whatever it was, brought back memories of last night, and those were some darn good memories.

She unlocked the door while he held her, and he shouldered it open. She thought he'd put her down once they passed into the hall, but he didn't. He carried her straight back to the bedroom.

"Maybe we should open a bottle of wine first," she suggested, hoping alcohol might ease her anxiety as much as it had last night.

"No," he said. "You're going to have to cope with your nerves. I want to feel everything, and I want you to feel it, too. And it's already after midnight. I'm not wasting any time."

He didn't sound like a guy who was just looking for a warm body, for whom any warm body would do. Eve didn't get that, since he fit the stereotype in every other way. "Why? Why does this night mean so much to you—without meaning anything at all?" she asked.

"You remind me of someone," he admitted.

Finally, she understood. *That* was why he wasn't interested in Noelle or another woman.

Eve wasn't thrilled to learn the truth, but at least he was being honest. "I see. What's her name?"

"I'd rather not say."

"Can you tell me where she lives?"

He put her down on the bed. "Does it matter?"

"You're the one who's acting like it does."

"Montana."

"Did you leave her or—"

"It didn't work out between us. She's married to someone else now."

Somehow that made this far less frightening than it had been a moment ago. It also made it less exciting to know he'd have his mind on someone else. But God, this guy could kiss. And once he started kissing her, it was easy to forget that she wasn't really the woman he wanted.

Eve was less like Laurel than Rex had thought. She talked differently, moved differently, responded differently to the things he did. At first he feared he'd built up the similarities between the two women so much that making love to Eve wouldn't be as satisfying as he'd hoped. But the more he touched her, the more he forgot about Laurel and the more he enjoyed exploring this new woman.

Physically, Eve was flawless, but he hadn't taken her to bed because of that. He was looking for something else and, even though she wasn't Laurel, she held a certain…promise. He liked that there was no history between them, none of the turbulence that had ended up tainting his relationship with Laurel. Despite the doubts he'd caused by being so secretive, Eve treated him as though he was what he seemed to be—a professional, successful thirtysomething businessman. That gave him a sense of freedom he'd never had with his best friend's sister. When he was with Eve, it was as if he'd never been "Pretty Boy," as The Crew called him. As if he'd never been the kid who'd screwed up and encouraged his little brother to jump off that ledge when they were cliff-diving or the angry teen who'd turned to drugs to numb the pain of being responsible for that brother's loss. Here, in this town, he could almost believe the image he saw reflected in Eve's eyes, felt almost as deserving of good things as everyone else.

"I can't imagine the devil kissing any better than you do," she told him.

"That's because the devil taught me everything I

know," he said, and nearly chuckled at the thought that she had no idea how true that statement was.

He ran his lips over her neck, reveling in the softness of her skin.

"What is it about me that reminds you of this other woman?" she asked.

"Don't talk about anyone else. I was stupid to mention it. I'm happy to be here with you."

"I'm curious."

"You smell like her. You must wear the same perfume." Maybe that was why he'd first made the connection. Last night, he'd been too drunk to realize it was merely a familiar scent.

"So do you want me to…to say something this woman used to say? Or…do something she used to do?"

He lifted his head. "No. Just be yourself." Having already removed her bra, he cupped her breast. "I like what I'm getting so far."

She closed her eyes and gasped softly as he lowered his head. "Then I'll…I'll relax and enjoy this."

He slid his hand down the flat plane of her stomach, searching for even more sensitive territory. "That's all you have to do," he said.

# 8

Eve wasn't sure why, but as their lovemaking progressed, she became determined to make Brent forget that other woman. She didn't want to be a fill-in for some old flame. She wanted him to remember *her* long after this night was over. But that meant throwing all reservations and self-consciousness aside, which wasn't something she considered herself particularly adept at. She figured most good girls had a problem with letting loose. She could only do it this time because he didn't really know her, and this was a one-night deal. Whether it went well or it didn't, they would never be together again. He'd move out of the B and B and go wherever he planned to go, and that would be the end of what had started at the bar.

She suspected it was their utter abandon that made the sex so spectacular. She wasn't drunk, but she wasn't feeling quite sober. She got the impression that what Brent felt wasn't a common occurrence for him, either. The more excited she got, the more excited he got, and when they finally reached that pinnacle of pleasure, it was by far the best intimate experience she'd ever had.

"I guess you're good at more than kissing," she said as he fell back onto the pillows and tried to catch his breath.

"That was amazing," he agreed.

He wasn't the type to lavish undue praise, so she assumed she could take him at his word and smiled as he curled around her.

He dozed off immediately, but she couldn't sleep. All she could think about was that she could be pregnant with this man's child.

Eve had expected Brent to be gone by morning. He'd certainly been in a hurry to get out of her bed yesterday. But last night he'd seemed to need something beyond sex. Or else he couldn't get enough of it, because at various points during the night when they'd both awakened, they'd made love again—and again. Now, according to her digital alarm, which was the first thing she saw when she opened her eyes, it was after ten and someone was banging on the door.

"Eve? Are you okay? There's a white SUV we don't recognize at the end of the drive. Do you know who it belongs to?"

Her father! Panic shot through her as she bolted upright. But it was still dark. Why would her clock say ten?

Then she realized. Brent had pulled down the blinds last night—something she rarely bothered to do. She didn't live close to anyone except her parents, and her bedroom window faced nothing but several acres of raw land.

"Damn it," she muttered as another knock sounded.

"What is it?" Brent didn't open his eyes. He brought his hand up to her breast and urged her to lie down again.

"Eve?" her mother called.

"Who's that?" he mumbled, but he didn't act particularly concerned.

She removed his arm so she could get up. "It's Adele and Charlie!"

*"Who?"*

"My parents!"

He raised his head, instantly alert. "Were you expecting them?"

"No, but they…they live in the house in front of mine. They come by whenever."

*"And you didn't mention that?"*

"Why would I?" she said. "I never dreamed you'd stay over!"

"I stayed over yesterday, didn't I?"

"Yes, but you woke up at the crack of dawn! That's a couple of hours before they usually roll out of bed. Besides, I didn't have to worry about them yesterday. They were gone, traveling in that RV you probably noticed when you parked."

"I wondered where that came from. Figured it belonged to your neighbors. It never occurred to me that those neighbors were your parents." He pushed himself into a sitting position and shoved a hand through his hair. "So what now?"

"I'm not sure." She was digging through her drawers, looking for a sweat suit to put on. "It's not like you can hide. They've seen your car."

"We could act like we're just friends. Like I slept on your couch…"

"My parents know all my friends. They'll guess the minute they see you that you're the guy I brought home last night."

"You said they were gone. How did they find out about last night?"

"I had to tell them."

*"Why?"*

"Because they were going to hear about it, anyway."

"Shit!" He kicked off the covers. "Maybe I should throw on my clothes and sneak out the back."

"No way! That'll make me look even worse. Just... just act as if we have some genuine interest in each other. Once you leave town, I'll tell them you dumped me."

He was up and putting on his clothes but he paused long enough to cast her a dubious frown. "And if you're pregnant?"

"They'll be glad. They want grandkids."

"They'll be pissed!" he corrected. "They'll want me to marry you!"

"And I'll tell them you gave me a number that's disconnected but you left me some money."

"Oh, fuck..."

She almost laughed in spite of their predicament. "Why does it matter what they think of you?" she asked. "After today, you'll never see them again."

"Eve, are you there?" her mother called.

Her father quickly followed up with, "We're coming in!"

"No, wait!" she called back. "Give us a minute!"

*"Us?"* Brent echoed, clearly unhappy.

"It's not my fault we slept in."

"It's mine?"

"You pulled down the blinds! You can suffer through a few minutes with them. All you have to do is be polite so they won't think I'm an idiot for letting you in my bed. Maybe this is a good thing," she added, considering it from a different angle. "Then they can tell my baby, if I have one, that they met you. I'd like that, and it might be good for the baby."

He looked as if he was about to curse again, but she ignored him. She glanced in the mirror to make sure her clothes were on straight and hurried out.

"Whoa!" she heard him say. "I'm not dressed!"

She was halfway down the hall when she looked back to see him hopping on one leg as he pulled on his jeans. "Shut the door and come out when you're ready."

"Tell me your father doesn't own a shotgun."

That hadn't been an entirely serious statement, so she didn't respond. She could see her parents' faces through the glass oval in the door, and was too intent on what might happen in the next few minutes.

With a smile, she poked her head out. "Hi!"

Her parents stared at her. "You're okay?"

"Of course."

Her father, aka Charlie, gestured toward the end of the drive. "So...who owns that Land Rover?"

"It belongs to Brent." She lowered her voice for emphasis. "The man I met the other night."

Her mother's eyes widened. "I thought that was a one-time thing," she whispered, "but...he's back? Did he go to San Francisco with you?"

Eve could feel a blush rising up her neck. "No, he came by after."

A creak in the hall indicated that Brent was emerging from the bedroom, but Eve kept the conversation going. "We were about to have some breakfast." She pushed open the door. "Would you like to join us?"

She was hoping they'd say no. Surely they could tell this was a bit awkward. But she was their only daughter, and they were far too curious about the new man in her life to butt out quite so soon.

"We'd love to," her father said, and the next thing Eve knew she was making introductions.

"It's very nice to meet you." Brent shook hands with both of them. Then they all filed into her small kitchen, so she could start breakfast.

"How do you like your eggs?" she asked Brent.

He raised his eyebrows. That small change in his expression gave away the fact that he wished he was *anywhere* else, but she pretended he was happy to be included.

"Over easy?" she suggested as if she was saying, "Just a little while longer..."

"Coffee's enough for me," he mumbled.

"I'll have scrambled," her father said.

She turned to her mother. "Mom?"

"Whatever you prefer to make, honey." Adele couldn't take her eyes off Brent. Eve thought she could serve her mother a *raw* egg and Adele would have no complaints.

Her father claimed the seat directly across from her guest. "So where are you from?"

Brent cleared his throat. "Los Angeles originally."

"And what do you do?"

"I own a business."

"What kind of business?" her mother asked.

Eve shot her parents a look, warning them to back off, but she was pretty sure they hadn't noticed. These were normal questions to ask a man your daughter was dating, so she could understand why they wouldn't feel they were doing anything wrong.

"Landscaping."

That caught Eve's attention despite her anxiety and distress. Brent didn't strike her as a landscaper. His hands weren't nearly calloused enough—and she would know. She supposed he could have work crews do the physical labor, though....

"Do you have any siblings?" Adele asked.

"A brother who's a surgeon and one who's a chemical engineer."

Her father's chair scraped the floor as he adjusted his position. "What brings you to this area?"

"I'm on vacation and thought I'd try my hand at gold-panning."

"Isn't it a bit cold for that this time of year?"

Eve cringed as her father continued to drill him—but at least the coffee was ready. She poured everyone except herself a cup. She was too filled with nervous energy as it was. And in case she *was* pregnant she planned to avoid caffeine.

"Not really. The weather's mild here compared to most other places."

"That's true," her mother conceded, weighing in on Brent's side. But her mother was a romantic, just like Eve. She saw that Brent was a handsome man. Articulate, too. That made her willing to overlook certain gaps in the information he'd provided. After all, Adele wanted to see her daughter married. But those same gaps were things her father wouldn't be so prone to overlook.

"Have you found any color?" Charlie asked.

"Not yet," Brent replied, "but I haven't been here long."

"Meeting someone like Eve is striking gold," her mother insisted. "You won't find a sweeter girl anywhere."

When his gaze shifted to her, Eve sent him a look, pleading with him to play along for a few more minutes.

"She must take after her mother, then," he said smoothly.

Adele's laugh sounded more like a giggle. "How nice!"

Eve hoped that the situation would begin to feel more natural, but Charlie broke in almost immediately. "Where do you live now?"

The hesitation was barely perceptible, but Eve picked up on it and was afraid her father had, too.

"Bakersfield."

"Thought you'd come north for a while, huh?" That was her mother, offering more support. Eve felt bad for deceiving Adele, but she told herself she had no choice.

"I heard it's pretty here," Brent told her.

"And do you agree?"

He didn't reply. He didn't get the chance, since Charlie was at him again. "How long will you be in town?"

Determined to take charge of the conversation—and put an end to all the questions—Eve answered before Brent could. "He's only here for a few days, Dad. He's got a business to run and has to get home."

Steam rose from Brent's cup as he lifted it in one hand. It looked as if he took his coffee black, and that somehow fit the minimalist he seemed to be. "Actually, my sister, Scarlet, is coming out to stay with me until after the holidays."

Eve felt her jaw drop. He hadn't mentioned having a sister when her mother had asked him about siblings a few minutes before. Not only that, but he'd made his departure from town sound imminent. The fact that he'd been renting a room at her B and B and had asked to stay just one more night seemed to confirm it. "What do you mean?"

"I've leased two rooms at Mrs. Higgins's house. Do you know her?"

"Of course!" her mother said. "She's a wonderful woman. Sad about Buck, though. He passed away a year ago. I know she misses him."

"So you're here until after Christmas?" As sorry as Eve was for Mrs. Higgins, she couldn't quite assimilate this new information—not just the sudden addition of a sister but the fact that Brent would be in town for several more weeks. By the time Christmas was over, she'd know if she was pregnant, which definitely changed how she'd imagined this scenario. Maybe he'd decided to stay that long so he could reclaim his money if she wasn't going to have a baby.

He took a sip of his coffee. "Looks like it."

"I'm so glad," her mother said. "Then we'll have more of a chance to get to know you."

"What about work?" Her father's eyes had narrowed as if he wasn't buying that any man would leave his business for all these weeks without a better reason than panning for gold in the middle of winter. Or maybe it was the inconsistent sibling information....

"I've been managing it remotely, and it seems to be running well." Brent shrugged. "We'll see how things go."

Eve stood with the spatula in one hand, her heart thumping. Why hadn't he told her he'd be staying for the whole month? And what did that mean for her?

He didn't think they'd continue to see each other, did he? If he was moving on, she'd rather not get any more involved with him. Even if he wasn't, there were too many inconsistencies in what he said and did, not to mention downright evasions. "I'm surprised you didn't say anything."

He grinned at her. "Got distracted, I guess."

She wanted to give him a dirty look. No doubt he found his allusion to what they'd done funny—his revenge for making him sit through this farcical little breakfast. But with Charlie and Adele in the room she knew calling him on his excuse would only create more embarrassment.

After a quick sip of his coffee, he pointed at the frying pan. "You might want to turn those eggs. Smells like they're burning."

# 9

Eve had beguiled him. That wasn't a word Rex had ever used before. He wasn't even sure how it had become part of his vocabulary. But it seemed to fit this particular situation. What else could explain his behavior? He'd already made love to her a number of times, including twice without protection. He should never have gone back to her house last night, and he should *not* have had breakfast with her parents.

As he drove away, with their invitation to join them later for a birthday dinner in Eve's honor echoing in his brain, he couldn't help cursing his own weakness. He knew better than to make a splash in this small community; he knew better than to make a splash anywhere. The same went for developing close personal ties. He'd been in hiding ever since he'd defected from The Crew. If anyone had learned how to survive, it was him.

But…

He sighed as he watched the set of mailboxes in front of her house grow smaller and smaller in his rearview mirror. So what if he knew *how* to survive? He no longer believed he could continue to do everything that avoiding The Crew required. He was coming to the conclusion that a life spent without any human attachment wasn't worth living.…

* * *

Because of her birthday Eve had planned to take this Saturday off. So after Brent left, she scrubbed down the shower and straightened the rest of the house. But then she thought she'd go to the inn, after all. She didn't want to lounge around anymore. That gave her too much time to think. And there was always more she could do to make her business a success.

But as she passed through town, she spotted the expensive baby boutique that she generally tried not to notice. The Cat and the Fiddle was only a couple of blocks from her B and B, but unless she had to purchase a gift, she didn't go in there. It made her too aware of the fact that she was still single and childless at thirty-five, when that wasn't the way she wanted it.

Today, however, she pulled to the curb and went inside.

"Oh, my God! That's darling!"

Eve was holding the sweetest pink dress she'd ever seen when that voice intruded and she turned to find Noelle Arnold standing behind her. Her heart nearly skidded to a halt for fear Noelle would guess the nature of her interest. But that didn't happen. Before she could respond, Noelle followed up with, "Are you going to get that for Cheyenne's baby?" Eve breathed a sigh of relief. Thank God for that excuse!

"I was thinking it might be nice if she has a girl," she replied, and hung the dress back on the rack.

"She doesn't know what it is?"

"Not yet. She wants a boy. Dylan wants a girl. They'll wait until she delivers to find out. So…I'll have to wait on the dress, too."

"You'll be giving her a shower, won't you?"

Of course. They were best friends. But…was Noelle angling for an invitation?

That would be *so* like her. She'd never taken responsibility for what she'd done to steal her sister, Olivia's,
boyfriend, never apologized for it. She just kept spinning
lies in an effort to make everyone believe she hadn't purposely seduced Kyle.

"Probably not till the baby's born," Eve said.

"Makes sense." Noelle started looking at other clothes.
"I've got to get her something, too. That's why I came
in here."

Sure she did. If Eve had her guess, Noelle had seen
Eve's car out front and wanted a chance to gloat over the
bad behavior she'd witnessed on Thursday. "What do you
think?" She held up a knitted cap with Viking horns that
was so cute it would've made Eve laugh if she'd been
standing there with anyone else.

Eve reached out to touch the soft yarn. "Since we don't
know the gender, it's hard to say."

"Sometimes a bag of diapers is the smartest thing to
get. A new mother can always use those. But…I could
never be that practical," she added with a dramatic sigh.

Eve glanced at the door. She was trying to come up
with a polite way to end the conversation so she could
escape when Noelle brought up the night in question.

"About what happened at Sexy Sadie's…"

*Here we go…* "I'm glad we can talk about that," Eve
said. "I've been meaning to thank you. I just…wasn't
sure where to start."

"No worries. You were so drunk I had to do *something.*"

Eve cringed. "Right. I'm embarrassed about that, of
course, about all of it. But I'm grateful to you for getting
me home. It…it was nice of you to help out."

"Don't be embarrassed! A girl deserves to have *some*

fun, doesn't she? And I won't tell a soul, so you have nothing to worry about there."

That was an outright lie. Noelle had already blabbed to Kyle and at least one other person. Kyle had told Cheyenne as much.

"You haven't?" Eve couldn't resist pressing her to see if she could flush out the truth, but it was a waste of time.

"Nope," Noelle said solemnly. "So if it gets out, it won't be my fault. But then…I wasn't the only person who saw you falling all over him."

She hadn't fallen "all over him" inside the bar. And no one else knew she'd taken Brent home. They'd walked out separately. But what was the point in arguing?

"Who are they to judge?" Noelle was saying. "What girl in her right mind could say no to *that* guy, anyway? God, was he hot! Having someone like him in your bed sort of makes up for what Ted did to you last year, doesn't it?"

Noelle had to rub her nose in that, too?

Through sheer willpower, Eve managed to keep her smile in place. "Deep down, I knew Ted and I weren't meant for each other, Noelle. I'm glad he and Sophia are happy."

"Sure you are," she said with a disbelieving snort.

"It's true," Eve insisted.

"Fine. If that's what you want me to believe. But—" Noelle grinned and nudged her with a sharp elbow "—tell me this. Who's better in bed?"

Eve longed to give Noelle a piece of her mind. Noelle had that effect on most people. But she didn't want her running around town saying they'd gotten into an argument over Thursday night. "I was so out of it I couldn't say," she told her instead.

"What a shame. Maybe you should invite him over again—when you'll be able to remember it."

Eve fidgeted uncomfortably but didn't respond.

"Or maybe I will," Noelle said with a suggestive laugh. "He new in town?"

Something akin to possessiveness raised the hair on the back of Eve's neck. *I have no claim on him,* she reminded herself. But she didn't like the idea of him sleeping with Noelle, even if she'd been the one to suggest it the night before. "Just visiting."

"For how long?"

"He'll be gone in a matter of…days." He'd surprised her at breakfast by saying he'd be in town through Christmas, but that was information Noelle didn't need to have.

"Too bad," Noelle said. "I was hoping he might be the man of your dreams. I know how badly you want to get married."

And the hits kept coming…. "You do?"

"What else is there in this town?" She rolled her eyes. "But take it from me. Marriage is highly overrated."

Eve couldn't believe she'd say that. Her ex was one of Eve's best friends, and Eve knew that Noelle had made Kyle's life absolutely miserable during the six months they'd been together.

"I'd really like to get out of Whiskey Creek," Noelle confided.

"So why don't you move?" It wasn't easy to ask that question without sounding too eager.

"I would if I had the money."

After four years of paying an exorbitant amount of spousal support, Kyle had gone to court to see if he could have it lowered. He'd won his case last month, which was probably why Noelle was now waiting tables as well as punching a time clock at the dress boutique where she'd worked, on and off, for years. She'd never been one to save money or use it responsibly, and had spent a great deal on clothes, jewelry and various surgical enhancements.

"I guess you'll have to save up if you're serious about it."

"Or marry a rich man." She chuckled, but Eve couldn't appreciate the humor, not with the way Noelle had taken advantage of Kyle.

"I'd better be going," she said. "I have to get back to the inn."

Cecilia was covering for her today, but Noelle didn't know that. Usually, Eve had only Sunday and Monday off.

"Before you go…" Noelle reached into her purse and pulled out a slip of paper. "The guy you were with left this in my backseat. I haven't seen him since, but I thought you might be able to return it to him."

It was a piece of stationery from a motel in Placerville, another Gold Country town about forty-five minutes away, with a number on it. Eve didn't recognize the area code, but cell phones weren't always tied to a particular area so that didn't mean anything. Although it was written in what looked like the same hand as the numbers jotted on the pad in Brent Taylor's room, there was no name, nothing to indicate that it was of any importance.

"What makes you think he wants it back?" she asked.

Noelle picked up some cute little booties. "Maybe he doesn't. But I thought I'd try to return it, to be nice."

Noelle didn't do anything to be nice, which made Eve wonder if she'd already called the number and knew it belonged to another woman. But she managed a polite "Thanks" as she pocketed the paper.

"No problem. Maybe I'll see you at Cheyenne's shower, huh?"

"Maybe so," Eve said, and turned to walk out the door.

Fifteen minutes later, she was sitting in her office in the back of the B and B, staring at the number Noelle had given her. Brent had checked out; she'd gone up to see. He'd said he'd be staying at Mrs. Higgins's, so she could run this over to him. But she didn't want him to think she was creating an excuse to see him again—the way Noelle had created an excuse to approach her. Now that he was gone, she was done with him. It would be easier on both of them if she tried to forget what had happened between them. Unless she was pregnant and couldn't, of course. Then they'd have to decide what to do. For him that would amount to monthly payments, she supposed— if he followed through and actually paid them.

And for her… It would change her life. But she'd always wanted to be a mother, after all.

Tossing the paper in the wastebasket, she turned on her computer. She had a couple of hours to kill before her parents' birthday dinner and figured she might as well get caught up on what she'd missed.

But she couldn't stop thinking about Brent Taylor, which made her far too curious about that number….

As soon as her email filled the screen, she bent down to dig it out of the wastebasket.

Could this be important?

After first blocking her own number, she dialed the ten digits. She wanted to know who'd answer. Maybe it would be a call girl or a business of some kind, and she could toss the number without worrying that she was disposing of information Brent might need. If this slip of paper had indeed belonged to him, he must've brought it from the motel in Placerville for a reason….

But the person who answered wasn't an employee of some business. Eve doubted it was a call girl, either. A woman picked up and, from the breathless sound of her voice, she'd rushed to get the phone.

"Hello? Hello?" she repeated when Eve didn't say anything. Eve was about to hang up when she heard, "Rex? Is it you? If so, *please* don't hang up. Talk to me. Your brother's at the hospital. He had a patient go into cardiac arrest. But I *know* he'd like to hear from you. The family's been torn apart long enough, don't you think? No one blames you for what happened to Logan. No one blames you for anything. That was so many years ago, anyway. Just…if you won't say anything to me, at least call back when Dennis is here, okay? He may not be able to say it, but he loves you. He—"

Eve hung up. She shouldn't have listened that long, but she'd been absorbed by the entreaty in the woman's voice. Whoever it was had sounded so sincere, so eager to put something right. But surely that woman had no connection to Brent Taylor. She'd been pleading with a person named Rex….

Again, Eve threw the number away. Maybe Noelle had been mistaken and someone else had dropped it in her car. Or maybe this was a business associate of Brent's who'd assumed she was receiving a personal call because it had come from a blocked number.

Except…Brent had said that one of his brothers was a doctor. That struck her as odd. And the handwriting looked so similar to what she'd found in his room.

Was it all a coincidence?

Eve called up the notes section on her phone. She'd recorded the phone number on the tag attached to Brent's luggage. She was glad now. Should she block her number again, muffle her voice so he wouldn't recognize it and ask for Rex? See what he said?

Butterflies whirled in her stomach as she considered the idea. She'd spent two nights with him and could be carrying his child. She deserved to know if Brent was his real name, didn't she?

Taking a deep breath, she blocked her number, covered the phone with one hand and prepared to talk in a high voice. But he didn't answer. She got a recording saying the number had been disconnected.

"Who or what are you hiding from?" she murmured as she set the phone aside. But then she pressed a hand to her stomach. The details of Brent's life didn't matter. For better or worse, they'd done what they'd done—and now she could only march on and accept whatever came of it.

# 10

Rita Higgins was probably seventy-five and lived all by herself in a well-kept 1950s rambler tucked away in the hills surrounding Whiskey Creek. She was listening to Christmas music while decorating her tree when Rex let himself in the front door, using the key she'd given him when he signed the month-long lease. He would've arrived earlier in the day, but he'd spent the past three hours having lunch alone, then nursing a cup of coffee at Just Like Mom's while waiting for Scarlet to join him. She'd said she'd be there by one, but it was after two when she finally returned his many calls to admit she wouldn't be coming to Whiskey Creek until Monday. She was having a hard time abandoning her usual life, didn't really want to believe she could be in serious danger.

Rex had run up against that kind of denial before, with other clients. Human beings were nothing if not resilient. Somehow, now that she'd had some time to rebound, she'd managed to cope with the shock of having her home invaded and had convinced herself that whoever had stolen her panties wouldn't harm her.

Rex hoped she was right—but he wasn't so sure. He tried telling her that this type of behavior could escalate, that it could even be deadly. But she wanted to join her friends at a Christmas party tonight and take a young girl she mentored shopping tomorrow, and she insisted no one had the right to steal that from her.

"I won't let some bully do this to me," she'd said while they were arguing about her decision.

Rex didn't feel she had any choice except to protect herself. But he couldn't force a client to do what he suggested; he could only advise her and hope that, for her own safety, she listened to him.

Considering his own decisions of late, he couldn't criticize her for disregarding his advice, anyway. Ever since he'd come to Whiskey Creek, he'd been disregarding his *own* advice. He couldn't remember a time, at least not once he'd gotten his life into some semblance of order, when he'd been this reckless. Since he'd met Eve, he'd done just about everything wrong. He'd drawn attention to himself and raised her suspicions, and he hadn't left when he should have. He felt it was only a matter of time before he dropped his guard completely and decided to live the way he wanted to, even if that meant taking his chances with The Crew. Although, he was ultimately drifting in that direction, he couldn't reveal himself, couldn't let go of his current identity yet. He didn't want The Crew to spoil this perfect place.

"There you are!" Mrs. Higgins was hard of hearing and hadn't realized he'd come in until she saw him. He found her teetering on a stepladder in an attempt to get her angel tree-topper on the highest bough. So he set down his luggage—this time he'd remembered to rip off the tags—and insisted she trade places with him.

"Look at that!" she said when it took him only a couple of seconds to put the angel where she wanted it to go. "It's *so* handy having a man around again." She craned her neck to peer through the front window. "Where's your sister? I was looking forward to meeting her."

"Something came up and she won't be able to join me until Monday."

She'd better come *then,* he told himself.

"Oh, well. Monday will be here before you know it."

He nodded. "You're doing a great job with the tree, by the way." His mother had always taken great pride in things like that....

The memory of his childhood home made him miss his mother so deeply, so poignantly, he almost couldn't breathe.

"I didn't get the tree up last year," Mrs. Higgins nearly shouted. "I just wasn't in the mood after my husband passed away. But now that there's going to be other people in the house, I thought it might be worth the effort."

If she was doing this for him and Scarlet, she didn't need to. He didn't require Christmas decorations, didn't want to be reminded of all those Christmases he'd spent with his own family. But this seemed important to her. And, for all he knew, the tree and the stockings lining the mantel would cheer Scarlet, too. He couldn't help thinking of his mother, anyway, especially at Christmas.

"It's nice of you to go to all this trouble," he told her.

"If you have time, maybe you could string some Christmas lights on the front of the house," she suggested. "There's a box of them in the garage. I'd do it myself, but I don't even know where to start. Buck always took care of the outside."

Buck. He'd heard that name before, from Eve's mother. Buck was Mrs. Higgins's deceased husband. "When did you lose him?" Rex asked.

"Just after Thanksgiving a year ago. We were sitting

at dinner when he looked up at me as if he was startled by something. Then he gasped and slumped over."

"So it was...his heart?"

He wished he hadn't asked when she began to tear up. "Took him that fast," she said with a snap of her fingers.

"I'm sorry."

"Maybe I could've handled it better if we hadn't already lost our only son to a drunk driver."

"When did that happen?"

"It's been twenty years. Buck and I got through those years together. We were married for fifty, you know."

"That's a long time to share your life with someone."

"There's no avoiding death. But—" her voice softened "—the reality of that doesn't make me miss him or our boy any less."

"I'm sure it doesn't."

She seemed to master her emotions. "So what do you say about the lights?"

Rex checked his watch. Why not? Now that Scarlet wasn't coming to town right away, he didn't have anything else he needed to do this afternoon. The weather was cold but clear, nothing that would make the job more difficult.

"Sure," he said. "Let me get settled in, and I'll see what I can do."

"How wonderful." Her weathered face split into a grateful smile. "When you're done, we'll have some hot cider and cookies. I bake the best gingerbread you ever tasted. I put up jams and jellies, too, so we'll see that you get plenty of those while you're here."

Slightly alarmed that she'd accepted him into her life so readily, he nearly told her that wouldn't be necessary. He didn't want this poor woman to latch on to him, to think he'd somehow be able to replace her dead son or fill the hole in her heart caused by the loss of her husband. If she did, it would just bring her more pain and disappointment when he moved on. But, with "The Little Drummer Boy" playing in the background and the lights twinkling on the tree, he couldn't allow himself to dampen her mood. She wasn't the only one who could use a little holiday cheer.

The last thing Eve expected was that Brent Taylor would show up at her parents' house for dinner. So when she drove home from the B and B and saw his Land Rover, she stomped on the brakes and sat there gaping at it.

"You've got to be kidding me," she muttered. What about all those excuses he'd given when they'd invited him to come this morning? He'd said he was waiting for his sister, Scarlet, to join him—to which her parents had said he could bring Scarlet ("the more, the merrier"). Then he'd said he had several things he had to get done on his computer—to which her parents had said he had to eat sometime ("It's fine if you want to drop by for just a few minutes"). *Then* he'd said he'd join them if he could, but Eve had assumed that was merely an attempt to get them to give up. What could they say to "I'll try," except "We hope to see you"?

Apparently "We hope to see you" had been enough to persuade him.

And that wasn't her only surprise. Dylan's Jeep was parked not far from Brent's Land Rover. Her parents hadn't mentioned inviting Chey and Dyl, but of course this meant her best friend and her best friend's husband would meet the man she'd been sleeping with. They'd be curious and very interested in seeing how he treated her.

The added scrutiny was one thing she didn't need.

Brent had already told her that he wasn't open to a relationship, and she'd adjusted her expectations accordingly. So why was he here, socializing with her friends and family? She didn't want them setting their hearts on something that wasn't going to happen....

Maybe this was about the money he'd given her. Maybe he'd decided it was a significant enough sum that he'd stick around until he knew whether he'd be getting it back....

"You could've communicated with me," she grumbled, and hit the gas. She feared that if she sat there any longer, someone would spot her through the window and the whole party would come pouring out to see what was wrong.

After pulling into her carport and cutting the engine, she climbed out. Originally, she'd intended to show up at dinner in the leggings, oversize sweater and boots she was currently wearing. She hadn't seen any reason to get dressed up to have a home-cooked meal with her parents, even if it was a bit of a celebration. But that had changed the instant she saw Brent's Land Rover. If he was going to be there, pride demanded that she look her best. Once he "dumped her" as planned, she'd rather not have anyone in her life thinking she hadn't done everything she could to avoid losing another man. The way her love life had gone lately, they had to be wondering if there was something wrong with her....

Clutching her purse to her chest, she dashed inside and searched frantically through her closet, finally settling on a pair of pencil-leg black slacks with a glittery top and new flats. Then she threw on her fake fur coat and hurried down the drive to her parents' house.

Taking a deep breath, she opened the door.

As the chaos of the party enveloped her, she inhaled

the wonderful smell of her mother's cooking. If Brent stayed long enough to eat, he'd be glad of it, she told herself.

"Eve! There you are." Her mother came over first and gave her a hug. "Happy birthday, honey."

Eve lifted her wrist. "I love the watch. I wear it everywhere."

"I'm so glad." She turned to indicate Brent, who was standing off to one side with Cheyenne and Dylan. "Look who managed to take a few minutes out of his busy schedule."

Eve had decided to act as if finding him here wasn't a *complete* surprise, so she smiled warmly. "I promise you won't be disappointed," she said to Brent. "No one can make tamales and enchiladas like my mother. You'd think she grew up in Mexico."

"Oh, stop," her mother said. "All you have to do is find some good recipes and practice. That's what I did."

Brent returned Eve's smile, both of them pretending that everything was as simple as it appeared to be and they didn't already know their relationship was doomed. "I'm anxious to taste them."

Cheyenne hugged her next. "You look great!"

"Thanks. You do, too."

"Stop being nice. I'm as big as a house," she said with a self-deprecating laugh.

"You should be big when you're about to have a son or daughter."

Cheyenne rubbed her tummy as if she really didn't mind, and Dylan stepped between them. "Happy birthday. *Again,*" he said.

"This seems to be the birthday that won't end," she whispered when they embraced, and was rewarded with one of his knowing grins as they parted.

"Would you like a glass of wine, babe?" Her father held up the bottle and almost started to pour before she could respond.

"No, thanks."

He frowned, his arm still in pouring position. "Are you sure? I bought your favorite chardonnay."

She wanted a drink. But as long as there was any possibility she might be pregnant, she wasn't going to have one. "Maybe later," she said, so he wouldn't find it odd that she'd refuse. She accepted a glass of sparkling water instead.

As her mother went into the kitchen to finish the last-minute preparations, they stood around visiting. Eve thought she was doing an admirable job of taking Brent's presence in stride. But, if his being here was for show, he didn't seem to be making much of an effort to fit in. Although the conversation often revolved around him, since he was new, he gave monosyllabic answers when he could and skipped all extraneous details when he couldn't. Otherwise, he didn't speak. Eve wondered why he bothered to stay. He could drop by her place to discuss his money later on....

She decided she'd talk to him privately and suggest he do just that. She excused herself to use the restroom and purposely remained detached from the group, replacing an ornament that had fallen off her mother's tree. But he didn't approach her as he could have. It was Dylan who walked over. As he acknowledged her with a nod, she glanced at Brent standing against the wall, holding the beer he'd requested instead of wine. He was watching them, watching *her,* as he'd been doing ever since she arrived. But she couldn't figure out what was going through his mind. Some deep emotion seemed to move under his skin, and yet his expression remained inscrutable.

When their eyes locked, he didn't smile, but she could feel a jolt of heat in his gaze, and it sent chills of awareness racing down her spine. He was here because he still wanted her, she suddenly realized.

That was as shocking as it was exhilarating. But if he wanted her so badly, why did he keep trying to push her away?

She had no answers. She only knew he was impossible to reach—and equally impossible to resist.

Her father walked up to Brent, inadvertently cutting him off from view, which was fortunate since she couldn't seem to peel her eyes away on her own. She'd felt puppy love for her high school boyfriend, and she'd fallen in real love with Ted. But their relationship had been more about respect and admiration and trust than arousal. What she felt for Brent was too new to be about more than chemistry and raw desire, but that desire was overpowering enough to leave her rattled.

"Eve?" Dylan said.

She curved her lips into a smile as she shifted her attention, but that unexpected exchange between her and Brent had played out right in front of Dylan, and she had no doubt he'd noticed. "What?"

"You really like this guy, huh?"

Eve cleared her throat and turned so that, even if her father moved to one side, Brent wouldn't be in her line of sight. "He's nice, I guess."

*"Nice?"* Dylan repeated, as if he could see straight through her.

"Okay, he's got to be the most beautiful man I've ever laid eyes on. But if this is where you warn me not to get my heart broken, don't worry. I'm not expecting anything permanent with Brent. He's only in town for a short time."

Cheyenne's husband took another sip of his beer as he considered her response. "Is that for real? If so, it's the best news I've heard all night."

She and Dylan had gotten off to a rocky start when he'd first begun dating Cheyenne, but these days Eve thought so highly of him and his opinion that she couldn't help being disappointed by what he'd just said. "Why don't you like Brent?"

"I didn't say I didn't *like* him. I'm sure he's great... in lots of ways."

"But...*something* has you concerned."

"Everyone who cares about you should be concerned. He's completely closed off. One hundred percent defensive. Constantly in fight or flight mode."

It wasn't like Dylan to be this opinionated, not so soon after meeting someone. "How can you tell?" she asked.

"Trust me. You trade punches with enough guys, you learn to identify the dangerous ones."

He was referring to the days when, after his father had gone to prison, he'd become an MMA fighter in order to support his four younger brothers. His level head and vast experience with fighting lent him credibility. But she couldn't believe Brent was *dangerous*. He'd touched her so gently, and she'd never felt the slightest bit scared—

The memory of when he'd awakened and slammed her onto her back suddenly came to mind. He'd scared her then, hadn't he? In that moment he'd seemed perfectly capable of violence. Even afterward, he'd acted oddly cautious, as if he expected someone to jump out of the closet and threaten his life.

"What is it?" Dylan's expression showed fresh concern.

"Nothing," she replied. "Nothing at all. He's had plenty of chances to hurt me and he's been nothing but—" she flashed him a grin to throw him off track "—accommodating."

"Don't let that pretty face fool you, Eve. That or whatever other assets he's got." The last part was the response she'd been looking for when she started to tease him. She'd been hoping he'd lighten up. But his levity came and went that quickly. When he spoke again, he was serious. "This guy's a hard-ass. I wouldn't be surprised if he's done time."

"That's crazy!"

Dylan shrugged. "I could be wrong, but…he's on edge, and that puts me on edge."

Maybe Dylan was right. But did that mean they should all turn their backs on him?

Eve was convinced that Brent needed someone and she couldn't keep herself from responding. *My life feels empty enough,* he'd said when she suggested he get with someone like Noelle.

But if she was pregnant, and he wasn't capable of loving her or being a good father, even at a distance…

"I told you, he's only in town for a short time," she said.

Her mother called them all to the dining table, but Dylan grasped her arm before she could move away.

"Just keep your eyes open," he said. "A lot can happen in a short time," he said.

If only he knew what had already happened—and how it might affect her future. "I'll be careful," she promised.

# 11

He'd fallen into a snow globe, Rex decided, into one of those perfect little Christmas scenes he'd peered into so often when he was a child visiting his grandmother's house. All that was missing was the snow.

He told himself a million times to leave Eve's parents' house. He had no business being here. He couldn't even say why he'd come, except that he hadn't wanted to make Eve look bad by proving to be so much less than the kind of man they'd expect her to bring home. He'd had enough disapproval over the years and didn't want to face it here, just when his life felt like a clean slate again. Also, his behavior reflected on her—there was no escaping that—so he'd planned to put in a brief appearance, to spend enough time that they wouldn't wonder if she'd lost her mind in allowing him to be so intimate with her.

He'd already stayed longer than he'd meant to, however. The food smelled so good, the house felt so warm and comfortable and the people seemed so happy that he couldn't resist wanting to be there, to belong to something magical like this again. Since he'd destroyed his own family, this was the closest he might ever get to what he'd once enjoyed.

Almost everyone treated him as if he was more than

welcome. The only person who seemed to recognize him for what he was—a wolf in sheep's clothing—was Dylan Amos. Every time Dylan caught his eye, he seemed to issue an unspoken warning: *Don't you dare hurt these people.*

But that didn't offend Rex. If he'd been in Dylan's shoes, he'd be doing everything he could to protect those he loved, too. The man had good instincts.

"So where does your family live?" Cheyenne asked as Eve's mother circled the table, serving the enchiladas.

Eve's pregnant friend, Dylan's wife, had taken the seat across from him and was watching him curiously.

"Los Angeles, for the most part," he said.

She tucked her long, honey-colored hair behind her ears. "Will you be joining them for Christmas?"

"No." There was nothing to go back to. Mike, his oldest brother, had moved to San Diego years ago. He was married, had two kids and a job heading up the engineering department of a plastics company. Rex spoke to him occasionally. Mike didn't seem to blame him for what had happened to Logan as much as their older brother did. Dennis, a heart surgeon in L.A., was also married and had three kids. Dean, their father, lived in Los Angeles, too, an hour south of Dennis. According to what Mike had told him several months ago, their father was finally getting past their mother's death and was even beginning to date.

Rex was glad for him but the idea of Dean with someone else felt so foreign that he couldn't imagine it. He missed his father the most. Despite how profoundly he'd disappointed his mother, how much he regretted that she was gone and that he'd never have the chance to ask her forgiveness, it was his relationship with his father—or lack thereof—that had caused him the most pain. But

Logan had been their father's favorite. Whenever he'd contacted Dean, which had only been a handful of times since he'd left, it just reminded him of how and why he'd lost his youngest son, and everything Rex had put him through.

"His sister will be joining him here any day," Eve's mother volunteered.

Rex had almost forgotten about Scarlet. With her dark hair and large, luminous eyes, she didn't look anything like him. But he guessed that didn't matter, not in the age of the blended family.

Cheyenne gave him a gentle smile. "I bet that'll be nice. Sometimes smaller groups are less stressful. Not *all* families are the havens they're supposed to be."

That comment took him by surprise. He'd expected her to be as untrusting as her husband—or as suspicious as Eve's father had been when they'd first met this morning. Coming here tonight had taken the edge off that at least.

"Are you speaking from experience?" he asked.

She laughed. "Yes. Not these days, but…I had an interesting childhood."

Rex thought it was nice of her to try and make him more comfortable. He would never have imagined that everything hadn't always been perfect in her world—because it certainly seemed perfect now. Her husband acted as if she meant everything to him.

"Fortunately, people don't have to be related to become a family," Charlie said, covering Cheyenne's hand with his own.

Cheyenne sent Eve's father a grateful smile. Rex could appreciate Charlie's obviously paternal love for someone who wasn't actually his daughter and he admired Cheyenne for being so kind. But he wasn't in the situation she assumed. There was nothing wrong with his family—except him.

"Do you have any other siblings, Brent?" Cheyenne asked.

He was so distracted by his food, by having a home-cooked meal in front of him, he didn't answer. It wasn't until everyone went still and looked up expectantly that he realized she'd been talking to him. Although he'd used various aliases since dropping out of The Crew, he still had to use a fictional surname. Right now that name was Taylor, but he'd gone back to Rex three years ago, and was no longer used to answering to anything else. Unless he was paying strict attention, "Brent" occasionally threw him.

"Sorry," he said. "What'd you say?"

The tension eased when he made it seem as if he hadn't heard her.

"I wondered whether you have any siblings besides your sister."

"He has two brothers, as well," Eve announced, her answer so quick and to the point it gave Rex the impression that she wanted to keep the questions to a minimum as much as he did. "One's a chemical engineer and the other's a doctor," she added, offering those details before her friend could ask. She seemed to think that should be the end of it but, of course, it wasn't. Cheyenne was too eager to get to know him.

"And you said they're both in L.A.?"

"Just Dennis," he replied, "the doctor."

When Eve stiffened at his side and glanced over at him, Rex sensed that what he'd just said had taken her by surprise or was somehow significant to her. But he couldn't imagine why. She didn't even know his real name. There was no way she could connect him to one of the many, many doctors in SoCal. "Do you know a Dennis in Los Angeles?" he asked.

Eve took a drink of water. Then she smiled, although it looked strained, and shook her head. "No, we have a good friend who lives there, though. She married Simon O'Neal, the actor? You've probably heard of him."

"You're not talking about one of the biggest movie stars in America?"

"Actually, I am."

"That's like casually mentioning that you're friends with Brad Pitt."

Cheyenne laughed. "We're all friends with Simon, because of Gail. We grew up with her. After college, she moved down south to open a publicity firm and that's how she met him. She used to represent him."

"Gail flies our whole group of friends out to stay with her when she has the time," Eve said.

"This summer she's taking us all to Italy," Cheyenne put in. "Simon will be filming a movie there—although I don't know if I'll get to go. My baby might be too young to travel that extensively and I'm not sure I'll want to leave him. Or her."

Rex wondered if Eve would be too pregnant to go. He hoped not, for both their sakes.

"Your baby's father could probably manage without you for a week," Dylan said. "Not that it'll be easy."

Fortunately, from there the conversation revolved around Simon, how Gail coped with the crazy antics of his ex-wife, how happy they were together and how cute their children were. Eve promised to take him to see the mansionlike cabin they owned, overlooking the Stanislaus River near New Melones Lake.

Rex couldn't tell if she was sincere about that invitation or just playing the role of cordial host, but before long he began to relax and enjoy her friends and family far more than he'd anticipated. He even stayed to play cards with them. It wasn't until eleven, when Cheyenne and Dylan were preparing to leave, that he said he had to go, too.

"Can you walk me home first?" Eve asked as she pulled on her coat.

"Of course."

Her mother was in the kitchen, loading the dishwasher, since she'd put that off to play cards with them. Her father had brought in all the dishes for her, but was now changing the channels on the TV, eager to find Sports Center.

"It was very nice to meet you both. Thank you for dinner," he told Eve's parents when her father stood up and her mother came out to say goodbye.

"You are such a nice young man," Adele said.

Not many people would describe him so favorably. The people who knew him well usually said he was his own worst enemy. He'd presented them with good reasons for that assessment. But time seemed to be healing those old wounds, to a certain extent, making it easier for him to behave well.

Her father shook his hand. "I'm glad Eve has a new friend."

"Thank you, sir."

"Don't call me 'sir,'" he said with a laugh. "We're too casual in Whiskey Creek for that."

"Since you won't be joining your own family, we'd love to have you and your sister here for Christmas dinner, if you're available," her mother told him.

He shouldn't have deepened his relationship with them, especially since that invitation was much more appealing than he wanted it to be. "I appreciate that," he said. "I'll check with Scarlet and let you know."

"You do that."

Her parents stood on the steps and waved as they walked away, and Eve slipped her arm through his.

"You have nice folks," he said.

"I do."

The door closed behind them and the porch light snapped off, but there was a full moon to light their way and a black velvet sky filled with stars. "I can see why you like it here."

"In Whiskey Creek?" She gave him an impish grin. "Be careful. If you hang out with me much longer, you might not want to leave when the time comes."

In some ways, he was already reluctant. But he couldn't stay indefinitely. Because his past would follow him wherever he went.

When they reached her doorstep, Eve told herself to let him go on his way. But she wasn't ready, despite Dylan's warnings. And Dylan didn't even know about that moment of panic when Brent had suddenly pinned her to the bed. Or that Brent had initially told her his name was Jared. Or that he hadn't mentioned having a sister when he told her parents he had two brothers. She guessed he'd say Scarlet was adopted if she asked, but…would it be true?

Eve didn't know what to believe. Brent Taylor might not even be his real name. Tonight, he'd identified his brother in Los Angeles as Dennis, which had immediately jumped out at her. When she'd called the number Brent had left in Noelle's car, she'd heard what sounded like Dennis's wife pleading with her brother-in-law, whom she called *Rex.* So if Brent's second brother *wasn't* named Rex, Brent could easily be him. The fact that he was rambling around with that number in his pocket and seemed to be estranged from his family certainly suggested it was possible.

And yet, as true and frightening as all of that was, he still held a real fascination for her. Whenever their eyes had met at her parents' house, she'd felt a zing of pleasure—and the way his gaze had followed her, she sensed that he was experiencing the same giddy attraction.

Was it only because she reminded him of that other woman?

Eve hated the thought....

"Lust is an interesting thing," she told him.

Taking hold of the lapels of her coat, he turned her and pressed her up against the door. "Now *there's* something we didn't discuss at dinner." His teeth flashed in a grin. "Why don't you tell me about it?"

Studying his perfectly shaped lips, she moistened her own. "It's far more powerful than I ever dreamed it could be."

His grin slanted to one side. "Is it?"

"To be honest, I'm not sure I've ever really felt it before, not like now."

He nipped at her lips. "I like where this is going."

"The thought of you, of what you can do to me, is driving me crazy," she admitted.

His hands slid inside her coat, curled around her bottom and brought her up against him as if he had every right to do whatever he pleased. "Does that mean what I think it means?"

She felt like someone else, someone far more daring, when she lifted her mouth to his ear and dropped her voice. "It means I want to feel you inside me again...and again," she whispered. "All night long."

He groaned. "If you're trying to make me hard, I'm already at rock level."

Giving him a seductive smile, she stared into his eyes while lowering her hand to feel the evidence. "I just have one question."

He sucked in his breath as she touched him. "What?"

"Is this for me…or for that other woman?"

"What other woman?" he asked.

"The woman who married someone else. The woman you wanted. Last night, you said I reminded you of her."

"No." He shook his head. "Only at first."

She eyed him, looking for deception. "You mean it?" He nodded.

"That's nice to hear," she said. Then his mouth came down on hers, warm and wet and demanding, and she slipped her arms around his neck. If they weren't careful, they wouldn't even make it inside, she thought as the passion built. But he pulled back.

"What about your parents?"

"I don't think they'll find it surprising if you stay over, seeing as they nearly walked in on us this morning."

He didn't seem convinced.

"What?" she said when he scowled.

"That seems too…disrespectful on my part."

His response surprised her. He cared about the impression her parents had of him? No matter who or what he was, he couldn't be all bad. "I'd say we could go to the B and B, but we have no vacancy this weekend," she told him.

"Jackson's not far."

"You want to go to the next *town?* You're kidding, right?"

"Not at all."

"But we can stay here for free."

"And feel self-conscious the whole time? No, thanks. I don't want anything holding me back." After another hungry kiss, he grabbed her elbow and propelled her along with him as, muffling their laughter, they carefully skirted her parents' windows and hurried to his SUV.

When Eve woke it was pitch-black, she was in a strange room—and she was alone. Had Brent abandoned her after they'd made love? Had he walked out and driven away, left her in an unfamiliar B and B in another town and without a car?

She sat up and stared into nothingness, her heart pounding in her ears as all her doubts about him, all the things she'd shoved into the back of her mind, bombarded her.

He said he lived in Bakersfield and owned a landscaping company, but she wasn't sure she believed it. He'd never mentioned the name of his business.

She didn't have any details on his background. Was he a high school graduate? A college graduate? If so, what was his degree?

She'd always had the cell phone number of any man she'd been intimate with. But the one she'd found on his luggage tag had been disconnected and he'd never given her *any* number. Other than knowing that he was staying temporarily with Mrs. Higgins, she had no way of contacting him.

And—she'd recognized this before but it was probably the most salient point—did she even have his real name? Was it Jared or Brent or Rex?

The only thing she had that she guessed *might* be accurate was a number for his brother in Los Angeles. And he hadn't provided that. She was pretty sure he wouldn't want her to have it if he knew, so she hadn't brought it up. She'd been afraid that would scare him off. But her own hesitancy to end whatever they had worried her as much as anything else. *Why* would she ignore so many danger signals?

Because she wanted to be with "Brent" more than she'd ever wanted to be with any other man. And it had surprisingly little to do with the fact that, with him, she'd experienced the best sex of her life. He couldn't fulfill her physically if there wasn't more to it. She wasn't someone who could be satisfied with an encounter that held no meaning. In the dark, when it was just the two of them and he was caught up in what he was feeling, he was surprisingly vulnerable and she couldn't help responding to that.

She might have thought she was crazy for reading such sensitivity into a remote man like Brent, a man who could rebuff the very kindness he craved. But the reverent way he'd touched her, especially the last time they'd made love, convinced her that there was more depth to him than her fear urged her to believe. He needed human contact—needed *love*—and it was that emotional element that undermined her caution. He made her feel close to him, in all the ways that really mattered, despite the many things she didn't know.

Even now, thinking about him evoked yearning. But if he couldn't be there for her during the day, not just at night in the privacy of a bedroom, she'd never ultimately be happy having a relationship with him. If he even permitted anything approximating a relationship. He'd already rejected the possibility in no uncertain terms.

And yet she was beginning to hope. Damn it! She knew better than to get involved with a man like Brent. But she'd tried his opposite when she dated Ted— someone steady, successful and reliable whom she'd known her whole life—and that hadn't worked out, either.

She was just throwing back the covers to climb out

of bed and get dressed, reclaim her cell phone and ask someone to pick her up—that wasn't going to be a fun call to make—when she heard the doorknob turn. She froze as Brent quietly let himself in. She would've assumed he'd gone to the bathroom, but this was a B and B like hers, where each room had been remodeled to include the modern conveniences most people preferred when they traveled.

That meant he'd been outside. Doing what, she couldn't fathom. It had to be three or four in the morning. But she could see in the dim light of his cell phone that he was fully dressed.

"Where'd you go?" she asked.

"I got a call."

"From…"

"My sister."

"In the middle of the night?"

"She's having trouble with an ex."

"She's okay, though, isn't she?"

"Shh…yeah, she's fine. I've got it handled. You don't have to worry."

When he stripped off his clothes and climbed back into bed, she rolled away from him, onto her stomach. She didn't like the way her arms ached to hold him. It was too much, too soon. If she let herself fall in love with the wrong guy yet again, maybe she'd miss the right guy when he came along.

Problem was…she couldn't imagine anyone appealing to her more. The only thing she didn't like was his reluctance to love her in return—and his secrets.

Closing her eyes, she tried to level out her breathing. She'd sleep until morning, and then she'd get away from him for good, she told herself, like she should have done from the beginning. But it wasn't ten seconds later that she felt his hands move over her body.

He started by massaging her back. She ignored that, thinking he'd eventually go to sleep. But he didn't seem to require her participation. He acted as if he was content just to touch her, and that slowly broke down her resistance, made her glad when he began to stroke her in other places.

By the time she felt his mouth close over her earlobe and his hand slide between her thighs, she'd lost all desire to refuse him. And before long he was whispering that she was the most beautiful woman he'd ever seen while cupping her breasts and taking her from behind.

# 12

When Rex opened his eyes, he found Eve lying on her side, studying him in the sunlight streaming through the crack in the blind. "Morning," he murmured.

"Morning."

He reached over to move a strand of hair away from her face. "You sleep okay?"

"I did. You?"

"I feel great." He'd slept deeply for the first time in… he couldn't remember when. He'd just completely sacked out, and being able to do that had felt almost as good as making love to Eve beforehand.

"What about your sister?" she asked.

He stretched, wondering if he'd ever been so relaxed. Not in recent memory. But he generally didn't allow himself the kind of intimacy he was enjoying with Eve. "What about her?"

"You said something happened during the night."

"She's fine," he told her, but that missed call, when he forced himself to get up and check, just in case, had frightened him. He'd thought Scarlet might be in trouble. But he'd awakened her when he called back, and she'd apologized for not leaving a message. She'd said that she'd needed her phone for navigation just when his voice mail came on and had planned to call back. But once she arrived at her girlfriend's house, she forgot until she was going to bed, and then she figured it was too late. "She wanted to let me know she was staying at a friend's." Which he felt was wise.

Eve nodded solemnly and they continued to stare at each other for several long seconds.

"No smile this morning?" he asked.

"I'm thinking."

"About…?" He was almost afraid to ask. He could tell it was something he'd rather not address.

"Last night was even more incredible than the night before," she said.

He hadn't expected a compliment. He would've been relieved—except that she didn't sound remotely pleased.

Hoping to lighten her mood, he grinned. "You nearly woke the whole inn when you cried out. Most people would be happy to come so hard."

She hadn't been *that* loud. He was teasing her, hoping to avoid where this was, in all likelihood, going. But she didn't take the hint. "Maybe I would be happy if I wasn't so confused," she said.

The sense of well-being he'd awakened with dissipated, and the old restlessness returned. "You shouldn't be confused. I've told you what to expect," he said.

"Essentially nothing."

He shifted. "Last night was nothing?"

She propped herself up against the headboard. "That's not what I meant, and you know it."

He supposed this was inevitable. He couldn't expect someone like Eve to sleep with him, again and again, no questions asked. "Then what do you mean?"

She folded her arms, keeping the sheet in place over

her breasts. "Why didn't you say you had a sister when you told my parents about your brothers?"

That was an oversight. "Because she wasn't part of the original picture."

"You're saying she was adopted?"

He hated lying to Eve, especially when so much of what had happened between them felt so...refreshingly honest. His desire for her was real. And her response to him? It was unmistakably innocent and unguarded. Although he felt moments of regret, when she reminded him of the man he could've been had his life taken a different course, she also brought him a great deal of comfort.

But the truth could get him killed—and her, too. He had to do what he could to protect them both. "She was a foster sister, at first. My parents adopted her later."

She didn't seem entirely convinced, but let it go. "And all the other stuff you've told me? That you live in Bakersfield? That you own a landscaping company? Is that true?"

He grimaced. He hadn't covered very well because he hadn't really wanted to mislead her. Now that reluctance and the half-assed lies he'd told were coming back to haunt him. "What does it matter?"

Her eyes widened in outrage. "I hope you're kidding!"

He sat up. "We're not getting married, Eve. I was clear about that from the beginning."

"And that rules out honesty? If we're not being honest with each other, what's the point?"

He got up and pulled on his pants. "We're just enjoying the fun as long as it lasts."

"And that's enough for you?"

It had to be enough. It was all he could have. "As far as I'm concerned, it's better than nothing. But I'll take you home, if you don't agree."

His terse words had hurt her. He could tell when she got up and started yanking on her own clothes. But she had to understand his limitations or she could be hurt much worse later on. "Fine. Take me home," she said. "It's got to end some time."

He felt helpless standing there, holding his shirt in his hands, watching her.

When she'd finished dressing, she went over to get her handbag from the chair, but he tossed his shirt aside and stepped toward her. "Don't let it end like this." Circling her waist with his hands, he brought her close and rested his forehead against hers. "You're all I want, even if it's just for a short time."

She moved to push him away, but he held her tight and kissed her cheeks, her forehead and her lips before whispering, "Come on. What's three weeks? You can give me that much, can't you?"

Finally, the tension left her body and she stopped resisting. But when he lifted his head, he could see the doubt in her eyes. "Three weeks?" she repeated.

"That's all," he said. "After Christmas I'm gone."

"Why *me?* There's Noelle and…and other women here."

He kissed her forehead again. "I told you. I want you. We're good together. You make me feel whole."

She shook her head. "See? That's the type of thing I don't get. Why wouldn't you be whole? What's happened?"

"Life," he said. "It's just life."

He released her and began to turn away, but she caught his arm. "Are you dangerous, Brent?"

That was the trickiest question she'd asked him yet. There'd been times in the past when he'd had to do things he didn't want to do. If The Crew confronted him, he could be forced to kill again. But he'd never hurt any-one he hadn't *had* to hurt in order to save his own life or someone else's. "I've never harmed an innocent."

Lines appeared on her forehead. He wasn't doing much to ease her concerns. She'd probably never met anyone who'd taken a human life, except maybe a soldier, and that type of killing didn't happen on American soil. His name, his occupation. Those were extraneous details. They described the shell of a person, weren't represen-tative of that person's heart, so they didn't count for all that much. But he couldn't lie to her about the kind of man he was. That was going too far.

"An *innocent?*" she repeated. "Maybe you don't real-ize it, but most men don't talk like that."

"I'm not most men, Eve. I admit it. I can't give you the home and family you deserve. I can't give you much of anything—except the next three weeks." He framed her face with his hands. "But I hope that'll be enough. That we can at least enjoy the time we've got. And I hope you know I'm *not* dangerous, not when it comes to you."

She rubbed her temples as if she couldn't decide, as if knew she should tell him to take a hike but was torn.

He raised her chin. "What do you say?"

Again, she didn't answer, but after another brief hesi-tation she sighed, then pressed her lips to his bare chest, to his neck, his jaw and, in the end, his mouth.

They'd slept too late to catch breakfast at the B and B where they'd stayed, so they drove to a greasy spoon in Jackson to eat. They were just looking over the menu when Rex received an incoming call from an area code he recognized as from back east.

"Go ahead and order," he told Eve, sliding out of the booth. "I'll have the eggs Benedict. I've got to take this."

After punching the talk button, he strode outside so he could have a conversation without being overheard. "Virgil?"

"There you are," his friend said. "Where the hell have you been? You scared the shit out of me."

"Why? Have you been trying to reach me?" They kept contact to a minimum, just to be safe. Virgil hadn't wanted Rex to return to California. He thought it was asking for trouble. So the last thing Rex wanted was the risk he'd taken to lead The Crew to Virgil and his family. Virgil was more like a brother to him than his real brothers.

"I've called your office several times this week," Virgil said.

"What for?"

"To see how you're doing. But a Marilyn Burrows keeps telling me you're 'unavailable.'"

"Why didn't you leave a message? She would've gotten it to me."

"Just because *you* trust her doesn't mean I do. I don't trust anyone I don't absolutely have to. That's how we stay alive, remember? So I wasn't about to say anything that might tip her off to the fact that you have a friend in New York."

"She's never even heard of The Crew."

"But if something about you or your business comes to their attention, that doesn't mean they won't contact her."

True. He and Virgil could never be too careful. "Then I'm glad we finally connected."

"Me, too. I was getting ready to buy a plane ticket so I could come out there and look for your ass."

Virgil would've dropped everything and done it, too. "There's no need for you to leave your family," Rex said. "I'm fine. But God, it's good to hear your voice."

There weren't many things he missed about being incarcerated, but the camaraderie he'd shared with Virgil Skinner was one of them. Virgil had gone to prison at eighteen for murdering his stepfather. Although he was exonerated when certain crucial pieces of evidence came to light, he'd spent fourteen years behind bars for a crime he didn't commit.

Rex couldn't even imagine how angry that would have made *him*. At least he'd been guilty of the drug charges he'd been put away for a few years after Virgil went in. "How're Peyton and the kids?"

"Great. Brady and Anna are growing like weeds. We're thinking about having another baby."

"Why not?" he said. "You guys are the kind of parents that should have several."

"How's your business going?"

"Can't complain. Plenty of people out here need a little muscle and are willing to pay for it. What about yours?"

"Hired three more bodyguards last month."

"That brings you to ten, doesn't it?"

"So far. Any word from your family?"

"My *family?*" Rex repeated.

"Yeah. Your father. Your brothers. Remember them?"

He kicked a small rock as he began to pace on the sidewalk. "You know we barely talk."

"I know they're the reason you returned to California. So why aren't you spending more time with them?"

He hadn't been able to figure out how to bridge that gap. Still wasn't sure. "It's complicated. And they're *not* the reason I returned." Deep down he knew that was a lie, but his pride demanded he sell it, even though part of him wanted nothing more than to mend those old fences.

"Then why'd you do it? You're certainly not any safer there."

"I like this state. It's home to me. And the weather sure as hell beats that refrigerator *you* live in." He also hated to let The Crew dictate where he settled, so maybe there were several reasons.

Virgil laughed. "I like New York, but I can't argue with you about the cold winters. Anyway, what's going on? Your email said you'd heard from a mutual friend."

"Mona."

"Livingston?"

He pivoted and headed back toward the restaurant. "That's right."

"She still with The Crew?"

"She is. At this point, I don't think she'll ever get away from them. Or escape her addiction." If getting off crank was half as bad as getting off OxyContin, Rex almost couldn't blame her. He'd never forget the terrible days he'd spent all alone, shaking and sweating and throwing up in a bathtub in some fleabag motel in the worst part of L.A. That was the price of getting clean. He'd paid that price, but he wouldn't wish so much suffering on his worst enemy. Just the memory of it was enough to keep him from backsliding, even though—after four years of sobriety—that old craving occasionally welled up, especially when he was stressed or feeling particularly lonely.

"She's been a decent friend, despite her problems," Virgil said. "I wouldn't be alive if it wasn't for her. And you."

Thanks to Mona, Rex had arrived in the nick of time to save his best friend's life soon after he'd given up drugs. They both owed her a lot. "Well, she's got more news."

"From the tone of your voice, it's not *good* news. But if she's still with The Crew, are you sure it's safe to remain in contact?"

"After she helped us before, I gave her a number where

she could leave a message any time she was in trouble. It's a Google number that goes to my email, nothing that could ever be traced to my physical location. Anyway, I hadn't heard from her in so long, I forgot I'd even set that up. Until two weeks ago. Then I saw that I had a new message waiting for me."

"From Mona."

"That's right. But she wasn't asking for help. She was warning me that certain members of The Crew claim to have new information on my whereabouts. She didn't say anything about you, but…I wanted to give you a heads-up, in case they're on the hunt again."

"They can't find me."

"Come on. It's not impossible. They know we're in the protection business, because that's what we were doing when they found us in D.C. And what else are we going to do? What else are we qualified for?"

There was a long silence. Then Virgil said, "I hear ya. Just when we think it's over, huh?"

"Those bastards won't give up. If only we'd known how badly we'd want out when we joined them."

"Don't beat yourself up about that," Virgil said. "We didn't have any choice. Not if we wanted to survive. You remember what it was like in prison."

He did. All too well. Without The Crew, he wouldn't have had a prayer of getting through those years without being used by any number of men. The "bulls" in prison liked his appearance almost as much as the women he'd met outside, which was why The Crew and everybody else in Corcoran had called him Pretty Boy. "At least I deserve whatever I get. I was guilty of what they put me in for. I really was dealing drugs. That's how I supported my own habit. But you? You shouldn't have been in prison to begin with."

"Life isn't always fair, or you wouldn't have ended up there, either. Prison wasn't the answer for someone like you. But we can argue about that shit another time. What are you going to do about this latest development?"

"I'm already doing it." The wind was picking up. Holding the phone in place with his shoulder, Rex zipped his coat. "I'm going to lie low for a while, see if there's actually anything to be worried about."

"How will you know?"

"If they've found my house or my business, they'll come poking around before too long. I have security on both that I can check via my computer. And Marilyn will call if anything odd comes to her attention."

"She's running the business while you're away?"

"She's helping. I'm within driving distance, so I can take care of anything she needs me to do."

"If that's true, you're vulnerable."

"So?"

*"So?"* Virgil repeated. "Do you like the idea of being shot?"

"No, but I'm tired of running. I'm tired of hiding, too."

"Don't talk like that. We do what we do because we have no choice."

Rex sheltered the phone from the noise of a large truck rumbling past. *"You've* got no choice. You have to look out for Peyton and the kids. Me? Some days I feel like walking into their damn clubhouse just to flip them off."

"You do that and you'll go down in a hail of bullets."

"It puts an end to it."

"Don't let them win, Rex. Whatever you do, *don't let them win.*"

He pivoted and started walking in the other direction. "I won't," he said, but sometimes it was a seductive vision—when he allowed his temper to get the best of him.

"You mean that, buddy?" Virgil asked, clearly concerned.

With a sigh, Rex turned to gaze through the window of the restaurant, where he could see Eve talking to the waitress. How was it that some of the most important decisions of his life had been made before he even knew what he was choosing? Before he even realized what he'd be forced to give up?

"Yeah, I mean it," he said. "How's Laurel?"

There was another long pause.

"You're not going to answer?"

"It's been years since the two of you were together, Rex. Don't tell me you're still thinking about my sister."

"I'll always care about her. That won't change."

"Caring is one thing, but—" Virgil blew out an audible sigh. "Never mind. She's fine. She and Miles are happy, in case that question's coming next. So…if you're waiting around, hoping they'll split—"

"No, I wouldn't want that," Rex interrupted, and he meant it. "I know he's made her far happier than I ever could."

"She had a hard time getting over you, too. Don't think it was easy for her."

"You don't have to justify her actions. I get it. Any woman in her right mind would've chosen Miles. The good sheriff comes with fewer…complications."

"She's lived a messed-up life, too," Virgil said. "Between both of you, there was too much shit that'd gone down. But someday you'll meet the woman who's right for you."

"A nice girl I can introduce to the fact that I'm being hunted by my old gang? Hardened criminals who wouldn't hesitate to put a bullet in me? That I'm an ex-con, ex-addict and being with me puts her in danger? I'm quite the catch, wouldn't you say?"

He'd been joking, but Virgil didn't seem to find any humor in what he'd said. "Peyton and I are making it work."

"If you call living in fear that The Crew could find you at any moment making it work."

"If anything happens to Peyton, or the kids, it's war," he said. "I hope those bastards know that."

They didn't care. They'd welcome the violence. They lived for upping their body count.

"I'm with you," Rex said. War, he could handle. After living as he'd been living, it would almost be a relief to confront his enemy. He would already have driven to L.A. and barged into whatever shit-hole their leaders were occupying these days if he thought he could put an end to the stranglehold they had on his life or Virgil's. But he and Virgil had confronted The Crew on several occasions. They'd even killed in self-defense. And it hadn't changed anything. More thugs just filled the shoes of the ones who were removed.

"I know you are, buddy," Virgil said. "I've always been able to count on you."

They still had the friendship that'd carried them through so much. But...

Rex turned to glance at Eve again. He wasn't about to drag a woman into the crossfire. He'd lost too many people he cared about over the years. He couldn't risk losing another.

# 13

While Eve was waiting for Brent and the food she'd ordered, a text came in from Cheyenne. Chey had tried calling earlier, but Eve hadn't picked up. She hadn't wanted to talk to her best friend in front of Brent. She wasn't sure she should respond even now that she had some privacy. She knew she was probably making a mistake getting involved with him. All the signs were there. Even Dylan, who didn't cry wolf unless he perceived a real threat, had tried to warn her....

She felt as if she was hurtling toward the sun, trapped by its gravitational force and unable to change course.

At least it was quite the cosmic ride, she told herself. Especially exhilarating for a small-town girl who'd known most of the other people in her life for years and years. An attractive, enigmatic, here-and-then-gone man like Brent was quite the novelty. And the possibility of being or becoming pregnant intensified the risks *and* the rewards. But the possibility of having *his* baby was beginning to take on special significance—further proof that she was too wrapped up in a man who had already put her on notice that he wouldn't be part of her life for more than a few weeks.

How'd it go last night? Cheyenne had asked.

After checking the entrance of the restaurant to make sure Brent wasn't on his way back in, she wrote, I've climbed aboard the big roller coaster.

That response makes me a little nervous. Want to explain?

Having Brent in my life is both thrilling and frightening.

Frightening is not very reassuring. Did he stay with you last night?

Yes. And it was crazy good....

There's that. So when did he leave?

He didn't. We're in Jackson, about to have breakfast at Jemima's Kitchen.

He's there now?

He stepped out to take a call.

This time there was a slight pause before Cheyenne responded—long enough that Eve took a sip of her orange juice and smiled politely at the waitress as she passed by. Finally, a telltale ping alerted her to another incoming text.

There's no guarantee Dylan's right, Eve.

So Dyl had voiced his concerns to his wife, which meant Cheyenne was worried, too, and trying to compensate for that. Or she was trying to get Eve to open up so she could warn her again.

There are definitely reasons to be concerned, she admitted.

Specifically...

I don't know a lot about him.

That's usual when you just meet someone.

Which was why she'd been foolish to sleep with him that first night. He's also as guarded as Dyl says.

At one point you were worried about the kind of man Dylan was, because of his reputation, remember? And look how well it's turned out for us. This thing with Brent doesn't have to end badly.

But it's going to, she wrote, then she erased it and put, Right. I guess we'll see.

Just take your time. Don't get in over your head.

Brent walked in before she could respond. Not wanting him to see what she was texting, she slipped her phone in her purse.

"Sorry that took so long," he said as he sat down.

"No problem. That wasn't your sister again, was it?"

"No."

"You must be relieved. Something come up at work, then?"

"It wasn't work, either. I just heard from an old friend."

She didn't bother questioning him further. She could

tell by his throwaway tone that this was all the explanation she was going to get. If she wasn't mistaken, he was upset or frustrated or angry.

"Did you order for us?" he asked, drinking some of his coffee.

"I did." She straightened her silverware. "The food should be here any second."

"Good. I'm hungry." He shifted several times, then started to bounce his knee.

"Are you okay?" She was about to tell him they didn't have to stay for breakfast, that they could try to cancel their order, but he spoke first.

"When will you find out whether you're pregnant?"

"In a week or two. At least, that's what I learned when I looked it up on the internet."

He nodded.

"Why?" she asked.

"Just curious."

She picked up the empty sugar packet and twisted it in her fingers. "Will you be terribly upset if I am?"

"Yes," he said—immediately and unequivocally. "I will."

Breakfast turned out to be an uncomfortable affair. They ate and Brent paid the bill. Then he drove her home, all without more than a perfunctory comment here and there.

When he pulled into her drive, Eve started to climb out, but paused with her hand on the door latch. The person Brent had been last night had been easy to want, easy to connect with. She was infatuated with *that* man. But *this* man... This man would always be a stranger to her because he wouldn't let anyone be more than that. "You're a difficult person to read. You know that."

A muscle moved in his cheek. "You don't have to read me. I've been up front."

"About…"

He wouldn't look at her. "Just don't get attached."

She stared at him for several seconds. "That's it? Don't get attached? After making love so many times? I've never had a man act as if he wants me with that same intensity. It's more like…like you *need* me. Like it's a gut reaction you can't control. And I can't help responding in the same way." It was so potent. "When you're like that it makes me feel…valued and desired. But then morning comes and—"

"And what?" he snapped. "I'm gone in three weeks, Eve!"

She gaped at him. "I know! I'm not trying to keep you here. But I thought we'd reached a point where the days we did have would be…I don't know…different. Or are you just passing time, trying to distract yourself from your normal life, whatever it is?"

When he didn't answer, just dropped his head and pressed his thumb and finger to the bridge of his nose, she laughed without mirth. "Never mind. Forget it. I can't take the contradictions. I don't think even *you* know what you want."

Once she finished climbing out, she slammed the door. She wanted him to come after her, hoped he'd revert to the sensitive man he'd been last night. That person was someone special, someone worth fighting for. No matter how many unanswered questions she encountered, she still believed he possessed so much potential.

But he didn't chase after her. He sat in her drive for several minutes. She could hear his engine from where she stood listening in the hall. Then he drove away.

* * *

Eve rubbed her arms against the chilly air as she took Ted down to the basement. He'd called her not long after Brent had dropped her off to see if she could meet him at the B and B. He'd wanted to spend some time studying the layout of the murder scene, and she'd been so upset about how her night with Brent had ended that she'd agreed to do it right away, to distract herself from the frustration and disappointment.

"I can see why you don't like to come down here. It's creepy, all right." Ted poked around the old boiler, which hadn't been in use since the previous owner installed central heating and air.

"Any basement in a house this old would be a little off-putting," she said. "But the murder of a child makes this one downright disturbing."

He left her standing at the foot of the stairs and threaded his way among dozens of pieces of old furniture, most of them draped, to reach the workbench her father had used when he maintained the property. "Not all of it's old," he mused, examining her father's tools.

"We haven't changed much, just that small corner. My dad built a work area so he'd have a place to store his tools and extension cords, that type of thing. He uses it if I need something fixed and he's in town to do it. But he's gone so much these days that I usually hire James Reed."

"I know James," he said. "He helped build the guest-house behind my place." He turned to look around him. "What do you plan to do with all this furniture?"

"Nothing, for now. I'm just hanging on to it, in case I need it later."

"So where was Mary found?"

She pointed to the closet behind her, under the stairs. "Right there."

"What made her father look for her here?" he asked when he reached it and opened the door to peer inside. "Did she come down here often? Because I tend to believe that this dark basement would frighten even a child of the Victorian era, especially one who's only six years old."

Eve had meant to get him the collection of newspaper articles a team of researchers had dug up for *Unsolved Mysteries*. They would tell him almost as much as she could, since that was where she'd gotten the bulk of her information. But she'd been too preoccupied with Brent the past couple of days to search the attic, where she'd put them. "He told the police it was because she liked to play with a train set he kept down here, out of harm's way."

"Harm's way?"

"He apparently said it wasn't for her use. And with the boiler…this wouldn't be the safest place for a child to play."

"You think he might have killed her for touching something he considered off-limits?"

"That *could* be what triggered his temper. According to the reports I've read, that's what some people believed. He carved the various pieces of the train himself, and they were quite intricate. There was a picture of one in the paper. Actually, it was a hand drawing."

"Has any of the train survived?"

"No. The day after he died, his wife threw his train set and all his papers in the hearth and burned them up."

"I'm sure some found that symbolic."

"I would imagine."

Ted scratched his neck. "When and how did John Hatfield die?"

"He fell down these stairs and broke his hip soon after World War I began. He was never the same after that."

"If Mary died in 1871, he must've been old by then."

"Seventy-something. I'm sure his age didn't help his recovery."

"Did Harriett stay here long after he passed?"

Eve bent to peer under the stairs as he was doing. She hadn't opened that door since *Unsolved Mysteries* filmed here. "No. But no one's really sure where she went."

The door at the top of the stairs suddenly slammed shut, and Eve froze as her gaze met Ted's. "See what I mean?"

"It could've been a draft."

"That slammed it with such force?"

He didn't seem convinced, either, but he shrugged as if it was possible. They waited to see if anything else was going to happen, but when nothing did, she went back to what she'd been saying about Harriett Hatfield. "Anyway, John's nephew Willard, and his young wife, Betsy, came all the way from Boston for the funeral and were planning to stay indefinitely and help Harriett with the house. But before they could even bury John, she slipped out, made her way to Sacramento where she could catch the train and…disappeared."

"Without saying a word to anyone."

"If you're asking how she bought a ticket if she wouldn't talk, I don't know. Maybe she only talked when she had to."

"No one knows where she went?"

"Most people think she went to live with her sister in South Carolina, where she was from."

He took the flashlight she'd brought down with them, turned it on and angled the beam into the corners of the closetlike space where Mary's body had been found. "She was strangled?"

"And beaten."

He grimaced, no doubt feeling the same distaste she did. "So what happened to this place after Harriett left?"

"John and Betsy tried to stay on. They'd brought all their belongings. But they didn't last long before heading back. Betsy didn't like it here."

"Do we know why?"

"The locals blamed it on Mary's ghost. Said it wouldn't give her any peace, since both she and her husband were strong advocates for John. They put the house up for sale but couldn't get any offers. No one wanted to live in a haunted home, so it sat empty for several years and fell into disrepair—until it was purchased for half its value by an eccentric widow from Portland named Luddy Lewis. She came to live here, alone, in 1925."

"Luddy didn't mind living with a ghost?"

"The whole reason she bought the place was to put Mary's ghost to rest. She said she could be the poor girl's 'voice' and reveal her murderer."

Ted turned off the flashlight, and the basement seemed even dimmer than when they'd first entered. "How did she plan to do that?"

"Claimed she could converse with the dead."

"Was she a fortune-teller?"

"No, just…eccentric, like I said."

"Where did she get her money?"

"That, I couldn't tell you. I suppose from her dead husband's estate."

"And did she learn anything from Mary after she moved in here?"

"You can't be serious…."

"I'm curious as to what she might have claimed."

"She didn't point a finger right away. But after several months, when a newspaper reporter confronted her, she said it was the boy next door. That he raped and killed Mary."

Ted straightened. "Really! What did the boy next door have to say about that—assuming he was still alive when this happened?"

"The records aren't complete enough to indicate which boy she was talking about. During the time Mary lived here, there were children, boys and girls, on both sides, so it seemed like a convenient answer to the puzzle— a way to come up with something original that couldn't be disproved."

Turning the flashlight back on, Ted pointed it at the corners. "Did Harriett ever accuse her husband? Outright accuse him, I mean?"

"Not that anyone's ever said."

"She didn't come forward, even after he died?"

"No."

"Don't you think she'd do that, if she truly believed he was to blame for murdering their child? If he was the reason she wouldn't talk, why wouldn't she advertise the truth once he was gone and could no longer punish her?"

"Maybe she thought it was too late. Or she blamed herself. Felt guilty for not leaving him when she first learned he was dangerous or for being unable to stand up to him and protect her daughter."

"I guess it's also possible that she suspected but didn't really know," he mused.

"True."

"Has anyone ever tried to figure out where she went? Spoken to her family? Hunted down all the boys who were living nearby at the time to follow up on Luddy's theory?"

"Why would anyone bother to do that? Luddy was basing her accusations on something she said she heard *from a ghost*. You don't believe there's anything to it, do you?"

"Of course not. But it'd be worth talking to everyone who might have some memory of the incident—or who knew someone with a memory of it."

"I don't think *Unsolved Mysteries* went that far. Time is money for them, and they were chiefly interested in coming up with enough for a good segment, because it meant they could feature Simon, which was the real draw for them."

"They got the ratings boost they wanted."

"And we got what little information they managed to dig up, but it certainly doesn't answer all our questions."

"That doesn't mean the answers we want aren't out there." Eve prayed he was right. In recent years, she'd despaired of ever solving the mystery, but his interest gave her renewed hope. It seemed as though everything he touched turned to gold. Maybe he'd have luck in this, too, and Mary's murderer would be identified despite the passage of so much time.

"Let's get out of here," he said, and Eve gladly led him up the stairs.

As they reached the main floor, she expected him to say goodbye and leave her so she could go find those documents in the attic, but he didn't. He stopped before they could reach the front door and gave her a searching look.

"What is it?" she asked.

"Sophia heard something at the salon when she was getting her hair cut that has us both worried."

Feeling immediately defensive, Eve crossed her arms. "So?"

"You're not even going to ask what it is?"

"I know what it is." Noelle had been gossiping. Eve had expected that. But it was a little disconcerting to hear

that the rumors had reached Shearwood Forest, where
they'd likely be regurgitated for weeks. "And I don't think
it's any of your business."

He stiffened. "Maybe not as a past lover. But I was
your friend before I was anything more, and I hope I'm
still your friend."

"Stop that," she said. "Of course we're friends. We'll
always be friends. I told you, I'm just going through a
rough patch."

"This rough patch…it's because of the guy you met
at Sexy Sadie's, right?"

"It's because I'm turning thirty-five and don't know
what to do with the rest of my life!"

"You were never confused before."

She didn't have an answer for that. She didn't understand why she suddenly felt so listless and dissatisfied.
Maybe it was because Brent had shown her what she
*could* feel, and it was heady and wonderful and more
fulfilling than anything she'd experienced so far.

"Is he the guy who was staying here?" Ted asked.
"The one who came up and whispered in your ear when
we were talking in the parlor?"

"Does it matter?"

"Just curious." He scowled at her. "God, why are you
so defensive?"

"Sorry." She thrust her hands in her pockets. "Yeah,
that's him."

"What's he doing in town?"

"Taking a vacation for the holidays."

"All by himself?"

"His sister is coming to join him tomorrow. Why?"

"I thought maybe he was here on a job—you know, to
protect someone, and I couldn't imagine who it might be."

"What are you talking about?"

"He's a bodyguard, right?"

A stab of foreboding made her uncomfortable, and she instantly thought of those odd scars on his body. "No. He owns a landscaping company in Bakersfield."

Ted's eyebrows went up. "You sure?"

She wasn't. She wasn't sure about anything when it came to Brent. "I think so. Why?"

"Apparently Noelle asked whether or not it was wise to leave you alone with him, and he said she didn't have to worry, that you'd be safe with him. That's when he said he was a bodyguard."

"He was drunk, probably didn't even know what he was saying." Besides, that sounded like a typical Noelle flirtation. If she'd *really* been worried about Eve's well-being, she wouldn't have dropped them off together, no matter what Brent said, especially when he'd had too much to drink. What murderer was going to admit his next victim wasn't safe?

But there was a note of authenticity in this that bothered Eve. Brent wasn't particularly bulky, but he came across more like a bodyguard than a landscaper. Plus, Dylan had reacted to the wariness in him. And that moment when Brent had pinned her down on the bed made her think he was used to physical confrontations. So did the way he constantly scanned a room, as if assessing any potential threat.

"Even if he was drunk, why would he lie? Personally, I think that's when he'd be more prone to tell the truth."

"Maybe he was being facetious!"

"Right. That makes sense." He said that as though it didn't make any sense at all, but Eve could imagine a man joking that way. *I'll look after her. I'm a bodyguard.*

Regardless, Ted moved on. "So how long will he be staying in Whiskey Creek?"

"Until after Christmas."

"Will you be seeing him again?"

As if she hadn't had enough warnings, Brent had given her another one just that morning: *Don't get attached...* No," she decided. "I won't."

# 14

Rex hadn't been able to reach Scarlet. He'd tried several times. She'd ducked his calls yesterday, when he'd been waiting for her at that home-style restaurant in Whiskey Creek. But she'd had a reason to avoid him then. She hadn't wanted him pressuring her to leave the Bay Area and go to a town she wasn't familiar with, hadn't wanted to face the reality of the danger she was in. Now that he wasn't expecting her until tomorrow, she should know he was just trying to check in—and that he'd worry if she didn't pick up.

So what was going on?

With a curse, he tried for easily the tenth time. Then he called Marilyn at home. "Have you heard from Scarlet?" he asked without even saying hello first.

"No. But it's Sunday, in case you haven't noticed. I don't work on Sunday."

"You get the emergency calls." Ordinarily, they came to him, but he'd asked her to take on that duty and to let him know if anything important developed. "This kind of work can't be scheduled into office hours. I explained that when I hired you, and when I asked you to take on some additional tasks while I'm gone."

"I know. It's just…it's been stressful since you left.

And I didn't get any sleep last night. I was at the vet clinic with my dog. He cut himself on the fence out back."

"I hope he's okay. I wouldn't ask this if I was any closer. But Scarlet's life could be in danger. I need you to drive by her place, see if you can find some sign of her. Meanwhile, I'll call the police and the hospitals."

There was a slight hesitation, but when Marilyn responded, she sounded almost as concerned as he was. "You're really worried."

"Shit, yeah, I'm worried."

He heard the jingle of her keys. "I'll leave now. I'll call you as soon as I get there."

"Thanks."

Mrs. Higgins was listening to her Christmas music again and baking in the kitchen. Rex could smell the gingerbread and wished that Scarlet had taken his advice— and come to this safe haven when she'd had the chance.

No one had died in the attic, but it could be as unsettling as the basement, with its musty smell and all the dust and cobwebs, not to mention the clutter and nostalgic memorabilia. Eve's own cradle was stored up here, along with several boxes of her old clothes and toys. Her parents had put her brothers' childhood belongings here, too, hoping that any grandchildren they might have would benefit from what they'd saved.

Eve wondered if they might finally get the grandchild they'd been waiting for come August but wouldn't allow herself to dwell on that possibility. Because then she'd also think of Brent, and thinking about him weakened her resolve not to see him again.

Maybe it would be easier once he left....

"Look at this stuff," she muttered aloud. She wasn't even sure her parents were aware of everything that had been shoved up here, but they'd said that some of it hailed all the way back to when the Victorian was first built. Harriett Hatfield, one of the original owners, hadn't taken much more than a suitcase full of clothes with her. And John's nephew and his wife, Betsy, sold all the household furnishings before they left, but probably hadn't been willing to drag several big boxes across the country with them, especially boxes full of stuff that was essentially worthless. The buildup had started there. Then Luddy had bought the place, refurnished it and piled *her* cast-off items on top of what John's nephew and Betsy had abandoned. Toward the end of her life, she probably hadn't been strong enough to haul box after box down the narrow stairs that were the attic's only access.

When Luddy died—it was in the 1950s if Eve remembered right—her only son came from San Francisco. He tried to open a flower shop in Whiskey Creek but couldn't get a foothold. According to what her parents had heard, he'd gone through the attic and sold the antiques, along with some of his mother's possessions, before returning to the city. But even he didn't go through all the boxes of journals and pictures. Or if he did, he didn't know what to do with them so he just left them behind like everyone else.

The Victorian had changed hands quite a few times after that—until 1984, when her parents bought it in order to turn it into a B and B. No doubt more of the storage had been sold off or thrown away during the gap between Luddy's ownership and the time the Victorian came into her family, but the attic was never completely cleaned out. Eve guessed no one wanted to toss things that might have some historical value. At least that was the reason her parents gave for not getting rid of it all.

Eve felt the time had come to put this place to rights,

but she wasn't in any hurry. A thorough cleaning would require a lot of work and time spent in the attic, which she couldn't afford through the Christmas season. Besides, the attic wasn't a comfortable place to be. It had no heat or air-conditioning, and several townspeople claimed, as far back as Mary's death, to have seen a figure standing in the window up here—when no one would admit to being in the attic. Two years ago, the woman who owned the dress shop in town told the *Gold Country Gazette,* when they did their usual Halloween article about the haunted B and B in town, that she saw someone holding a candle in the highest window, late at night, just the previous summer.

Although Eve had always coped with the possibility that she shared the B and B with a ghost, she wasn't eager to spend much time in the attic or the basement, especially alone. She didn't think she'd ever grow accustomed to the unease that made her feel slightly clammy. But she hadn't expected retrieving the records *Unsolved Mysteries* had left to take very long. She'd been fairly certain she'd put them close to the door, but she'd been searching for nearly thirty minutes and hadn't been able to locate them.

"What the heck did I do with those things?" she muttered as she worked her way deeper into the stacks of tax records and old toys, baby items, photo albums and decorations for seasons other than Christmas. She and Deb had dragged all her Christmas decorations out of here and had moved other stuff around in order to do it. That must be why the box of information wasn't where she'd expected to find it.

Seeing the coffin and skeleton she'd bought for Halloween several years ago gave her a jolt.

"Come on, Eve," she said, laughing at her own reaction. But she couldn't help sending a nervous glance at the window where everyone said the mysterious "ghost" appeared. Had those people really seen something that indicated paranormal activity? Or was it all imagined?

Eve preferred to believe the latter. She was a pragmatist at heart. If she couldn't trust what *she'd* seen and heard, how could they? But it was a bit disturbing that no one could get to that particular window, not without moving a lot of junk that looked as if it hadn't been touched in decades.

Eve decided to make a pathway now. Why not? With any luck, she'd come across the research from *Unsolved Mysteries* in the process. And if she looked out, maybe she could ascertain what people were actually seeing when they said they'd spotted Mary's ghost.

Once Eve reached the window, she had to smile at the thought that someone would probably see her and claim yet another ghost sighting. But as she gazed out over downtown, she quickly forgot about Mary, the records, even her anxiety about the unexplained, when she saw Brent's Land Rover tearing down the street. He was going faster than he should and accelerated in a sudden burst, scooting through a yellow light. Then he skidded around a corner and disappeared. Where was *he* going?

It looked to her as if he was heading out of town.

So maybe he'd changed his mind about staying through the holidays. Maybe he was leaving early.

That wouldn't bother her, Eve told herself. She'd just been thinking it would make things easier.

But if that was her honest response, why did she suddenly feel so heartsick when she went back to digging for those records?

* * *

Rex was sitting beside Scarlet's hospital bed when she opened her eyes. Her parents had been there earlier, to greet her when she first got out of surgery. But they were gone now, getting a bite to eat. Rex had promised to sit with her, and he was glad of it. This afforded them a few minutes alone.

"Hey," he murmured, approaching the bed when he realized she was conscious. "You gave us all quite a scare."

Her eyes filled with tears. "I should have listened to you. That woman was there, when…when I went home to change and get more stuff." She choked up. "She… stabbed me…almost killed me."

Rex had heard, from the police and Scarlet's parents, that the person who'd been stalking her was a woman by the name of Tara Wilson—the jealous girlfriend of one of Scarlet's old love interests. Tara didn't have a history of violence, and no previous complaints had ever been filed against her, so the police had never even suspected her.

Rex had to admit, like the police, he'd 100 percent assumed it was a man. Tara had been clever enough to make it appear that way, what with that picture of a penis and stealing Scarlet's underwear. The sexual aspect had sent them in the wrong direction. So who knew how long the torture might have continued if Scarlet hadn't surprised Tara at the house?

"The good news is that she didn't," he said. "And she won't get away with what she's done. The police have her in custody. It's over. She'll go to prison for assault with a deadly weapon, and once your stitches are out, you'll be fine."

"But why would she *stab* me? What have I ever done to her? Nothing! I only met her once, briefly, when I saw the two of them at a birthday party for a mutual friend."

"Maybe she panicked and felt she had to kill you or you'd identify her."

"But I don't understand what made her fixate on me in the first place. I don't even care about Tom anymore. He calls every once in a while, but we haven't been to-gether—not in *that* way—for years."

"It's possible he never got over you."

"Did she say that?"

"She told the police he has pictures of you all over his apartment and throws you up to her as the love of his life whenever they argue. She resents living in your shadow."

"That makes no sense," Scarlet insisted. "Tom creeped me out a little when we broke up. I've never seen a man cry and beg like that. But…he's been fine since. When he calls, we don't even talk about intimate things. I ask how his life is going. He asks about mine. No big deal."

"You probably wouldn't have taken his calls other-wise."

"So it was all an act?"

He wiped a tear from her cheek. "A lot of situations like this *don't* make sense. At least you're safe now, and you'll be able to spend the holidays with your family without constantly worrying about what you might find when you go home."

She gazed around the stark hospital room. "You mean I'll be able to enjoy the holidays after I get out of here."

"That won't take too long. Somehow, miraculously, that knife missed your vital organs. You should heal quickly."

She sniffed. "This wouldn't have happened if I'd gone to Whiskey Creek with you."

"True. I wasn't pleased that you ignored my advice. But if you hadn't, she might never have been caught. I'm just happy it's over for you."

She adjusted the tube going into her IV so she could use her arm to push the hair out of her face. "How did you find out I was here?"

"I've been calling you all day, trying to check in. When you wouldn't pick up, I had the woman who runs my office drive by your place."

"Marilyn."

"Yes. She saw the cop cars, so she called me and I drove over."

"That's almost a two-hour drive."

"I know."

She reached for his hand. "It was nice of you to come so far."

He let her thread her fingers through his. "I feel bad for not being there when you needed me."

"It was my choice to stay in the city for another couple of days." She managed a rather pitiful smile. "So don't worry. I'm not going to ask for my retainer back."

He chuckled at her joke. "I do have one question."

"What's that?"

"How long has Tom been with Tara?"

"A year or so. Why?"

A year? That couldn't be. "How long did they know each other before dating?"

"A week or so after we bumped into each other, he called to say hello and told me he met her at work a few weeks before they got together."

"Then who was stalking you before?"

A look of confusion crossed her face and, once it cleared, her jaw dropped. "God, I must still be groggy from the anesthetic, because you're right. It couldn't have been her. Not the last time. She didn't even know me when I was being terrorized back then."

"Shit," he said. "She's not your stalker."

"Are you sure?"

"The chances are way too small that you picked up *two* stalkers, especially with such similar behavior."

"But she was *in* my house. She came at me with a knife."

"Maybe she was there looking for proof that you and Tom were together recently. Because my money's on him," he said, and called the police.

"I found them." That evening, Eve sat in her office at the B and B with the box from *Unsolved Mysteries* at her feet. She would've phoned Ted to notify him as soon as she'd hauled it down from the attic, but she'd spent the past several hours reading what it contained. If it wasn't so late, she would have gone through the entire box, but she knew Ted was expecting her to call before bedtime.

"That's great!" he said. "Where were they?"

"In the attic, like I thought. Took a while to find them, though. I have no idea how they got shoved so far in the back."

"Thanks for going to so much trouble. I'm sure the historical society will thank you, too, once I finish my book."

"They have copies of a lot of these documents already but I've been meaning to let them go through all this stuff to see if they're missing anything."

"Sure, we can do that at some point. Should I pick them up from your house or—"

"No, come to the B and B," she said. "I'm still here."

"When I left, I thought you weren't going to stay much longer. Isn't Sunday your day off?"

It usually was, but she wasn't in any hurry to go home. She was afraid she'd just mope around, thinking of Brent, and she refused to be *this* disappointed over a guy she'd met only a few days ago. With Ted she'd had a long history and a commitment of sorts, so there'd been something substantial to mourn.

Anyway, she'd decided to finish the December menus Cheyenne had begun, check the pantry for supplies and place an online order for anything they might need. Why not get an early start instead of leaving the inn vulnerable to delayed deliveries caused by the typical Christmas congestion?

"You know what owning a business is like," she said. "Yours is a different kind of business than mine, but it still takes a lot of time, effort and energy. It's more than just writing the books."

"You've put your heart and soul into that B and B," he said, ignoring what she'd said about him and his business. "Are you still thinking of leaving it behind?"

"No." At least, not if she was pregnant. If she was going to have a baby, she'd want to stay right here and provide a wonderful life for that child. Being a mother wasn't all she wanted; she preferred to be a wife, too. But she'd done everything she could to find a husband and—no luck.

"Glad to hear it," he said.

He arrived at the B and B fifteen minutes later, while she was still reorganizing that box. Pamela, who split all the nightshifts and the days Eve was off with Cecelia, walked him back to her office.

"I didn't even realize she was here," Eve heard Pam exclaim.

"Considering how much she works, it can't surprise you."

"No," she responded with a laugh. "Maybe that's why I didn't notice her come in."

Pam hadn't been anywhere in sight, but Eve didn't comment. She merely glanced up as Ted entered the room.

"There you are," he said.

"And here's what you're looking for." With a smile of appreciation for her employee, she shoved the box in Ted's direction. "I hope it helps. I've read through most of what's in there and didn't find anything new, but you'll be able to document certain facts. There are deeds, legal descriptions, death certificates, birth certificates, copies of journals, newspaper articles and old photographs they somehow collected. So…it's all yours until you're done and don't need it anymore. Then I'd like to get everything back so I can go over it with the historical society, like I said."

"Of course. But before I go, I have a little something for you." He put an envelope on her desk.

"What's this?" she asked as she picked it up.

"I had Chief Bennett do me a favor."

"The police chief? What sort of favor?"

"I had him run the plates on your new friend's Land Rover."

"Without probable cause? Isn't that illegal?"

"It's not like we searched his room, Eve. Chief Bennett doesn't need probable cause to run a license plate. He does it routinely while he's driving behind people. Most cops do."

"But Brent hasn't done anything wrong. Why would Chief Bennett agree to do such a thing?"

"Because I wouldn't ask unless I had some sincere concerns."

Eve glared at him. "How do you even know Brent drives a Land Rover? When you mentioned him earlier, you acted as if you'd seen him just that once, when he came in while we were talking in the parlor."

"That *is* the only time I've seen him. But the discrepancy in what he told you and what he told Noelle had me worried, so I called Cheyenne to see what she thought of the situation."

"*What* situation?"

"A strange man in town possibly taking advantage of someone we both care about. If it was another woman, another member of our group, wouldn't you expect us to look out for her? Why wouldn't we do the same for you? Anyway, Dylan got on the phone and said he wished we could do some sort of background check. He'd made a note of Brent's license plate number. But he didn't have the relationship with Bennett to ask him to access the DMV records, so I offered."

"I see." Eve came to her feet. "And how do *you* have a relationship with Bennett? He hasn't been in Whiskey Creek that long himself. What's it been—a year?"

"He's from Jackson, which isn't far, so he's got a similar background." He grinned. "He's also a big fan of my books."

"Isn't *that* flattering," she said. "You must be very proud of yourself. But did it never occur to you or Dylan that you were meddling in something that's none of your business?"

He scowled, but she could tell by the stubborn set of his mouth that he felt he was well within his rights. Of course Ted, being Ted, would have thought it all out. "It did," he said. "Neither of us *wanted* to do this. But… the guy could be a serial killer for all we know. There's nothing wrong with making sure he's a legit character, is there? We don't want to let him victimize you or anyone else in town."

That actually wasn't so unusual. These days lots of women ordered background checks on the men they dated. Being cautious was considered wise. But checking up on Brent without Brent's knowledge, especially when it involved contacting the police, felt...intrusive. Disloyal. It also made her fear for him, worry that it might cause him to be arrested, which was crazy. If he was what he said he was, there'd be nothing for either of them to fear.

"I've never snuck around and checked up on anyone before," she grumbled.

He tilted his head as if she was being difficult for no reason. "Neither have I. Because it hasn't been necessary until now. Here in Whiskey Creek, we know everyone's background. But he's new, and he's not exactly an open book."

She sighed as she turned the envelope over in her hands. "Shit."

"What? Are you really mad at us?"

"No. I understand that you have my best interests at heart." She also knew they had a valid reason to worry. "I just feel terrible—slimy—looking at what's inside this envelope."

"Don't feel slimy," he said. "It doesn't tell you much. Except that he's been lying."

Her blood ran cold even though she'd suspected, almost from the beginning, that Brent hadn't been telling the truth. "About?"

"Dylan said he told everyone at your parents' house yesterday that he owns a landscaping business in Bakersfield."

"You're saying he doesn't?"

"He might, I guess. But that Land Rover is registered to a company called All About Security, Inc., which has a P.O. box in the Bay Area."

Her mind reverted to those numbers Brent had jotted down on the pad by his computer. They all had Bay Area prefixes....

But a few phone numbers didn't amount to a smoking gun.

"That doesn't tell us anything," she said stubbornly.

"Check out the webpage for All About Security, Eve. It tells us he's more likely a bodyguard than a landscaper."

Then he picked up the box of papers and walked out.

# 15

After Ted left, Eve pulled up the All About Security, Inc., website and combed through every page. Sure enough, it was a bodyguard service. But what she read didn't tell her a whole lot. There were no names mentioned, not even the owner's. There was some generic contact information, the range of services offered, the prices for standard jobs, plus a link a visitor could use to get a quote for full-time protection. She also read a blurb about the dependability of the AAS bodyguards and some endorsements from business leaders and city officials who had hired this company to provide security at certain events.

"So why wouldn't you just say you were a bodyguard?" she asked despite the fact that Brent wasn't around to answer. She wasn't sure if he'd be coming back, or if watching him drive out of town had been the end of it. She'd been trying to wait and see, didn't want to let her obsession with him leave her any more disappointed, any sadder, than she already was. But her curiosity wouldn't let her rest. So she got Mrs. Higgins's number from her mother and called.

"This is Eve, over at Little Mary's," she said when the older woman answered.

"Oh, yes. Adele's daughter. What can I do for you?"

"Mr. Taylor left something behind when he was staying at the B and B, and…he's your new renter, isn't he?"

"You mean Brent. Yes. What a nice young man."

Eve could only hope so. "Is he around?"

"No, dear. I'm afraid he went out earlier and said he wouldn't be back until late."

"But his things are there?"

"His what?" she said.

Eve spoke louder. "His belongings. Are they still in his room?"

"I suppose so. He wasn't carrying anything, but… just a sec."

There was a long pause before Mrs. Higgins came back on the phone. "Yes. His suitcase is in the corner, where he keeps it. Did he say he was leaving for good?"

"Not that I know of, I…saw him drive out of town and thought he might be going back wherever he came from."

"Not yet. Not until after Christmas."

"Right."

"Would you like me to tell him you called?"

Eve *didn't* want that, but she knew it would seem strange for her to say he'd left something behind and then not give her number, so he could retrieve it. She had no choice. "If you wouldn't mind."

"Not at all."

Fortunately, Mrs. Higgins didn't seem to have heard the rumors that were floating around. Maybe she wouldn't. But it was always possible. She got her hair done at the same place most people did, shopped at the same grocery store and went to the same gas station. So maybe she just hadn't made the connection between Brent and the stranger Eve had taken home from Sexy Sadie's.

"Thanks," she said, and hung up.

Eve was on the internet, looking for what else might pop up in a search for Brent's name, his brother's name and All About Security, when her cell phone rang.

She was tempted to ignore it. She was engrossed in what she was doing. But then she saw that it was Cheyenne and was perturbed enough by what Dylan and Ted had done to answer.

"Did you know your husband and our dear friend Ted had Chief Bennett run Brent's license plates?" she asked.

"I did," Cheyenne replied. "I'm sorry. I wasn't sure how I felt about going that far, but…Dylan and Ted convinced me we should."

"Is this payback?"

"Payback?" Cheyenne echoed.

"For when I was worried about you getting involved with Dylan?"

Cheyenne laughed. "No. Not at all. The truth is that none of us wants to see you get hurt. And if that means being extra…vigilant, well, I figured it was better to err on that side. It's not like we owe Brent anything if he isn't going to be honest with us."

There *was* that. Why was he lying? Was there something in his past he felt he had to hide? Even if there was, it didn't seem as though he was trying to take advantage of her, not when he kept warning her about his limitations. He'd also handed over five thousand dollars just in case she was pregnant.

"He might be honest in the areas that really count," she said, speaking her thoughts aloud.

"Telling you he's a landscaper from Bakersfield when it looks like he's a bodyguard from the Bay Area *doesn't* count?"

She'd been talking about *emotional* honesty. "Not if he doesn't intend to hurt me."

"How can you base any kind of relationship on that?" she asked.

Cheyenne had a point. But what Cheyenne, Dylan and Ted didn't understand was that Brent hadn't shown any interest in the things a life-wrecker or con artist might be hoping to gain. He wasn't after her money. He hadn't tried to ingratiate himself that way, wasn't trying to latch on so he could live off her. He'd told her repeatedly not to expect a relationship. He wasn't after sex, or not exclusively. He could easily get that from other women without the obligations—like having dinner with her parents— that came with seeing the same woman over and over.

So what *did* he want?

From what she could tell, he was hoping for a little human kindness, a chance to lose himself in someone he enjoyed and wanted to be with, someone who was at peace and could offer him a brief respite from whatever he was going through. He'd described his life as empty. She got the impression he was trying to fill it—even if the relief he sought was short-lived.

"I'm not sure," she told Cheyenne. She didn't believe he was dangerous in the same way they did. But that didn't mean she could trust him with her heart.

By the time he returned to Whiskey Creek, Rex was exhausted. He didn't want to disturb Mrs. Higgins by letting himself in so late. Like him, she struggled to sleep at night; he knew that because he'd seen the Ambien on the counter. That wasn't something people generally kept in full view unless it was a daily necessity.

Going back to the house also meant he'd probably spend hours pacing the floor, being tempted by that sleep aid, which he couldn't take, not after his addiction to

OxyContin. He was afraid even one pill would start him down the wrong road again.

But he had no other place to go. He didn't dare show up at Eve's. Although he wanted to be with her, more tonight than ever, since they hadn't parted well, he couldn't justify continuing to intrude on her life. He couldn't give her what she wanted, and there was no getting around that. So he entered as quietly as he could and sat in Mrs. Higgins's living room, watching the lights twinkle on her tree and thinking about last night, particularly the hour following his call to Scarlet. Making love to Eve that time had been especially tender. He liked remembering it, the slow, soft way she'd kissed him and how they'd slept tangled up with each other afterward. The coziness of that memory made him sleepy, and yet he had so much nervous energy running through his body.

That was usually the problem. The damn nervous energy. The unpleasant memories that assaulted him. The blood of the past…

He unplugged the tree, then went into his room and fired up his laptop to check on his house. After what had happened to Scarlet, he half expected to find evidence that his own place had been trashed. But the cameras he'd installed showed every room as he'd left it, all the sensors on the doors and windows green.

So what the hell was he doing out here in this small town where he didn't belong? Had he let Mona spook him into stepping out of his regular life for nothing?

He'd been coping so well. Better than ever.

And then this.

Clicking away from his house, he checked his email and voice mail and responded to everything. Then there was nothing to do but try to get some sleep. That was when he saw the note, written in Mrs. Higgins's shaky handwriting, on his nightstand. "Eve Harmon called at 8:33 p.m."

He stared at those words for several seconds. What did they mean? Did she want to see him?

He could call her to ask. Mrs. Higgins had jotted down her number.

Rex scratched his head as he tried to talk himself out of waking Eve. It was nearly two in the morning.

But he lost that internal argument. With only so many days in Whiskey Creek, he wasn't willing to waste any more of them.

"Hello?" she said when she picked up after several rings, her voice huskier than usual—proof that she hadn't been sitting by the phone, waiting for his call.

"Eve, it's me."

"Brent?"

He grimaced at the name but had to answer to it. "Yeah."

"Where are you?"

"Home."

"You okay?"

"Fine."

"It's the middle of the night, isn't it?"

"I'm afraid it is."

"Why are you returning my call so late?"

He tightened his grip on the phone. "I want to see you," he admitted. "We don't have to make love. I just… I'd like to hold you if that's okay. I…I need some sleep." He hadn't meant that last part to slip out, but it was true; he'd discovered that he rested better with her next to him. There was a long pause—long enough to make him realize he was asking for more than he deserved.

"Never mind," he said. "I'm sorry. It was rude of me to disturb you."

He started to hang up, but she caught him. "Brent?"

"What?"

"I'll unlock the door."

Brent had told her they didn't need to make love, but that was the first thing they did. Eve instigated it. When he got into her bed wearing boxers, probably to assure her that he'd be true to his word, she pulled them off, and her eagerness to feel him and touch him somehow ignited a frenetic, desperate need. He yanked up her nightgown the second she removed his boxers and nearly ripped her panties, trying to get them down. It was almost as if the two of them had been kept apart for a long time, she thought distantly, and had just found each other again.

"That feels good," she gasped as soon as he put on a condom and thrust inside her. He didn't respond to her words. But his touch was instinctive and uncalculated, and that marked a change from their previous encounters. He'd always made sure she was satisfied first. While she appreciated the unselfishness, his actions now seemed more…significant. For once, he was completely lost in the moment. That took him beyond thought, beyond anything other than responding to what he was feeling. Eve loved knowing that she could push him outside his usual boundaries. She also loved that the man who kept telling her not to get attached, as if it was so easy to order one's heart around, suddenly couldn't hold back.

When he said her name, she couldn't tell if he was asking for permission to go ahead and finish, or apologizing for how fast it had gone so far. There hadn't been *any* foreplay. But Eve wasn't complaining. She didn't want him to back away. So she sank her nails into the rigid muscles of his back and arched up to meet him— and when he heard her groan in pleasure, it threw him into a climax powerful enough that she felt his whole body shudder.

After he slumped over her, they didn't speak for several minutes. She could feel his chest rising and falling against her own, could hear the rasp of his breathing, since his mouth was so close to her ear, and smiled. He was beyond exhausted; she could tell. But he tried to rouse himself. "Let me...let me do you before we go to sleep," he said.

"Tomorrow," she told him, and kissed his temple as she eased him off to one side, so that they remained close but she wasn't bearing as much of his weight.

"Okay, tomorrow." He seemed relieved to be able to give in to his fatigue without feeling guilty about it. Turning his face into her neck, he pulled her even closer and fell asleep within seconds.

Brent was still asleep when Eve woke up. She was glad he seemed to be getting some rest. She'd seen how much he needed it and sensed that he was a troubled soul who couldn't quite find peace. She just wasn't sure what *she* was doing entertaining a man with such obvious problems.

She stared at the ceiling for several minutes, asking herself that question, but ultimately put it aside. Three weeks. They'd agreed on three weeks when they were at the restaurant yesterday. She'd allow herself to spend the Christmas season with him. Why not? It wasn't as if they could keep their distance while he was in town. They were too attracted to each other.

But she wasn't going to take any of it seriously. Then she wouldn't be disappointed when he left. It was all a matter of expectations, she told herself, and he'd let her know right up front where her expectations should be.

Careful not to wake him, she slid out of bed to use the bathroom. But as soon as she'd washed her hands, she heard a knock at the front door.

"Eve! You're never going to believe what I found."

This time it wasn't her parents. Thank God. But she wasn't any happier to have Ted show up at her house right now, while Brent was in her bed. Not after he'd asked Chief Bennett to run the license number on the Land Rover. She didn't think Brent would appreciate Ted's involvement. And she didn't want Ted to know she'd ignored his warning about Brent. That would only invite more doubt and speculation by her friends.

"Don't tell me it's your parents," Brent mumbled as she grabbed her robe.

"No, it's a friend. Go back to sleep."

"Just a second," she called to Ted. They knew each other well enough that she was worried he might retrieve the key from under the mat and let himself in before she was ready to greet him. Since he used to come here and sleep with her himself, he knew where it was. She should've found a new hiding place for the sake of privacy, if for no other reason. When she finally opened the door, he scowled at her. "You're not dressed? It's after ten!"

"Last I checked, Monday was my day off. Sunday *and* Monday, remember?"

"Oh, right. But even if you're not going to work, you're usually up early."

That was when she managed to get some sleep. Recently, she'd been too busy with Brent. But Ted didn't seem to realize she had company and, when she looked down the drive, she could understand why. His Land Rover was nowhere in sight. He probably hadn't wanted her parents to see it, so he'd parked some distance away and walked back.

"What'd you find?" she asked Ted.

He held up an envelope. "This."

"What is it?"

He frowned when she didn't throw the door open and invite him in the way she normally would. "If you'll give me a cup of coffee I'll show you," he said.

She tightened the belt on her robe. She preferred to deal with this later, but she knew it would seem odd for her to suggest that. He'd assume she wasn't as curious about his find as she should be, given her interest over the years in solving Little Mary's murder.

But her hesitation had nothing to do with her interest. She'd just decided that it would be better if the life she normally lived in Whiskey Creek didn't intersect with her temporary fling. Then, once Brent was gone, she'd pick up where she'd left off.

That meant keeping her friends out of her love life, however, and maintaining a level of privacy she'd never bothered with before.

"Sure. I've only got a minute, though. I have to go over to Cheyenne's this morning."

He followed her inside and sat at the kitchen table while she put on the coffee.

"So what's all the excitement about?" Although she had her back to him, she could hear the crinkle of paper and guessed he was flattening whatever he'd removed from the envelope.

"Come take a look."

Suddenly self-conscious, for fear of some telltale sign or other that she'd just been with a man, she leaned over, careful not to get too close.

"See this?" he said. "It's a letter from someone named Doug Hatfield to the producers of *Unsolved Mysteries*."

Eve hadn't come across that when she'd been searching through the box. It must've been among the papers she hadn't had time to finish. "And? Is he a descendent of John's?"

"He is."

"What does Doug say?"

"You can read it. There's not much there. But he does indicate that his mother's been deeply involved in genealogy for years and has contact information for the great-granddaughter of Harriett's sister."

"Harriett had a sister?"

"She did. A woman by the name of Mabel Cummings. She always lived in South Carolina, never in California, which is probably why no one knew about her."

"Was there anything from the great-granddaughter in the stuff I gave you?"

"No. And I've gone through all of it. But look." He pointed to the date on Doug's letter. "This is only a month before *Unsolved Mysteries* came out for the shoot. I'm guessing they either didn't follow up on his information, or they sent a letter to the great-granddaughter, hoping to confirm his facts, and didn't hear back."

"Or they could've heard from her after they'd already finished taping, which is why there's nothing from her in the records they left with me."

"Exactly. At that point, it probably wasn't a high enough priority that they'd even bother to forward it to you."

"So where does this great-granddaughter live?"

"South Carolina."

Eve skimmed Doug Hatfield's letter. "You realize she may not know anything."

"She should be able to tell me where I can find the rest of the family—or at least a few members. Hopefully, *some* pieces of Harriett's life remain. Previously unpublished pictures, her journal. Anything like that would be great to include in my book. And maybe Harriett told someone in her family—perhaps on her deathbed, if not before—that John killed Mary."

"Once John died, it's possible she started speaking again. But if she did make that kind of accusation, it seems odd that no one here heard about it."

"Communication then wasn't what it is today," he said with a shrug.

"That's true. I guess it's not like Harriett had any friends in Whiskey Creek. She'd been isolated for too long." She played with the ends of her belt. "I'm glad you have a fresh lead. That's more than I was expecting when you decided to write about Little Mary."

"Me, too." He slouched in his chair with a satisfied smile. After a few seconds of silence, however, he straightened. "So…are you okay?"

"Of course I'm okay."

He studied her. "You're acting sort of…remote. Like you might be mad at me. I know you like that Brent dude. And I can see why. Even Sophia says he's good-looking. But I hope you'll listen to me and stay away from him."

She had her own hopes right now—namely, that Brent couldn't hear them. But she was fairly certain he could. Her house wasn't that large. "I'm a big girl, Ted. I can take care of myself. Here, let me get your coffee."

She stood up to grab a mug from the cupboard, but the coffee wasn't finished brewing.

"Just so you don't think I was being too hard on him, I did an internet search on landscaping companies in

Bakersfield last night," Ted told her. "His name isn't attached to any of them."

She lowered her voice. "That doesn't mean anything. Maybe he doesn't have a web presence."

"I called some of the companies I did find on the Net just before I came here. None of them ever heard of a Brent Taylor. Don't you think *one* of them would've run across the competition at some point?"

"Not necessarily. Bakersfield isn't like Whiskey Creek. There's got to be a quarter of a million people there. Anyway, I appreciate your interest, but have to ask you to butt out, okay?"

He scowled. "Eve, please listen. I know you're angry with me for what happened last year. I'm sorry we didn't work out as a couple. I was an asshole for starting what I did, but at least I made an honest mistake. I wasn't *lying* to you about anything. I wasn't *using* you, like this guy. I was trying to fall in love with someone I admired and knew would be good for me."

"But you just couldn't manage it." She rolled her eyes. "Thanks. I feel a lot better."

"Come on. You have so much to offer, but I was already in love and didn't know it. Anyway, I've always cared about you, and I'm worried about you now. You're saying things you wouldn't ordinarily say. All that talk about leaving Whiskey Creek to figure out what you want to do with your life. Since when were you so unhappy? Not since you started sleeping with some guy who—"

The sound of her bedroom door hitting the inside wall cut him off. Ted's eyes widened, and his eyebrows rose when he realized they weren't alone.

Brent shuffled into the kitchen, wearing only a pair of faded jeans. "Morning." He gave her a sleepy smile before hooking an arm around her neck and planting a

very deliberate kiss on her mouth. "Coffee smells good."
He let go of her and turned to face Ted. "You must be the
good friend I've heard so much about. You're some kind
of big-deal author, right?"

When Ted's gaze shifted from him to Eve and back
again, Eve wasn't sure what to do. Normally, she wouldn't
have been afraid that a confrontation like this would erupt
in a fight. Ted was a thinker, not a fighter. But Brent was
definitely putting Ted on notice to mind his own business,
and she'd never seen anyone challenge Ted before. Everyone in Whiskey Creek had too much respect for him.

Ted stood up. "At least I am who I say I am," he said
and walked out.

Brent's lazy charm fell away as soon as the door
slammed. A glower descended, and he turned to stare
out the window, apparently watching Ted drive away.
"Sorry about that," he grumbled.

Despite the apology, he remained stiff and defensive.
"I should've stayed in the bedroom," he said. "But the
shit he was saying—that I'm ruining your life—it was
hard to take."

Eve poured him a cup of coffee. "I'm going to have a
shower. Cheyenne's planning a Christmas party, and I
promised we'd make the invitations today. Help yourself
to anything in the fridge, if you're hungry."

"You have no comment on what I said to your ex?" he
asked as she moved toward the bedroom.

"I would've preferred my friends not know we were
still seeing each other. That would have made it a lot
easier to step back into my regular life once you leave."

He rubbed a hand over his face. "Well, I blew that."

"It's okay. I suppose trying to hide the fact that I'm
sleeping with someone is pretty unrealistic in a town
this small."

"For what it's worth, I'm *not* using you," he said. "I'm not entirely sure why I'm here when I know you'd be better off if I left you alone, but…" He shoved his hands in the pockets of jeans. "It's not for the reason your friends seem to think."

"Last night was my decision," she said. "I'm not holding you accountable for that. Not to sound egocentric, but I don't think many guys in your situation would've refused."

"It's not just sex for the sake of sex, Eve. I've been with other women since Laurel. Sometimes only something intensely physical can take my mind off other things. But I've never been with the same woman more than once. Since Laurel, I've never even wanted that. Until now."

She could've pointed out that he'd just mentioned the name of the woman he'd loved, which he hadn't been willing to give her before. But she was trying to keep this in perspective, and the only way to do that was not to take any of it too seriously. She'd already told herself that. She was available, convenient—and lonely. Eve knew she'd be a fool to get excited about the fact that he'd wanted to be with her more than once. "So are you over her?" she asked, purposely ignoring the more personal implications of what he'd confessed.

"I think so. But it's not only that. Something about you sets you apart. I don't want to see you hurt. I want the opposite."

She waved a hand. "It's okay. You're not going to hurt me. You told me—don't get attached. And I'm not. So you have nothing to worry about, and neither do my friends."

"You mean that?"

She did. She'd been trying to make her relationship with Brent too important, because she wanted what Cheyenne and her other friends had. But lowering her expectations and accepting what he could offer brought relief. She could stop questioning his feelings and hers, stop hoping and simply enjoy the next three weeks.

"Completely," she said. "What we're doing, it's just short-term fun, right? Three weeks. One Christmas. It'll end soon enough. There's no need to overanalyze a sexual attraction. In the end, it's nothing but a pleasant way to pass the time." The possibility of a baby was never far from her thoughts, but for the moment, she set it aside.

She left him standing in the kitchen, staring at her as she hurried to her room. Last night had felt like a lot more than nothing. But it was the best things in life that often didn't last. And now that she'd made her decision, she didn't want to ruin the time they had by worrying about the time they didn't.

# 16

"Are you really going to have us build gingerbread houses at the party?" Eve asked Cheyenne as they sat at Cheyenne's dining table, stamping and pasting. Dylan was at the auto body shop he owned with his four younger brothers, so they had the place to themselves. "That'll be a lot of prep time."

"But the party's only two days before Christmas and what could be more Christmassy?" She tucked a stray wisp of hair behind one ear. "Maybe we can have a contest with a prize for the most creative."

"What kind of prize?"

"A stocking full of nuts, fruit and candy, or a box of chocolates—or an ugly Christmas sweater as a badge of honor that could be worn at every future Christmas party. What do you think would be best?"

"Whatever you decide will be great."

Cheyenne leaned forward. "Hey. Did you even hear the part about the ugly Christmas sweater?"

Eve glanced up. "What ugly sweater?"

"Caught you." Cheyenne chuckled. "You're *so* preoccupied. Are you okay?"

She sounded like Ted. "I'm fine. Why?"

"You're just not yourself lately. What's going on?" She

lowered her voice for emphasis. "Are you thinking about Brent by any chance?"

As a matter of fact, she had been. She couldn't forget the way he'd walked up to her this morning and casually kissed her—with Ted watching. He'd looked so fresh-out-of-bed-sexy in nothing but those blue jeans it had made her heart race. And, whether she wanted to admit it or not, she liked the possessiveness of that move, liked that he was bold enough to stand up and show interest in front of her friends.

She just hoped it wouldn't cause Ted to get their entire group riled up in a protective frenzy. She didn't want him telling all of them that business about Brent being a bodyguard in the Bay Area and not a landscaper in Bakersfield. There was definitely *something* going on with Brent. She couldn't question that. But she wasn't going to press him for answers. She'd already made up her mind to surf the wave she was riding all the way into shore—shore being the moment Brent left Whiskey Creek for good. Yes, she'd crash in the foamy surf. But he wouldn't be around to see it, and it wasn't the crash that mattered. It was having the guts to stay on the board.

Eve looked over at the clock. "I'm surprised that we've been doing this for an hour and you've only mentioned him now."

"I figured you'd talk about him when you were ready. I was trying to give you time to work up to it."

"Thanks. But there's not much to say."

"You're still seeing him, though?"

*Seeing* him? Certainly not in the traditional sense. She "saw" him at night. But they hadn't been on a single date—unless she counted the breakfast they'd shared yesterday morning in Jackson.

Eve added the invitation she'd just finished to the stack

beside her. "Ted didn't call you the minute he left my house this morning?"

Cheyenne looked confused. "Ted went to your house? What did he want?"

"He's writing about Little Mary's murder. He's in the process of gathering information."

"Finally! He's been meaning to explore that mystery for ages."

"Right. I just wish it wasn't now."

"You're not happy that he's gotten around to it? You've been curious about Little Mary since your folks bought that place. I've been curious about it, too. Maybe he'll come up with something new."

"I hope so. But I don't need him sitting in the front row, watching what's going on in my life right now."

"You mean because he doesn't approve."

Eve slumped lower in her seat. "No one does."

"Maybe we don't like the risks."

"But it might not be as bad as it seems. Maybe Brent *used* to be a bodyguard but is planning to start a land-scaping company in Bakersfield."

"That's a generous interpretation."

"It's possible," she insisted.

"Look, I like Brent. He's wary of people but…he kind of reminds me of Dylan, so I could be predisposed to give him the benefit of the doubt. From his standoffish behavior, I'm guessing he's been through a lot. Anyway, have you *asked* Brent about the bodyguard thing?"

"No."

"Because…"

"If he wanted me to know his situation, he would've told me to begin with."

Cheyenne's eyebrows shot up. "You don't have a problem with being left in the dark?"

"Of course I do. It's just…we're attracted to each other. That's all. It's not like we're planning to get married."

Cheyenne straightened the pile of envelopes. "I thought you *wanted* to get married."

"I do. When I find the right man. But I think we can agree that a man who can't tell me what he really does for a living isn't the right man."

"I'm glad to hear you say that. But it begs another question."

"And that is…"

"Are you sure you want to risk your heart on someone who can't or won't give you the happily-ever-after you've been waiting for?"

Eve eyed her friend's big belly. "Maybe he's not a candidate for marriage, but he can give me…other things."

Cheyenne's hands froze as she was about to glue another red "berry" button on the card she was making. "Sex?"

Eve drew a deep breath. "There's a chance I could be pregnant, Chey."

*"No…"*

"Yes."

Cheyenne dropped the button, then wiped the glue off her fingers. "Raising a child alone isn't easy, Eve."

"You think I don't know that? It wasn't a risk we planned to take."

"So it was an accident."

"If you call getting too drunk to take the proper precautions an accident."

"That's too bad," Cheyenne murmured.

"Why is it too bad?" Eve asked. "I know it's…not how things are normally done. But if you can use your brother-in-law to have a child, I guess I can have a baby out of wedlock and raise it myself."

A blush suffused Cheyenne's cheeks. "Please don't ever mention that again, or…allude to it or anything else. As far as I'm concerned—and Aaron, too—this baby belongs to Dylan."

"Would Dylan feel that way if he learned it was really his brother's child?"

"I hope so," she said quietly, and Eve sensed that she was afraid to put a voice to the truth. "But I don't see why he ever has to learn, which is why I don't want to talk about it. He's been through enough hardships in his life, given so much, protected all those he can. Why would I make him suffer because of this, too? So what if I decided to shield *him,* for a change? To ensure that he got what he wanted without making him feel he's less of a man because he can't get his wife pregnant? I didn't *sleep* with Aaron. It was an artificial insemination performed by my sister—legit in every way, except that Dylan doesn't know it required someone else's genetic material. To me, that part doesn't matter. We're the ones who'll love the baby and care for it. Aaron doesn't even want to be reminded of his…donation."

Eve felt terrible for bringing it up. She wasn't sure why she had, other than to make herself feel better about her own situation. "I'm sorry," she said. "I won't ever mention it again."

Cheyenne reached across the table to squeeze her hand. "Eve, I know you've felt a bit lost since things didn't work out with Ted. It couldn't have been easy watching him get married, especially when he expected you to be such a big part of the wedding, as a friend, like the rest of us. Somehow you managed that. You stood tall and smiled through the whole thing. I've been proud of you for bearing up under the disappointment. But don't let that tempt you into screwing up your life."

"You think having a baby will screw up my life?"

"I think falling in love with the wrong man can *definitely* do that—and having his baby will only make it harder to get over him."

"I'm not falling in love with Brent," she said.

Cheyenne didn't respond. She just sat there, looking at her.

*"What?"* Eve snapped.

"Then why are you making so many compromises?"

Rex was waiting for a call from his sergeant friend, Eddie, in the San Francisco police department regarding Scarlet's case. He sat at the small desk in his room at Mrs. Higgins's and clicked through the various feeds on the cameras he'd installed in his house. There was no change from the last time he'd checked, which was good, but it also made him believe that he'd banished himself to Whiskey Creek for no reason. The longer he went with no sign that The Crew planned to make a move on his life, the more he began to wonder if Mona had been mistaken. He'd emailed her back, hoping for confirmation, but…so far, nothing.

She was probably on another drug binge.

"Damn it, Mona," he grumbled. Should he quit playing hide-and-seek and return to work?

He was sorely tempted. He couldn't bug out at every false alarm. Already his past was affecting his present far more than he wanted. But being in California required an added amount of caution, especially when the person warning him had warned him before—and been 100 percent accurate about the danger he was in.

His phone rang. "At last," he breathed, and answered, anxious to hear what the police had found while searching Scarlet's former boyfriend's apartment.

"Her panties were there," Eddie confirmed. "Stuffed between the box springs and the mattress of the bed."

Rex drummed his fingers on the desk as he continued to gaze at his living room via a live feed. "But was it Tom or Tara who took them?"

"I can't believe *she'd* do it. She's consumed with jealousy as it is."

"Did she say that?"

"As you know, I'm not on the case. And from what I heard, she lawyered up pretty fast. But Detective Rollins indicated that she said it in so many words before she stopped talking. Like you, he thinks Tom's our man. But we'll do the homework—make sure it's his DNA on the letters and not Tara's. That should clinch it."

"And if Tom used gloves?"

"Rollins will find physical evidence somewhere. They haven't had a chance to go through the bastard's computer yet. But there's that, too. If that penis picture was sent from an account he created, it'll make for a solid case."

"Don't forget the bedsheet he urinated on. I had Scarlet save it."

"I know. She turned it in."

"That should have some DNA."

"No doubt it'll have his. Have you ever heard of a woman trying to pee on something like that? She'd need a shower afterward," he said with a chuckle.

"That's a little more than I'd like to imagine, but good point."

The sergeant laughed again.

From what Rex could tell, Scarlet was in good hands. At least he could breathe easier about *her* welfare. "By the way, has anyone established why there was such a long break between when she was being tormented before and when this started up again?"

"Until the bastard admits it and tells us, which he may never do, we won't be able to explain that gap. But whoever was doing those things before has to be the person who was doing it more recently."

"I agree. Still, it would be nice to have more to rely on than our gut instinct."

"We've learned he was seeing a psychologist during that time," his friend said. "That could account for it. Maybe she was helping him control his behavior and obsessions."

"He's not going to her anymore?"

"No. He quit just a few weeks before Scarlet started being harassed again."

"Why?"

"Psychologist says his girlfriend kept nagging him about the money. She was pushing him to get married, get a house, have a family. The pressure could have set him off. About the same time, he nearly lost his job for making sexual innuendoes to a coworker, and he got into a fight with his sister over a piece of furniture he felt he should have received when his grandparents died. I'm guessing it just all came together."

"Sounds plausible to me. Okay, I'll hope for the best. Let me know how it goes."

"Of course."

A soft knock sounded at his door as Rex ended the call. "Yes?"

Mrs. Higgins poked her head into the room. "Something smells like it's burning out here. I'm afraid there might be a short in the lights on the tree—and as dry as those poor needles are, that's dangerous, isn't it?"

"You just bought that tree a week ago, didn't you?"

"I did, but they cut them down so early these days they're dead before you can even drag them into your house," she complained. "That tree's already dropping its needles. Anyway, would you mind checking to see if you can smell it, too?"

When Rex had rented this room, he hadn't planned on helping his elderly landlord decorate for Christmas. He hadn't planned on eating gingerbread cookies with her so she could feel appreciated. And he hadn't planned on becoming the "go to" guy for anything that might need fixing. But she had no one else. And it brought him an odd sort of pleasure.

"Sure. I'll be out in a sec," he told her.

"Thanks." She seemed genuinely relieved. "Oh, I wanted to ask if you'll be here for dinner. I'm making my chicken and crescent rolls with mushroom gravy. Any chance you'd like to join me?"

It was probably hard for her to eat alone every day. "You bet. Sounds delicious."

She smiled as he passed her on his way to look at the tree, then followed him into the living room.

"Do you smell it?" she asked.

"I'm afraid I don't," he replied.

"Are you sure?"

He bent closer and checked to make sure there wasn't an obvious short. "Positive. These lights seem fine. But we can unplug them for a bit if you're worried."

"No, that's okay. It must've been my imagination."

Or her desire to have a good reason to interrupt him....

"We'll eat in a couple of hours," she said and patted his shoulder.

"That'll be great. I have a few things I need to do on my computer, so just call me when it's ready."

"I will. Get your work done so you can relax."

She seemed so grateful for his company that he couldn't help being glad he'd agreed. He returned to his room so that he wouldn't have to entertain her for longer than the hour or so it would take to have dinner. He didn't want to create too many ties here. But he really didn't have much to do. Since he couldn't take on any protection jobs, and he couldn't train the new guy or manage the others, he was left to the paperwork side of All About Security, and he'd been taking care of that for over a week.

The good news was that he'd never been more caught up. The bad news was that he was growing as bored as Marilyn had predicted he would. Staying busy was what kept him going.

But he wanted to call Scarlet, and he wanted to make a decision on what he'd learned from Mona. Was he hiding for nothing? Now that Scarlet wasn't coming to town, he felt he might be wasting his time here.

He called Scarlet first. She seemed to be recovering quickly, but she couldn't talk long. The doctors wanted her to rest. So he hung up and checked his house on the computer again, even though he'd just checked it a few minutes earlier.

Nothing had changed. He stared at the images for a while—then he pulled up the message Mona had sent him and listened to it for probably the hundredth time.

She must have been high when she left him that message, he decided. Enough waffling on his part. He was going home tomorrow, if only to keep from getting too close to Eve. He couldn't go through the kind of thing he'd been through with Laurel, not again. Not after all the other shit he'd had to deal with. His heart didn't have any more breaking left in it.

*Don't get attached.* That was his mantra.

Since he was still waiting for dinner, he entered Mona's name in a search engine on a fluke, just to see if he could pull up some contact information for her. He wanted to actually speak to her if he could. See how convinced she was about what she'd heard. Learn the context. Ask if she knew the bangers who'd said it well enough to ascertain whether or not they were truly committed to his murder—and if they had the balls to go through with it.

He also wanted to convince her to get into a good rehab—although he hadn't had much success with that when he'd tried in the past.

Several links appeared. He didn't get the chance to look for contact information, however. What he saw shocked him too badly—and made contacting her a moot point, anyway.

"Oh, my God," he mumbled as he read "Mona Livingston, thirty-two, found dead in South Central L.A. Shot twice in the back of the head."

He couldn't believe his eyes. They'd killed her. She didn't get out when he'd told her to, when he'd offered to help, and it had ended up costing the poor woman her life, just as he'd feared it would.

*Damn it, Mona!* He clicked on the excerpt so he could read the rest. The coroner suspected she'd been "executed" last Friday by an unknown assailant.

Rex was willing to bet that assailant wasn't entirely unknown to *him*. But Mona had died only four days ago, and the timing bothered him as much as the fact that she was gone. Why *now*? Why would she be killed after all these years of managing to survive despite her associates and her addiction?

The obvious answer put a hard lump in Rex's stomach. Was it because someone inside The Crew had figured out that she'd tipped him off?

# 17

$W$as Scarlet in town?

Eve hadn't heard from Brent all day, so she assumed he was preoccupied with his sister's arrival. She was tempted to call him at Mrs. Higgins's, to see if he and Scarlet had plans for dinner. Thanks to years of experience at the B and B, working with chefs and helping with meals, she felt she was a pretty good cook, and she was looking forward to meeting someone who'd been part of Brent's life for much longer than she had. Maybe Scarlet would be more forthcoming about the kinds of details he refused to share. At the very least, Eve should be able to find out whether his second brother was named Rex. What she'd heard when she'd made that call to L.A. was so unsettling because she was afraid that woman had been pleading with the man she knew as Brent. It made Eve want to see whatever had gone so wrong in his life put right so he could be reunited with his family.

But she hesitated to invite him and Scarlet over so soon. She'd just been with him this morning. She didn't want to seem pushy or overeager.

In the end, she decided it would be better to give him time to get his sister situated. He'd call if he wanted to see her.

Now that she had a night on her own, however, Eve found herself at loose ends. What had she done before he came on the scene?

She'd often stayed at the B and B until late if she didn't have plans with one of her friends, and, as they got older, she had plans with them less and less often. So it was her work that typically filled those extra hours. But work suddenly seemed like a poor substitute for the excitement, pleasure and heady emotion she felt when she was with Brent.

Tomorrow would be soon enough to tackle the remainder of what she'd missed on her days off. She pulled up the website for All About Security again, only this time she jotted down the phone number listed in their contact information. It was after five, so she doubted anyone would answer. But placing a call to this company might connect her with a voice mail system that would let her access a directory of its employees....

If that happened, would there be a Brent Taylor?

She decided to find out.

After she dialed, and it rang three times, she heard the recording of a woman's voice.

*"You've reached All About Security, where licensed and trained executive protection specialists are available around the clock to see to all your security needs. If this is an emergency and you'd like to speak to a specialist after hours, press one and leave your number. You will receive a call back within thirty minutes. If you would like to speak with someone tomorrow, during regular business hours, press two. If you would like to learn more about All About Security, feel free to visit our website."*

Eve *had* visited the website. It didn't tell her what she wanted to know.

She rocked back in her chair as she disconnected.

What was she doing? She didn't want to be the type of woman who'd check up on a love interest behind his back. It just felt…wrong. She'd certainly never done anything like it before. And yet she was so curious about Brent— curious enough to wonder how the woman in Los Angeles would respond if she called again and asked for Scarlet. If that number went to Brent's brother's house, and the woman she'd spoken to before was the brother's wife, she would surely know Scarlet. That would confirm his relationship with Dennis, make Eve feel she was holding one piece of the puzzle that was Brent's life.

After a few minutes of wrestling with her reluctance, Eve blocked her number and called again.

"Hello?" This time it was a man who answered. Judging by the authority in his voice, Eve guessed it was Dennis himself.

"Doctor?" she said, to be sure.

"Yes?"

She heard a degree of hesitancy in his response. He was probably wondering how one of his patients had managed to get his home number. "Is Scarlet there?"

*"Who?"*

"Scarlet. Your sister."

"I don't have a sister."

"That's strange," she said. "You have a brother who's an engineer, right?"

"I do, but his wife isn't named Scarlet. Anyway, how do you know Mike? *Who is this?*"

She gave him the first name that popped into her head. "Jessica."

"Jessica who?" he asked. "How'd you get my number? It's not even listed."

He sounded suspicious and slightly upset, and she couldn't blame him. "Sorry for bothering you," she muttered, and hung up. Then she got to her feet so that she could move around, give herself an outlet for the nervous energy that was flowing through her.

"Shit!" Calling Dennis had done anything but put her mind at ease. She was now more confused than she'd been before. He *had* to be Brent's brother. He had the right name, he was a doctor, he lived in L.A. and his number had come from Noelle's backseat after Brent had been there.

But if he was Brent's brother, why didn't he know Scarlet? And if Mike was the engineer in the family, who was Rex?

Rex couldn't sleep. Not after what he'd learned about Mona. He kept thinking of the day he'd watched some worthless john The Crew had prostituted her to toss her in the street like garbage. He'd walked over to find her scraped and bruised and crying. It had been a pathetic sight. But his own situation was pretty bad back then. He'd understood what falling that low was like. Just remembering those days made him grateful he'd somehow found the strength to build a better life, to get away from what he'd settled for during that period of self-hate. He had Virgil to thank for giving him someone to care about and for encouraging him. They'd gotten out together.

Gratitude for his best friend overwhelmed him for a moment. Everyone needed a hand now and then. And he feared he hadn't been persistent enough in offering that helping hand to Mona. Worse, he feared she wouldn't have been killed if she hadn't tried to warn him. The timing was just too coincidental.

But what more could he have done? The day he found her in the road eight years ago, he'd driven her to her sister's house, hoping the sister would provide a place for her to live until she could dry out and get into rehab. He hadn't been able to stay with her; his own life had been in jeopardy. But he'd hoped that dragging her away at that pivotal time would give her a new start.

Unfortunately, that didn't happen. Mona hadn't been ready. Or maybe she hadn't been capable. Either way, he couldn't really fault her. As many battles as he'd fought—in prison, in his family, in the gang, even with Laurel when they were trying to manage a relationship—he'd never fought one tougher than the battle against Oxy-Contin.

With a sigh, he cycled through the live feeds of his house, which he'd been doing all night. He felt sick sitting there, thinking about Mona and what a tragic waste her death was while staring at his laptop, wondering when The Crew would turn up in his own life again. Because he was now convinced they would.

He'd sent an email to Virgil, letting him know about Mona, but when he opened his in-box to see if Virgil had answered, the new message waiting for him wasn't from his best friend.

It was from his brother Dennis.

You okay?

Fine, he wrote back. He thought that would be the end of it. Their exchanges were usually just that brief and impersonal. But Dennis kept the email chain going.

Do you know a Jessica?

Jessica who?

She didn't say.

No. Why?

A woman by that name called here this evening. She asked for someone named Scarlet. Said Scarlet was my sister.

Eve. It had to be her. Who else thought he had a sister named Scarlet? No one who would be interested enough—or concerned enough—to follow up. But how the hell did she get his brother's number?

Shoving back his chair, he got up and went through the pockets of all his pants. He'd written Dennis's number down when he was in Placerville. Mike had emailed him with it, asked him to check in. He hadn't done so, but he'd walked around with that number in one pocket or another for several days. Had Eve taken it?

When he couldn't find it, he could only assume she had.

Shit. It was happening. Real life was barging in, before he could even enjoy his three weeks. He'd been crazy to think he could steal these days, find a brief refuge from what his life had become.

The thought of not seeing her again made him feel worse. But he'd known what his limitations were. He should never have let himself hope for more.

When he returned to his computer, there was another message from Dennis.

I wouldn't have thought anything of it, but she also mentioned Mike, so I checked with him. He has no idea who Scarlet is and doesn't know a Jessica, either. It all seemed a bit weird. As soon as I pressed her as to how she got my number, she hung up. Made me think you might be in trouble again.

Again. He just *had* to add that. His brother thought he was always in trouble, and he laid the blame for everything that had happened squarely at Rex's feet.

Rex would be the first to admit he deserved it, but his brother's unyielding attitude and self-righteous behavior didn't go very far toward improving their relationship. Dennis didn't trust that he'd really changed. Dennis assumed his old problems would be gone if he had. But he didn't understand The Crew, the position Rex had played inside the outlaw organization or why the current members felt such a strong desire for revenge. Gangs had never been part of his privileged existence—other than what he saw on the news reports on TV—and he resented that Rex hadn't led the same kind of uncomplicated, pristine life. Instead, Rex had made their parents suffer, and Dennis resented him for that, too.

Maybe his brother would have understood, at least slightly, if Rex had ever bothered to fully describe the chain reaction that had been set in place so long ago. But he couldn't even talk about it because he couldn't talk about Logan—not to anybody—and that was where it all started.

It was impossible to get close to his brothers without endangering their lives, anyway. So there was little point in putting any effort toward changing their opinion of him. He figured he served them best by staying away, and that was what he tried to do.

That didn't mean he didn't miss Dennis and Mike, though—or that it was easy flying solo so much of the time, especially at Christmas when the memories of what once was crowded close and reminded him of all he'd lost. Eve had been such a welcome respite—a gift. He craved her touch, her warmth, her steadiness.

If only he could lose himself in her one more time....

But he couldn't spend three weeks with her and remain a mystery. She was trying to figure out who he really was. And the more she pressed, the more dangerous things would become—for both of them.

I'm not in trouble, he wrote to Dennis. But the reality was that he was beginning to think his "trouble" would never end.

A noise in the living room alerted him to the fact that Mrs. Higgins was up, walking the floor. Apparently the sleeping pill hadn't done its job.

He felt for her. Some nights seemed to last forever. But he couldn't keep her company.

After closing his laptop, he got up to pack.

# 18

He was gone. He had to be. Eve had driven past Mrs. Higgins's place a number of times—twice late at night—and had yet to find Brent's Land Rover. She hadn't heard from him, either, not in a whole week, which meant the past seven days had passed as slowly for her as any on record. He'd told her not to expect more than three weeks with him, but he hadn't warned her that it might be much shorter than that.

Had something terrible happened to his sister? Some altercation with her ex? Or had something else come up?

Eve hoped it wasn't the fact that she'd called Dennis and Dennis had alerted Brent. But that was what the timing suggested. If it was anything other than what she'd done, Brent would've called to say goodbye, wouldn't he? The last time she'd seen him, he'd told her she was the first woman he'd wanted to be with, really be with, since Laurel. A guy didn't go from that to nothing without *some* trigger.

Maybe, since she'd approached their eventual parting so flippantly that day in her kitchen, he figured she wouldn't care. But she only said those things because she'd thought she'd have more time to cope with his leaving, because she hadn't wanted to face it right then.

"This sucks," she muttered as she sat alone at Just Like Mom's. She wasn't even sure what she was doing at the restaurant. It was nearly ten, which was when they closed on weeknights, and she'd had supper at home. She just knew that Brent liked this place. He'd said as much the day they'd had breakfast together in Jackson, had asked if she wanted to eat here instead. So Just Like Mom's felt like somewhere he might go if he ever came back, and then she'd get to see him and possibly learn why she hadn't heard from him.

"This is crazy, Eve," she told herself. "What do you think—that he's going to come strolling through the door at any moment?"

Maybe in a perfect world. But it didn't happen. Her waitress didn't appear, either, although Eve had been waiting to pay for her pie and herbal tea for at least ten minutes.

She opened her wallet to see if she had enough to cover the bill so she could leave it on the table and scoot out. But she didn't have the cash.

"Damn it," she grumbled—and wanted to swear with even more vigor when Noelle Arnold walked in. Noelle had a friend with her. They were both dressed in the skimpy uniforms they wore at Sexy Sadie's, so Eve guessed their shift had just ended.

The second Noelle spotted her, Eve wished she could slip under the table—or somehow disappear—but that was impossible, since her waitress hadn't collected her credit card yet.

"Hey!" Noelle came up with her friend lagging behind by half a step. "How's it going?"

Eve managed a smile. It was, no doubt, a frail imitation of her usual smile, but the best she could muster under the circumstances. She hadn't been this depressed in ages. "Fine, thanks."

"You still seeing that guy you took home a couple of weeks ago? God, he was hot. I don't think I've ever seen a better-looking guy in my life!"

Eve gritted her teeth, trying to control her emotions so she could speak. "No. We were never together. He was just…passing through." But she could be pregnant with his child. She hadn't done the test yet. She'd been waiting until she felt she'd be able to rely on the results. But she'd driven halfway to Walnut Creek to purchase a pregnancy test where no one knew her. It was there, waiting, under her sink.

"Bummer!" Noelle cried. "I'm *so* sorry! I could tell you were really into him. You've had such bad luck with men lately, haven't you?"

"I don't mind being single," Eve lied. "I've hardly missed him. You know how Christmas is at the inn. It's my favorite time of year."

Noelle must've heard the tears in her voice, because she cocked her head to one side as if the sudden change in pitch surprised her. But before she could follow up, her friend grabbed her hand and started yanking her toward a booth. "Enough socializing. Come on! I'm *starving!*"

"Okay! Okay!" Noelle allowed herself to be led away but turned back to make a parting remark. "At least you got to sleep with him while he was here. The rest of us could only dream about it!"

Was that what she'd been reduced to? Being glad she'd had sex with some guy who didn't care enough to even let her know he was leaving town?

"Pathetic," she whispered, and that pertained to her *and* Noelle. She was about to get up and track down her waitress, who was probably cleaning up in the back instead of taking care of her final table, when the bell rang over the door a second time—all the more noticeable since the restaurant was almost empty.

When Eve realized it was Ted and his wife, she nearly groaned aloud. If there was anyone she'd rather not see, other than Noelle, it was Ted. Ted *with* Sophia only made matters worse.

*I can't catch a break.*

"There you are!" he said as he led her replacement in his life over to the table.

"You've been looking for *me?*" Eve pretended as if she hadn't been ducking his calls. She'd been avoiding *all* her friends, except for Cheyenne. She couldn't avoid someone she worked with. Cheyenne had definitely tried to question her about Brent, but Eve had managed to skim over his sudden absence as if they were still in touch by phone, and she hadn't given anyone else the chance to discuss it with her. For the second week in a row, she hadn't attended coffee on Friday and, although she'd received several texts asking where she was, she'd responded to everyone with the same few lines. She was so busy this time of year, just couldn't make it—that sort of thing.

No one knew she was walking the floor night after night, waiting and hoping Brent would call.

Texting was a godsend when it came to these situations; it allowed her to reassure everyone without having to confront them face-to-face. But she hadn't sent off the same pat message to Ted. In the text he'd left her, he'd said he had news to share about Little Mary and wanted to talk to her. That suggested he had more to say than he was willing to type into a phone. So she'd put off responding. She'd had to. She was afraid he'd call the second she texted him, because then he'd know she had her phone with her and that it was turned on.

"Have you checked your messages lately?" He gave her a disgruntled look. "I've been trying to get hold of you."

"I'm sorry. I've been meaning to call. Just been so busy."

"Good thing I saw your car out front."

*Yeah. Good thing,* she thought sarcastically. She was interested to hear what he'd learned about Little Mary. But even a conversation that started out on another subject would eventually turn into questions about Brent, and she didn't want to talk about him, didn't want to acknowledge that he was already gone and she'd been a fool to get involved with him—just like Ted and everyone else had told her.

"What's up?"

Sophia gave her a sympathetic look, as if she could see right through her, which didn't help. Eve didn't want them feeling sorry for her, any more than she wanted them feeling smug about so clearly being right.

"I got in touch with Mabel Cummings's great-granddaughter," Ted announced, obviously proud and excited. He gestured for his wife to slide into the booth so he could, too. "Her name is Emma Wright, and she lives in Virginia."

Eve sent another glance toward the kitchen, once again cursing her waitress. She was pretty sure she'd been forgotten; no one had come out to greet Noelle and her friend, either, let alone take their food order. The women were getting so impatient and vocal that Eve guessed the noise would bring someone out soon—but not soon enough for her to escape this get-together with Ted and Sophia.

Eve turned her water glass in a circle. "Nice! It's wonderful that you were able to track her down. What did she have to say?"

"That her great-grandmother's sister—Harriett— never claimed it was John."

"So she spoke again?"

"Apparently so. Once she returned to her family in South Carolina, at least. She told her sister that he was innocent and one of the most 'misunderstood' people she'd ever met."

"Then…why did she burn his train set?"

"Who knows? Mable couldn't answer that, didn't even remember hearing about a train set. But she said her great-aunt told her grandmother that John wasn't to blame."

This captured Eve's attention in spite of everything else that was going on in her head and her heart. "Then who was?"

"She had no idea."

"And she claimed John was misunderstood? That's an interesting way to characterize someone who was so disliked by the people in his community."

"It certainly doesn't lead me to believe she blamed him for her daughter's death."

"No, but it sounds like she didn't suggest any other possible culprits. And, blame or no blame, that could be her opinion. Doesn't mean he was innocent. Maybe she loved him so much she couldn't bear to consider the possibility that he'd murder their child."

"I could see that kind of blindness on the part of a wife," Sophia chimed in.

Because of her great love for Ted, of course. Eve barely resisted making a face. "Did Emma know her great-grandmother's sister turned into a recluse after

Mary's death?" Eve asked, to distract herself as much as anything else.

"I gather she did," Ted replied. "She told me that Harriett remained very withdrawn until the day she died."

"In South Carolina?"

"Yes."

"Did you mention the neighbor theory?"

"I did. Mable liked the idea. She'd rather not think Harriett's husband did the deed. But she's never heard anything about the neighbors being involved, so if one of them was to blame, Harriett probably didn't know it."

"Are you going to try and track down the names of the boys? Follow up with their families?"

He pursed his lips. "Eventually. But I'm going to look in what I think is a more fertile area first. I still have so many of Harriett's relatives to approach. Emma gave me a whole list, including another of Harriett's nieces who's almost a hundred years old. I think my time is better spent finding out what she might know."

"Wow! A centenarian? Does she still have her memory?"

"According to Emma, she's as sharp as ever."

"That's fabulous!" Eve felt some genuine excitement. This was more information than anyone else had dug up. Ted was actually talking to people who'd been alive when Harriett was! "Now I can see why you're happy. When will you get to talk to her?"

"She's in assisted living. Emma's going to set up an appointment for me to see her."

"Where does she live?"

"Alabama."

"You're really going to fly clear across the country? Can't you…Skype or something?"

"She doesn't own a computer. It'll be easier for me

to communicate in person. That way I'll get to see any memorabilia she still has, too."

Eve nodded.

"Would you like to go with me?"

"Yes, except I can't leave the inn right now. Not at Christmas. And I'm sure you don't want to put it off until after."

"I'd rather not wait."

"Then go. You're doing a thorough job. You can update me when you get back."

"If you'll answer your phone."

When she offered him a sheepish smile, he winked at her. "That wasn't so painful, was it?"

"Ted, stop," Sophia chided him, but Ted had known Eve his whole life and wasn't about to let his wife dictate how he interacted with her.

"It wasn't *too* painful," Eve said, "as long as it ends there."

His eyebrows rose. "So you don't want me to tell you what I know about Brent?"

The waitress finally appeared, looking flustered. "I'm sorry," she said. Then she lifted a finger to indicate she'd be right over and hurried to take Noelle's order first, a wise decision given that Noelle was ready to storm out.

"You don't know anything about Brent," Eve said.

"Then maybe that was someone else I followed out of town."

This took her aback. "You followed him? *Why?*"

"Because it was three in the morning, and I found it strange that he'd be out and about."

Eve folded her arms. "No stranger than *you* being out and about."

"Except that I have a stepdaughter who was having

such painful cramps she was in tears and needed some
ibuprofen."

"Yet you took the time to follow Brent."

"I thought you might thank me."

She couldn't deny that she was curious. "What night
was this?"

"Last Monday."

"Where'd he go?"

"I tailed him to Jackson. Had to drive that far to find
a store that was open, anyway."

"And then?"

"It looked as if he got a room at that B and B on the
edge of town. I can't remember the name." He looked to
Sophia for help.

"You said it was the one that's painted blue," she reminded him.

Eve broke in so they wouldn't belabor that small detail. "I know which one it is," she said. How could she
not? It was the place they'd stayed when they went to
Jackson together.

"Right. Anyway, his car was there when I headed past
on my way back about fifteen minutes later, so I can only
guess that he stayed the night," Ted said.

Was he still there? Eve wondered. So close?

But she knew chances of that were slim. "Why didn't
you tell me sooner?"

At the impatient tone of her voice, Ted brought a hand
to his chest. "You're kidding, right? How many of my
messages have you ignored?"

Seeing that the waitress was on her way over, Eve
grabbed her purse and stood before handing her the credit
card. "You know where I work."

"I wasn't all that eager for you to have the information, to be honest," he admitted.

"Then why tell me now?"

"Because Cheyenne feels you two have unfinished business. She mentioned that he didn't say goodbye. As far as I'm concerned, you deserve the chance to confront him about that, especially if he's going to act all possessive while I'm at your kitchen table, as if I have no right, as one of your best friends, to warn you about him."

"So this is a pissing contest?"

"I'm trying to hold him accountable for his words and his actions." He got to his feet, too, and so did Sophia, but something—probably Eve's sense of purpose—made him narrow his eyes. "Where are you going?"

"Home," she said. But it was a lie and she was sure they knew it. She was heading to Jackson. It was a long shot that Brent would be there after a whole week, but if he was, she had to know if his sister was okay—or if she'd chased him away by calling his brother.

# 19

Thunder rumbled across the sky, loud enough to shake the walls. Rex had been home for a week, but his house didn't feel like the same place he'd left. Maybe that was because his approach to furniture and decor suddenly seemed less calculated in its practicality and more devoid of the things that brought comfort and reassurance, especially when he compared it to the coziness of Eve's bungalow, her B and B, even the rest of Whiskey Creek. It was also nerve-racking to have to watch his back much more carefully now that he was back where The Crew might expect to find him. It felt like the old days.

"When will this end?" he muttered to himself as he stood to one side of the window and peered out through a crack in the blinds at the storm lashing his small backyard. If The Crew had somehow managed to learn his address, this would be the perfect night to strike. Provided they came in sufficient numbers, they could swarm his house, break in from more than one point of entry—and his neighbors wouldn't even hear any shots that were fired.

He wondered how long it would take for Marilyn or someone else to find his body. A day? Two? He hated the idea of her coming upon such a gruesome scene. She wouldn't know how to get hold of his family, he realized, and pulled his phone out of his pocket so he could leave her a message.

"Marilyn, it's me," he said when he got her voice mail. "I'm calling to tell you that if anything happens to me, you need to contact my brothers. I've never mentioned them, but I have two. You'll find my will in the safe at the office. Everything's to be split between them." He'd had that drawn up when he first returned to California. There were things he'd change now if he could. He'd want to give Eve more than the five thousand dollars he'd left with her, if she was pregnant. And he'd want to provide something for his employees. But he hadn't known her or them when he'd made plans for his estate, and if something happened tonight it was too late for that.

Once he'd left Marilyn his brothers' phone numbers, he considered giving her Virgil's, too. He'd want Virgil to know as soon as possible that he'd been killed. But he didn't dare leave any clues, even verbal ones, that could be traced to New York. Once he was dead, The Crew wouldn't bother hurting his family. There'd be no point. But they'd continue to search for Virgil. The few emails he and Virgil had exchanged about Mona's execution were all they could safely afford at the moment.

He took a minute to write a letter to Dennis, telling him to give a woman named Eve Harmon from Whiskey Creek any money she needed. He could only hope Dennis would honor that wish. Planning to mail it in the morning, he slipped it in his pocket. Then he went from his study to the living room to check the front of the house and yard.

He could see the Christmas lights on the house across the street—colorful blurs through the rain. Most people were caught up in the holidays, buying gifts, throwing parties, preparing for the end of the year, while he was preparing for the end of his *life*.

*Shit.* He was tired of staring out the windows and monitoring those cameras on his laptop. If The Crew was coming, he wished they'd arrive and get it over with. He had his gun in his waistband, wouldn't go down without a fight. It wasn't as if he *wanted* to die. But this was no way to live.

When his cell buzzed, and he had to get it back out of his pocket, he wondered if one of his clients was in the middle of an emergency. But it wasn't any of the bodyguards. It was Marilyn. She must've received his message much sooner than he'd intended. He'd thought she'd be asleep. The day he'd returned, he'd reprogrammed the phone system at the office to alert him and not her to all after-hour calls. She was officially off duty at four if she came in early, as she usually did.

"'Lo?" He thought he saw movement in the yard and almost drew his weapon. But when he looked closer, he realized it was the bough of a tree, being tossed in the wind.

"What's going on?" she asked.

"Nothing," he said, still keeping a close eye on the moving shadows caused by the swaying trees.

"Then why'd you give me your next of kin?"

"Just…in case."

"In case of what?"

"I told you. In case something happens."

"That scares me."

"I'm sorry," he said. "I don't have anyone else to leave that information with."

She cleared her throat. "It also makes me wonder if I should tell you that…we got sort of a strange message today."

The tension tightening his shoulders increased. Was this "strange message" the beginning of the end? He'd been waiting for something unusual, something that would tip him off that The Crew was closing in. "Why didn't you give it to me? You left before I did, and I've been monitoring the phones ever since."

"It came in around three, when I was on another line and you were at the bank, but I thought it was just a wrong number."

"Who was it for?"

"Someone named Brent."

Eve's face conjured up in Rex's mind, making him hope, as much as he also had to hope against it, that she was trying to contact him. "Was it a woman?"

"No."

"What made you think of it now?"

"When you called me a few minutes ago, I was reminded of it. For some reason it gave me a funny feeling. I began to wonder if maybe you've been using that name for whatever reason."

Irritated that she'd assume he didn't need to know about that message, for *whatever* reason, he stepped away from the window and focused on the conversation. "Marilyn, you can't keep *anything* from me. I don't care who it's for or who it's from."

"Why? That's what I don't get?"

"Because it could wind up getting me killed. Do you understand?"

There was a long silence. "See? Thanks to comments like that, I can't sleep at night."

He didn't mean to spook her, but he had to impress upon her the importance of telling him everything. Who could say what small thing would warn him of the presence of his old gang? "We work in protection. That pits us against some dangerous people, and some of those people like to go after revenge."

"Is that what's happening? Because you've never left town for two and a half weeks before and had me secretly meet you to sign checks. You haven't even taken a vacation. And you've never used a different name."

Little did she know that the name she called him wasn't his real name—not his surname, anyway. He'd been through several incarnations of his identity. The first—when he, Virgil, Peyton, Laurel and her two kids went into WitSec and moved to Washington, D.C.—had been Perry Smith. He'd hated that name. It had never quite fit, had always left him feeling as if something important had been stolen from him. But he'd been through five others since and didn't like those any better—which was why, when he returned to California, he'd gone back to Rex. He'd believed there were so many people in this crowded state that one Rex wouldn't stand out. He'd missed being who he really was. And, at that stage, he hadn't heard anything from The Crew or Mona since a guy called Ice had found Laurel in Montana over a year earlier.

"Someone's out to get me, Marilyn."

*"Who?"*

"Someone I've come up against in the past. That's all you need to know. So what was this mysterious message?"

He could tell she didn't like being kept in the dark. She seemed to think his refusal to give her the details of the danger he faced meant he didn't trust her. That was true, to a point. But only because he couldn't expect her not to give The Crew his home address if she had a gun to her head. And how much more quickly would she talk if it was her husband in danger?

She was a loyal employee, but The Crew did everything possible to exploiting one's vulnerabilities. Asking her to die in his place was out of the question. "Well?" he prompted.

"It was from someone named Dylan."

The only Dylan who knew him by Brent was the one he'd recently met with Eve. "Any last name?" he asked, just to confirm what he suspected.

"No. All he said was 'Brent, you bastard. You didn't have to effing prove me right.'"

That message had definitely come from Cheyenne's husband. With the help of Eve's friend Ted, Dylan had figured out where Rex really worked. But what Marilyn had said didn't quite fit the image Rex had of a tough guy like Dylan. "Did he really say *effing?*"

She lowered her voice. "I didn't want to repeat it *verbatim*. My mother-in-law's sleeping in the next room and *bastard* was bad enough."

He would've laughed. Marilyn didn't shy away from harsh language at work. But he supposed he wouldn't drop an F-bomb within hearing of his mother-in-law, either, if he had one. He'd never used bad language in the presence of his own mother, not even in his worst days. All his anger had been turned inward. "He didn't leave a number?"

"No. I didn't get the impression he was expecting a call back. But the number he was calling from showed up on the screen, so I jotted it down."

Rex knew he should let this go. He'd be a fool to respond. If he called Dylan back, Dylan and Ted would both know that he was, after all, associated with All About Security. But they weren't buying the story he'd concocted for them about being a landscaper in Bakersfield—and the recklessness he'd been feeling lately reasserted itself.

So did his desire to rebel against the strictures under which he had to live his life. *Bring it on,* he thought as he imagined, for the millionth time, his final confrontation with his old gang.

"Give me the number," he told Marilyn, and walked back into the office to get a pen and paper.

Two minutes later, he blocked his number and called Dylan.

Cheyenne answered. "Hello?"

"Is your husband there?" Rex asked.

"Who's this?"

He hesitated. He preferred not to identify himself to her, but he doubted she'd get Dylan if he didn't. "Brent."

"Oh, um, Brent. Right. Okay, just a sec."

She sounded flustered, but she didn't ask why he'd left so suddenly when he was supposed to have stayed through Christmas. Neither did she mention the fact that his sister had never shown up—or that he'd driven off without even telling Eve goodbye. She hurried to get her husband; he could hear her calling Dylan's name in the background.

Dylan's voice came through a few seconds later. "Brent?"

"You think I should've stayed?" Rex asked without preamble. "Is that what you think?"

There was a long silence. Then, instead of railing at him as Rex had expected, Dylan spoke quietly, calmly. "No, I think you would've liked to stay, or you wouldn't have made this call."

"Maybe so." Why deny it? Who wouldn't want to remain in a place that seemed so safe and homey and protected from all the bad things that threatened him? Whiskey Creek was a place out of time and going there had *almost* felt like a second chance.

"So why'd you leave?" Dylan asked.

"Because it was impossible for me to do anything else, okay? I did Eve a favor by walking away. I did you *all* a favor." He was about to end the call. He'd just had to let Dylan know that he hadn't used Eve, that he wasn't *that* kind of bastard. Or perhaps he'd wanted an outlet for his frustration and anger, a fight that didn't have life-and-death stakes. If so, that desire had been quashed by Dylan's insightful response.

Dylan spoke before he could. "What kind of trouble are you in, Brent? Is this about your sister?"

Rex raked a hand through his hair, which was already mussed from the many times he'd done that tonight. "No. I don't have a sister. Scarlet was a client. I was going to bring her to Whiskey Creek so I could look after her, but that situation resolved itself."

There was another long silence. Then he said, "What else did you lie about?"

"Practically everything," he admitted. "But what's happening in my life…it has nothing to do with the police, if that's what you're getting at."

"Then it has to do with people who are not the police, and that means they can help you."

"They've tried. There's nothing they can do. I'm better off on my own."

"What, then? You testified against someone? Or—"

"Something like that," he broke in.

Rex was pretty sure Dylan was surprised they were even having this conversation. Rex was surprised, too. They barely knew each other—and he hadn't reached out to anyone before, for understanding or anything else. Why Eve and her friends would be different, he couldn't say, but their good opinion mattered to him. He still wanted to see Eve, to explore what he felt when he was with her.

"Whatever you're dealing with, you have to stop running sometime," Dylan said.

Rex chuckled without mirth. If he hadn't arrived at that decision himself, he would never have left Whiskey Creek. "Exactly. But, trust me, you don't want me to stop running in *your* town," he said, and disconnected. He couldn't have kept talking, even if he'd wanted to. He hadn't seen anyone pull into his drive. But a lone figure approached his door.

His breath caught in his throat as whoever it was knocked, and he reached for his gun. Maybe this would be the end of it.

# 20

Brent had checked out of the B and B in Jackson the same day he checked in. That was information the manager at the Bluebell probably shouldn't have given Eve, what with the privacy laws these days, but the woman recognized her as having been with him before and didn't even bring up any legal issues. Eve was grateful the information had come so easily. Knowing she hadn't just missed him soothed her anger at Ted for waiting so long to tell her.

But she had so little to go on, she'd never be able to find Brent. From what she'd learned, he'd checked in at the Bluebell very late, slept for a few hours and taken off to…only God knew where. Why hadn't he just stayed at Mrs. Higgins's place those final few hours? Maybe he thought Mrs. Higgins would try to talk him out of leaving if she saw him with his luggage. That was Eve's guess, although it was also possible that he'd set off, realized he was too tired to drive all the way to his destination and decided to sleep at the only place familiar to him that wasn't in Whiskey Creek.

But if his "sister" had been harmed, if that was the reason he'd left in the middle of the night, stopping so soon was odd. Why wouldn't he have some coffee or take a couple of NoDoz capsules to help him stay awake so he could go right to her?

Eve sighed. Who could say? He'd made no secret of the fact that his relationship with his family was strained. Perhaps he didn't feel comfortable rushing to Scarlet's aid because other family members had gotten there first but was too upset to remain where he was.

There was just one problem with the whole sister-in-jeopardy theory. Eve was now convinced that Dennis was Brent's brother, that Brent's real name was Rex and that Scarlet wasn't his sister. Dennis had acted as if he didn't even know a Scarlet.

God forbid she was Brent's—er, Rex's—girlfriend.

"You said you weren't a cheater," she muttered aloud as she drove into Whiskey Creek. But could she believe that?

It started snowing as she reached the outskirts of town. Winter had been late this year. There'd been plenty of rain but this was the first snow. Normally, she would've been excited at the prospect of a white Christmas. There was nothing more charming than her quaint little town resting beneath a blanket of snow. But she didn't feel any Christmas spirit this year.

At the moment, she was just eager to find her bed—so she wasn't happy when she turned into her drive and saw Dylan's Jeep. His backup lights were on, as if he'd come to visit, found her gone and was leaving.

Was Cheyenne with him?

It was too dark to tell.

The second he spotted her, he parked again, even though he was blocking the carport. Normally, that wouldn't have bothered Eve. But she didn't want to talk about Brent. Not to Ted and Sophia. Not to Cheyenne and Dylan. Not to anyone. She felt sick at heart, whether she had any right to or not, and needed time to cope with her disappointment. There was still the fear of what that pregnancy test in her house would reveal, of course. Her emotions were in such upheaval, she wasn't sure how she'd feel about having a baby. She only knew that she hadn't been ready to give Brent up when he left, and she hadn't thought she'd have to, not for three more weeks.

The driver and passenger doors opened at the same time, which answered her question as to whether Cheyenne was with Dylan.

Maybe Ted had called to tell them she'd left the restaurant upset, and they were here to see that she was okay.

"What are you two doing out so late?" she called to them. She'd parked to one side so Dylan could get around her when they went home.

Dylan's keys jingled in his hand as they walked over to her. "We've been trying to call you."

She reached back into the car to get her purse, so she could check her phone. It was dead. "Oh, I guess I'm out of battery." She'd been so consumed with her mission to find Brent/Rex that she hadn't even noticed.

"The lights were on in the house, so we thought you might be home—that maybe you lent your car to someone else." Cheyenne knew Pam, at the B and B, had a car even older than Eve's. Whenever she had engine trouble, she borrowed the Mercedes if Eve didn't need it.

"No, not tonight." She'd left the lights on when she went to Just Like Mom's because she hadn't planned to be gone very long and, as a single woman, found it more reassuring to return to a house that wasn't completely dark. "But you still haven't told me why you're here."

"Brent called Dylan," Cheyenne announced.

Eve's heart skipped a beat. "He did? Why? And...how did he get your number?"

There was a slight pause. Cheyenne was waiting for her husband to field this question.

Dylan gave Eve a look that suggested he wasn't all that happy with the answer. "I called his business this afternoon and left him a message."

"You *what?*" Eve said.

"I knew he was lying about owning a landscaping company, and I wanted him to know it," he explained. "I was also pissed that he'd come crashing into your life only to walk away as if it was nothing. You deserve better."

Since she felt angry with Brent—Rex—for the same reason, she appreciated Dylan's desire to stand up for her. But that reaction came in a distant second to the curiosity his news had aroused. "So you called All About Security."

"Yeah."

"And he called you back…"

"Which was as good as admitting that we were right," Cheyenne said, pointing out the obvious.

They were getting wet, so Eve motioned them to the front door. "He must've realized that."

Dylan nodded as they hurried inside. "He did."

She led the way to the kitchen. "He said so?"

"He said he left because he had no choice. That's what I wanted to tell you. I thought it might help with…the suddenness of his departure."

"He left because of his sister and the problems she's been having with her ex?" she said. "Is that what he told you?"

"No. He doesn't have a sister," Dylan replied. "Scarlet was just a client he'd been hired to protect but, according to him, her situation has since 'resolved itself.'"

Eve breathed a sigh of relief at finally learning who

Scarlet was. So she wasn't Rex's sister *or* his girlfriend. Now the fact that Dennis hadn't recognized her name made sense. She wished that didn't please her as much as it did, but...

"Whatever trouble he's in now is *his* trouble, not Scarlet's," Dylan added. "But he claims that trouble doesn't involve the police."

"He's told me the same thing." Setting her purse aside, Eve removed her coat. "Do you believe him?"

"I do," Dylan said.

"Why?" she challenged. "When he's told so many lies?"

"If you'll remember, he didn't volunteer those lies. He didn't really want to say anything. We forced those answers out of him. And he didn't need to call me back if he was just going to offer up more of the same. He seemed sort of...resigned, if you want the truth."

Eve wished *she* had talked to him. "Did he say anything about me?"

"Not directly. But that whole call was about you."

"Yet I wasn't mentioned," she said as she sat down on a kitchen chair.

"He wouldn't have bothered if he didn't care about you." Dylan helped Cheyenne with her coat and put it on top of his. "That's why we're here. I don't think he wanted to leave Whiskey Creek, and I felt you should know that."

What Dylan had said soothed her wounded pride—but it also made her want Rex back. "Is he safe?"

Dylan frowned. "I got the impression *he* doesn't think so."

Suddenly as cold as if she was still standing outside, Eve clasped her hands in her lap. "He would know, wouldn't he?"

"I'm guessing he would." Dylan's response was grudging. Eve could tell he didn't really want to think about that aspect.

"Is there anything we can do?" she asked.

He sat across from her and stretched out his legs. "Stay out of the line of fire, I guess. He doesn't want to bring whatever danger he's in to Whiskey Creek. And I can't say I'd like to see that myself."

But if he wasn't safe, who was going to help him? "You're saying we just let it go, let him handle whatever it is on his own?"

Dylan shrugged. "I'm sorry, but I don't see any other way."

As she sat there, looking at Cheyenne's swollen belly, she could understand why Dylan might choose to play it safe. Eve knew she could be carrying a child herself. She didn't want to see anyone hurt—but that included Rex.

Rex had nearly shot his neighbor. Never had he imagined that Leigh Dresden, half of the couple who lived next door, would show up on his doorstep at one in the morning, in the worst storm to hit San Francisco so far this winter. It wouldn't have been such a close call if she hadn't covered the peephole with her finger as a friendly joke. But he could see why she wouldn't expect something like that to put her in danger. And he was pretty sure Leigh didn't know what the hell she was doing. From her giddy laughter, and the way she swayed on her feet, she'd had too much to drink. Maybe that was why she'd braved the wind and the rain to show up with a platter of decorated sugar cookies. She'd covered them with plastic wrap, which revealed some presence of mind, but she wasn't even wearing a coat. And this kind of behavior wasn't like her. She had two kids, two little boys, and had always seemed so circumspect and devoted.

"Made you these," she said, slurring her words enough to add further proof to his "she's drunk" observation.

He could feel the weight of his gun in his right hand. He'd turned on the porch light, but he hadn't turned on the light in the entry, so he was standing in shadow. From what he could tell, she hadn't yet noticed that he was holding a pistol. She was too busy looking at his face—and smiling.

"That's nice of you." He hid the gun behind his back. "What made you do that in the middle of the night?"

She stood on her tiptoes and glanced over his shoulder into his house, apparently curious as to what she'd find there. "I thought you might like them. You seem so isolated and remote over here, you know? I never see you bring anyone home. You never entertain friends or...or anything."

"You've been watching me that closely?"

Her laugh sounded slightly nervous, as if that question had brought a moment of clarity. "Things have changed since Marcus and I split."

The breakup was news to him. "You and your husband are no longer together?"

She gave him a funny look. "No. We haven't been for six months. He decided he preferred the eighteen-year-old bimbo he met at the gym."

Rex rubbed his free hand over his chin. "I'm sorry about that. I guess I'm a little behind on neighborhood gossip."

"I guess so," she said. "I didn't think anyone had missed hearing *that* story." She laughed again but then sadness wiped the smile from her face. He was bringing her to the house. It was Ben, across the street, who told me what was going on."

"Ouch."

She looked sullen, but then managed another smile. "Anyway, I saw that all your lights were on, and I know you're usually up late, and…" She gestured sloppily. "I couldn't sleep, so…I thought I'd walk over to see if you'd like a cookie." She seemed to focus on his mouth. "Or… maybe you'd like to come over for a drink and then have a cookie. We've lived thirty feet apart for two years and yet we barely know each other."

And she thought *now* was the time to get acquainted?

"Where are your kids?"

"They're home, asleep." She lowered her voice and fluttered her eyelashes at him. "They won't bother us."

She obviously wanted more than conversation. Rex wasn't interested. But he couldn't send her away and have her fall and get hurt or run into a member of The Crew on her way home. So he shoved his gun back into his waistband and pulled his shirt down, shielding that action with his body. "I'm afraid I was just getting ready for bed, so we'll have to have a drink another time," he said as he took the cookies and set them aside. "But, here, let me walk you home."

She slid her arm through his and leaned her head on his shoulder almost as soon as he stepped outside. He hadn't grabbed a coat. Although it was freezing, he'd been too nervous about a woman standing on his front stoop when he was expecting to be attacked. He just wanted to get her home safely, but she was so drunk she could hardly walk. Her lack of coordination and the wind fighting them at every step made progress slower than he'd planned.

"Don't you ever get lonely?" she asked wistfully, blinking as she turned her face up to his.

He thought of Eve. The only time he hadn't been lonely was recently, when he was with her. "Yes," he said.

Her smile broadened and her gaze returned to his lips. "Then why aren't you more sociable?"

"I'm busy."

"A man's got to have *some* downtime. You have to eat and sleep and do...*other* things occasionally."

They'd finally reached her doorstep. She didn't seem troubled by the weather, but he didn't enjoy getting soaked. "Here you are. You'd better go inside before you catch a cold."

"Come in with me," she said with a pout, and opened the door to tug him through it.

"Leigh, I'm sorry." He let her pull him inside but stood in the entry. "I've got to get back."

She closed the door behind him and lifted his hand to her breast. "Why? You won't find anything over there like you'll find here."

"I'm sorry, Leigh," he said again, removing his hand. "But I'm in a relationship with someone else." He almost couldn't believe those words had come out of his mouth. He and Eve weren't in a "relationship." He couldn't offer her anything. And yet...she might be pregnant with his child.

His neighbor linked her arms around his neck. "You never bring anyone home," she responded, jutting out her bottom lip. "I know. I've been watching you since my husband left."

"She lives somewhere else."

"In another state?"

"There's no need for you to worry about that." He gently extricated himself. It was clear she was going through a difficult time. Christmas probably brought back a lot of memories of when she was with her husband, and yet she had to put on a happy face for her kids.

He could see why she might get drunk and seek comfort and pleasure where she could find it.

But just as he stepped away and started to open the door, he saw a car drive by—going very slow—and stop at his house.

Quickly closing the door again, he drew the dead bolt.

"What is it?" Leigh asked.

He didn't answer. He hurried over to the window, where he watched four men get out. From the way they stalked purposefully to the house, sheltering something under their jackets, he guessed they were carrying guns.

# 21

Banging on the door woke Eve from a restless sleep. She sat up, wondering if she'd imagined the noise—or mistaken it for something in one of the many dream sequences she'd been having.

Then it came again. Solid and distinct. Someone wanted to rouse her. It couldn't be her parents, could it? It wasn't even six in the morning!

Slightly anxious—she'd had such a bad night already—she grabbed her robe and her cell phone and crept out to the living room. The sun hadn't yet made its appearance. Maybe it wouldn't make much of one today. Judging by the wind howling through the eaves, the weather hadn't cleared since the previous night, when Dylan and Cheyenne had paid her a visit. She wasn't sure if it was still snowing, but the storm certainly wasn't over.

She went to the window and peered out. The snow had stopped but she could see no car in her drive.

"Who is it?" she called, her finger hovering over the send button for 9-1-1.

"It's me," came the response.

Eve's heart nearly dropped to her knees. Brent! No, *Rex*. She had to get used to his real name—but first she needed to confirm it.

"Rex?"

"Yeah."

She managed a slight smile after she opened the door. "It's nice to finally meet the real you."

"I'm sorry, Eve. I've tried to stay out of your life."

He was pale and drawn, much paler than she'd ever seen him. She wondered if he was sick but figured it was exhaustion. His hair had been whipped around and was noticeably tangled, he had more beard growth than usual and his eyes were bloodshot. "I don't want you out of my life," she said, and pulled him inside, where it was warm.

"I can't stay," he told her. But she ignored that. He needed sleep and good food and a little TLC before they even considered anything else.

"You look like you haven't been to bed tonight."

"Not yet."

"Not *yet*? It's nearly morning!"

She began to lead him to her bedroom, but he pulled back. "You'd be smarter to send me away. It should be safe for you now—for both of us—or I wouldn't be here. But at some point they'll find me again."

*They.* She didn't know who "they" were. And she didn't know what he might have done, if anything, to cause the danger he was in. But she didn't dare ask him. Not right now. There was something ragged about him, something watchful and defensive, that made her heart ache.

"We'll talk about that later," she said. "After you've had a chance to rest."

"When do you leave for work?"

"I have to be there by nine, so if I'm gone when you wake up, just make yourself at home and shower, eat, whatever. Do you need to borrow my car?"

"No. I have a rental. It's parked down the road half a

mile or so. I didn't want your parents to see it and wonder what was going on."

"And your bags?"

"I don't have much, but what I do have is in the car."

He let her strip off his shirt. But when she started to unbutton his jeans, he stopped her, and she realized it was because he had a gun.

She froze as he removed it, but he didn't immediately set it aside. He paused, as if he thought the sight of it might upset her enough that she wouldn't want him to stay. "It's for self-defense, Eve," he said. "I would *never* hurt you. You believe that, don't you?"

She did. It wasn't as though he was threatening her with it. But there were other reasons he possessed such a deadly weapon, and they scared her. "Have you ever had to use it?"

She'd known he was in trouble, and that it was serious trouble, but a handgun? That brought the reality home. He was talking life and death!

Instead of answering, he slid the weapon back into his waistband. "I shouldn't have come here, shouldn't be including you in my problems."

Part of her, the part that recited what her parents and her friends would most likely say, told her she should let him go. But the other part, the part that cared about him and felt his exhaustion and his pain, couldn't bear the thought of his leaving without the rest and comfort he needed.

"Don't go," she said. "I admit it's a leap of faith for me to have a gun in the house, but…put it down and come to bed. I want you beside me. I want to hear your heart beating and know you're with me, solid and safe."

When he hesitated, she reached for the gun, but he guided her hand away and put it on the nightstand himself. Then Eve took off her nightgown. It wasn't because she wanted to make love. She didn't feel he was emotionally capable of that right now. She wasn't sure *she* was. But she craved the feel of his skin against hers and, when she crawled in with him, he seemed just as eager to be close.

"I love the way you smell," he murmured as he gathered her to him.

She liked a lot more than that about him. She couldn't say why. She didn't know him all that well—not to mention that what he'd originally told her wasn't true. But she felt satisfied when she was with him in a way she'd never been satisfied before. It was almost as if something had been missing in her life, and he provided it. "I'm glad you came back," she said, and shifted to press her lips to his temple.

He seemed to drop off almost instantly but Eve didn't. She didn't want to sleep. She knew these minutes were numbered, that she'd be lucky if he stayed more than a day or two. So she lay there, listening to him breathe and memorizing the features of his gorgeous face as the sun came up. She wanted to store every detail in her memory, since memories were probably all she'd ever have.

Unless he'd given her a baby...

When Rex woke up, the house was quiet. Eve had to be at work. He lifted his head to gaze around the empty bedroom, with all its feminine frills, then fell back onto the pillow when he remembered how badly The Crew had shot up his house and Land Rover last night. They'd assumed he was at home.

He needed to shower so he could run his errands and, when she returned from work, have her take him to the airport. He had to get out of California as soon as possible. He also needed to figure out how he was going to sell his business and his house and then rebuild his life. He knew he should be grateful that he'd survived the night, that his neighbor had given him reason to leave his house at that precise moment. But it was difficult to face the destruction of everything he'd built—especially since he'd thought he'd finally reached a point where this wouldn't happen again. Until the final message from Mona, he'd believed that as long as he was careful, the past would continue to fade away.

He shouldn't have assumed he was clear of it. Then maybe the disappointment wouldn't taste quite so bitter. He'd never escape The Crew entirely. Which was why he couldn't linger in Whiskey Creek.

A noise at the front door made him sit up. Although he saw no way The Crew could have traced him to Whiskey Creek, he was rattled enough by what had taken place to grab his gun.

"Don't worry, it's just me!" Eve called out. "I've brought you some lunch!"

He noted the caution she'd used because she knew he was armed.

"I'm still in bed," he called back, and placed his Glock in her top drawer so she wouldn't have to see it the second she walked into the room.

She appeared in the doorway, looking as beautiful as ever in a fitted gray dress with black trim and black stockings. "Good. I hope you slept well. You needed it." She smiled at him. "You hungry?"

"Starving." He let his gaze range over her, starting with her dark hair and those pretty cornflower-blue eyes and moving over her slender figure. "But maybe we could have dessert first."

Instead of capitulating, she raised an eyebrow. "I sense

some avoidance going on here. Some *more* avoidance,
I should say."

He grimaced. "Does that mean you want to talk?"

"What do you think?"

"We have very limited time. Why waste it?"

"Finding out what's going on wouldn't be a waste to
me." She came over to sit beside him on the bed. "Are
you going to trust me enough to tell me?"

He was so used to hiding his past, his true identity
and so many of the events that had shaped him. It felt
strange to even consider opening up. And yet all those
secrets created such a heavy burden. She was the first
woman since Laurel to know even this much about him,
little though that was.

"What's the use of keeping me in the dark?" she prodded, as if she understood the battle he was waging in his
head. "Why not let me know the real you?"

With a sigh, he shoved the pillows against the backboard to give his spine some support. "My real name is
Rex McCready. That's the name I was born with. Since
then I've been Perry Smith, Jackson Perry, Taylor Jackson—" He'd started to tick them off on his fingers, but
she interrupted.

"And Brent Taylor. I think I see a pattern here," she
said with a wry smile.

"I figured it would be easier to remember my own
name if at least part of it was familiar."

She nodded, encouraging him to continue. He grimaced again. "Sometimes even I don't know who I am."

"That goes deeper than a name."

"Maybe."

"What I need to know is *why*," she said. "Why all the
different identities?"

This was the tough part, the part he preferred to avoid.

"I did something when I was a teenager, Eve, something I will always regret." He still couldn't bring himself to go into any detail about Logan's accident. "It cost my family a great deal, drove a wedge between us and filled me with self-loathing. I just…couldn't cope with it, with the fact that I was responsible for something so tragic. There are still moments when it eats me up inside." His voice dropped in anguish. "I would give *anything* to turn back the clock, but…"

"That's impossible," she said softly.

"Yes." He'd hoped his answer had seemed contemplative. Resigned. That was what he was striving for. But she somehow understood who he really was, and that made it harder to keep the truth locked in the "do not open" compartment in his brain.

Her eyes searched his face. "You're not going to tell me what that tragic event was?"

He summoned the mask that normally hid his deeper emotions. "It doesn't matter, not to the rest of the story."

She must have heard the "no" in his statement because she didn't press him on that. "So this self-loathing caused you to act out."

He nodded.

"In what way?"

"I started getting into fights, ditching school, taking drugs. First it was pot. Then I worked my way up to harder drugs. Pretty soon I was dealing to support my habit. And not long after I turned eighteen, I got busted."

"And then you did time."

He rubbed a hand over his face. "Yes."

"Dylan guessed as much. Said you were…leery."

"It's that obvious, huh?" He chuckled without mirth. "Prison is a hell of a place for a kid as angry and self-destructive as I was, because it only makes you angrier and more self-destructive. I probably would've been killed if I hadn't joined a gang called The Crew." Which was what made it so ironic that *they* were the threat now.

"A *gang?*" she repeated.

He tried to comb some of the tangles out of his hair with his fingers. "I can imagine it sounds shocking to someone like you, someone who's never encountered what I've encountered. But…prison is a world all its own, Eve. Inside, you either click with other guys, or you face all comers alone—and you're not going to last very long doing that." She didn't need to know *all* his reasons for joining, not the least of which was that he hadn't expected to reach his thirtieth birthday. If he wasn't going to survive, the future was of no concern to him. There didn't seem to be any reason *not* to join and at least take a spot at the top of the food chain for a while.

"You're saying it was a necessary evil."

"Felt that way at the time. But these men, these gang members, they become your brothers. What you would live and die for gets twisted, but you love them so much that you'd give your life for them. I felt like I was unworthy of my real family, and yet here was this fiercely loyal group of brothers willing to accept me, and they weren't any better than I was. It was the first time in ages that I felt as if I belonged to something important, was someone who mattered. I wasn't about to lose that."

"But…"

"Then came Virgil."

"Another inmate?"

"Yeah. After a few months, he became my cell mate."

"He was in this gang, too?"

"Eventually." He rested his head against the backboard as he talked. "He was in prison for murdering his abusive SOB of a stepfather."

She blanched. "This…friend of yours, he *murdered* someone?"

"No. But he served fourteen years before they found the real killer. That was some sad bullshit." He felt his muscles tense. "I still feel angry at the system when I think of what he went through—for no good reason. Like me, he was only eighteen when he went in. He'd gotten there first. He's a few years older than me. But he was different, a good person, and we became close. Then he was exonerated."

"So he got out before you did."

"Not by much. I was released weeks later. There was just one problem."

"What's that?"

He took her hand. He knew this wasn't what any woman would want to hear. "Once you join a gang, you're in it for life, Eve. They don't let you walk away."

"You wanted to leave The Crew once you got out of prison?"

"Not me. Not at first. Like I said, those guys were the only family I had. My own family had basically disowned me. But Virgil had a new chance at life. He wanted to start over, and he knew he couldn't do that unless he had some way to protect his sister."

She stared down at their entwined fingers. "How did his sister get involved?"

"If the gang can't get to you, they'll take out the people you love—hurt you however they can."

When she recoiled, he feared he'd gone too far. But he'd never told anyone this story, and he had to finish. He didn't want to feel as if he was still lying to her by telling only part of the truth. It was important to find out if she could still look at him the same way once she saw what lay behind his pretty face.

Although he couldn't imagine she would.

"It wasn't just his sister," he said. "It was her two kids. She was divorced and struggling to make it on her own, no longer had a husband to look out for her, protect her."

"And every woman needs a man."

"Are you being sarcastic?"

She laughed. "Of course. These days most of us believe we can take care of ourselves. But your background puts that comment in perspective, so I guess I can't hold it against you."

"You think you could shoot a man?" he asked.

"Probably not," she admitted. "But I don't think most of the men I hang out with could, either. Anyway, what did Virgil do?"

"He cut a deal with the California Department of Corrections. Agreed to go undercover to help them bust up an even worse gang in a different prison if they'd put Laurel into Witness Protection."

"So Laurel is Virgil's sister," she said, recognizing the name.

"That's how I met her."

"Makes sense." She shifted on the bed. "But I'm shocked that they'd allow him to endanger himself like that."

"A judge had just been killed by a member of this gang, so they figured it would save a lot of lives in the end. And no one was going to be more convincing than Virgil. He was tough. He had prison experience. He had gang experience, too. And he didn't smell like a cop. They thought he was perfect for the job."

"Was he able to do what they wanted him to—and get out alive?"

"Yes and no. There were things that went wrong. The Crew found his sister and nearly killed her and her kids.

They would have, if I hadn't been there to stop them." He didn't tell her that was the moment he'd had to make his own decision—between the path Virgil had taken and the one he was on and ultimately left behind. That day had changed everything.

Eve seemed wary. "How did you stop them?"

He slid open the drawer of the nightstand and her eyes widened with understanding when they landed on the gun. "I see. You shot someone."

Was she going to ask him to leave when this was over? He wouldn't blame her if she did. He knew how bad he must sound, especially to someone who lived in Whiskey Creek. "I had no choice, Eve. You should have seen what he was trying to do to her."

Her throat worked as she swallowed. "And then?"

"After that we had no choice but to go into WitSec—all of us. Virgil had helped break up the Hell's Fury at Pelican Bay—"

"Pelican Bay is a very notorious prison!"

"For good reason."

"And he survived that."

"Yes. But we barely managed to escape with our lives, hence the WitSec decision. Last thing we needed was for The Crew to come after us again."

"They must have, or we wouldn't be having this discussion."

"Yes. They found us in D.C. We escaped a second time, just as narrowly. Then we left WitSec, thinking we might be safer on our own. That was when Laurel moved to Montana to start over without us."

"Where did you go?"

"Farther up the east coast. I stayed to help Virgil reestablish the personal security company we'd opened in the D.C. area."

"You weren't with Laurel at the time?"

"Not anymore. We'd broken up. That was part of the reason she left."

She smoothed the bedding before meeting his gaze again. "Why didn't it work out between you? You obviously loved her very much."

He wasn't sure how honestly he wanted to answer that question. But he'd had enough of lies. "It was my fault," he said. "I wasn't ready for the kind of relationship we both wanted to have. When my mother died, I screwed up again, even though I'd promised her I wouldn't."

"Screwed up in what way?"

He noticed the subtle tension around her mouth and eyes. "Started using again."

"You're talking about drugs."

"Yes."

"What kind?"

"OxyContin. Prescription pain meds. That shit is so addictive. I fought it for a number of years."

She hesitated for a moment. Then she said, "And now?"

"I've been clean for nearly four years. Can't even remember the last time I was drunk—until Sexy Sadie's."

"You try to be careful about alcohol, too?"

"I watch for triggers. I don't want to go back to that place."

She folded her arms. "I see. So none of you were married when Laurel moved to Montana."

"Just Virgil." Revealing so much would probably change her feelings toward him, but Rex had to grin when he thought of Virgil's no-nonsense wife. He'd always liked Peyton. "He married the deputy warden from Pelican Bay, met her while he was there under cover, if you can believe it."

She gave a surprised laugh. *"What?"*

"It's true. They have two kids and are happy—really happy, which does my heart good. Except that they have to watch their backs just like I have to watch mine."

"Where do they live?"

"Not in California."

She studied him. "That's an interesting answer."

He thought of Mona, but decided not to burden her with that part of the story. "It's better if you don't know certain things."

"You think I'd tell?"

"The Crew would torture you if they ever got a hold of you and believed you could provide any useful information. I'm trying to protect you as much as Virgil."

The color drained from her face. "What you're talking about…it's all so foreign to me. I mean…the biggest problem I've faced is how to meet the right man so I could start a family."

He couldn't help it; he glanced at her belly. "And how's that family thing going?"

"If you're asking if I'm pregnant, I haven't taken the test. When I do, I want to be sure that it's accurate."

"You told me it'd be accurate in a week. So it should be accurate now."

She nodded. "I bought one a few days ago. I'll take it soon."

The silence stretched for a minute or two. Realizing she must be freaked out, he finally broke it in an attempt to reassure her. "So now you know why I lied, why I left and why I have to leave again. I don't want my past to catch up with me, especially here. I don't want you hurt."

She stood and began to pace. "They can't *still* be looking for you. You've been out of prison for what…five years?"

"Eight."

"That's crazy!" She stopped to face him. "Surely they've forgotten about you by now."

He chuckled bitterly. "They haven't forgotten, Eve. I doubt they ever will."

"Why? Why do they care so much?"

"You have to understand what's important in their world. There's a lot of street cred in taking Virgil and me out. We killed several of their leaders, and we walked away. They can't let that go unpunished. The banger who puts a bullet in us will be a hero, and that gives every asshole in the club incentive to try. After what happened before, Virgil and I are like…like two giant bucks that several hunters have seen but none have been able to bag. They talk about us, daydream about us, make plans for how they'll be the ones to claim the prize…."

She started pacing again. "Still. How do you know they've found you again—"

"They shot up my house and my car last night, Eve. That's how I know."

Her hand covered her mouth. "No."

"Yes."

"Where were you when it happened?"

"At a friend's down the street." He didn't see any reason to let her believe he might've been having sex with someone else by mentioning that "friend" was the recently divorced woman who lived next door.

"So your car was at your house."

"Yes. That, the late hour and the fact that the lights were on is what made them think I was home. They probably wouldn't have busted in and shot up the place otherwise. You should've seen what they did to my bed—and everything else once they realized they were wrong and I wasn't home."

"Better your car and your house than you! What if your car hadn't been there? They would've waited for you to come home, right?"

"Probably."

"You don't seem very relieved that they didn't kill you," she complained.

"It's all getting old, Eve. I'm tired of it, don't know how much longer I can keep fighting this battle."

She pivoted at the foot of the bed. "You have no choice!"

"I *do* have a choice. It's just not a choice most people would expect me to make."

She rubbed her arms as if he'd given her goose bumps. "That sounds suicidal."

"I'm *not* suicidal. I want to live as much as anyone. But the longer I run, the longer they're going to chase me." He shrugged. "Problem is…I've tried standing and fighting. That doesn't get me anywhere, either. The more of them I kill, the more they'll send."

"Kill…" she repeated.

He said nothing.

"Did you call the police?"

"Someone did. But I didn't stick around to talk to them. There's nothing they can do for me, Eve. That's what I've been trying to tell you."

"They *have* to be able to help!" she insisted. "I mean… there has to be *someone* you can turn to."

"Not unless I go back into WitSec and, at this point, I doubt the government would even be willing to spend the money. We walked away from the program last time. I'm not interested in returning, anyway."

"So what happens next?"

"I'll have to disappear, reestablish myself somewhere else. And that starts with getting a new computer this afternoon and some clothes. I lost everything." Fortunately, he had the money to pay for those items. He'd pulled all his money out of the bank when he returned to San Francisco, and The Crew hadn't found it. They hadn't been looking for money; they'd only been looking to do as much damage as possible. So once they took off, he'd gone in and retrieved it. He probably could've salvaged some of his clothes and other belongings while he was there, but he'd heard the sirens and knew he had to get out as soon as possible. He couldn't afford to be delayed answering questions when answering those questions wouldn't help, anyway.

"What about your business?"

This was another difficult subject. All About Security was the one thing he had. It had given him focus, a measure of success—success he'd established independent of Virgil—a sense of importance. And that had pulled him through. He'd have to say goodbye to all his bodyguards and Marilyn, never talk to them again. He'd been careful not to get too close to anyone, in case it came down to this, but it was impossible not to connect on some level. "I need to sell it, cut ties."

Her sympathetic expression suggested she understood what starting over would cost him. "Cutting those kinds of ties won't happen overnight."

"I can only hope I'll be able to make the arrangements in a short amount of time, which means I'll have to sell cheap."

She rubbed her forehead as she walked back toward him. "How long can you stay here?"

"They won't be able to follow me right away," he said. "There's nothing at my home or office that leads to Whiskey Creek. My administrative assistant knows I was here before, but I was in other towns, too. And I left a message for her this morning saying I was going to Arizona. I don't think she'll expect me to return to Gold Country, not without notifying her." Why would she? As far as she knew, this place had been nothing more than a stopover, a dot on the map, where he'd found shelter for a few days. She didn't know that he'd gotten involved with Eve, didn't know how much he liked the town, because it hadn't meant all that much to him when she'd come out to have him sign those checks.

He was glad of that now, or he wouldn't even be able to allow himself this reprieve before the inevitable new name, new place, new business.

"At least now I understand," she said.

"I'm sorry the truth is so ugly."

"I can't say you didn't try to warn me." She managed a forgiving smile, but seemed a bit shell-shocked and tentative, as if she'd just learned that the cat she'd been petting for days had rabies. "Let's eat," she said, beckoning him toward the kitchen. "I have to get back to work."

He would rather have had her climb into bed with him, rather have had the chance to hold her. Maybe they had no future, but they had today.

Or was he just thrashing around, trying to find something or someone to hang on to? That would be a natural reaction. No one felt comfortable being cast out or isolated, even by circumstance. He'd been wandering in that wilderness long enough to know how lonely it could get. But he didn't want to be the kind of bastard who'd drag a woman down with him—especially Eve. "Yeah, let's eat."

# 22

"So he's at your place *now?*" Cheyenne had arrived at work twenty minutes earlier—she was only on the schedule for four hours on Tuesdays—but they'd spent every one of those twenty minutes talking about Rex.

"If he hasn't left." Eve rearranged the items on her desk while Cheyenne finally removed her coat and scarf. "He was there when I took him some lunch, but he could be gone by dinner. I don't know what I can rely on—and I was afraid to ask. After what he confessed, I wasn't sure which answer I wanted to hear."

"That's understandable." Cheyenne used her desk to support her as she leaned over to drape her coat and scarf across the filing cabinet.

"I can hardly believe all the things he told me," Eve said. "I know that lately I've been anxious—maybe overanxious—to meet someone. And hooking up wasn't the best way to do that, but—"

"A man like Rex would make any woman do a double take," Cheyenne said.

"For me, it's not just his appearance, Chey. There's something about him—something about how he talks and moves and looks at me. When he touches me, it's unlike anything I've ever experienced before." Eve took some lip balm out of her drawer and smoothed it on. "Do you think it's karma for trying to force what I want? For lowering my standards enough to bring home a complete stranger?"

"No. Not at all. Think of the good things you do—and have always done. That should bring you *good* karma, not bad."

"But my luck couldn't get any worse. Last year I fell for a guy who was in love with someone else, and now I've humiliated myself in front of our entire group of friends—in front of the whole town."

"That's not true," Cheyenne said.

"Yes, it is. And Noelle reminds me if I ever start to forget."

"Noelle's jealous. You deserve to find a great guy. I hate to be mean, but she'd drive any decent person to drink. Kyle can tell you all about that."

Eve raised one hand to let Cheyenne know she hadn't meant to send them off on a tangent. "Noelle will probably be on her second marriage before I have a first."

"With her track record, she'll probably be divorced in no time, too."

"At least she hasn't fallen for some guy who has armed gangbangers trying to kill him. That sounds like something on TV—*Sons of Anarchy* or...or *Breaking Bad.*"

Cheyenne chuckled. "That guy on *Sons of Anarchy* is hot, too."

"But that sort of thing shouldn't happen in real life," Eve argued. "Not to me. And not here."

"Things happen here, too. If you were thinking clearly you'd remember some of them. Anyway, I feel bad that Rex is in this mess. I liked him when I met him at your parents', I really did. But you can't allow what's destroying his life to destroy yours, too."

"You're saying I have to let him move on."

"You have any choice?"

"What about *him?*" she asked, coming to her feet.

"What about him?" Chey repeated, frowning up at her. "I don't want to play judge, but…there are people who'd say he put himself in this situation."

Eve rested her hands on her hips. "When he was a teenager, Chey! How many of us haven't made *some* stupid mistake when we were young?"

"You. That's why you deserve better. And we're talking about more than a stupid mistake, Eve. He dealt drugs. He got busted. He went to prison. He joined a gang. He had to kill to get out of it, and because they won't let him go, there could be other…repercussions. That's all very serious!"

But something had started all this, something he did as a teenager, that had affected him so profoundly he wouldn't even share it.

"Are you listening to me?" Cheyenne asked. "You can't have the life you want with a man like that."

Eve picked up a pen she'd dropped earlier. "What if I'm pregnant?"

Cheyenne rocked back in her chair. "I assumed, if you were pregnant, you would have said something by now."

"You haven't asked."

"I've been afraid to!"

"So you were hoping it wasn't an issue."

"I'm still hoping that. I can only imagine how a baby would complicate an already complicated situation."

"I haven't done the test yet," she said. "I figured it might be smarter to hold off, to know for sure whether he's going to be out of my life for good before I deal with the consequences of having met him and…and behaving the way I did."

Cheyenne gripped the arms of her chair as she leaned forward, suddenly intense. After everything she'd suffered growing up, she hated to put anyone down. That was one of the things Eve loved about her. So she knew Chey was really worried when she weighed in against Rex. "How can there be any question? He told you himself he has to start over somewhere else."

"I can't write him off that easily, just let him become a victim of his past mistakes. If I were him, I wouldn't want anyone to do that to me." She used a higher, mocking pitch. *"This is your own fault. See ya!"*

Cheyenne tilted her head. "But you don't have any control over his situation, and neither does he. That's the problem."

"It doesn't mean he's not worth fighting for."

"You mean *risking your life* for?"

Eve considered what Rex had told her about his friend Virgil. "The other guy, the one who was exonerated, is married. Has kids, too."

"Do you want to take on the same problems *his* wife has?"

Eve couldn't say with certainty what sacrifices she was willing to make. She didn't know Rex well enough to decide. But she refused to let the threats he faced stop them from being able to explore what they were both feeling. "To be honest, I don't know. I would do a lot for love."

Cheyenne grimaced. "Don't use that word quite yet. It's only been a couple of weeks."

Maybe it *was* too soon for "love." But what she felt was compelling enough to make her want to be with him in spite of everything. She'd been miserable since he left. And she couldn't bring herself to turn him away when he'd shown up at the door last night. That would've been the time to do it. "I don't want him to walk out of my life."

Cheyenne sighed. "I understand. For some couples there's just an undeniable...spark, and it happens quickly."

"It was like that for you and Dylan, wasn't it?"

"Sort of."

"I guess he was right about Brent. About his past."

"Dyl's not going to say 'I told you so.'"

It wasn't Dylan she was worried about. "I'm just glad Ted's out of town."

"You're not going to tell him what you told me?"

"Heck, no! And neither are you. Don't you *dare* tell a single soul."

"But Ted knows something is up. It's not like you'll really be hiding anything."

Eve shook her head. "It would be too hard to put up with his disapproval."

"I didn't even realize he was gone," Chey said. "Where'd he go?"

"South Carolina to chase down a lead on Mary's murder."

"When did he leave?"

"A couple of days ago."

"Lucky timing—except, if he was here, you know he only wants what's best for you."

Eve couldn't argue with that. In spite of her brief romantic entanglement with Ted, and the disappointment that had resulted, he'd always been her champion. He was a good example of the point she'd been trying to make earlier: *everyone* made mistakes. Even the great Ted Dixon had, in his desperation not to fall for the wrong woman, managed to hurt her when she would otherwise have remained an innocent bystander. "Maybe what's best for me isn't what it seems," she mused.

Cheyenne bit her lip. "Wishful thinking?"

That wasn't the answer she'd been looking for. "Perhaps, but regardless of what you think, you can't tell anyone about Rex's situation, okay? He can't be subjected to the kind of gossip we get here, can't risk that some word of where he is will get out. It might leak back to his old gang, or someone who knows someone who knows someone in The Crew, which is why he didn't tell me the truth in the first place. He wasn't expecting us to get so...involved."

"Did he say that?"

"Basically."

Cheyenne seemed pleased to hear that he felt some concern for Eve. "Of course. I won't tell anyone if you don't want me to. But none of our friends would give him away."

Rex's comment about The Crew's methods of extracting information came to mind. That had shaken her so much she decided against repeating it. "It's just better if no one else knows."

"Except for Dylan, I won't say a word. I swear." Cheyenne placed her arms on her swollen stomach. "But I want you to do something for me."

"What's that?"

"Find out."

"About..."

"Whether there's a baby!"

An anxious tingle raced through Eve. She wasn't sure if it was excitement or dread. She'd been putting off the moment of truth.

What if she *was* pregnant? If, by some miracle, Rex stayed in Whiskey Creek, would she eventually have to send him away for the sake of their child? What if The Crew showed up, without warning? What if she and Rex had to move again and again?

Eve wouldn't want to keep uprooting a child, any more than she'd want to give up associating with her family and friends—everyone who was now a part of her life. How would her parents feel about finally having a grandson or granddaughter and never even seeing the child? And it could come to that. Rex had indicated that he'd had to start over many times. Did she want to be put in a position of choosing a man over everyone else she loved?

"Don't you think there's enough going on in my life?" she asked Cheyenne.

"I think a child should figure into any decision you make, don't you?"

Grudgingly, Eve nodded.

"So…"

"I'll take the test tonight," she promised.

Cheyenne levered herself out of her chair and grabbed the coat she'd taken off. "I'll go down to the drugstore and get what you need right now."

"No." Eve gestured at her friend's very obvious condition. "Look at you. Anyone who saw you would know you're not buying it for yourself. And with the rumors about me and Rex, and considering how close you and I have always been, the truth will be obvious."

"If you're pregnant you won't be able to hide it, Eve. Not for long."

"But if I'm *not* pregnant, there's no need to give people any more reason to talk. These past couple of weeks, I've been featured prominently enough."

"Hold on!" Cheyenne said. "I have one at my house. I have several, actually, from before, when I was testing so often. I'll double-check the expiration dates, but I'm fairly certain they last for quite a while."

"I have one, too—at the bungalow," Eve said. "I might as well wait and use that."

"And if Rex is there when you get home?" Cheyenne challenged.

Eve couldn't help hoping he would be—but she wouldn't want to take a pregnancy test while he was. If she was carrying his baby, she'd have to look at everything through different eyes, and she knew that would probably include denying herself what she wanted most.

"Okay," she said. "Go get one from your place and—" she swallowed hard "—we'll see what the future holds."

# 23

Eve was shaking so badly she could scarcely open the box. "I really wish you'd let me put this off," she told Cheyenne, who was standing outside the bathroom door.

"Procrastination won't help anything," her friend responded, speaking in a low voice so no one at the B and B would wonder what they were doing hanging around the bathroom together. "It's better to know."

"I'm not entirely convinced of that." If she *wasn't* pregnant, he might be reassured by the news. At this point, *she'd* be reassured, too. Then she could enjoy spending the holidays with him without worrying about how it would impact another life. But what if she was?

"You got it?" Cheyenne asked.

"Quit rushing me!" she snapped.

"I'm just wondering if you need any help!" Cheyenne sounded equally perturbed.

"I can figure out how to do…you know, what we want." She sat on the lid of the toilet seat as she read and reread the instructions. The steps seemed simple enough. But the outcome…

"You're stalling," Cheyenne accused her. "I can tell."

"Obviously you won't give me any peace until I do this, so…" Taking a deep breath, she set the instructions aside and got out the plastic piece that tested her urine and did what she needed to do.

"Well?" Cheyenne asked as she finished.

Instead of answering, Eve set the plastic indicator on the vanity, smoothed her dress down and unlocked the bathroom door.

"Come and see for yourself."

When Cheyenne walked in, she looked as nervous as Eve felt. "I can't remember—how long, exactly, do we have to wait?"

"Two minutes. A line means I'm pregnant."

"God, Eve. What a mess." Cheyenne's eyes were riveted on the indicator but Eve was afraid to look.

Eve didn't say anything. She held her breath and counted to sixty before making herself peek at the results. Then she sank onto the lid of the toilet seat. "Oh, no."

"There's a line," Cheyenne confirmed.

Dropping her head in her hands, Eve tried to absorb the fact that she was going to have a baby—Rex's baby. And that it would be just one more reason they couldn't be together.

That evening when Rex heard a car pull into the drive, he got up to make sure it was Eve. Then he stood at the window, watching as she gathered up some groceries from the backseat. For a second, he allowed himself to imagine what it would be like to walk out and greet her as if he were a regular man with regular problems— problems they could overcome if they wanted to.

Then he glanced at his new laptop, which he'd purchased at an electronics store about an hour away— almost in the Bay Area—once Eve had returned to work. He'd also bought some clothes, shoes and a shaving kit at a mall that wasn't much farther, and then he'd come back to reload his programs and restore his files. He'd just downloaded what the cameras had recorded while The Crew trashed his house. Seeing that was enough to dispel his wishful reverie. The past always pushed what he wanted out of his reach.

He wasn't convinced Eve would be glad to find him still hanging around, anyway. Not now that she'd had time to think about what he'd told her. Surely, she would see the wisdom of getting rid of him as soon as possible.

He walked out to help her in spite of that. "Hey."

Her smile seemed strained. "I thought you might be gone."

He hesitated. "Is that what you were hoping for?"

She studied him for a few seconds. Then she shook her head. "No. I can't say I was."

He took the bags out of her arms, and she turned to get something else—a box—from the backseat. "You okay?" he asked. "You look a little...stressed."

"I'm fine." She hefted the box higher and led the way to the house. "Just tired."

"Why don't I make you some dinner? I'll move to Mrs. Higgins's afterward, so you can get some rest."

She didn't offer to let him stay with her, as he'd secretly hoped. Now that he was here, now that resuming his life in San Francisco wasn't an option, he wanted to spend as much time with her as he could. He understood that might make things more difficult on both of them when he had to leave, but he was so sick of fighting the same battle over and over. He needed a respite, a reason to recommit to outdistancing The Crew. If he had to move on in order to protect Eve, he could make himself do it. But saving his own skin no longer meant that much to him, not if he was only looking at more of what he'd endured for the past eight years.

"I was going to cook *you* dinner," she said.

"But I'm the one who got to sleep in."

She shot him a wry look as he leaned against the door, holding it open. "Because you were up all night."

He deposited the bags on the kitchen table while she put her box on the counter, and they began to unload the groceries. He didn't have any idea where most of the items went, so he stuck with the obvious—taking care of the food that needed to be refrigerated.

She nodded at his laptop, which he'd set up on the end of the table they weren't using. "Looks like you've been shopping."

"It's never easy to lose a computer."

"I hope you had everything backed up."

"I did."

"Thank God. But it still takes a while to recover so much information."

"That's no joke. It'll probably take most of the evening."

"You've got to be tired."

He was bone-tired, but not due to lack of sleep. He was struggling beneath an emotional load that was heavier than any he'd had to drag around before—except when he and Laurel had broken up. But that was back when he'd allowed himself to dull the pain with OxyContin.

There was no relief for this, except Eve's touch and smile and the warmth of her body beside him in bed.

"Did you file a police report?" she asked.

"I did. Not that it'll do me any good."

"They could catch the guys. Put them behind bars."

He hated to destroy her hope, but there was the crime—and then there was the practical side of the situation. "How long do you think they'd get for shooting out a few walls and light fixtures when rapists are typically sentenced to what…five, six years? And I can't give the police my contact information so—"

"Why not give them mine?" she broke in.

"That's the last thing I'd do."

She seemed surprised by his unequivocal response. "You don't think—"

"I wouldn't take the chance."

"You don't even trust the police?"

"The Crew has wives and girlfriends, sisters, uncles and cousins—not to mention parents, friends, former teachers and all the rest. They don't exist in a vacuum."

"Meaning…" She got out several cloves of garlic and the tomatoes so she could start dinner.

"They have a huge network, Eve. And all the people who love them feel some degree of loyalty, and hold various regular jobs. A few are probably even police officers or legal clerks or administrative assistants to various law enforcement agencies. You'd be surprised by the amount of information that flows into The Crew's organization. I was part of it, remember? I know how it works. I've only survived by playing it safe."

"But the police—"

"It was an insider who gave us away in the WitSec program. I learned my lesson the hard way—trust no one."

Lines appeared on her normally smooth forehead. "It's so frustrating that you're not getting the help you need."

"Gang violence is notoriously hard to stop. Look at it from this perspective—an average detective has worse crimes coming across his desk every day, murders for instance. And the victims have families call him up all the time, demanding justice. The police don't give a shit about the windows in my house when no one was actually hurt."

"*You* could've been hurt." Finished chopping the garlic, she looked up at him before grabbing the pan she needed. "You could've been killed. Someone should care about that."

"No. Not when I got myself into this mess."

"You had no idea what you were doing when you did it."

"It doesn't matter," he said, but he didn't want this conversation to continue. He'd spent eight years thinking about The Crew and cursing his situation. He'd had enough. He preferred to spend this one night focusing on the beautiful woman preparing him a home-cooked meal, so he changed the subject. "What can I do to help with dinner?"

She gestured to the box on the counter, which she hadn't emptied yet. "If you'll boil some water for the pasta, I'll make the sauce."

"I'm on it." The food was already beginning to smell good. He folded the sacks and held them up, a silent question as to where they should go.

She glanced over. "In there." She motioned toward a small pantry. "I hope you like artichokes," she said as he put them away.

"They're going in the sauce?" he called back.

"No. We'll start with some artichoke dip on crackers. Then we'll have a green salad and angel hair pasta with olive oil, tomato and garlic. I had Pam, at the inn, prep most of it, so we've got the dip and the salad. The rest won't take long."

"And for dessert?"

"I bought a big chocolate cake. And I have ice cream in the fridge."

He grinned. "Cake and ice cream? Sounds like we're celebrating your birthday again."

"No, we're definitely not."

She seemed preoccupied and distressed when he came up behind her. "Is there any chance you could do me a favor?" he asked, sliding his arms around her waist and pulling her against his chest.

At first she remained stiff, as if she was tempted to resist his touch. But as he kissed her neck, she softened and sank into him. "I'm almost afraid to ask what it is," she said.

"I don't want to talk about my problems tonight. I don't want to talk about my past or my family or what I'm going to do in the future. I just want this evening with you to…feel normal. Is that too much to ask?"

She set down the spatula she'd been using to brown the garlic and turned in his arms. She didn't say anything at first, just stared up at him. So he prompted her again. "Is it?"

"No," she said in a resolute tone. "That's not too much to ask. Fortunately, Victorian Days doesn't start until tomorrow, so I'm available."

"Victorian Days?"

She locked her hands around his neck. "It's a Christmas celebration the town hosts every year. We sing carols around the tree in the park and someone reads the story of Christ's birth. I open the inn and sell wassail and cookies, along with the ornaments from one of my trees. All the profits go to buy presents for the children of needy families. Then I wrap those presents, and my friend Kyle dresses up as Santa and delivers them to the individual houses a few days before Christmas. There are other vendors, too, who sell handmade items and other things. Quite a few people contribute. It's a lot of fun, something I look forward to all year."

"Sounds like it."

"But there's nothing going on tonight—unless you'd like to go over to Sexy Sadie's for a drink."

"I'm not looking for that kind of fun." His gaze fell to her mouth. "I just want a quiet night at home with you."

She seemed intent as she watched him. There was something serious going through her mind, but he didn't know exactly what it was and wasn't about to ask. He'd requested that this night not be spoiled by the dark things in his life.

"What do you say?" His heart was in his throat in case she rejected him. But she didn't. Taking his face in her hands, she stood on tiptoe and pressed her mouth to his.

# 24

Eve had planned to let Rex go over to Mrs. Higgins's after dinner. What with news of the baby, she had too much on her mind; she couldn't allow her feelings for him to complicate the decisions she had to make. So kissing him had been a mistake.

She should've known she couldn't stop there. Any contact with him was potent, so potent that, in almost no time at all, every thought of what would be best—even for her child—deserted her.

The baby wouldn't arrive for nine months. She'd figure everything out by then, she told herself. What they were doing was inevitable. They hadn't been able to keep their hands off each other from the first night they met. And that attraction hadn't gone away simply because she knew he had a checkered past. She wanted him in spite of that, and she suspected the season had a lot to do with it. At Christmas, everything seemed possible, all transgressions magically forgivable—at least if one wanted to be forgiven, wanted to change.

Or maybe that was just an excuse. Either way, she'd felt desire burn like fire through her veins the moment he'd met her at the car to help her with the groceries.

Trying to forget that pregnancy test—there'd be plenty

of time for that later—she let herself focus on how pliable and warm his lips were, how expertly he used his tongue.

"It's a good thing not all men kiss like you do," she said.

"It's just my kisses you like? And here I've been trying so hard to impress you with my other talents."

She liked a lot of things about him. The way he looked was certainly one of them. But just about any woman would admire such uncommon beauty. Mostly, she loved the way he made her feel, as if all was right with the world as long as he was with her. "I'm impressed by the whole package."

"I love it when you talk dirty."

"That was talking dirty?" she asked in surprise.

"My package likes you, too."

She laughed, which further eroded her resistance. "You make it impossible for me to even *think*."

"Then *don't* think," he said. "And I won't, either."

He'd asked for a night devoted just to enjoying each other, and she saw no reason not to give him that. "Dinner," she muttered, vaguely remembering she had something on the stove that would be ruined if she didn't attend to it.

He reached behind her and turned off the burner. "How hungry are you?" he breathed against her mouth. "Can you wait for fifteen or twenty minutes?"

"I want you more than I want anything else." She felt his arms tighten around her, felt his kiss grow more purposeful and intense.

"You smell delicious," he told her.

"I smell like garlic," she said.

"Exactly."

"Sounds like *you* might be too hungry to wait."

His mouth moved down her neck as his hands sought her bra clasp. "Maybe I'll have you for dinner."

"That sounds promising."

"Then help me get rid of some of these clothes."

He was making quick progress on his own. Her blouse was already in a puddle at her feet. "We should go into the bedroom," she said. "I don't have blinds on these windows. What if my parents come down the drive?"

"Do they pop in very often?"

"Not really. They don't like all the ruts between the two houses. But…still."

"Let me get some cake first." He rummaged around in the carton until he found the cake in its bakery box and scooped up a handful of frosting. Then he pulled Eve around the corner, out of sight of the windows and spread it on her breasts. "Damn, this is going to taste good," he said.

Eve dropped her head back as his mouth closed over her. It *felt* good, too.

Rex had used a condom. He hadn't asked whether she was pregnant from that first night. He'd just ripped open the package and rolled it on before he pressed inside her, and that was enough to tell Eve he was assuming she wasn't.

So she didn't tell him about the test she'd taken at the B and B, with Cheyenne hovering anxiously outside the bathroom. Didn't tell him the test had been positive.

After drifting off for a few minutes, he stirred next to her. "You awake?"

She was so warm and languid snuggled up against him that she didn't want to move. She wished they never had to get out of bed. "Yeah."

"Because you're hungry?"

"Not really."

"Then what are you thinking about?"

"That's a loaded question, what with all the topics that are taboo for tonight."

"Maybe. But you seem too pensive for a woman who should be satisfied and relaxed. I can't help being curious."

"You won't want to discuss it."

"If it's about certain parts of my life, that's very likely."

She'd been thinking about their baby and his comment that he'd be "terribly upset" if she was pregnant. But because she had certain topics she wanted to avoid, too, she touched one of the scars on his chest. "This. How'd you get it?"

"From a security job I never should've taken."

"What happened?"

He shifted so she could settle more comfortably on his chest and ran his fingers through her hair as he talked. "Believe it or not, I've never been shot by The Crew. They've tried to hurt me, but they've never succeeded. All these scars are from when I was trying to start my business."

"Does that make them fairly recent?"

"If you call three years ago recent."

"They're from *one* event?"

"Yeah. Just after I moved to San Francisco and started All About Security."

She raised herself onto her elbows. "These look like they were serious injuries. How is it that you didn't die?"

"I nearly did. Spent a month in the hospital."

She hated the thought of such a close call, hated that he was still in danger. "Was there anyone in San Francisco to support you?"

"Support me how?" He acted as though the concept itself was foreign to him. She'd already guessed that he'd been alone for too long but this confirmed it.

"Come to visit you. Encouraged you during your recovery."

A wry smile twisted his lips. "What a girlie thing to say."

She gave him a hard nudge. "You can be so sexist!"

"Calm down. That softer side is what I love about you."

"Then why are you making fun of it?"

"'Support' isn't the first thing I would've thought of if you'd told me *you* nearly died." He tweaked her chin. "So get that offended expression off your face. I actually didn't have anyone to rely on, just Marilyn, my assistant, and the two bodyguards I'd hired up until that point. They came by once or twice. Virgil would've flown out, but I wouldn't hear of it."

"He should've come, anyway."

"He has kids. It's not easy to leave them. And Peyton worries whenever he's gone—for good reason."

"What about your family? Dennis and Mike?"

He sobered. "They didn't know. Still don't."

*"You never told them?"* She couldn't imagine going through something like that on her own. Her friends and family had always been so important to her, such a big part of her life.

"No. They're aware of the basics, but not many of the details."

*"Why?"*

"It's complicated."

"Since you're leaving soon, you have nothing to hide, remember? You can be an open book with me."

"I don't know if I'll ever be an open book."

She gave an exasperated sigh. "Fine. You don't like to talk about your family. Then will you tell me why you took that particular job? The one that got you hurt? Were you desperate for work or—"

"No. I was getting by. I just agreed to a contract with someone I shouldn't have gotten involved with. He told me he owed some dangerous people quite a bit of money. He had the money and was going to pay them off, but he wanted me to go with him to make sure it went smoothly."

"I'm almost afraid to hear the rest," she said.

"It didn't turn out too pretty. What he'd told me wasn't true. It was actually some kind of high-stakes drug deal that went bad. As soon as we got to the drop, several other cars pulled up and a bunch of guys jumped us both. I managed to get the bastard I was protecting back into his car before he could get hurt, him and his money, and then the driver took off, as he'd been instructed to do."

She bit her lip, tense even though this was something that'd happened in the past. "They *abandoned* you? Did they at least call the cops so you could get some help?"

"Are you kidding? What could they say without explaining why we were there in the first place? And the fact that I'd salvaged the money royally pissed off the guys who were still left."

"How many men were there?"

"Had to have been eight." He rolled over to show her some of his other scars—as if she hadn't already made careful note. "I was shot three times and stabbed twice."

"That asshole who misled you! I hope he's rotting in prison somewhere."

"I have no idea where he is. The worst of it was that he never paid me. When I tried to reach him later, his number was disconnected. Haven't been able to track him down since."

"He'd probably be surprised to learn that you were even looking, that you're not dead."

"It's a miracle I didn't die. If not for some homeless guy who stumbled upon me while he was searching for a place to sleep, I would've bled out, no question. Even if it had gone another five or ten minutes."

"Where were you?"

"In the yard of some warehouse."

"He went for help?"

"That's what the cops told me later. All I remember is someone turning me over, realizing I was alive and backing away. The next time I opened my eyes, I was in a hospital bed."

The dangers of his job had been overshadowed by the threat he faced from his old gang, but Eve knew his job alone would be difficult for any woman to contend with. "I'm not sure I like what you do for a living," she said.

He pulled her down against him. "Normally it's not too bad. Now that I know I'm not invincible, I'm a little more careful about the assignments I accept."

"Don't you have other bodyguards you can send?"

"I do. But I have to be even more careful when I involve them."

"Of course." She didn't like the idea of him taking the most dangerous jobs, but she could understand why he wouldn't want to be responsible for getting someone else injured or killed. "Have you ever had one of your men get hurt?"

"Back when Virgil and I were in business together, one of our bodyguards took a bad beating. And more recently an employee of mine was stabbed while trying to get a client out of a bar. He needed reconstructive surgery on his shoulder. His wife made him quit."

"No wonder."

"It's a job best suited to single guys. That's what I've decided."

"Single guys like you."

He rolled her onto her back and stared down at her with those intense green eyes of his.

"What?" she asked.

"I don't think I've talked so much in years. I'm sure I've met my yearly quota. We'd better eat."

She smiled but grabbed his arm before he could get up. "Are you ever going to tell me why you're estranged from your family?"

His open, playful mood seemed to evaporate. "We're not talking about any of that tonight, remember?"

"It must've been something bad, Rex."

For just a second, she saw a heart-wrenching expression on his face and regretted bringing it up. "It was," he said, his mind obviously a million miles away—possibly reliving whatever it was.

"I should tell you something," she said to bring him back to the present.

His eyes focused again. "What's that?"

"The first time I called your brother's house—"

"The first time?" he broke in.

"I called twice."

"Because…"

"I was curious. Why else would I call? I knew you weren't telling me the truth."

"What I don't understand is how you got my brother's number in the first place. Did you take it out of my pocket?"

She grimaced. "No. I would never go through your pockets."

"You went through my hotel room."

"I *cleaned* your hotel room. There's a difference. And

I'd asked you to leave. If you had, none of your stuff would've been there."

That devilish grin she liked so much appeared on his face. "So it was my own fault?"

She felt the heat of a blush. "I didn't get into your bag or anything."

"There are *some* lines you won't cross, huh?"

Throwing off her embarrassment, she pulled him in for another kiss. "Maybe not anymore."

Her impulsive action seemed to surprise him.

"What? You didn't want me to kiss you?" she asked.

"Actually, I liked. I liked it a lot."

"Good." She stared up at him, caught in some profound moment she didn't quite understand.

"If you're trying to distract me, it's working," he said.

"Distract you from what? Dinner?"

"How you got my brother's number."

She sighed and let go of him. "It must've fallen out of your pocket, into the backseat of Noelle's car. She ran into me a few days after she brought us home and passed it along, said it belonged to you."

He adjusted the covers, which were tangled around their legs. "And you didn't return it because…"

"I told you. I was curious about your true identity." She wasn't sure whether to say what else was on her mind, but she thought it might help him in some way, comfort him, to know what she'd heard that day. "And my curiosity only grew once I spoke to someone I assume was your sister-in-law."

He stiffened. "Why? What'd Connie say?"

"That Dennis would want to talk to you. That he loves you. She begged you to call back when he wasn't in surgery. She's hoping to bring the family back together again."

He sat up. "She thought *I* was calling?"

"I didn't speak the first time."

"But why would I call and not say anything?"

"Because you're lonely?"

A muscle moved in his cheek. "What I am is hungry," he said. "Let's eat. I don't want to get over to Mrs. Higgins's too late. She has a hard time sleeping since her husband died."

Eve watched as he got up and started to dress. Those scars were proof of the wounds he'd suffered on the outside, but she suspected he'd been hurt far worse on the inside—and yet he showed no kindness to himself.

"Connie also said that no one holds you responsible for what happened to Logan," she added.

For a heartbeat, he froze. Then he said, "I hold myself accountable," and the ragged edge in his voice broke Eve's heart. She wanted to tell him that maybe it was time to forgive himself for whatever he'd done, that Christmas was here and soon after would come New Year's—a perfect time for fresh beginnings. But he was suddenly so aloof she wasn't sure she'd reach him. And she was afraid that trying would only push him farther away.

So she got up and put on her clothes—and went out to finish preparing dinner.

The meal they shared passed in quiet contentment. When Eve got up to get more bread or to pour him more soda, she often touched him. Once, she even came up from behind, wrapped her arms around his shoulders and pressed her cheek to his for a few seconds before picking up the bowl and ladling more pasta onto his plate. The evening felt…perfect, he decided. She was peaceful and calm, *whole* in a way few people were. And that relieved the obligation he often felt to try to make the lives of those around him better. With that burden gone, it was easier for him to take refuge from his own thoughts and feelings.

Even Laurel, as much as he'd loved her, hadn't been able to offer him the same emotional steadiness. She'd been through too much herself. Eve grounded him, and that gave him a chance to catch his breath, to clear his head, to finally feel…at rest.

"How do you think The Crew found you?" she asked when they were nearly finished.

He'd wondered that many times himself. "I can only assume they're checking every personal security company in America, looking for me and Virgil."

She tore off a piece of her garlic bread. "How do they know what business you're in?"

"We were in the same business in D.C. Stands to reason we'd stick to what we're familiar with. We both went to prison before we could graduate from high school. I got my GED while I was inside, but it's not like we have college degrees or any other experience to fall back on. We have to make money somehow."

Her eyes were troubled when she responded. "That means you won't be safe even if you leave Whiskey Creek. Or the state."

He took her hand, loving the way her fingers fit so comfortably between his. "If I change my identity, I should be fine. Gangs have practical concerns, too. The Crew can't send people out to get a visual on every body-guard in the country. That would cost them a fortune. I shouldn't have gone back to my first name. That's probably what tipped them off."

"Why did you?" she asked. "It's not like Rex is all that common."

"It gets old when you can't be yourself," he said with

a shrug. The renegade inside him had tempted fate. That was classic behavior for him.

She held her water glass loosely in her free hand. "So you'll change your name and move...where?"

"Don't know yet. Wherever I land. Coming back to California was another mistake. Virgil tried to talk me out of it, but...I wouldn't listen. It was my attempt to reclaim what I felt was mine, I guess. My name. My home. The Crew operates out of L.A., so I came north and thought that would put sufficient distance between us."

"Why didn't it? What went wrong?"

"Who knows? The only thing I can think of is that my discovery came from some prison inmate."

"How?"

"The Crew has members in prisons all over California. Some are probably even in the federal system by now, but that's beside the point." He brushed some crumbs off the table. "Anyway, say they have a member in San Quentin, right there by San Francisco. They could've got someone who was visiting that guy to find out if the owner of All About Security is the Rex they remember."

"But there's no address on your website. Your name isn't listed there, either. They'd have to start with that, wouldn't they?"

"They probably did. I'm guessing they randomly check security companies, hoping to get lucky. Maybe, for some reason, All About Security landed on their list of possibilities. All they would've had to do is have someone call in and act like a client. It wouldn't be unusual for a client to hear my name. Maybe someone they know went so far as to hire me and, at some point, took a picture they could compare to my mug shot. Boom. They have identification."

"That still doesn't give them your address."

"So maybe that client continues to work with me. I can't do security one night, so I assign one of my bodyguards. They become friendly, and the bodyguard casually mentions where the office is located."

"And then they wait outside and follow you home."

"There you go."

"But they came to your house in the middle of the night, after you were already home."

"They might have tried earlier and pulled out at the last minute because there were too many people around. I have neighbors who have kids. So they decided to hit late at night. Fewer witnesses and the cover of darkness gives them better odds of getting away."

"And then you left and came here."

"They weren't figuring I'd have my own mole. I'd received word that they were getting close, so I took off."

"So once they knew where you lived, they just sat tight."

"Assuming I'd be back eventually. Yes. They didn't know where I'd disappeared to, so all they could do was wait."

"Who tipped you off?"

"I had a friend who was still associated with them. She sent me a message to warn me."

"*Had* a friend?"

He waved her off. "You don't want to know."

She fell silent again. "There's nothing that could lead them to *this* area," she said at length.

"Not right now. I wouldn't be here if there was. I wouldn't endanger you."

"I'm saying you could probably stay, if you wanted to. How would they ever find you?"

"My money won't last forever, Eve. How would I get work?"

She didn't have a chance to answer. Her phone rang, distracting her. She ignored it and stood up to do the dishes. But then a text came in and, when she read it, he heard her gasp.

"What?" he asked.

"Cheyenne's having her baby!"

He'd just started carrying dishes to the counter. At this, he hesitated. "Is everything okay? I mean…she's close to her due date, right?"

"Her due date is the twenty-eighth, so she's about ten days early. I don't think that's anything to worry about, but…I hope she and the baby are going to be okay."

"Where is she going? Is there even a hospital around here?"

"Sutter Amador's in Jackson."

"Does she expect you to be there?"

"Of course. And I want to be. I'm sure all of us will go to support her."

"All of whom?"

"Our group of friends. That text was from Dylan. He would've alerted Kyle, Riley, Callie and the others, too."

"Will you go into the delivery room with her?"

"No. She can only have two people. Dylan and one other. They don't want a crowd getting in the way. Her mother was planning to be here, but she lives in Colorado and won't arrive until after Christmas. So now…"

He put the dishes in the sink. "Looks like that slot has opened up."

"Even if it has, her sister, Presley, moved back to town not long ago. She'll take it. I'll just wait in the lobby with the rest of our friends."

He stopped her as she was hurrying to retrieve her purse and find her coat. "Do you want me to go with you?"

Yes, because otherwise she was afraid he'd be gone by the time she got home. She hated that feeling of never knowing when he might decide to move on. But she was also nervous for her friend, afraid that something about the baby would give away Cheyenne's secret—a birthmark that only Aaron possessed or anything else that might make Dylan suspicious. She wasn't sure what Chey would do if the truth came out, couldn't imagine what she must be thinking now that the big day had arrived. Was she worried about the lie—well-intentioned though it was—that she was living? Even if she was, Eve couldn't do anything to soothe her fears. Cheyenne had made her promise not to bring up the subject of her baby's true paternity ever again. And Eve intended to fulfill that promise.

"If you don't mind," she said. "I'm so jittery I'm not even sure I can drive." The fact that she was pregnant probably had something to do with it. She'd be going through all of this come summer, only she'd be doing it *alone*.

"I don't mind," he said. "I like Cheyenne. Do you have everything you need?"

"I think so."

"Great. I'll drive you over."

# 25

Ted was the only member of their weekly coffee crew who didn't show up at the hospital. No one seemed to know where he was, and he hadn't been answering his phone, so when Sophia and her daughter, Alexa, came into the waiting room, Eve hurried over. "Ted's not coming?"

"He's going to hate missing this, but I'm afraid he's still out of town."

"I thought it would be a quick there-and-back trip," Eve said in surprise. He'd been gone for four days.

"No. He's learning a lot, but it's taking him all over the United States."

Eve smiled to reassure Sophia. Sophia was always a little tentative with her these days, but Eve had had a harder time forgiving Ted than Sophia. She hadn't been as close to Sophia. And Sophia had been through so much with her former husband that Eve couldn't blame her for wanting someone like Ted. What Skip had pulled when he tried to disappear and leave Sophia with all the debt he'd created was shocking. Eve couldn't believe that any man could be so selfish when it came to his wife and daughter. She was glad Sophia had finally found peace and happiness—even if it was, to some degree, at her expense. "Only Ted would be that thorough," she said.

The twinkle in Sophia's eye told Eve how proud she was of him. "Yes."

"I hope he can figure it out," Alexa added. "I've always wondered what happened to Mary. All the stories about her ghost…they sort of freak me out."

"Me, too," Eve admitted, and glanced at the clock. Cheyenne had been in labor for two hours.

"Has anyone called Gail?" Callie asked, joining them. "Or Baxter?"

"I assumed that Dylan got in touch like he did with us," Eve said, but she texted them to be sure, and Baxter called her almost immediately.

"So tonight's the big night?" he said as soon as she answered.

"It could be tomorrow. Labor can take quite a while, especially with a first baby."

"That's what Dylan said when he texted me, so I was planning to come in the morning. Do you think I'll miss it if I do?"

"There's no way to tell." Eve saw movement at the doorway and, hoping it was a nurse with some kind of update, glanced over.

It was Aaron. He walked in, holding his three-year-old son in his arms. His fiancée, Presley, was presumably in the delivery room with her sister. The three younger Amos brothers trailed after him. So did his father, his father's wife and her daughter.

Everyone said hello and tried to make room for the newcomers, but there weren't any more seats, so Rex got up, saying he was going to get something from the vending machine in the hall. Several pairs of eyes followed him, then looked questioningly at her, but Eve ignored their interest, grateful she was on the phone.

"Dylan's family just got here," she told Baxter.

"Including his father and his father's crazy bitch of a wife?"

It was hard not to laugh. Baxter rarely held back, and his frankness was often funny, because he was almost always right.

Turning away, she lowered her voice. "The whole gang." If Baxter knew that the real father of Cheyenne's baby was in the waiting room and not the delivery room, he'd die!

"I'm sure he'll be pleased to have their support."

This time she allowed herself to laugh at his sarcasm, but she sobered the second she glanced up and her eyes met Aaron's.

Was there a flicker of trepidation in them?

She thought so. Then his expression turned stoic and, after nodding hello, he pulled his gaze away. She figured he had to be at least as nervous as Cheyenne. From what Cheyenne had confided, he'd been reluctant to get involved in the artificial insemination. He'd only agreed because he felt he owed his older brother so much.

They had nothing to worry about, she told herself. Nothing could go wrong. Aaron looked like Dylan. All the arguments Cheyenne had used to justify her actions came to mind, but there was still that niggle of doubt, and it was enough to put Eve on pins and needles.

"Hello? You still there?" Baxter said.

Eve hadn't realized she'd let her end of the conversation lapse. She was holding the phone to her ear, but hadn't been listening to a word Baxter said.

She cleared her throat. "Yeah. Sorry. I got distracted."

"Not because the baby's been born…"

"No, not that we've heard."

"Then I'm on my way. I don't dare wait."

"I'm glad," Eve said. "It'll be good to have you with us."

There was a slight pause. Then he said, "Are Noah and Addy there?"

"Yes. But that doesn't matter because you're over Noah, right?"

"Of course. I got over him a long time ago."

She highly doubted that. He'd been in love with Noah for most of his life. Something with that kind of longevity wasn't going to disappear overnight. "Are you bringing Scott?" she asked.

"I don't think so. I don't want him nagging me to leave before I'm ready," he said, and hung up.

That brought up another issue—her concern over Scott and the lack of interest Scott showed in Baxter's lifelong friends—but she couldn't dwell on that right now. Until she saw Cheyenne's baby, Eve knew she'd have a knot in her stomach, and she guessed that Aaron, Presley and Cheyenne were every bit as terrified as she was.

Rex hovered around the periphery of the crowd that had gathered to support Cheyenne. He couldn't imagine having so many friends interested in his life that they were willing to spend the night in a hospital waiting room. Like he'd told Eve, when he'd been shot and stabbed and was fighting for his life in the weeks that followed, he'd had a couple of employees drop by once or twice, and that was it.

But he'd had to limit his social contacts, had to become a loner. And, for the most part, he functioned fine that way. It was only when he saw the contrast between his world and Eve's, saw how full life could, be, that he grew envious. That was when he wondered what he might've been like had he never taken Logan to the river that day. He'd been sixteen, so young and cocky.

Poor Logan had been even younger, only twelve.

*I made that jump myself last week...*

He cringed every time he remembered saying that, every time he remembered the admiration—and then the determination—on his baby brother's face. He *had* made that jump, more than once, but it didn't matter. Logan must've veered off to the left or the right or just landed oddly, and that one mistake had cost them everything. Sometimes the regret Rex felt was so tangible he nearly threw up.

"What are you doing?"

Eve had approached him where he was leaning against the wall. "Just waiting, like you." He offered her some of the coffee he'd been sipping. "You need a jolt?"

"No. I'm too jittery for caffeine. I can't drink it black, anyway."

"I can get you a cup of your own."

"It's okay. I'm bouncing off the walls as it is."

He studied her delicate features, the long sweep of her thick eyelashes, her dark hair with its dramatic widow's peak. "Don't be worried. Women have babies every day."

She glanced over her shoulder toward someone else in the room, seemed about to say something, then changed her mind. "There are things that could go wrong. But you must be exhausted after what you've been through. Do you want to leave so you can get some rest?"

"No, it's too late for me to go over to Mrs. Higgins's. Especially since she isn't expecting me. I don't want to give her a heart attack thinking someone's breaking into her house."

"Why not go back to my place?"

"And strand you here?"

She gestured at the room full of people. "I can get a ride."

He wanted to pull her to him, to rest his chin on her head and close his eyes for a few minutes. He would have, except he was already getting too many curious looks from the people he hadn't met until this evening. "I won't leave you."

"But it might be a while yet. I feel bad, now, that I asked you to come."

"It's fine," he insisted.

"What time is it?"

He checked his watch. "Midnight."

"Baxter should be here by now."

"*Baxter?* Is that the baby's name?"

She laughed. "No. That's a friend who's coming from San Francisco."

"As long as he arrives soon, he should make it. This baby doesn't seem to be in any hurry."

"A baby's always on its own clock."

Was *she* pregnant? As much as he'd tried to forget about the possibility, he couldn't entirely avoid it. She hadn't said anything when he'd used a condom since then, hadn't told him the effort was futile. But he had no idea what she was thinking. Neither of them had planned to be in their current situation.

"Will you be in here in nine months, doing the same thing?" He hadn't intended to ask. He'd told himself he'd leave without knowing, that he'd ask later, when he'd adjusted to the changes ahead of him. He wasn't any good for Eve. But the words had slipped out and they'd caught her unawares, too. Her eyes flew to his face and her lips parted, but before she could answer, Baxter walked in and, following a slight hesitation, Eve hurried off to greet her friend.

After that, there was too much commotion to talk about anything serious. Everyone was eager to catch up with the newest addition to the group. Then their friend Gail called from Los Angeles and she and her movie star husband spoke to everyone on someone's speakerphone. An hour or so after that, Baxter managed to separate himself from the others and walked over to the corner Rex and Eve were occupying.

Rex smiled because they'd already been introduced, but Baxter didn't speak directly to him. He gave Rex a once-over before shifting his attention to Eve. "This guy looks like he could model for Armani, doesn't he?"

Eve went a little red. Rex could tell she wasn't quite comfortable with Baxter's approach. "He's definitely handsome."

Rex wasn't quite comfortable with the compliment himself. He had no idea what to say. "Thank you" seemed awkward, since Baxter hadn't been speaking to him. But he couldn't exactly pipe up with something self-deprecating like "Yeah, well, you should see how screwed up my life is," either.

Fortunately, he didn't need to say anything because Baxter didn't give him the chance. "Where'd you find him? Because if he has a twin brother who happens to be gay I want his number."

*"What?"* Eve said. "You have a partner, remember?"

A hint of sadness entered his face, but he quickly masked it with a sneer. "Yeah, well, maybe not anymore."

Eve sobered instantly. "What does that mean?"

"Scott stormed out while I was trying to get packed so I could come here."

"Why?" Eve cried. "Did you get into an argument or—"

"It always causes an argument when I want to see you guys. He didn't want me to come. Said I should wait until morning, and then we would both drive out for a few hours to see the new baby."

"For a few hours," she repeated. "He doesn't like us."

"He doesn't like that you mean so much to me. And he *hates* staying with my parents."

"Do *you* hate staying with them? Because I could always give you a room at the inn, if there's an opening."

"I could never stay anywhere else. It would break my mother's heart. She doesn't understand that it's still a bitch to be around my father. He's trying so hard to be accepting—or at least his version of accepting, which isn't quite accepting at all."

Rex felt he shouldn't be part of such an intimate conversation. He'd barely met "Bax." But he couldn't walk away without seeming rude.

"Are you okay?" Eve asked.

Baxter nodded. "I'm fine. I think. Scott'll be back. Maybe."

"Do you really want him to come back if he's that possessive?" Rex asked. He wasn't sure where that had come from. He'd just decided he had no business contributing anything. But he saw how much these people meant to one another and hated to see any of them dragged away from the group.

Baxter didn't seem to mind that he'd involved himself. He glanced over his shoulder to where a guy named Noah was talking to his wife.

"It's better to be wanted than not, right?"

Eve clutched her friend's arm. "There's got to be someone out there who'll love you for you *and* embrace your family and friends," she said. But she didn't get the chance to say more. Dylan appeared in the doorway at that moment and announced that he was the proud father of a healthy, strapping nine-pound, two-ounce baby boy.

After everyone had clapped and hugged one another, Baxter wandered across the room, drawn in by the excitement—and probably eager to avoid the subject that had just been broached. Chaos took hold for a few minutes, until Dylan raised his hands for silence. Then he looked at his brother—Eve had clued Rex in on who was related to whom, but that one was pretty obvious—and choked up a little.

"Cheyenne insisted that I name the baby," he told everyone.

"So what's it going to be?" someone called.

"Kellan Aaron Amos," he replied. "Actually, she suggested Kellan because she saw it on some baby-name site and we both liked it, but…you know where I got the rest."

When Eve whispered, "Oh, God!" and her gaze cut across the room to Aaron, who went white as a sheet, Rex wasn't sure that honor was everything it was meant to be. But Dylan was so caught up in all the additional back-patting and good wishes, and assuring everyone that Cheyenne had come through labor and delivery like a champ, he didn't seem to notice.

The awkward moment passed so quickly Rex was almost convinced he'd imagined it.

When they finally left the hospital, it was after four. Eve was tired but happy. She'd had a chance to see her best friend, who looked relieved and every bit the excited new mother. Eve had also had the chance to hold the baby, who'd been so exhausted from the ordeal of his birth that he'd hardly whimpered.

After that, everyone had taken turns holding Kellan. Even Aaron had held his namesake, although Eve hadn't gotten the impression he was too thrilled when Dylan thrust the baby into his arms. He'd smiled and congratulated his brother but passed the newborn off as soon as possible.

Eve had glanced at Cheyenne, but Cheyenne had refused to look back at her. She'd kept a stubborn smile on her face as if nothing was wrong—as if she genuinely believed the baby was Dylan's and nothing would ever convince her otherwise. And Presley had rested a reassuring hand on her shoulder.

Eve supposed that was how Cheyenne would have to handle what had to be a trying situation. It was too late to tell Dylan now. For better or for worse, she'd made the decision and would have to keep the secret for the rest of her life.

After the first few months, maybe it would get easier. It would *have* to get easier—

"Why did you say what you did when Dylan announced the name of his son?" Rex asked as they walked from his rental car to her house.

That made her miss a step, but she acted as if the loose gravel in the drive had caused it. "I was…happy for Aaron, you know?"

"'Oh, God' is happy?"

"In this case."

"How so?"

She wasn't sure how she was going to explain her reaction, but to keep her promise to Cheyenne, she had to try. "The two brothers have an interesting history. They haven't always gotten along."

"What's interesting about that? The same can be said for most brothers."

"In this case, there've been some…extenuating circumstances. When they were young, their mother killed herself. Dylan's father couldn't handle it. He started drinking, let his business go and eventually got into a brawl at a bar in the next town, where he stabbed a guy who ended up dying."

"This place seems far too innocent for that."

"People are people. They make mistakes and create problems. It's the same wherever you go."

"So Dylan's father wound up in prison."

"He did. For a good long while. And that meant Dylan had to take over as head of the household when he was only eighteen, or his four younger brothers would've been split up and put into foster care."

"His father was there tonight, wasn't he? Didn't you introduce us?"

"Yes." She got out her keys to let them in.

"When was he released?"

"Last summer. Everyone's been trying to adjust ever since."

He held the door so she could pass through. "How did he meet that woman he's with?"

"Anya?"

"I couldn't remember her name, but she seems a bit young for him."

"She is, and they fight like crazy. Dylan thinks she only stays for the free rent. And she claims he's good in bed." She grimaced to show her distaste. "Which is information we'd all rather not have, of course. Dylan and his brothers don't know what to do with her. They'd kick her out—they'd probably like to kick their father out, too—except they feel sorry for Anya's daughter. The poor girl doesn't stand much of a chance with that mother dragging her down."

He locked up and checked the house to make sure it was secure. That reminded her of the danger he was in, but it also felt protective, as if he belonged in her house and had taken responsibility for her in some way he hadn't before.

"There isn't always a correlation," he said as he followed her to the bedroom. "I had a good mother."

"You're saying how you turned out is not her fault?"

"That's exactly what I'm saying."

"You're not very generous to yourself."

"I'm honest."

She thought he was far too hard on himself. But she was so surprised that he'd volunteered anything about his family, she focused on that instead. "Tell me about her."

He didn't avoid the question as he usually did. "She was tall, thin, beautiful. My father adored her. We all did." He shook his head. "She lived with a houseful of boys, each more eager than the last to protect her." He was silent for a second, then finished more softly. "Which is why it tears my heart out every time I think of how badly I hurt her."

She moved closer to him. "Like I said before, everyone makes mistakes, Rex. We *all* need second chances."

He shrugged off her hand as if he couldn't bear her kindness. "That sounds good—in theory. But some things can't be fixed."

"Sometimes the hardest person to forgive is ourselves."

He took off his shirt. "That might be true. But forgiving myself wouldn't be quite so hard if I hadn't caused so much damage. I can't blame my family for how they feel toward me. I earned that—and more."

She unbuttoned her own blouse. "But isn't that where love comes in? Love can compensate for anything." They hadn't bothered to turn on the light, but she could see the gleam in his eyes from the light spilling into the room and wondered what he was thinking. But he didn't answer her; he just walked over and slid his arms around her waist, and she rested her cheek against his chest.

"You make me feel…"

"What?" she prodded when he let his words trail off.

"Fresh hope," he said.

She wasn't sure how to take his response. Those words should have given her some reassurance. But he'd said it as if that was the most attractive and yet painful thing of all.

# 26

The following morning, Rex was up and working on his computer when Eve's alarm went off. She saw him at the kitchen table when she shuffled out to pour a glass of orange juice. She could smell the coffee he'd made, and wanted a cup, but had, of course, given it up for the pregnancy.

Just as she entered the kitchen, she realized it was Sunday, her day off, and she didn't need to get up quite so early. "Damn."

He glanced up. "What is it?"

"It just occurred to me that I could've turned off my alarm last night, but I forgot to."

"No work this morning?"

"I switched a few shifts around at the inn so I can be there for Victorian Days tonight."

"How long does that run?"

"Four days—Thursday through Sunday. What have you been doing this morning?"

He grimaced at his computer screen. "Trying to finish restoring all my files and taking care of a few things for Marilyn."

"She's your assistant, right?"

"Yeah. With me gone, she's having to backfill a job I

had this week. Christmas is a busy time of year. Lots of events that require security."

"Did you tell her you were going to close down the office and relocate?"

He had his hair pulled back with one of her ties again, which accentuated his good bone structure. "No. I can't give her bad news during the holidays."

"It must be hard to let your employees go." She knew what that felt like. When she was struggling to stay afloat, she'd had to consider laying off Pam and working those additional hours herself. In the end, she hadn't been forced to do that, but it had been a close call. "Do you think one of them might be able to buy the business?"

"No one has much money. It's not like they could give me a down payment. But I've got some savings, so maybe they could just make payments." He pursed his lips. "I'll see if one or more of them might be interested. Marilyn's husband has a good job, which gives her some security. Maybe she'll do it. She certainly knows how to run the place. The only problem would be the loose threads…."

"What loose threads?"

"The money could be traced to wherever I go next." He sat back and stretched out his legs. "And this is it, Eve. Wherever I go, this is the last time. I can't start over again."

The fatalistic note in his voice concerned her. "There's got to be some way to make the arrangements."

"I'll check it out, see what I can do. But…I don't want to leave anyone vulnerable. Come take a look at this."

Nervous about what she might see, she edged around the table as he fiddled with a video on his computer. When it started, she realized immediately what it was. The Crew, trashing his house. Those few minutes had been recorded by security cameras. One hooded intruder even spun around to a camera, giving it the finger and then took a baseball bat to the walls and windows.

It was one thing to hear about what had happened, quite another to see it. "They're filled with hate," she murmured.

"Only my death will satisfy them."

She couldn't watch anymore. These images made her sick. She turned away, but he caught her hand and gave her an imploring look.

"What?" she said.

"Aren't you going to tell me?" he asked.

She knew that he was talking about whether or not she was pregnant. She hadn't let herself think about the baby. The realization of how much her life would change, and what those changes would involve, crept into her mind in the quiet moments—like before she fell asleep. She couldn't ward them off forever. Sometimes she'd feel a trickle of excitement, sometimes a trickle of unease. But there was no going back now. She had to take one day at a time, and right now she was falling in love with the father of her baby, despite the fact that he was a man she couldn't have.

Even if they could figure out a way to be together, he might not be able to love her as deeply as she wanted. She had to face the possibility that he'd been through too much, was too damaged.

There had to be someone less complicated out there. Someone who could help her build a good life without the serious challenges Rex faced.

Maybe, but her heart argued with her constantly, always taking his side.

"Are you sure you want to know?" she asked.

His eyes probed hers, searching for the answer. "It'll

be easier to move on if I'm not aware of everything I'm leaving behind."

"Of course."

"But you would've told me if you weren't."

She bit her lip. "Are you upset?"

Her question served as confirmation, of course. If she wasn't pregnant, what would he have to be upset about?

Dropping his head into his hands, he began to massage his temples.

"Rex?"

"I'll cover the cost of the delivery—the doctor and the hospital and whatever else you need. And I'll send you money every month."

Eve lifted her hand. "I don't want you to do it because you feel obligated."

"That's not it. I want to participate in some way."

"Why?"

"I will not leave it all on you," he replied. Then he lowered his voice. "And I want to be a better father than I've been a son."

He needed to succeed at something besides business. Eve understood that. Maybe being a father would help him heal, help him understand how a parent could still love a child who made mistakes, even serious ones.

"Okay," she said, and bent to kiss his head.

Ted came over while Eve was making breakfast. She hesitated when she saw him at the door, wasn't sure whether he'd be civil to Rex, but ultimately let him in. She couldn't turn away one of her best friends. He'd just spent several days, and probably a couple thousand dollars, tracing down Harriett Hatfield's descendants for the benefit of her B and B and the other historical buildings in town.

When he strode into the kitchen, she held her breath. She wanted to warn him that he'd better be polite, but that would probably do more harm than good.

Fortunately, Ted nodded at Rex in greeting and Rex, tentatively, did the same.

"I didn't realize you had company," Ted said. "Where's the Land Rover?"

"Rex is driving a rental car," Eve said. "He parks it down the street."

A muscle moved in Ted's jaw. "He's called Rex now, is he?"

Eve felt her pulse pick up. "That's his real name."

"I see. And he parks down the street because…"

She could feel the tension in him, the disapproval, so she grinned, hoping to get him to lighten up. The contrast between what she was about to say and the gang-banger Rex used to be was sort of funny. "He's a little old-fashioned."

"I don't want to offend your parents," Rex clarified with a scowl.

Ted gave her a pointed look. "They don't know he's here?"

"Sure they do," she said. "They've seen us come and go. We've even waved at them a couple of times and stopped to talk."

"I'm not hiding from them," Rex snapped. "I just don't want to rub their noses in the fact that I'm sleeping with their little girl. To me, that's rude."

Ted placed his hands on his hips. "Am I supposed to be impressed by how considerate you are?"

"Ted!" Eve exclaimed.

He turned to her. "Why is this guy still here, Eve? You know he's been lying to you. First he's Brent. Now he's Rex? Is *that* even his real name?"

"Yes!"

"But if he can't marry you, be the kind of husband and father you want, why are you wasting your time with him?"

Rex shoved his chair back so hard it hit the wall. "Maybe I'm just that good in bed."

Anger flashed in Ted's eyes. "Or maybe you don't care about the damage you cause, as long as you get what you want."

Before Eve could intervene, Rex stepped right up to him. "Did anyone ask for your opinion?"

Eve had never known Ted to come up against someone who seemed as volatile as Rex did in that moment but, surprisingly, he didn't back down. "This is bullshit. Eve's one of my best friends."

"Guys, come on." Eve's heart pounded for fear this little confrontation would get worse. "Please, don't be assholes, either of you."

Ted turned to appeal to her. "You're not really going to throw your life away on this guy, are you?"

"Like I said, there are things you don't know. Just… please, calm down and be polite," she said, but it was too late to smooth over what had happened. Rex glared at Ted for several long seconds. Then he shut down his computer, grabbed his keys off the counter and walked out.

The slamming of the door echoed in the sudden silence.

"*Why* did you do that, Ted?" Eve started to go after Rex, then stopped. She knew it would be futile but was frightened by the thought that, even though some of his clothes were here, Rex might not return. It would be so easy for him to get into his rental car and disappear. So what if he left a few more things behind? He'd left much more in San Francisco.

How many times had he been forced to start over? He was used to it.

When he saw her distress, Ted began to pace, wearing a tortured expression. "Damn it, Eve. I don't want to create a problem between us. I really don't. But I let you down so badly last year. I can't let you get involved with the wrong guy. It could ruin your life!"

"How do you *know* he's the wrong guy?"

"You're joking, right?" He stared at her.

"You don't know him," she argued. "Not like I do."

"What I know about him is enough." He turned to the window, watching Rex stalk down the drive.

"I'm already in love with him, Ted," she said. "Nothing you can do is going to save me now."

With a curse, he banged his head against the glass. "Of course," he muttered to himself.

Eve took a deep breath. "Not only that but…I'm pregnant."

*"What?"* At this, he whipped around, pulled out a chair and sank into it. "Please tell me that isn't true."

"Rex isn't what you think."

"Exactly my point!" he cried. "He's not what any of us think! He hasn't told us a scrap of truth since he came here."

Smelling smoke, Eve hurried over to the stove, where she shoved the pan in which she'd been frying sausages off to one side. She'd forgotten it, already burned them. "He's had a shitty life, Ted. He deserves more."

"And you think you can give him that? *You* can change him, heal him, save him, when no one else has been able to do it?"

It might sound unrealistic, but all he needed was a chance to settle down, to redeem himself. He could achieve that with some consistency and unconditional love. "Everyone needs help once in a while." She folded her arms as she leaned against the counter. "Well, everyone except you. You've always done everything right. And it can be a little sickening to the rest of us."

He scowled at her. "Don't pull that bullshit on me. You've never done anything wrong in your life. Until now."

"*Someone* has to care about him!"

"I'm sure many women have tried."

"Don't! He's a good man. He may have made some mistakes, but he's been through hell, and it's time for that hell to stop."

"How can *you* stop it?"

"I'm not sure, but I'd like to try."

"You can't do anything if he won't tell you his real situation. Why's he here? What's he running from? Who's looking for him?"

She didn't want to tell anyone else about Rex's reality. She understood the need for extreme secrecy. But when it came to this type of confidence, she trusted Ted's discretion as much as Cheyenne's. "I'm aware of all of that," she said, and poured herself some more juice before sitting down to explain.

"What you just told me is supposed to *comfort* me?" Ted blurted out when she was done. "Learning that he's an ex-con who's got a dangerous prison gang after him? That you could get *killed* simply by being with him? God, Eve!"

"He was eighteen when he was put away, Ted. Eighteen! Do you remember how stupid we were at that age? And there was some…incident, something that hurt him so badly he can't talk about it to this day. Whatever it was sent him spiraling out of control, and that's why he turned to drugs."

"He was a dealer!"

"He was trying to support his own habit. It was the only way to anesthetize himself against the pain."

"Pain caused by an event you know nothing about."

"I told you! He won't tell me what set him off. But can you imagine how hard it would be, once you're on that path, to put your life together again? And yet he's managed to do it—as much as The Crew will let him."

Ted drummed his fingers on the table as he considered what she'd told him. "Does he know you're pregnant?" he asked.

She shifted uncomfortably. "Yes. I told him this morning, just before you walked in."

He cursed under his breath and shook his head.

"Don't do that," she said. "Don't go all muttery and disapproving. What, exactly, are you thinking?"

"You don't want to know," he grumbled.

"Yes, I do."

With a sigh, he stood up. "I'm thinking it'll be a miracle if he comes back so what the hell am I worried about."

When she flinched, he put a hand on her shoulder. "I'm sorry. When you want to hear about my trip, and who I think killed Little Mary, give me a call," he said. Then he walked out.

# 27

Although Eve was dying to learn what Ted had discovered, she had too much pride to call him, especially when Rex didn't come back that day. She knew Ted would ask if she'd heard from him. So she tried not to think about the murder that had cast such a long shadow over her family's B and B. He probably hadn't dug up anything definite, anything that would answer her questions, or the truth would have come out before now.

She'd always loved Victorian Days, more than all the other festivities that preceded Christmas. But her heart wasn't in it this year. She couldn't find it in her to care about the decorations or the food or the parties— all the things she usually enjoyed. But it wasn't only the holidays. She wasn't even paying attention to her occupancy rate, which was something she always watched very closely.

She just wanted to be with Rex.

At five o'clock, she forced herself to change her clothes and hurry over to the inn. But she should've been there much earlier.

"What's going on?" Pam asked when she entered the kitchen.

A deluge of guilt hit Eve for stranding her staff with all

the work, since they weren't used to performing without direction and support. Normally, everything had to have her touch. The inn was a showcase, especially at Christmas. "I don't know what you mean. I've been really busy today," she muttered to stave off the inevitable questions.

Cecelia came out of the pantry with a platter of their signature sugar cookies decorated like snowmen. "There you are! What's up? This time of year, you spend all day here, helping us bake. I tried calling but could never reach you."

Eve had seen those calls come in. She'd ignored them, which she'd justified by telling herself that her employees had it easy. Most of the time that was true. She was more of a workhorse than any of them, but she could at least have given them some idea of when she'd arrive. "I had complete faith that you guys would do a fabulous job."

Pam and Cecelia exchanged a look that suggested this was not the response they'd expected, that they couldn't believe she wasn't rushing around, tweaking everything they'd done.

"Cheyenne had her baby last night," she told them, partly to get out from under the magnifying glass through which they seemed to be studying her.

"Seriously?" Cecelia cried. "I hadn't heard."

In previous years, she'd had only one of them help her through Victorian Days, to avoid a lot of overtime when her employees were the least likely to want to put in those hours. Cheyenne worked with her for free, for the sake of the charity. But with her best friend so pregnant, she'd asked Pam, Cecelia *and* Deb to be on hand, and now she was glad she'd done that. She'd had no idea Cheyenne would go into labor early.

Pam removed the plastic covering the cookies. "What'd she have?"

"A baby boy. Weighed nine pounds, two ounces."

Cecilia smiled. "Wow. That's a big baby."

"So *that's* where you've been," Pam said. "Makes sense now. How's she feeling?"

Eve didn't correct her. She'd stopped by the hospital to visit, but much more briefly than they assumed. "Great. The baby's doing great, too. She'll stay over one more night—"

"Why?" Cecelia broke in, her face creased with concern. "Nothing's wrong…"

"No. She had the baby in the middle of last night, so she hasn't been there twenty-four hours yet. Her insurance covers forty-eight, so she's going to take advantage of that."

"Good. Maybe she'll be able to get some rest," Pam said. "My first baby was so colicky I couldn't get three hours of sleep in one stretch."

"Hopefully, little Kellan won't have that problem." Eve genuinely wished Cheyenne the best, but she'd had a hard time acting like herself when she'd been at the hospital earlier that day. She'd brought a plant and a card, then promised to call or text everyone on Cheyenne's guest list to let them know she'd had the baby early and wouldn't be having the Christmas party this year. The whole visit lasted only a few minutes, since she left with the excuse that she needed to get ready for Victorian Days.

But she hadn't gone directly to the B and B afterward. She hadn't returned home, either. She'd driven aimlessly around town, past Mrs. Higgins's and Just Like Mom's and any other place she thought Rex might be, which had turned out to be a waste of time. She hadn't found any trace of him.

*I'm thinking it'll be a miracle if he comes back…*

Was he gone for good?

"Eve?"

She blinked as Deb held out another tray of cookies. "Um, shouldn't we set these out?"

"Definitely." Assuming her usual sense of purpose, she took the tray and headed to the front. Fortunately, her staff had cleaned the inn from top to bottom, and all the Christmas lights were on and twinkling. The B and B was beautiful, even without all the extra attention she gave it. She loved it here, loved her work. And yet none of it meant what it had before, not since meeting Rex.

"I've got to snap out of it," she murmured.

"Did you say something?"

Eve turned from where she'd been putting down the platter. Sophia had come in. "No, sorry. Just…talking to myself."

"I came to volunteer. I figured that, with Cheyenne in the hospital, you could use some help tonight. The inn is such a focal point during Victorian Days."

Sophia could be thoughtful. Eve had to give her that. "How nice, but I'm fairly certain that we have it covered."

Sophia leaned a little closer. "Ted told me about this morning, Eve. I'm sorry. He feels terrible about it. He doesn't want to make you unhappy. He just…feels so protective."

"You mean he still feels guilty because he dumped me for you."

She winced. "Don't use that word. He didn't *dump* you. That's not how *I* look at it."

"Really?" Eve crossed her arms. "Then maybe you wouldn't mind explaining how you see things. I've always wondered."

Sophia clasped her hands in front of her. Since Ted and Sophia had appeared on her doorstep last Christmas to apologize, whenever they were around Eve simply pretended she and Ted had never been together. But that almost made it more awkward than addressing the reality. "I prefer to think that…that for whatever reason, Ted and I were meant to be together, and I'm grateful to you for being as gracious as you were when we…we realized our feelings for each other."

"I doubt that if I'd chosen to be less gracious, it would've made any difference," she said with a humorless laugh.

"That's not true," Sophia argued. "Your feelings mattered a lot to both of us. They still do." She clutched Eve's forearm. "You were kind to me when I had no one else, when I couldn't fall any lower. I will never forget that."

Impulsively, Eve hugged her. So what if the uncertainty of her current situation triggered memories of the rejection she'd suffered before? It was selfish to let what was happening in *her* life adversely affect her friends. "Don't worry about me. I'm fine. I'm just…"

"Pregnant?"

Sophia finished her sentence when Eve couldn't find the words to explain the angst and longing that were making her so miserable.

Eve glanced behind her. She didn't want anyone else hearing that, didn't want it getting back to her parents before she was ready to break the news to them herself. But the two of them were alone, and Sophia had spoken softly. "Ted told you about that, too?"

Sophia nodded. "Are you excited or scared or—"

"I can't say yet," Eve responded. "There's so much going on in my head and my heart. But…it'll be a good thing, no matter what happens."

"Of course it will. Just…know you won't have to go through it alone. I'll do whatever I can to make life easier. Help out here at the inn. Go to doctor's appointments with you. Babysit after the baby's born. You'll have Cheyenne's help, too, of course, but with her being a new mother and all, you might need someone else, and I want you to know I'll be happy to do anything I can."

She was *so* sincere. "That's a lot to offer when you'll probably be having a baby of your own soon." Eve couldn't help remembering Ted's statement to Cheyenne when they were feeling her baby move.

"I'm thinking we should put it off for a year or so, get you through this first."

Her response brought tears to Eve's eyes. "I've never heard *anything* so generous."

"You saved me that night you came over after Skip's death, Eve. Thanks to you, I'm so much happier—and able to offer my daughter the security she needs. I can't tell you what that means to me. I'll do anything for you. I promise."

"Then maybe you'll tell me what Ted found out on his trip," she teased.

"He didn't tell you this morning?"

Eve made a face. "We didn't get that far."

"It was Harriett."

*"What?"*

"Yes. Ted said it was John's descendants who had a story to tell, not Harriett's. John's great-nephew, a man by the name of Patrick Hatfield, claims Harriett killed Mary."

After believing John was the culprit for so many years, Eve had a hard time grasping this new theory. Harriett had told her sister he was innocent, but Eve hadn't really believed that. "Why? What would ever make a mother do something like that?"

"What makes mothers do that kind of thing these

days? Depression? Mental illness? Extreme narcissism? Rage?"

"Which was it?"

"We don't have all the details. It was just a fluke that Ted managed to locate Pat."

"I can't imagine Mary's descendants kept track of the Hatfields. So how did he do it?"

"It's convoluted, but the husband of one of Mary's cousins went to college with Pat for a year. They even played rugby together on weekends—never realizing they had a family connection until it came up one day. So when Ted contacted Mary's relatives, they put him in touch with Pat. To make the story even more spectacular, Pat lives in London now. He married a woman who was born there. But he makes documentaries and was in Toronto on a project. So Ted talked him into a quick meeting and flew up there to speak to him."

"Sounds like it was worth the time."

"It was. Pat says that Harriett was never quite right in the head, that John protected her and took care of her for years. He didn't feel he had any other alternative. He couldn't bear the idea of a woman going to prison. Back then, most people didn't believe that women could really be that terrible. And he thought an insane asylum would be even worse."

*"Despite what she did?"*

"Apparently she tried to warn him that she didn't like her own child, that she was jealous of his love for Mary and didn't want Mary in the house. He thought it was just more of the crazy things she sometimes said, never suspected she'd act the way she did. When she was herself, she was a wonderful person. But, according to what he told his brother, she had these dark moods. He didn't know what they were all about or how to get her the help she needed. Things back then weren't like they are today when it comes to depression and mental illness, you know? So John handled the situation the best he could, by keeping her separate from other people, making sure she couldn't harm anyone else."

"No wonder everyone thought he was the bad guy. He took total control of her. But…people reported seeing bruises on the rare occasions when she did get out."

"It probably became difficult, at times, to keep her under control. Maybe she tried to slip out, and he had to physically hold her down. Or her behavior frustrated him so much his temper occasionally boiled over. I'm not saying he was a saint. But he wasn't a murderer. From what Ted heard, she might even have hurt herself. She tried that sometimes."

"So why would she burn his train set?"

"Ted wondered the same thing. He thinks it reminded her of the basement and what she'd done."

"What a tragic situation." Somehow Eve found it worse to imagine Harriett as the culprit than John. Poor Mary!

"In every way," Sophia agreed. "That Harriett could do it, and that John would not only have to bear the grief of Mary's loss but care for a woman who was mentally ill for the rest of his life."

"John held the truth so close. Why did he finally tell his brother?"

"He had to. Once he fell down the stairs and broke his hip, he knew he might not be able to act as her guardian. If he died, someone had to take care of her, had to know she couldn't be trusted around children." She paused. "Willard, John's nephew, and his wife, Betsy, took over the house—with the stipulation that they look after Harriett."

"So she ran away because she feared she couldn't rely on his nephew to be kind to her?"

"It's possible he wouldn't have been. He was considerably younger, and he and Betsy were newly married. Anyway, that's what Ted believes."

"Wow." Eve shook her head. "Is Ted going to put all of this in his book?"

"He is. The pieces finally fit together. He won't be able to present any forensic proof, of course, but he'll do what he can to clear John's name—for Patrick and John's other descendants, and Mary, too."

Was that what Mary had been waiting for? Would the strange noises and disturbances now stop? Either way, Mary had died just before Christmas. Somehow it was fitting that the truth had finally come out at Christmastime.

"Thanks for everything," Eve said. "And please tell Ted how much I appreciate what he's done. The truth, despite its sadness, does bring some closure."

Sophia winked at her. "Maybe you'll call later and tell him yourself."

When Eve nodded, Sophia squeezed her hands and left.

Pam came out of the kitchen carrying the heated container of wassail. "I hope we get a good crowd tonight," she said.

Feeling teary-eyed, for Mary's sake and because of the friendship Sophia had just shown her, Eve averted her face and pretended to smooth a wrinkle out of the tablecloth. "I'm sure we will."

"It's been so hectic this season I haven't really taken the time to enjoy it," Pam said. "But I'm feeling the Christmas spirit tonight."

Although Eve couldn't look up—she didn't want Pam to see that her eyes were wet—she had to agree. This evening was dedicated to raising money for children who wouldn't get anything for Christmas otherwise. That, along with John's long-ago sacrifice for his mentally ill wife and Sophia's sacrifice in offering to put off having her own child, even though Eve would never encourage her to do that, was what Christmas was all about.

Rex watched Eve from a distance. She'd spent most of the evening in the front parlor at Little Mary's, providing hot drinks and cookies and nodding and smiling at everyone who visited her inn. He knew because the place was lit up with all the Christmas lights and, from where he was leaning against his rental car down the street, he'd been able to spot her occasionally through the window, milling about in the crowd. Her parents had been there for a while, too. Now that it was getting late, and there weren't many people left, she'd come out to enjoy the celebration herself. Arm in arm with Callie Something—he couldn't remember Callie's last name but she was one of the people he'd met in the hospital waiting room—Eve meandered from booth to booth.

"Hey."

Startled to hear a voice so close to him, Rex twisted around to see another of Eve's friends coming up from behind. He'd met so many people when Cheyenne had her baby, he couldn't remember the name of this guy, either. "Hi."

"Sort of removed from the action, aren't you?"

"Guess so."

"Why are you standing over here in the dark?"

"I'm waiting for Mrs. Higgins. I gave her a ride and I'll need to take her home." Some of the vendors were beginning to pack up. He didn't think it would be much longer before Mrs. Higgins was ready to leave.

"I'm Kyle." The other guy stuck out his hand. "We met last night."

"Yes. I remember." Rex shook hands with him, then leaned against the car again.

"My ex-wife is Noelle Arnold."

That was one name Rex wasn't likely to forget. "I'm sorry."

"I see you're familiar with her," Kyle said with a chuckle.

"I am."

"She mentioned that you and Eve, er, met at Sexy Sadie's, but I didn't realize you were…you know, actually seeing each other until last night."

Were they seeing each other? At this point, Rex would probably describe it more as a series of hit-and-runs. He knew he should leave her alone but couldn't stay away. "I won't be in town for long."

"Eve hasn't met up with us in three weeks. I feel as if I'm out of the loop on what's going in her life."

"Met up with *us?* You mean you and Noelle?"

"No. Eve and I belong to a group of friends who have coffee together every Friday at Black Gold."

Rex nodded, thinking it must be nice to have such a strong network. These days, people didn't stay put the way they used to, so something like that was rare. "Only in Whiskey Creek."

Kyle didn't seem to know how to take the comment. "You don't like it here?"

"I do. It's like…a snow globe," he said, voicing what he'd often thought of the place.

Kyle laughed. "Is that why you're standing over here, just watching everyone?"

He was standing to the side because he didn't belong,

could never belong, and didn't want to disrupt the lives of those who did. "No need for me to get in the way."

"Of the party?" he said with a scowl.

Of Eve's life, of everything she had to look forward to. When he drove out of San Francisco for the last time, he'd planned to stay only one or two nights, long enough to buy some clothes and get another computer. But he'd paid rent at Mrs. Higgins's through December. Given the fact that money might become extremely tight until he could get his business up and running again, he figured he should conserve where possible. What was the difference between leaving now or after Christmas?

"Of the relationships here," he replied.

"We're not as unfriendly to outsiders as we might seem." Clasping Rex by the shoulder, Kyle dragged him out of the shadows and into the flow of pedestrians.

Rex could smell alcohol on Kyle's breath and suspected the guy was a bit tipsy. But he wasn't falling-down drunk, and Rex couldn't help feeling a sense of relief at encountering a little friendliness.

"How 'bout we get you a drink?" Kyle said.

They stopped at a vendor selling beer, but before Rex could order, Kyle noticed that Eve wasn't far away and called out to her. "Hey, Harmon! Look who I found."

When Eve glanced up, she said something to Callie, who nodded and called Kyle over. A second later, they walked off, leaving her to approach him alone.

"I wondered if you were going to show up tonight," she said.

He offered her a lopsided smile. "Mrs. Higgins wouldn't hear of me staying home and missing the celebration."

She looked around. "Where is she?"

"I drove her here, but as soon I parked, she got out and

hurried off to help with some quilt for an orphanage or something. I haven't seen her since."

"That quilt is actually for our 'Sub for Santa' project. She and the other members of the historical society sew one every year."

"Nice."

"Yeah." Eve rubbed her hands against the cold. "Does that mean you're staying at her place?"

"For the time being."

"Because…"

"It's for the best, Eve. Don't pretend it's not."

"So that's it?"

"Better now than later. It'll only get harder."

She considered him for several seconds. Then she said, "Tell me something."

He met her gaze a bit reluctantly. "What's that?"

"Is it really your situation that's got you running so scared? Or is it that I'm going to have your baby?" She started to walk away, but he grabbed her arm.

"I'll still pay, if that's the problem."

"That's definitely *not* the problem. I don't even want your money."

"Then what are you accusing me of?" he asked. "I'm thirty-six, Eve. You think, at this age, I'd be afraid of the responsibility of having a child?"

She jerked out of his grasp. "I think you're afraid of getting too close to me or anyone else. That you believe you've failed your father, your mother, your brothers, Laurel, almost everyone who's ever really meant anything to you—and you're afraid you'll fail again. So you've locked your heart in a cage and you reject any love that comes your way."

"Don't try to psychoanalyze me, Eve," he said.

"Can you honestly tell me I'm wrong?" she asked.

"Have you ever wondered why you keep everyone at arm's length? Always hover on the periphery so you can make a quick exit? Tell the women you sleep with not to expect anything from you?"

"I don't need to wonder. The fact that my house just got shot to hell answers that question," he said. "This thing with The Crew—it isn't a game, Eve. And it's not me I'm afraid will get hurt!"

"Yes, it is," she insisted. "Maybe you're not afraid of bullets. You've proven that. But you're afraid of other things besides The Crew. If you weren't, you'd keep the name Brent Taylor and stay right here."

"I would."

She lifted her chin. "Yes. You want to, or you'd already be gone. You know Whiskey Creek would be good for you, probably the best place you've come across, at least recently. But you won't let yourself put down any roots, because you don't think you deserve it."

"That's bullshit," he growled.

"Is it? Tell me this. How is Phoenix or…or Portland or Seattle any better for you than here? Those places are just farther away. That's all."

"They offer me a chance to make a living!"

"What you do for a living puts you at risk of being found again. You admitted that's probably how they found you this time. You need to give it up and start over. *Really* start over."

"And do *what?*"

"You're smart enough to figure something out."

"So you want me to stay here? Want me to…what? Be with you? We only met three weeks ago!"

She shook her head in apparent disgust. "That's it, then? What we feel doesn't count because it's so new?"

"It's not much to base a relationship on!"

"And if you have your way, we won't get the chance to base it on anything more. You'll make sure of it."

"I don't have any choice!"

"Yes, you do. Fight for what we could have—for the chance to be a father. I believe you would if you thought you deserved the happiness it could bring. But you'll move on, and you'll keep moving on every time you meet someone who could mean something to you until... when?" she asked. "Where will it end?"

"Stop it," he replied. "I can't love you, Eve. That would only give me someone else to lose. Why would I put myself in that position?"

"Why did Virgil put himself in that position?" she asked.

When he didn't answer, she said, "Because having someone is worth the risk. But if you keep lying to yourself, keep telling yourself it's The Crew that's stopping you from making any sort of commitment, you'll wander through life alone."

# 28

She'd done the right thing, Eve told herself. Rex needed to hear the truth and she needed to face it. But Eve couldn't go home for fear that she'd stare at the ceiling all night, thinking about him. So she drove over to the hospital.

"How was Victorian Days?" Cheyenne asked as soon as Eve walked into the room.

Dylan was sitting in a rocking chair next to Cheyenne's bed, holding Kellan and watching him sleep in that love-drunk way so many new parents gazed at their babies.

"Fun." Eve forced a smile and asked to hold the baby. But after a few minutes, Cheyenne let her know she wasn't fooled by the small talk.

"Tell me what's wrong," she said.

"Nothing," Eve insisted.

Cheyenne gave her husband a pleading look. "Honey, is there any chance you could take the baby for a stroll through the hospital?"

Dylan had been running a finger over the peach fuzz on Kellan's head while Eve held him, and hadn't really been listening, which was obvious when he blinked and focused on his wife. "What did you say?"

She grinned at his preoccupation. "He's been like this all day," she explained to Eve. "It would be nice if you would take your son out of the room for a few minutes. I'd like to talk to Eve alone, if you don't mind."

"I don't mind." He took the baby from Eve, cradling Kellan as carefully as though he were made of glass and flashing her a proud but embarrassed smile.

"Your baby's beautiful," she told him as he left. Then she turned Cheyenne. "It looks like Daddy's happy."

"I want this baby to be…an uncomplicated joy for him. You understand, don't you?"

They were talking about the way she'd gotten pregnant. "I understand that you love him and did what you thought would serve him best. But…I just about had a heart attack when he named the baby after Aaron. Didn't you try to discourage that?"

"No. I couldn't say anything."

"Why *not?*"

Cheyenne dragged a hand through her hair. "Because it would've seemed strange. Aaron's always been the black sheep of the family. Now that everyone's maturing, things are getting easier between them, but Dylan wants to make sure all those old fences have been mended."

"He couldn't do that a different way?"

Cheyenne sighed. "He was so excited when he came up with the idea I didn't have the heart to tell him Aaron probably wouldn't be pleased."

Or that it would be a constant reminder of their secret, Eve thought, but she didn't say that.

Cheyenne angled her head to catch Eve's eye. "How did he react?"

Eve considered telling the truth—that Aaron had looked like he'd swallowed something difficult to get down. But she didn't see how that would lighten Cheyenne's concerns, and there was no point in adding to her worries. "He seemed fine with it. I'm sure that as time goes by, it'll get easier to…you know, forget."

"Yeah."

"And this baby will be a breeze for Dylan to raise, nothing like what he went through with his brothers."

"Dylan loves his brothers as fiercely as he loves that baby," Cheyenne said. "And they love him, or…or Kellan wouldn't be here."

"I know." Eve fiddled with the strap of her purse.

"Aren't you going to sit down?" Cheyenne asked.

"I don't think so. I just wanted to check in."

"I hope that doesn't mean you're leaving already!"

"I've got three more nights of Victorian Days ahead. I should get some sleep so I can be a little more engaged than I was today."

"Why weren't you engaged today?"

Eve gave her a look. "You have to ask?"

Cheyenne reached for her hand. "Did you tell Rex about the pregnancy?"

She nodded.

"And? What did he say?"

"Nothing. He made it clear from the beginning that he wouldn't be staying. Having a baby won't change his mind. He'll pay child support, and that's it."

"He said as much?"

Eve considered the conversations she'd had with him earlier and then the one tonight. "Yeah. He said as much."

"So where will he go?"

"I have no idea. And he won't be able to tell me."

"I'm sorry," Cheyenne said.

Tears burned Eve's eyes, but she blinked them back. "It's okay. I think. I'll get over him, right? That's what my mother would tell me."

"Maybe his situation will change, allow him to come back."

"I doubt it," she said. "He's running from more than The Crew."

Cheyenne looked alarmed. "What does that mean?"

"Nothing more than what you might've guessed. He's trying to protect himself from suffering like he did in the past—by shoving away all the people who'd care about him if he'd let them. And what kind of life is that?"

"Then maybe his leaving will be a blessing in disguise, Eve. You don't know that he could be a good father to your baby any more than he does. He has a lot of…issues."

"Sometimes people with 'issues' can overcome them. Look what Presley's done with her life, Chey. Look at Aaron. Aren't you glad you didn't give up on them?"

"I am. But I'd have to say they're the exception to the rule."

"Rex could do the same," she insisted.

Cheyenne moved a rolling table farther to one side so she could raise the head of her bed. "And The Crew? Whiskey Creek isn't that far from San Francisco."

"They'd have no reason to look here. Not if he got into a different line of work."

"He's in his thirties, Eve, and changing professions is easier said than done. What would he be able to do?"

"I don't know," she said. "But I'd rather he worked at a fast food joint than be at risk. Life is a series of compromises."

"That's a big one."

The door opened and a nurse walked in. "Sorry to interrupt," she said. "But I need to take Mrs. Amos's blood pressure."

"I'd better go," Eve told Cheyenne.

"Wait," Cheyenne said. "When are you going to tell your parents?"

She didn't specify "about the baby," but Eve knew what she meant. "Not now," she said. "Maybe after the holidays."

The nurse slipped the cuff onto Cheyenne's arm and began to inflate it. "Everything's going to be okay," Cheyenne said. "You've got me, and Dyl and all the rest of us."

Sophia had told her the same thing. At least, considering the way things were going with Rex, she wouldn't have to worry about leaving all her friends behind. Not to mention the B and B and her parents. If it came right down to it, she wasn't sure she could do that, anyway. "I know," she said. "Thanks."

"How come you're back?"

Cecelia, her night manager, was understandably surprised to see Eve at the B and B. It was after eleven.

"I'm too wound up to sleep," she said. "So I decided to get a few things done here."

"But you were exhausted when you left. You look exhausted now."

She shrugged. "Like I said…"

Cecilia's lips turned down. "Are you okay? You don't seem yourself these days."

Eve *wasn't* herself. She was in love with a man who was pursued by a dangerous gang, and she was pregnant with his child. Now he would leave, and she would probably never hear from him again. Not only that, but the news of her pregnancy would cause a stir in town. Her parents would have to defer the trip they had planned for this summer so they could be home for the birth. And she'd have to make an acceptable babysitting arrangement so she could continue to work after the baby was born—at least once the child got a bit older and wanted to run around.

"I just have a lot on my mind," she mumbled.

"Of course you do. You're a godmother now."

She was going to be a *mother* this summer. "Cheyenne's baby is beautiful," she said, mostly to change the focus of the conversation.

"No wonder you're excited. I can't wait to see him."

They chatted for a few minutes about Kellan and how proud Dylan was to be a father. Then Cecelia returned to the kitchen, presumably to handle her part of the food prep for breakfast as well as afternoon tea, which was something she did every night.

Eve remained where she was. A text had just come in from Ted. He was responding to a message she'd sent him earlier, amid the clamor of Victorian Days, thanking him for trying to protect her, for caring enough to get involved and for going to so much trouble and expense to solve the mystery of Little Mary's death.

You can be a pain in the ass sometimes, he'd written in reply. But I'll always be there for you.

She had to smile at that. That's your way of accepting my apology?

That was an apology? <G>

It was an olive branch.

I was never mad at you. Just worried.

I know.

Are you going to be okay?

Whatever happens, I'll get through it.

She'd dropped her phone back in her purse, intent on heading down the hall to the office, when the doorbell rang. For the sake of safety, whoever it was couldn't get in after eleven unless he or she was already a guest and had a key or a staff member opened the door. Having heard the bell, Cecelia poked her head out of the kitchen but Eve was closer and waved her off. "I've got it," she said.

Occasionally someone showed up late, looking for a room. Thanks to Victorian Days, they were nearly full tonight, but there was one room left. Eve would've been eager to book it, except that as soon as she opened the door, she knew she didn't want to let the four men standing on her porch inside. They smelled of alcohol, were covered in ink depicting immoral and violent acts and wore hard-ass expressions, indicating that their attitudes weren't any more appealing than their appearance.

"What can I do for you?" She offered what she hoped was a professional smile.

"What do you think?" the guy closest to her replied. "This is a B and B, isn't it?"

The others snickered at his rudeness.

"I thought maybe you'd like the wedding suite for you and whichever one of these men is your partner. Is this a celebration?"

His eyes flashed in anger when she drew more laughter than he had. "Fuck, no. Not that kind of celebration. Just give us a couple of rooms."

She almost said she was booked for the night. She doubted her current guests would feel comfortable sharing lodgings with such people. But as she opened her mouth to say the words, she noticed that the man who'd spoken had letters tattooed on the knuckles of one hand.

They were written in such elaborate script that it took her a moment to realize what they spelled. But when that word registered, her blood ran cold. *C-R-E-W.*

Swallowing hard, she backed up a step. "I'm afraid we don't have much available."

"What the hell does that mean?" he asked.

She almost told him he had to go, that she'd call the cops if he didn't. But the fact that he might react violently stopped her. So did the thought that it might be wiser to know where these men were than to send them away and then wonder.

"It means, because of Victorian Days, we're down to only one vacancy."

He stared at her for a second. Then he nudged the guy standing behind him. "Give me that photograph."

She hadn't noticed it until that moment, but the other guy held a manila envelope. He handed it over, and the first man pulled out a glossy eight-by-ten, which he shoved at her.

"You ever seen this guy?"

Eve's heart was pounding in her ear so loud she could barely hear above it. Trying to keep her hands from shaking, she took hold of what he was giving her, but she knew before she even looked that it would be Rex.

Sure enough, they had a picture of Rex exiting an office building. The image was slightly blurred, since he was in movement, but there was no question about his identity. She could easily make out his blond hair, his well-sculpted features, his lean, wiry build.

But she frowned as if she didn't recognize him and shook her head. "No. I'm sorry. He a friend of yours?"

"My long-lost brother."

The others laughed again.

"You *sure* you don't recognize him?" the first man asked.

"Positive," she replied. "If he lived in this area, I'd know it. I've been here my whole life."

"He don't live here. He's just passin' through."

She almost volunteered the fact that there was another B and B in town. She was nervous enough to let just about anything come out of her mouth. But she was afraid the Russos, who owned A Room with a View, or one of their employees, might've seen Rex around town and wouldn't know to claim otherwise. "If so, he's not staying here. I'd remember a face like that."

"'Course you would. Too bad he's got nothin' a little lower down."

Too bad she knew otherwise.

She handed the picture back. "So...would you like to book the room? I doubt you'll find anything else in town this late."

"Why not?" he said. "Asshole and Dickhead, here, can sleep in the car."

"Ah, *man!* That'll be a bitch!" either Asshole or Dickhead cried.

"Hey, who you callin' Asshole?" the other guy asked.

The one who seemed to be in charge turned to scowl at them both, and the complaints stopped.

"I'll just need to see some ID and a credit card," she said.

"I'll pay cash," he responded, as if that was all she should require.

Curling her fingernails into her palms, she told herself to stay calm. "You can pay with cash if you like, when you check out, but I'll need a credit card to book the room. And I'll need to see some ID, too, to prove that the credit card you're using belongs to you. It's nothing personal. Just our standard operating procedure. These days it's the same for practically all hotels and motels."

"Stupid whore," he muttered, and got out his wallet.

# 29

"Wasn't that quite a party?" Mrs. Higgins asked. They'd both been trying to sleep for the past two hours, but had somehow ended up in the living room together, her with a cup of tea and him just staring at the Christmas lights.

"I've always loved Victorian Days. They've been a tradition here since I was a child," she added.

Rex found it difficult to pull himself out of the mire of his thoughts long enough to respond. But he forced himself to do that because he really liked Mrs. Higgins. She was set in her ways, and lonely after the loss of her husband and son, but she was easy to be around, supportive, kind. It almost felt as if he was living with his grandmother.

He stretched out his legs and rested his hands on his abdomen. "Have you lived here your whole life?"

Her cup clinked on its saucer. "I have."

"You still love it." That was more of an observation than a question.

"Of course. It's beautiful, quiet, filled with wonderful people." She set her tea aside so she could get up and move one of the ornaments she apparently felt was out of place. "Why would I want to go anywhere else?"

"How do you know you couldn't find something better? There's a big world out there." At least that was what he kept telling himself. He had to make venturing out into it seem appealing, since staying put wasn't an option for him.

"There's no place like home," she said with absolute conviction.

How often had he heard that cliché? Somehow it didn't sound so trite this time. The very concept of home made him feel like a perpetual wanderer.

But could he blame all of that on The Crew? Maybe, as Eve had said, his behavior stemmed from something deeper than a physical threat. Maybe he devoted himself to his work because it was the only source of self-worth he had, and it gave him a sense of confidence he could cultivate and maintain. He was good at what he did, knew he wouldn't let his clients down. Despite the dangers of his job, there was a strange kind of safety in that.

Mrs. Higgins tightened her robe. With curlers in her hair and pink furry slippers on her feet, she reminded him of the old lady on those funny greeting cards, except that she was shorter and rounder. "I hear you've got your eye on that pretty daughter of Adele's," she said.

"Who told you that?" he asked.

"In case you haven't been warned before, nothing much happens in this town that doesn't get spread around."

He chuckled. "I guess that's one reason to go somewhere else."

"No place is perfect," she said. "You just have to find the place where you belong."

And if he didn't belong anywhere?

She cleared her throat. "My husband proposed a week after he met me."

He gave her a suspicious look. "And you're trying to tell me…what?"

"It doesn't always take months to know when you've met someone you want to spend the rest of your life with."

That didn't make Rex's decisions any easier. He couldn't stay here, and he couldn't take Eve away from Whiskey Creek. Not even if she'd go. What could he offer her? Who would run the inn? And what if something happened to her—or the baby—despite his best efforts to protect them? How would he live with himself?

He was just trying to figure out a good way to explain why he had to leave when a car came down the street.

He stood the moment he spotted the lights. This was a quiet road that saw very little traffic, especially so late. He grew even more concerned when that same car—a sedan—parked out front.

Was this going to be a repeat of what had happened in San Francisco?

"Were you expecting company?" He couldn't think of a single way The Crew could have traced him here, but the last thing he wanted was to put Mrs. Higgins or anyone else in Whiskey Creek in danger.

"No," she said. "I'm not sure who that could be, coming here so late. Good Lord, it's after one!"

"In the back. Hurry. And stay away from the windows." He started to go for his gun, which was in the bedroom. But the driver opened his door before Rex could take two steps and, because of the interior light, he recognized the man getting out.

Eve rubbed sweaty palms on her jeans as she waited at Ted's place for Ted to return with Rex. When those members of The Crew showed up at her inn, she hadn't known where else to go, who else to turn to. She couldn't call the police. The men who were looking for Rex hadn't done anything wrong—at least that she could prove. Yet. And she'd feared that if she went straight to Rex, he'd leave immediately, to make sure no one got hurt, and she'd never see him again.

Even with what she and her friends had planned, she knew he'd still have to go. But if they could pull it off, he'd finally be able to outdistance the past.

"Would you like a cup?" Sophia called, interrupting her thoughts.

After she and Ted had hung up with Kyle, and Ted had left, Sophia had gone into the kitchen to put on a pot of coffee. But Eve didn't need any coffee.

She went to the kitchen door so she wouldn't have to raise her voice. She didn't want to wake Alexa, who was, presumably, sleeping in the upstairs bedroom they'd added after they were married. "I'm fine, thanks."

Sophia gave her a sympathetic smile. "Don't worry, okay? I'm glad you came here. You know Ted. He'll do all he can to help."

Eve would've gone to Dylan instead. He was another person who could solve just about any problem. But Kellan had been born so recently. Dylan deserved to enjoy his son's first days unmolested by her and her problems.

Besides, Ted had a different set of skills and resources. She doubted Dylan would have suggested the same solution, and she believed what they'd hit upon could really work—with Kyle's help.

"I wouldn't have bothered you this late if it wasn't so serious," she said.

"I know." Sophia got three mugs from the cupboard.

The minutes seemed to drag. Would Rex even get in the car with Ted? Or, after their encounter at Victorian Days, was he already on his way out of town?

When Sophia's phone buzzed on the counter, Eve held her breath.

"Hello?" Sophia looked at her while she talked and Eve could tell by the tone of her voice that it was her husband. "You did?…Good….I've got some coffee ready…. See you in a few minutes."

"What'd he say?"

"Kyle's on his way over."

"And does Ted have Rex?"

"Yes. They're coming, too."

Eve let her breath out slowly. That meant they would at least have a chance to explain what they'd devised.

But would he go along with it?

He'd be crazy not to, she told herself.

"I hope we won't disturb Alexa," she said. "It's bad enough that *I* barged in on you guys."

Sophia laughed. "Oh, don't worry. An earthquake wouldn't wake Alexa. She sleeps with her iPod on. We can hardly get her out of bed when her alarm's screaming three feet away. But she's not home, anyway."

"Is she at a friend's?"

"No, her grandparents—Skip's parents—took her to Disney World."

"That's quite a Christmas gift."

"You know them. Everything has to be big and splashy, even though they no longer have the money. They promised Alexa this trip, then told us they couldn't afford to take her. So we had to pay for her flight and their entire hotel stay."

"Does she know that?"

"No. There was no point in sending her if we were only going to upset her first."

"She won't miss Christmas?"

"Oh, no. She'll be home on the twenty-third, which

is…what?" She checked the calendar on her phone. "Sunday."

"I hope she's having a good time."

"Seems to be. She texts me quite often." Sophia wiped off the counter. "Can I get you a glass of water? Or some wine to help you relax? Wait…never mind. I forgot about the baby. That's going to take some getting used to."

"No kidding." Eve shook the tension from her hands. This was such a crazy year. "Anyway, water would be perfect."

The doorbell rang as Sophia reached for a glass. "I'll answer it," Eve said, and hurried across the living room.

Kyle stood on the stoop. "Thanks for coming," she told him. "I appreciate it."

His hair was sticking up on one side, proof that she'd hauled him out of bed, too. "If it was anyone else, I wouldn't do it," he teased, but she knew that wasn't the truth. He'd do what he could for any friend.

"So where's the ex-con?" he asked when she let him in and he saw that the living room was empty.

"Quit it!" she said. "He'll be here any minute."

He chucked her under the chin. "You're so uptight you're about to shatter. We've got this, okay? Relax."

She nodded and went to get him a cup of coffee.

Ted and Rex walked in shortly after she'd returned with it. Rex's gaze went to Kyle first, then settled on her. He raised his eyebrows, and Eve knew he was reacting to the fact that she'd pulled Ted, Sophia and Kyle into his business. To him, that created more risk where The Crew was concerned, but Ted hadn't told him four members of The Crew were in town and staying at Little Mary's. Ted had agreed he wouldn't give that away until they'd had a chance to discuss what they'd come up with as a solution.

"What's going on?" he asked when she didn't say anything.

"We think we have an answer to your…problem," Ted said.

Eve motioned to the couch. "Have a seat and we'll go over it."

Rex hesitated, but eventually walked over and sat down.

"Eve explained your situation," Ted said. "And we want to help."

"There's nothing you can do," Rex told him. "It would be foolish to even try."

Ted rested his elbows on his knees. "What we're about to propose comes with certain risks, but I think those can be mitigated."

Rex's eyes narrowed. "Why would you be willing to do anything? You've been warning Eve against getting involved with me from the beginning."

"Can you blame me?" Ted asked. "What would you have done if she was *your* lifelong friend?"

Rex didn't answer that question, but his attitude improved by several degrees. "So what do you propose? And why do we have to discuss it in the middle of the night?"

"Your buddies are in town," Ted said.

"My buddies?"

"Four members of your former gang."

Rex stiffened. "How do you know?"

Eve spoke up. "They came to the B and B about an hour and a half ago. They showed me a picture of you coming out of an office of some kind. Asked me if I'd ever seen you. I said no, of course, but if they show that around town too much, they're going to get a yes sooner or later. You've had dinner at Just Like Mom's, purchased gas at the Gas-N-Go, had a few drinks at Sexy Sadie's.

God forbid they ask Noelle. She'll lead them right to my doorstep."

"But…how'd they find me?" he asked, obviously stuck on the fact that he'd thought he was safe.

"I have no idea," Eve said. "I couldn't ask. I just gave them a room."

He jumped to his feet. "You *what?*"

"Well, I had only one vacancy, so technically two of the four—Asshole and Dickhead—are sleeping in the car."

"Asshole and Dickhead," he repeated in disbelief.

"That's what the guy called them. The one who told them they wouldn't get the room."

"Inside a gang, everyone gets a nickname, but Asshole and Dickhead are obviously insults, so…whoever those two are, they don't have a lot of clout."

"I got that impression," she said. "The other two were definitely in charge. One in particular. The name on his credit card was Eric Gunderson." That seemed such an innocuous name for a man like that. She wondered what his nickname might be.

"I don't know that name, but he might not have been part of The Crew when I was." He reached over and gripped her arm to add emphasis to his words. "You should've told them you were full for the night!"

"I considered that but figured it might be smarter to know where they are."

"And that was good thinking," Ted said. "It gives us an advantage."

"You have no advantage," Rex argued. "They have guns. They shot up my house a few days ago. Eve saw the recording. They'll shoot *me* if they can find me. And if you get in the way, they'll shoot you, too."

"So we should walk away from you. Leave you to fight this battle alone?" Eve said.

"That's exactly what you should do." Ted took control of the conversation then. "We'd rather try something else."

"And that is?" Rex directed his next comment to Eve. "I'm telling you those guys are dangerous. You don't want any part of them."

Ted lifted his hands in a placating gesture. "She gets it. We all get it. But after some deliberation, we've come to the conclusion that we could provide you with a unique opportunity."

Rex scowled in irritation that they weren't listening to him. "I can't go to the police, so don't even try to persuade me to—"

"That isn't what we plan to suggest," Ted broke in. "Although the police *will* be involved. So will the fire department."

"The newspaper will play a key role, too," Kyle pointed out, "unwitting though it may be."

This seemed to take Rex aback, so much that he sank down on the couch again. "I don't understand."

Ted smiled. "There are certain advantages to growing up in such a small town."

"And those are?"

"You generally know the right people."

"For *what?*"

"We're going to need your ID," Kyle said, and then he explained the whole thing.

Once Kyle had finished, Rex looked from him to Ted and then to Sophia in astonishment. "Why are you doing this?"

Ted stood and held out his hand. "Because that's what friends are for."

# 30

Eve arrived at the B and B at the crack of dawn.

"You look tired," Pamela said the moment she saw her. Pam came on at four in the morning to relieve Cecelia.

"It was a short night." She'd gotten barely three hours', but not because Rex had gone home with her. He'd given her a brief hug when he left last night but returned to Mrs. Higgins's to tell her what was happening so he could enlist her help and then wait for her to pack.

Pam gestured at Eve's eyes. "Look at those dark circles! You should've slept a little longer."

She couldn't. She wanted to witness the moment when those Crew members came downstairs, and she had no idea when that would be.

Fortunately, she'd seen their battered vehicle in the lot when she parked. She knew it was theirs because Asshole and Dickhead were asleep inside it. That they were still where she thought they should be gave her a measure of peace. "I'm fine. I didn't help out much for Victorian Days yesterday. So I thought I'd get an early start."

"Wow, you're really dedicated." Pam straightened the items at the front desk. "CeCe said we had a late arrival last night."

"We did."

"She didn't mark down what they want for breakfast."

"That was my fault. I checked them in but...forgot to ask." She'd been far too flustered and preoccupied.

"So what should we do?" Pam asked, as if that threw everything off kilter.

She smiled to reassure her that the world wasn't coming to an end. Considering what she and her friends were doing, there was the possibility that *her* world might sustain real damage, but that wouldn't affect her employees. "I'll handle it."

"Okay." She shrugged and went back to the kitchen as Eve headed to the office.

Glancing at Cheyenne's empty desk, Eve put her purse down and rummaged through it for her phone so she could text Ted. Are Rex and Mrs. Higgins safely out of the house?

They are. I have them comfortably installed in the guesthouse with Mrs. Higgins in the master. I assume they're sleeping because I haven't seen them yet.

Good. They'd stay with Ted until the coast was clear.

What's going on at the inn? Your "guests" still there?

Yes, thank God, since we need them to stay long enough to learn that Rex is here.

Remember not to change your story about that picture, though. It might seem suspect to them later. We don't want to do anything that could make them feel this is a setup.

I won't. I'll let someone else in town recognize Rex.

Good. The more people who tell those bastards that he's in town, the more convinced they'll be they've found him. That's exactly how we want it to play out.

True, but the waiting wasn't going to be easy. Do you think they'll hit Mrs. Higgins's house?

No. Moving her along with Rex is just a precaution. Very few people even know he was staying there. But no one, except you, me, Sophia and Kyle, know they're here. That tightens the circle a lot.

His reassurance calmed her fears a little, but she still had some concerns. If these guys do hear that he was at Mrs. Higgins's, will they believe he moved out to Kyle's place?

Her phone rang. It was Ted. Apparently he was tired of typing messages into his phone. "Why wouldn't they believe he moved out to Kyle's place if that's where his remains are found?"

"No one will have connected him to Kyle or Kyle's property."

"Doesn't matter. They'll think they shot up his place in between him staying with Mrs. Higgins and taking the house on the corner of Kyle's property."

"Makes sense." But it helped her to go through their plans, soothed her nerves. "I just hope it all happens right away. I don't like having them in town, let alone staying at my B and B."

"Whiskey Creek isn't that big. Someone will tell them he's here. If should happen fast from that point on."

Then The Crew would really dig in and Kyle would fire the house. "When they come down to breakfast, maybe I'll suggest they try Sexy Sadie's tonight," she said. "If Noelle's working, she'll give them the information they want."

"If you get the chance to talk to them. But don't push it. Don't be obvious."

She paced to the filing cabinet and back. "Do you really think we can make this seem real, Ted? I mean... faking someone's death only happens in the movies."

"Skip tried it, didn't he?"

Ted was referring to Sophia's late husband. "Do I have to remind you that he died in the attempt?"

"Stop worrying. It's all under control."

"Have you talked to Chief Bennett?" That was an essential piece of the plan.

"Yep. Met him at the station fifteen minutes ago. I'm on my way home now."

"He's willing to help?" Eve had to admit she was a little surprised. Ted commanded a lot of respect in this town, but the chief would be going out on a very thin ledge.

"He was skeptical at first, but I provided the name off that credit card you took, so he can check out the leader of those gangbangers. And I passed along the name of a guy with WitSec that Rex gave me who can confirm his story. Bennett said if everything checks out, he'll do what he can to help."

"It won't work without him."

"He'll be there for us. By the way, Rex figured out how The Crew might've found him. Did he tell you?"

They hadn't talked. Eve wasn't sure she wanted to say much at this point. She was just hoping to get The Crew out of his life. "No. What does he think?"

"That it's got to be his assistant."

*"What?"*

"She thought he was in Arizona. So she probably told

all his bodyguards that he went to Whiskey Creek. Trying *not* to give his secret away."

"And one of them talked?"

"Not necessarily. Maybe word just got around. Some client or call-in might've been told the same thing."

"Damn. So it was likely just a fluke?"

"Yep. Whiskey Creek might've come to mind because she knew he'd been here before—that type of thing."

Eve made herself sit and try to relax. "I hope we can pull this off."

"We can." He was about to hang up, but she stopped him.

"Thanks, Ted. I really appreciate it."

"If this works out, you have to forgive me for last year," he said.

She could hear the humor in his voice and laughed. "I already have."

Rex called while Eve was sitting in her office, having lunch. "Hey," he said.

She winced when she remembered how she'd confronted him at Victorian Days. "Wow. Look who's finally up."

"I don't have anything else to do. Might as well sleep. You've got me on lockdown for the day, remember?"

"Maybe two or three days," she said. "You agreed to go along with this, and I expect you to do it."

"I will." There was a pause. Then he said, "You okay?"

"I'm fine. What about you?"

"Worried, if you want the truth."

"About…"

"Your friends. It's nice of them to get involved, but… what if Kyle does something wrong when he sets fire to that house and ends up getting trapped or something?"

"Kyle knows how to handle himself."

"And he's really willing to lose that house?"

"He told you. He was planning to tear it down, anyway, so he can build an extension to his solar manufacturing plant. He would've waited until spring—but it won't hurt to prepare the site a little earlier."

"No one's renting it?"

"Not anymore. He had one of his workers in there, a guy who was going through a divorce. He was letting him stay for free, just to help him out. But then the roof started leaking and Kyle didn't want the liability anymore, especially because the guy would bring his kids over, and Kyle was afraid someone would get hurt."

"I see."

"That's why we called Kyle last night. We go to coffee with him every week, and had heard all about his plans, so it occurred to us that we could use that old place instead of burning down a house that has actual value."

"You really considered that?"

She would've offered her own bungalow if it meant saving him, but she saw no benefit in admitting that. The strength of her feelings would only scare him away. "Until we realized we'd go to jail for insurance fraud if we didn't pay to rebuild it ourselves."

"I would have sprung for that part."

"It's not cheap to build a house in California, so I'm guessing that wouldn't leave you much seed money."

There was a slight pause, then he said, "What do you expect when this is all over, Eve?"

Instinctively, her hand went to her stomach and her pulse sped up. "I don't expect anything, Rex."

"You're doing this…for nothing?"

"I am. I would never want you or any man to stay here out of a sense of obligation. I'm merely hoping this gives you a brighter future. What you do with that future is up to you."

Pam knocked on the office door. "Eve?"

Eve's chest felt as though there was a hundred-pound weight sitting on it, which made it difficult to breathe. This wasn't a good time for an interruption. But she asked Rex to hang on. "Yes?"

Her assistant manager opened the door and made a face. "There's a guy with a tattoo of a gagged woman getting her clothes torn off, and he's asking for you."

Tightening her grip on the phone, Eve covered the mouthpiece. "That's one of the two gentlemen who rented Room 4 last night."

*"You gave him a room?"*

"Is he causing trouble?" Eve asked.

"No, but...but he's making the other guests uncomfortable. He frightens me, too."

"I'll be right out," she said.

"What's wrong?" Rex asked. "Is it The Crew?"

"Yes. I guess one of your old friends is asking for me."

"Be careful."

"We just have to follow the plan and everything will be fine."

"What are you doing after Victorian Days tonight?" he asked. "Maybe I could hide out at your place."

"I hope I'll finally be getting some sleep," she said. "You should, too. I might see you tomorrow."

Eve stared at the phone for several seconds after she hung up. It hadn't been easy to turn down the opportunity to be with him. But she felt it was necessary, so he'd know she was serious when she said she had no expectations when this was over.

She only wanted him if he could love her as much in return.

* * *

Eve smoothed the oversize top she was wearing with a pair of leggings and took a deep breath before leaving the office. The man who'd booked the room last night was standing at the front desk, waiting for her. The others didn't seem to be with him.

"You wanted to see me?" she asked.

"Yes."

"I hope your room was okay."

His lip curled as he surveyed the lobby area, with all its festive decorations. "I'm not much for these kinds of places."

"I hope that doesn't mean you'll be checking out."

"That's what I wanted to see you about. I'm hoping you have another room for my two friends tonight."

"Actually, Room 3 should be checking out by eleven. Would you like to book that?"

"Isn't that why I'm standing here?" he asked.

Ignoring his rudeness, she called up the page she needed on the computer. "We'll get you a reservation, then. I just need to see your credit card again."

Grudgingly, he dug in his pocket and handed her the credit card and the driver's license he'd given her earlier, which identified him as Eric Gunderson.

"You're all set," she told him when she handed them back. "But you'll have to pick up the key a little later."

He didn't respond. As he turned to go, she said, "By the way, breakfast comes with the room. Do you plan on joining us this morning?"

"No, we've got things to do," he said.

"Well, if you do get hungry, Just Like Mom's is down the street. I highly recommend the food. And tonight is a big Christmas celebration, right here in the center of town. Everyone will be there."

"Wouldn't miss it," he said with a chuckle, and Eve was sure he intended to show up. What better place to search for Rex?

After he left, she called Ted. "Rex's old buddies will be at the celebration tonight. I suggest we have all our friends there, too, prepped to tell him they recognize the man in his picture if they get asked. Do you know if Mrs. Higgins is going to attend?"

"She is. She mentioned something about working on a quilt."

"Good. If she could watch for them and bump into them somehow, I doubt they'd ever suspect such a sweet old lady of being a plant. She might even tell them that Rex was staying with her until he moved out to Kyle's rental."

"Great idea!" Ted said. "If she can't manage that, one of us will have to cross paths with them."

"Now we just need to be sure Chief Bennett's going to do his part."

"He called me a few minutes ago. That name you gave me—Eric Gunderson? He has a rap sheet a mile long. And someone from the LAPD confirmed his gang affiliation. Bennett doesn't want any gang activity in this town."

"So we'll make sure they think Rex is dead, and they'll leave."

"Bennett's confirmed the bad guys, but he still has to hear from Rex's contact in WitSec before he feels confident."

"Just pray that guy isn't on vacation."

Eve had butterflies in her stomach when she hung up. Tonight would be the night. She called Kyle and Rex, just to give them a heads-up.

# 31

"Can you take the pile?" Mrs. Higgins asked.

Rex studied the twenty or more cards in his hand, searching for a pair of eights. They were passing the time by playing canasta, a game Rex had never played until now but Mrs. Higgins had often played with her husband.

"No."

"Then you need to discard," she told him. "A black three will freeze the pile."

He had a couple of black threes, and black threes didn't seem to be much good for anything else in this game, so he threw one. He felt bad that he'd had to dislodge Mrs. Higgins from her home, and right before Christmas, too, but she didn't seem to mind. She loved the excitement and secrecy of what they were doing—and having his undivided attention.

"There you go. See? Now I can't take the pile." She spread six nines in front of her, which he thought was probably a better hand than his.

"That's a lot of nines," he said, scowling at the fact that she was so much closer to ending the hand than he was. "That doesn't bode well for me, does it?"

She gave him a sympathetic grimace. "It's only one away from the seven nines I need in order to have a straight canasta, remember? I'll probably win this hand, especially if you can't get down."

It would help if he knew exactly what she meant. He wasn't catching on to the game all that quickly. He was too preoccupied with the call he'd just had from Eve, telling him that Eric Gunderson and his three companions would be attending Victorian Days, and that her group would have ten people milling around, hoping to be asked about that picture. Would they be able to execute what they'd planned?

Rex had to admit it sounded great in theory. Ted was a smart guy, and Kyle certainly seemed capable. But what if it *did* work? How would he feel then? He'd been looking over his shoulder for eight years—ever since he was released from prison, and he'd gone to prison at eighteen. He'd never had a normal life, not since he was a young kid. Would he even know what to do without that constant threat?

"How do you go out again?" he asked Mrs. Higgins, referring to the game.

She got up to pour herself another cup of coffee as she explained. When she sat down again and settled her reading glasses back on her nose, she squinted at him over the top of the frame. "Eve and her friends are such good people, aren't they?"

He surveyed the guesthouse, where they were staying. It wasn't large, but it had two bedrooms and two bathrooms and a small kitchen/living room area with a fireplace. Everything Ted had was nice, but particularly the big house he lived in. "Definitely. Ted doesn't even like me and yet he's trying to help."

"It isn't that he doesn't like you. He likes everyone. He's just protective of Eve. They grew up together. And you're an unproven entity."

"Would they do this kind of thing for anyone?" he asked.

"I'd like to think they would—anyone who's worthy of it," she replied. "So don't feel too guilty."

"I feel—" he almost said "like shit" but changed it out of respect "—terrible that my coming to town is disrupting so many lives. Especially *yours*." He didn't deserve the sacrifices involved. He'd barely met these people, and he'd spent the time he'd known them pushing them away.

"I don't mind." She looked up from studying her hand to smile at him. "I feel useful trying to entertain you while everyone does their part."

"But it's Christmas, and I'm sure you'd be more comfortable at your own place."

"This is what Christmas is about, isn't it? Peace on earth, and goodwill to all men. Anyway, I wouldn't be too comfortable at home if The Crew decided to pay me a visit. I think I'd rather hang out here with you," she said with a laugh.

"You're not going to Victorian Days?"

"Oh, yes, I have to finish the quilt. I'll go over when Sophia does. I mean until then." She tossed him a seven. "Can you take that?"

Rex held three sevens in his hand. "Actually, I can."

Eve kept an eye out for Eric Gunderson and his companions. But she worked most of the night at the inn without seeing them once. She was just starting to panic, to think they might not be asking around about that picture of Rex, when Ted showed up.

"How are things here?" he asked.

She glanced over at Deb, who was packaging the items she'd been ringing up. "Busy. How's the rest of the celebration?"

"One of the best yet. Every year we get more people, which means more money for the charity and the vendors."

"We've had a steady stream," she said.

He leaned close and whispered in her ear. "Any chance I can have a moment alone with you?"

She handed her current customer the sack containing her purchases. It was a woman she'd never seen before, but Victorian Days drew people from all over. "Can you manage without me for a few minutes?" she asked Deb. "I'm going to take a quick break."

"Of course. It's almost ten, anyway. Things should be slowing down pretty soon."

Eve was glad—except that she didn't want the evening to end until they'd achieved what she'd set out to achieve. "Thanks," she said, and walked Ted back to her office, where she shut the door behind them.

"So? Any sign of The Crew?" she asked.

He frowned. "Not that I know of. They haven't come back here?"

"No. I've been watching for them all evening." She bit her lip as she considered their options. "Have you had someone go by Mrs. Higgins's place, just in case?"

"Kyle checked it a few minutes ago. All quiet."

"Where could those bastards have gone?"

"There were a lot of people out tonight," he replied. "Maybe they were in the crush but we somehow missed them."

"They stand out too much for that. Especially here."

Ted took Cheyenne's chair. "True. It's really frustrating because we have the go-ahead from Chief Bennett."

"He told you that?"

"He did. He pulled me aside earlier and said he's not excited about reporting something that isn't true, but by the WitSec guy's own admission, Rex has been through enough. If we can't stop what's happening in an honest way, it's time to stop it *any* way."

She rubbed her temples to relieve the headache starting behind her eyes. "I can't believe we have everything in place, including the piece I thought would be the hardest to get—and these idiots aren't running around town, showing everyone that damn picture. I was so sure they would."

"Like I said, maybe—" His phone, which he was holding in one hand, rang, and he paused to check it. "It's Sophia," he said, and answered.

"What's up?...You have?"

When he looked back at her, Eve read the excitement in his face. She guessed someone had finally encountered Gunderson and his cohorts, and she clenched her hands in anxiety, curiosity and impatience.

"Where?...Who said that?...Wow! That takes balls the size of coconuts....Okay, I'm at the B and B. I'll tell her, and I'll call Kyle myself. You and Alexa head home right away and have Rex keep an eye out....Love you, too."

He sighed as he ended the call.

"They've been spotted?" Eve asked.

"They had the nerve to ask Chief Bennett if he'd ever seen the man in the picture," he said with an incredulous chuckle.

"No..."

"Yes. I guess they figured if anyone would keep track of new faces in this town, it would be law enforcement."

"But...what excuse did they give for looking for Rex?"

"They said he was Gunderson's brother. Sophia told me Chief Bennett believes they're intoxicated."

"So they were probably out at Sexy Sadie's."

"Chances are good that they were."

"Did Bennett tell them he *had* seen Rex?"

"No."

*"Why not?"* she cried.

"He didn't feel it would come off as credible, and I have to agree. A man in his position wouldn't give that information to four obvious gangbangers, who are strangers and drunk to boot. But he told Sophia, who just told Mrs. Higgins, where he saw them, and Mrs. Higgins is going to walk by."

"You think she'll be safe?"

"I do. They're not in a dark alley or anything, and they have absolutely no reason to harm her, since she's going to give them the information they want."

"Not directions, though."

"No, and that'll buy us the few minutes we need to stay ahead of them."

Eve bit her lip. "That means this could happen in the next hour. You'd better call Kyle."

He was already punching in the numbers.

Rex sat in Ted's darkened living room, peering out the front window. By now, Mrs. Higgins was probably asleep in the guesthouse; Sophia was upstairs in the master bedroom. He could hear the drone of the TV drifting out of that part of the house.

"Come on, come on," he muttered, growing more anxious by the second. Kyle should've been able to check in by now, but Rex hadn't heard anything. Of course, he no longer had a cell. They'd put it in the house so it would die at the same time he supposedly did. But there was always Ted's home phone.

When the call came, he let Sophia answer it and waited with bated breath to hear how things were going.

It took a few minutes, but she finally appeared at the top of the stairs. "Rex?"

"Yes?"

"Can you pick up? It's Eve."

Relief ran through him as he strode into the kitchen and used the extension. "Hello?"

"It's done."

He kneaded his forehead. "And? How'd it go?"

"Kyle just called. He said it was quite a blaze."

"Why did it take so long to get a report?"

"He had to wait until the building was totally destroyed before notifying anyone. We didn't want some brave firefighter rushing in to save you and losing his life."

"So the fire's out?"

"For the most part. And Chief Bennett's on-site, since Kyle made a point of telling 9-1-1 that your rental car's sitting in the driveway."

"The fire never threatened the car or anything else…."

Leaving the car in such close proximity was a chance they'd felt they had to take. Parking it far away for no apparent reason would seem odd. "No. It's been so wet out that there was no danger of it spreading."

"That's good." Rex wondered how she was holding up under the strain of what was going on. "How are you feeling?"

"Cautiously hopeful."

"Me, too," he said. "Have you seen Gunderson?"

"No. They haven't come in, which worries me a little. Where could they be?"

Rex knew where *he'd* be if he was still one of them. "I'm guessing they're watching the blaze. They might even be poking around in my rental car while everyone else is rushing around making sure the fire's out."

"Good. Then they'll see Rex Taylor's name on the rental agreement in the glove box."

"That's why we left it."

"I'll stay here until they come in and I'll call you before I go home to bed."

"Eve." He caught her just before she could hang up. "I'd like to see you."

"Not tonight," she said, and then she was gone.

Gunderson and his friends came in about thirty minutes later. Eve pretended to be busy doing something at the front desk, but she was too tired to accomplish any real work. She'd reverted to playing solitaire while waiting for them. But she was glad she'd stayed. She could smell the fire on them when they walked in, knew exactly where they'd been.

"Did you attend the Victorian Days celebration?" she asked, offering them a warm smile.

Gunderson shot her a dirty look. She thought he was going to continue to his room without responding, but then he paused and turned around. "That guy I asked you about?"

She blinked innocently. "What guy?"

"The one in the picture."

"Oh, your brother or...something like that."

"Yeah. You really haven't seen him?"

"No, why?"

"Plenty of other people in this town have."

She frowned. "So...that's good, isn't it? Didn't you want to find him?"

"I *will* find him—if he's still alive," he said.

"Still alive?" she repeated.

"Never mind."

Once he and his friends had gone to their rooms, she

hurried back to the office, closed the door and called Kyle. "What's been happening?"

"The fire department's gone," he replied.

"What's left of the house?"

"Not much. Just a scorched shell."

"So you'll be able to finish knocking it down easily?"

"Oh, yeah. And it won't require nearly as many trips to the dump."

"There's a bright spot. Is Chief Bennett still there?"

"No."

"Is he okay with saying he believes Rex Taylor died in the blaze? That's pretty important if this is going to work."

"We had a cup of coffee before he left. He told me he doesn't like the lie. But if it's the only way to save a man's life.... There's what's technically right, and there's what's morally right, he said. The moral side of things is what matters most to him. He's a good man."

"He is. Did he find Rex's cell phone in the rubble?"

"No. They can't search for anything like that yet. Everything's still hot. But Ed Hamilton was out here, taking pictures of the fire. The story will be in this week's paper for sure."

"How'd he hear about it?" Eve asked.

Kyle grinned. "As a newspaper man, he's supposed to be monitoring the police scanners for emergency calls, but he was at his in-laws' and had fallen asleep on the couch. So...I may have called him."

"You're kidding."

"No. I told him I knew he wouldn't want to miss something like this. It beats another article on the town Christmas tree."

"I bet he was appreciative."

"He was. Said he'll have his wife bake me some cookies. I'm going to feel guilty taking them."

Too tired to laugh, Eve smiled instead. "He doesn't get many things like this to report. He'd be even more interested in the real story, though."

"He's not going to find out about that. Neither is anyone else."

"Did you see Eric Gunderson and his buddies out there?" she asked.

"No. But that doesn't mean they didn't come. I was too busy trying to make sure everything happened when it was supposed to."

She stared at the wall, halfway in a daze. "I can't believe we did what we did."

"Neither can I," he admitted. "I've never set fire to anything in my life. Wait, I take that back. I once helped my grandfather do a weed burn when I was a teenager. But this…this was totally different. Damn, an old house can go up quick. I'm still a little freaked out by the power of that blaze, and relieved that it went exactly as planned."

"Thanks for doing it, Kyle. I appreciate it. You're a true friend."

"No problem. So…are you okay with the fact that even after everything we've done, you won't be with Rex? I mean, he can't stick around here. Not after so many people went out on a limb to fake his death."

"We killed an identity, an identity that was false to begin with."

"He's still got to go somewhere else and start over, Eve."

She knew that. But at least this should be the last time. "Of course. And I'll be fine." She wasn't really sure she would be. She felt shell-shocked and uncertain about what tomorrow might bring—whether or not they'd really get through this as cleanly as they hoped. She also wondered if Rex would miss her, and if he'd make the most of the chance they were trying to give him.

"He seems cautious with people, afraid to open up," Kyle said. "But I guess that's understandable, under the circumstances. I like him."

"Kyle?"

"What?"

She closed her eyes, battling the effects of all the adrenaline of the past few days. "I'm going to have his baby."

There was a long silence. Then he said, "Does he know that?"

"Yes."

"I see. Well, you're going to be okay. We'll make sure of it."

She straightened her spine. "No one has better friends than I do."

She had a lot to be grateful for, she told herself. At least when she thought of Rex in the future, she'd be able to imagine him living without the constant threat of The Crew—and know that she and her friends had been the ones to set him free.

# 32

The next few days proved to be an agonizing wait for Rex, because he couldn't go anywhere or even do much, except communicate with Virgil via email and play card games with Mrs. Higgins in the guesthouse.

Eve was so busy with her work he hardly saw her. But he received a call from her when she overheard Gunderson and the others at breakfast the day after the fire, talking about whether or not he'd been killed in the blaze. Then he got a call from Kyle when The Crew showed up at his place with the photo to confirm that he was indeed the person who'd rented the house that burned. And on Saturday morning, he had a call from Chief Bennett when Gunderson and friends showed up at the police station to ask if a man by the name of Rex Taylor had died.

Chief Bennett told The Crew that the fire was so hot, there wasn't much left in the way of remains, but what little they'd found was being sent for DNA testing. Then he'd asked them if they could help him locate some next of kin, since no one had seen or heard from Rex Taylor since the fire and the person who died must surely be him.

They declined, of course, but that seemed to satisfy

them, because when Eve called him again, it was to say that they'd checked out.

So it wasn't until Sunday morning, when Eve and Kyle showed up at Ted's place with a copy of the *Gold Country Gazette,* that Rex realized the past eight years—that entire era of his life—was really over. No one had actually died in that fire, but the man he'd been before had died in a figurative sense. Now he had the chance to become anything he wanted.

"What do you think?" Ted asked.

They were all sitting in Ted and Sophia's kitchen while Sophia made them a late breakfast.

Rex glanced up but he was fighting a sudden surge of emotion so he quickly returned his attention to the picture on the front page, which showed the charred remains of Kyle's old rental. The heading below it read Man Believed Killed in Fire Caused by Faulty Wiring. "This looks legit," he said. "I don't think anyone would question it."

Ted leaned forward to clink his orange juice glass against Rex's. "Success."

Rex smiled. He was grateful to Eve, Kyle, Ted, Mrs. Higgins, Sophia—all of them. But with Eve, he felt a lot more than gratitude. He couldn't take his eyes off her.

"So now what?" Kyle asked. "Where will you go?"

"I have a friend who lives on the East Coast," Rex said. "I'll stay with him until I can create my new identity."

"And how will you do that?" Ted asked.

"When you've been to prison, you generally learn who can get you a fake ID."

"A good one?" Kyle asked.

"Undetectable."

"This particular contact isn't associated with The Crew…" Ted began.

"No. Not even remotely."

"And then what?" Sophia asked.

"I'm not sure." Initially, he and Virgil had split up to make it harder for The Crew to find them, but now that Rex was supposedly dead, he no longer had to worry about bringing any danger to Virgil and his family. He supposed he could stay there indefinitely....

Rex wished he could offer his friend the same release from the past Eve and her friends had made possible for him. But faking two deaths—especially so close together—would strain the bounds of credibility. "Virgil also has a personal security company," Eve explained. "So Rex will have work right away."

"Your friend's giving you a job?" Kyle asked.

Rex nodded. "One I'll take until I can get financially stable. I've decided to leave my own business to my employees since there's no way, as a dead man, I'll be able to sell it. I've written up something that Eve will send to my assistant—dated the day I returned here, just to be safe." He'd brought all his money to Whiskey Creek, so he had a sizable amount, but it wouldn't be enough to start his own business. He'd be lucky if it carried him through the immediate process of reestablishing himself. He needed to save.

But at least this would be the last time he'd ever have to begin from scratch.

"When will you leave?" Kyle asked.

Obviously it would be better to leave sooner rather than later. Virgil had bought him a plane ticket. But, with the holidays, Rex couldn't get out until the red-eye on Christmas Eve. "Late tomorrow night."

"You'll be staying in the guesthouse until then?"

"Unfortunately not," Ted said. "Alexa's coming home from Disney World tonight, and we don't want to have to explain who he is or why he's been here. No need to burden someone so young with such a big secret."

"Do you need a place?" Kyle leaned back so that Sophia could ladle some eggs onto his plate. "Because you could stay with me."

"No way," Ted insisted. "He's not going anywhere near there. What if one of your workers happened to see him? They're always showing up at your house."

"They don't come by that often," Kyle said. "And I live alone. Besides, it's only for a night and a day. Where would he be better off?"

"My place," Eve said. "He'll be coming home with me after breakfast. The inn is closed the twenty-fourth and twenty-fifth, so…I'll be home."

"That's nice. Then you two will have a little time together before he has to go. But what about your parents?" Kyle asked. "They live so close to you."

"I had to bring them in on the secret," she answered. "My mother was just too upset when she thought Rex had died. It didn't seem fair to them, especially when I know they'd never tell a soul."

"I would've done the same," Ted admitted. "But we can't tell anyone else. We're all in agreement on that, right?"

"Absolutely," she said.

"Have you chosen your new name?" Sophia asked as she carried the pan back to the stove.

"I told Eve she could pick it," he said.

"Well?" Ted prompted. "What's it gonna be?"

Eve took a sip of her juice. "I like the name Lincoln."

"For his first or last name?" Kyle didn't seem overly impressed.

"His first name."

"Where'd you come up with that?"

"I've heard it around. It's not so unusual."

"What about a last name?"

"McCormick. Lincoln McCormick. It's sexy yet distinguished—not too old or too young."

"It sounds like a lawyer," Sophia said with a laugh, and took her seat at the table. "What do you think, Rex?"

Rex let his gaze linger on Eve. "I like it. At least she didn't name me Sue," he added with a grin.

"Well, there are definitely worse names," Kyle agreed.

"I wish you could wait another day or two before you go," Sophia told him. "Spending the night on a plane won't be much of a Christmas."

"The airlines were all booked. I had to take what I could get," he said. "But, thanks to you guys, this will be the best Christmas I've ever had."

That was true on the one hand. On the other? It wasn't going to be easy to leave Eve.


Eve's final day and night with Rex felt like a honeymoon. She'd never made love so many times in such a short period. Even when they weren't making love they stayed in bed and talked. But she grew sad whenever she saw the clock and realized how quickly the minutes were ticking away.

"We only have a few hours left," she said as they lay curled up together Monday afternoon. "And right now those hours feel like seconds."

"I'd bring you with me if I could," he said, but she wasn't sure he meant it. At the moment, he was in no position to take on a wife. And leaving Whiskey Creek would've been so difficult for her. Without her income, she wasn't even convinced they'd survive financially, for the first while, anyway.

When the time came to drive Rex to the airport, however, she felt she could give up anything except him.

"Be happy," she told him when she let him out of the car.

He picked up the small duffel bag that contained everything he owned—his computer and the few clothes and personal belongings he'd purchased after San Francisco—and came around the car to her side.

She got out to kiss him.

"I'm sorry I have to leave you." He rested his forehead against hers and slid a hand over her stomach as if he was remembering that she wasn't the only one he was leaving behind. "I'll call you occasionally, tell you how I'm doing. And I'll send more money for the baby."

She nodded and blinked fast, trying to stanch the tears that suddenly welled up. She'd promised herself she wouldn't make their parting any more difficult by crying.

Before the desperation she felt to hang on to him could get the best of her, she forced herself to let him go. "Forgive your family. And, for whatever you did wrong that had such an impact on your life, forgive yourself." She started to get into her car, but he pulled her back into his arms.

"I encouraged my little brother to...to make a jump into a lake that ended his life," he whispered into her ear. Then he released her and, without looking at her again, slung his bag over his shoulder and started for the entrance.

"How old were you?" she called after him.

After a slight hesitation, he turned to face her again. "Sixteen."

"How old was he?"

A muscle moved in his cheek and his voice sounded choked when he eventually spoke. "Twelve."

He glared at her as if, now that she knew, she'd condemn him, but she felt nothing except pity as she stood there, clinging to the edge of her open door. "Did you intend for something like that to happen?"

The pain on his face nearly wrenched her heart from her chest. "Of course not!"

"Then quit beating yourself up," she said. "I mean it, Rex. Enough penance. Just let it all go—at last."

Tears filled his eyes, but she didn't stay to see if those tears ever spilled down his cheeks. She knew he was a proud man, that he wouldn't want to break down in front of her or anyone else, and she didn't want him embarrassed by his attempt to finally share his pain. So she did what she could to preserve his dignity. She climbed into the driver's seat and drove off.

When Christmas dawned, Eve opened her eyes to a stream of pale yellow sunlight shining through her window and reached across the mattress, remembering what it had been like to have Rex there for the past couple of days.

How long would it take him to get used to the name Lincoln McCormick? she wondered.

She could only imagine how hard it had to be to change something *that* integral to one's identity. It was hard for her to even think of him with yet another name.

Her phone rang, and she scrambled out of bed to pluck it off its charger. She hoped it was Rex—*Lincoln*—checking in to let her know he'd arrived safely at his destination.

But it was her mother.

"Merry Christmas!" Adele chirped as soon as Eve hit the talk button.

Eve dropped back onto the bed. It felt like an insur-

mountable task just to get up. "Same to you," she said
with a yawn and a stretch, but went back to staring help-
lessly at that little ray of sunshine. She'd get through this,
she told herself. Somehow, she'd pick up and go on, for
the sake of her child, her parents and her friends, if not
for any other reason. Unlike Rex, she'd always had a lot
of support.

"Did you get Rex off to the airport okay?"

Eve remembered the tears in his eyes and once again
understood what it had taken him to share that painful
history with her. "I did," she said, but she couldn't dwell
on Rex or she'd end up in tears again. "When do you and
Dad want to exchange gifts?"

"The sooner, the better as far as we're concerned."

"You sure sound chipper," Eve said.

"Aren't *you?* You and your friends pulled off quite a
feat and gave Rex a new lease on life. That's the perfect
Christmas gift."

*Chipper* wasn't the word to describe her state of mind
at the moment. "Yeah, well, I'm happy about it."

"You should be. Can you get ready and come over
now?" her mother asked.

Eve let her breath seep out quietly so Adele wouldn't
hear the sigh it would have been otherwise. She didn't
want to leave the house, didn't want to celebrate Christmas. But she couldn't ruin the holidays for everyone else.

"Sure." She did her best to inject some energy into
her voice. "Give me an hour, okay?" Hopefully, a hot
shower would get her moving, because she'd never felt
more lethargic.

"Hurry," her mother said. "I want to see if you like
what I got you."

Whatever it was didn't matter. It could be the moon

and the stars, and it wouldn't be enough to fill the joyless vacuum Rex had left. "I'm sure I will," she said.

Somehow, Eve managed to shower and dress. Then, because she'd let all kinds of things slide this past month while she was occupied with Rex, she had to wrap the robotic vacuum she'd purchased for her mother and the wallet she'd gotten for her father. When she finally finished that herculean task, she trudged down the drive.

"Isn't it a beautiful Christmas morning?" her father asked when Eve walked in. He was sitting in his recliner, watching football. "Feels almost like summer."

It was definitely deep winter in her heart. "I've seen prettier," she grumbled, but she purposely said it in a low enough voice that her father didn't hear her. When Charlie raised his eyebrows as a way of asking her to repeat what she'd just said, she agreed it was a gorgeous Christmas.

"I've got homemade egg nog," her mother announced. "Come on into the kitchen and I'll get you a glass."

"Okay." She placed the presents she'd brought under the tree and dutifully followed her mother, and she was soon glad she had. Life was somehow easier when she was sitting at the table, basking in the love and comfort of being in her mother's presence. How many Christmases had she spent with her mother hurrying about, doing the cooking, and her father enjoying a good football game in the other room?

"Should we open presents after breakfast?" Eve asked.

"I was thinking we should do it before," her mother replied.

"Right now?"

"As soon as I get the turkey in. I've just been seasoning it. I like to cook it low and slow."

Eve got up to lift the heavy pan for her—something

her father would have done if she hadn't been around—and then closed the oven.

"Should we go into the living room?" her mother asked.

Eve was a little excited about the robotic vacuum. Her mother's present cost quite a bit more than her father's, but she felt it was the ideal gift for both of them. These days, her father probably did more vacuuming than her mother, since the vacuum was heavy, so he'd benefit from Eve's gift, too. "Sure."

Eve got the presents she had for her parents, but they set them aside instead of opening them. "We want to give you yours first," her mother said. "But you need to close your eyes."

"You didn't wrap it?" she teased.

"It was much too big for that." The way her father grinned told her it was going to be good. But she was still completely unprepared for what happened next. When she closed her eyes, she heard a creak in the hallway—her mother going to get whatever it was. Then there were more creaks, and instead of putting something down in front of her, her mother pulled her to her feet.

"Can I open my eyes?" she asked.

"Not quite yet," a male voice replied, and a large pair of hands cupped her face just before Rex kissed her.

When he raised his head, she stared up at him, too shocked to even ask what he was doing there.

"I couldn't leave you," he explained. "I got to Phoenix and had Virgil book my flight back. I don't want to go to New York. I don't want to go anywhere without you."

Her heart was racing, filling with hope despite what was going through her mind. "But you can't stay here! Someone could recognize you," she said, but there was no real conviction in those words because she wanted him, more than anything, to convince her he could.

"Not here." His thumbs moved gently over her cheeks as he spoke. "But if I change my name like I'm already doing, start a different kind of business and alter my appearance a bit—cut my hair and grow a beard—we could live in Jackson or Placerville or Sutter Creek. Those places are close enough that you'd be able to see your family, even work at the inn. The only difference would be that, at the end of the day, you'd come home to me."

If he did those things, anyone from Whiskey Creek who happened to bump into him there probably wouldn't connect Lincoln McCormick with the Rex Taylor who'd supposedly died. And the risk of that would drop dramatically as the years went by.

"But...you like what you do," she said. "You don't really want to give it up."

"It's time," he said. "I don't know how I'll replace that income, but...I'll figure it out."

She stepped back to look at her parents, who were positively beaming. "Isn't this the *best* Christmas ever?" her mother asked, her hands clasped in pure joy.

"Yes," Eve said. "I've never loved anyone so much or wanted anything more."

Rex—Lincoln—went to the tree and pulled a small gift out from under the others. "I left this for you. I ordered it online and had it come to Ted's house. But since I'm here now, I'd like to see you open it."

Eve felt as though she was living a dream. Could it be? Was he really going to stay with her? Make a life with her?

She had no qualms about moving to another town, not if they could remain close to Whiskey Creek and she could still see her family and friends whenever she wanted. "But I don't have anything for you," she protested.

He smiled. "You've given me enough."

Everyone watched her tear off the paper. Inside was a small velvet box that held a gold necklace with an angel pendant.

He didn't have to explain why he'd chosen it for her. She understood.

"Thank you. I *love* it," she said. Then she decided that now might be a good time to tell her parents about the baby....

# Epilogue

Lincoln couldn't stand still as he and Eve waited on the doorstep of his brother's upper-middle-class rambler in Valencia.

"Relax," she muttered, squeezing his hand. "Everything's going to be okay."

Somehow, if Eve was around, everything *would* be okay because it always was. He had to remember that. He'd never been happier in his life than in the past four months, since they'd gotten together and he'd started his landscaping business. But it had been so long since he'd seen his brothers and his father, and they were all going to be here tonight to celebrate his father's birthday. Lincoln wouldn't have come, if not for Eve's urging him to accept Mike's invitation. Although his brothers knew he'd changed his identity once again and was living a new life, they were somewhat skeptical, so he'd shared only that much.

But perhaps it was time for more, time to put in the effort required to change their minds....

The door opened and his oldest brother stood in the entry. "Well, well," he said as he looked from Lincoln to Eve. "You two seem to be doing well."

Lincoln held his father's present but lifted the hand that still clasped Eve's. "Mike, this is Eve, my wife."

"You emailed a few months ago to say you were getting married, but you didn't tell me she was so beautiful." Lincoln hadn't mentioned the baby, but Eve was five months along and beginning to show. He knew his brother had noticed when his gaze moved to her stomach before returning to her face.

"Welcome to L.A., Eve."

She surprised Lincoln, and probably Mike, too, by stepping forward to give Mike a hug. "I'm so glad to finally meet you," she said.

Lincoln had no plans to hug anyone other than Eve. In that moment, he was damn glad he was holding the present. But he hoped that, too, would come with time. "Is Dad here?"

"He is. And he's anxious to see you," Mike said. "Come on in."

\* \* \* \* \*

# REQUEST YOUR FREE BOOKS!

## 2 FREE NOVELS
## FROM THE ROMANCE COLLECTION
## PLUS 2 FREE GIFTS!

**YES!** Please send me 2 FREE novels from the Romance Collection and my 2 FREE gifts (gifts are worth about $10). After receiving them, if I don't wish to receive any more books, I can return the shipping statement marked "cancel." If I don't cancel, I will receive 4 brand-new novels every month and be billed just $6.24 per book in the U.S. or $6.74 per book in Canada. That's a savings of at least 22% off the cover price. It's quite a bargain! Shipping and handling is just 50¢ per book in the U.S. and 75¢ per book in Canada.* I understand that accepting the 2 free books and gifts places me under no obligation to buy anything. I can always return a shipment and cancel at any time. Even if I never buy another book, the two free books and gifts are mine to keep forever.

194/394 MDN F4XY

| Name | (PLEASE PRINT) | |
|------|----------------|---|

| Address | | Apt. # |
|---------|---|--------|

| City | State/Prov. | Zip/Postal Code |
|------|-------------|-----------------|

Signature (if under 18, a parent or guardian must sign)

### Mail to the Harlequin® Reader Service:
**IN U.S.A.:** P.O. Box 1867, Buffalo, NY 14240-1867
**IN CANADA:** P.O. Box 609, Fort Erie, Ontario L2A 5X3

**Want to try two free books from another line?**
**Call 1-800-873-8635 or visit www.ReaderService.com.**

* Terms and prices subject to change without notice. Prices do not include applicable taxes. Sales tax applicable in N.Y. Canadian residents will be charged applicable taxes. Offer not valid in Quebec. This offer is limited to one order per household. Not valid for current subscribers to the Romance Collection or the Romance/Suspense Collection. All orders subject to credit approval. Credit or debit balances in a customer's account(s) may be offset by any other outstanding balance owed by or to the customer. Please allow 4 to 6 weeks for delivery. Offer available while quantities last.

**Your Privacy**—The Harlequin® Reader Service is committed to protecting your privacy. Our Privacy Policy is available online at www.ReaderService.com or upon request from the Harlequin Reader Service.

We make a portion of our mailing list available to reputable third parties that offer products we believe may interest you. If you prefer that we not exchange your name with third parties, or if you wish to clarify or modify your communication preferences, please visit us at www.ReaderService.com/consumerschoice or write to us at Harlequin Reader Service Preference Service, P.O. Box 9062, Buffalo, NY 14269. Include your complete name and address.

ROM13R

# BRENDA NOVAK

| | | | |
|---|---|---|---|
| 32993 | INSIDE | ___ $7.99 U.S. | ___ $9.99 CAN |
| 32904 | WATCH ME | ___ $7.99 U.S. | ___ $9.99 CAN |
| 32886 | DEAD GIVEAWAY | ___ $7.99 U.S. | ___ $9.99 CAN |
| 32831 | KILLER HEAT | ___ $7.99 U.S. | ___ $9.99 CAN |
| 32803 | BODY HEAT | ___ $7.99 U.S. | ___ $9.99 CAN |
| 32725 | THE PERFECT MURDER | ___ $7.99 U.S. | ___ $8.99 CAN |
| 31591 | COME HOME TO ME | ___ $7.99 U.S. | ___ $8.99 CAN |
| 31546 | TAKE ME HOME FOR CHRISTMAS | ___ $7.99 U.S. | ___ $8.99 CAN |
| 31423 | WHEN SUMMER COMES | ___ $7.99 U.S. | ___ $9.99 CAN |
| 31371 | WHEN SNOW FALLS | ___ $7.99 U.S. | ___ $9.99 CAN |
| 31351 | WHEN LIGHTNING STRIKES | ___ $7.99 U.S. | ___ $9.99 CAN |
| 28858 | DEAD SILENCE | ___ $7.99 U.S. | ___ $9.99 CAN |

*(limited quantities available)*

| | |
|---|---|
| TOTAL AMOUNT | $ _____ |
| POSTAGE & HANDLING | $ _____ |
| ($1.00 for 1 book, 50¢ for each additional) | |
| APPLICABLE TAXES* | $ _____ |
| TOTAL PAYABLE | $ _____ |

*(check or money order—please do not send cash)*

To order, complete this form and send it, along with a check or money order for the total above, payable to Harlequin MIRA, to: **In the U.S.** 3010 Walden Avenue, P.O. Box 9077, Buffalo, NY 14269-9077. **In Canada:** P.O. Box 636, Fort Erie, Ontario, L2A 5X3.

Name: _____

Address: _____ City: _____

State/Prov.: _____ Zip/Postal Code: _____

Account Number (if applicable): _____

075 CSAS

*New York residents remit applicable sales taxes.
*Canadian residents remit applicable GST and provincial taxes.

**H** HARLEQUIN® MIRA®
www.Harlequin.com

MBN1114